GIRL, WOMAN, OTHER

'Bernardine Evaristo is the most daring, imaginative and innovative
of writers, and *Girl, Woman, Other* is a fantastic novel that takes fiction
and black women's stories into exciting new directions'
Inua Ellams, author of *The Half-God of Rainfall*

'For a fresh and inspired take on writing about the African diaspora,
there's nothing like a new book by Bernardine Evaristo. Somehow she does
it every time!' Margaret Busby, editor of *New Daughters of Africa*

'Bernardine Evaristo is without doubt one of the most important
voices in contemporary British literature. Her phenomenal
writing gets at the heart of what affects and concerns us most
in these times' Jacob Ross, author of *The Bone Readers*

'*Girl, Woman, Other* is brilliant. I feel like a ghost walking in and out
and in again on different people's lives, different others. Some I feel close
to, some I feel I must have met and some are so "other" that I have
to stretch myself to see them. Mind-expanding' Philippa Perry

'The finest chronicler of black lives in Britain: yet everything with Evaristo,
like her headrush of language, like her dancing style, reaches outward
to distant shores and far-flung imaginations, searching for rupture, affiliation'
Daljit Nagra, author of *Look We Have Coming to Dover!*

GIRL, WOMAN, OTHER

Bernardine Evaristo

HAMISH HAMILTON
an imprint of
PENGUIN BOOKS

HAMISH HAMILTON

UK | USA | Canada | Ireland | Australia
India | New Zealand | South Africa

Hamish Hamilton is part of the Penguin Random House group of companies
whose addresses can be found at global.penguinrandomhouse.com.

First published 2019
006

Copyright © Bernardine Evaristo, 2019

The moral right of the author has been asserted

The lines quoted on page 254 are by Grace Nichols, 'We the Women', from *I is a Long Memoried Woman*
(Karnak House Publishers, 1983). Lines reprinted by kind permission of Grace Nichols.

Set in 12.5/16 pt Fournier MT Std
Typeset by Jouve (UK), Milton Keynes
Printed and bound in Great Britain by Clays Ltd, Elcograf S.p.A.

A CIP catalogue record for this book is available from the British Library

ISBN: 978-0-241-36490-1

www.greenpenguin.co.uk

Contents

For the sisters & the sistas & the sistahs & the sistren
& the women & the womxn & the wimmin & the womyn
& our brethren & our bredrin & our brothers & our bruvs
& our men & our mandem & the LGBTQI+ members
of the human family

she thinks back to when she started out in theatre

when she and her running mate, Dominique, developed a reputation for heckling shows that offended their political sensibilities

their powerfully trained actors' voices projected from the back of the stalls before they made a quick getaway

they believed in protest that was public, disruptive and downright annoying to those at the other end of it

she remembers pouring a pint of beer over the head of a director whose play featured semi-naked black women running around on stage behaving like idiots

before doing a runner into the backstreets of Hammersmith

howling

Amma then spent decades on the fringe, a renegade lobbing hand grenades at the establishment that excluded her

until the mainstream began to absorb what was once radical and she found herself hopeful of joining it

which only happened when the first female artistic director assumed the helm of the National three years ago

after so long hearing a polite no from her predecessors, she received a phone call just after breakfast one Monday morning when her life stretched emptily ahead with only online television dramas to look forward to

love the script, must do it, will you also direct it for us? I know it's short notice, but are you free for coffee this week at all?

Amma takes a sip of her Americano with its customary kick-starter extra shot in it as she approaches the Brutalist grey arts complex ahead

at least they try to enliven the bunker-like concrete with neon

Chapter One

Amma

Amma
is walking along the promenade of the waterway that bisects her
city, a few early morning barges cruise slowly by
to her left is the nautical-themed footbridge with its deck-like
walkway and sailing mast pylons
to her right is the bend in the river as it heads east past Waterloo
Bridge towards the dome of St Paul's
she feels the sun begin to rise, the air still breezy before the city
clogs up with heat and fumes
a violinist plays something suitably uplifting further along the
promenade
Amma's play, *The Last Amazon of Dahomey*, opens at the National
tonight

*

light displays these days and the venue has a reputation for being progressive rather than traditionalist

years ago she expected to be evicted as soon as she dared walk through its doors, a time when people really did wear their smartest clothes to go to the theatre

and looked down their noses at those not in the proper attire

she wants people to bring their curiosity to her plays, doesn't give a damn what they wear, has her own *sod-you* style, anyway, which has evolved, it's true, away from the clichéd denim dungarees, Che Guevara beret, PLO scarf and ever-present badge of two interlocked female symbols (talk about wearing your heart on your sleeve, girl)

these days she wears silver or gold trainers in winter, failsafe Birkies in summer

winter, it's black slacks, either baggy or tight depending on whether she's a size 12 or 14 that week (a size smaller on top)

summer, it's patterned harem pants that end just below the knee

winter, it's bright asymmetric shirts, jumpers, jackets, coats

year-round her peroxide dreadlocks are trained to stick up like candles on a birthday cake

silver hoop earrings, chunky African bangles and pink lipstick

are her perennial signature style statement

Yazz

recently described her style as 'a mad old woman look, Mum', pleads with her to shop in Marks & Spencer like normal mothers, refuses to be spotted alongside her when they're supposed to be walking down the street together

Yazz knows full well that Amma will always be anything but normal, and as she's in her fifties, she's not old yet, although try

3

telling *that* to a nineteen-year-old; in any case, ageing is nothing to be ashamed of

especially when the entire human race is in it together

although sometimes it seems that she alone among her friends wants to celebrate getting older

because it's such a privilege to not die prematurely, she tells them as the night draws in around her kitchen table in her cosy terraced house in Brixton

as they get stuck into the dishes each one has brought: chickpea stew, jerk chicken, Greek salad, lentil curry, roasted vegetables, Moroccan lamb, saffron rice, beetroot and kale salad, jollof quinoa and gluten-free pasta for the really irritating fusspots

as they pour themselves glasses of wine, vodka (fewer calories), or something more liver-friendly if under doctor's orders

she expects them to approve of her bucking the trend of middle-aged moaning; instead she gets bemused smiles and what about arthritic flare-ups, memory loss and hot sweats?

Amma passes the young busker

she smiles with encouragement at the girl, who responds in kind

she fishes out a few coins, places them in the violin case

she isn't ready to forgo cigarettes so leans on the riverside wall and lights one, hates herself for it

the adverts told her generation it would make them appear grown-up, glamorous, powerful, clever, desirable and above all, cool

no one told them it would actually make them dead

she looks out at the river as she feels the warm smoke travel down her oesophagus soothing her nerves while trying to combat the adrenaline rush of the caffeine

forty years of first nights and she's still bricking it

what if she's slated by the critics? dismissed with a consensus of one-star reviews, what *was* the great National thinking allowing this rubbishy impostor into the building?

of course she knows she's not an impostor, she's written fifteen plays and directed over forty, and as a critic once wrote, Amma Bonsu is a safe pair of hands who's known to pull off risks

what if the preview audiences who gave standing ovations were just being kind?

oh shut up, Amma, you're a veteran battle-axe, remember?

look

she's got a fantastic cast: six older actresses (seen-it-all vets), six mid-careerists (survivors-so-far) and three fresh faces (naïve hopefuls), one of whom, the talented Simone, will wander in bleary-eyed to rehearsals, having forgotten to unplug the iron, turn off the stove or close her bedroom window and will waste precious rehearsal time phoning her flatmates in a panic

a couple of months ago she'd have sold her grandmother into slavery to get this job, now she's a spoilt little prima donna who ordered her director to pop out and fetch her a caramel latte a couple of weeks ago when it was just the two of them in a rehearsal room

I'm so exhausted, Simone whinged, implying it was all Amma's fault for making her work so hard

needless to say, she dealt with Little Miss Simone Stevenson in the moment

Little Miss Stevenson – who thinks that because she's landed at the National straight out of drama school, she's one step away from conquering Hollywood

she'll find out
soon enough

at times like these Amma misses Dominique, who long ago
absconded to America

they should be sharing her breakthrough career moment together

they met in the eighties at an audition for a feature film set in a
women's prison (what else?)

both were disillusioned at being put up for parts such as a slave,
servant, prostitute, nanny or crim

and still not getting the job

they railed against their lot in a grotty Soho caff while devouring
fried egg and bacon slathered between two slabs of soggy white
bread washed down with builder's tea alongside the sex workers who
plied their trade on the streets outside

long before Soho became a trendy gay colony

look at me? Dominique said, and Amma did, there was nothing
subservient, maternal or criminal about her

she was über-cool, totally gorgeous, taller than most women,
thinner than most women, with cut-glass cheekbones and smoky
eyes with thick black lashes that literally cast a shadow on her face

she wore leathers, kept her hair short except for a black fringe
swept to one side, and rode about town on a battered old butcher's
bike chained up outside

can't they see I'm a living goddess? Dominique shouted with a flamboyant gesture, flicking her fringe, adopting a sultry pose as heads turned

Amma was shorter, with African hips and thighs

perfect slave girl material one director told her when she walked
into an audition for a play about Emancipation

whereupon she walked right back out again

6

in turn a casting director told Dominique she was wasting his time when she turned up for a Victorian drama when there weren't any black people in Britain then

she said there were, called him ignorant before also leaving the room and in her case, slamming the door

Amma realized she'd found a kindred spirit in Dominique who would kick arse with her

and they'd both be pretty unemployable once news got around

they went on to a local pub where the conversation continued and wine flowed

Dominique was born in the St Pauls area of Bristol to an Afro-Guyanese mother, Cecilia, who tracked her lineage back to slavery, and an Indo-Guyanese father, Wintley, whose ancestors were indentured labourers from Calcutta

the oldest of ten children who all looked more black than Asian and identified as such, especially as their father could relate to the Afro-Caribbean people he'd grown up with, but not to Indians fresh over from India

Dominique guessed her own sexual preferences from puberty, wisely kept them to herself, unsure how her friends or family would react, not wanting to be a social outcast

she tried boys a couple of times

they enjoyed it

she endured it

aged sixteen, aspiring to become an actress, she headed for London where people proudly proclaimed their outsider identities on badges she slept rough under the Embankment arches and in shop doorways along the Strand, was interviewed by a black housing association where she lied and cried about escaping a father who'd beaten her

the Jamaican housing officer wasn't impressed, so you got beats, is it?

Dominique escalated her complaint to one of paternal sexual abuse, was given an emergency room in a hostel; eighteen months later, after tearful weekly calls to the housing office, she landed a one-bedroom housing association flat in a small fifties block in Bloomsbury

I did what I had to find a home, she told Amma, not my finest moment, I admit, still, no harm done, as my father will never know

she went on a mission to educate herself in black history, culture, politics, feminism, discovered London's alternative bookshops

she walked into Sisterwrite in Islington where every single author of every single book was female and browsed for hours; she couldn't afford to buy anything, and read the whole of *Home Girls: A Black Feminist Anthology* in weekly instalments, standing up, as well as anything by Audre Lorde she could get her hands on

the booksellers didn't seem to mind

when I was accepted into a very orthodox drama school, I was already politicized and challenged them on everything, Amma

the only person of colour in the whole school

she demanded to know why the male parts in Shakespeare couldn't be played by women and don't even get me started on cross-racial casting, she shouted at the course director while everyone else, including the female students, stayed silent

I realized I was on my own

*

the next day I was taken aside by the school principal
you're here to become an actor not a politician
you'll be asked to leave if you keep causing trouble
you have been warned, Dominique

tell me about it, Amma replied, shut up or get out, right?
as for me, I get my fighting spirit from my dad, Kwabena, who was a journalist campaigning for Independence in Ghana
until he heard he was going to be arrested for sedition, legged it over here, ended up working on the railways where he met Mum at London Bridge station
he was a ticket collector, she worked in the offices above the concourse
he made sure to be the one to take her ticket, she made sure to be the last person to leave the train so she could exchange a few words with him

Mum, Helen, is half-caste, born in 1935 in Scotland
her father was a Nigerian student who vanished as soon as he finished his studies at the University of Aberdeen
he never said goodbye
years later her mother discovered he'd gone back to his wife and children in Nigeria
she didn't even know he had a wife and children
Mum wasn't the only half-caste in Aberdeen in the thirties and forties but she was rare enough to be made to feel it
she left school early, went to secretarial college, headed down to London, just as it was being populated by African men who'd come to study or work
Mum went to their dances and Soho clubs, they liked her lighter skin and looser hair

she says she felt ugly until African men told her she wasn't
you should see what she looked like back then
a cross between Lena Horne and Dorothy Dandridge
so yeh, really ugly

Mum hoped to spend their first date going to see a film and then
on to her favourite spot, Club Afrique, right here in Soho, she'd
dropped enough hints and loved to dance to highlife and West African jazz
    instead he took her to one of his socialist meetings in the back-
room of a pub at the Elephant and Castle
    where a group of men sat guzzling beers and talking independence
politics
    she sat there trying to act interested, impressed by his intellect
    he was impressed with her silent acquiescence, if you ask me

    they married and moved to Peckham
    I was their last child and first girl, Amma explained, blowing
smoke into the already thickening fug of the room
    my three older brothers became lawyers and a doctor, their obedi-
ence to the expectations of our father meant I wasn't pressurized to
follow suit
    his only concern for me is marriage and children
    he thinks my acting career is a hobby until I have both
    Dad's a socialist who wants a revolution to improve the lot of all
of mankind
    literally

    I tell Mum she married a patriarch
    look at it this way, Amma, she says, your father was born male in

Ghana in the 1920s whereas you were born female in London in the 1960s

and your point is?

you really can't expect him to 'get you', as you put it

I let her know she's an apologist for the patriarchy and complicit in a system that oppresses all women

she says human beings are complex

I tell her not to patronize me

Mum worked eight hours a day in paid employment, raised four children, maintained the home, made sure the patriarch's dinner was on the table every night and his shirts were ironed every morning

meanwhile, he was off saving the world

his one domestic duty was to bring home the meat for Sunday lunch from the butcher's – a suburban kind of hunter-gatherer thing

I can tell Mum's unfulfilled now we've all left home because she spends her time either cleaning it or redecorating it

she's never complained about her lot, or argued with him, a sure sign she's oppressed

she told me she tried to hold his hand in the early days, but he shook her off, said affection was an English affectation, she never tried again

yet every year he gets her the soppiest Valentine card you can buy and he loves sentimental country music, sits in the kitchen on Sunday evenings listening to albums of Jim Reeves and Charley Pride

tumbler of whisky in one hand, wiping tears away with the other

*

Dad lives for campaigning meetings, demos, picketing Parliament and standing in Lewisham Market selling the *Socialist Worker*

I grew up listening to his sermons during our evening meal on the evils of capitalism and colonialism and the merits of socialism

it was his pulpit and we were his captive congregation

it was like we were literally being force-fed his politics

he'd probably be an important person in Ghana if he'd returned after Independence

instead he's President for Life of our family

he doesn't know I'm a dyke, are you kidding? Mum told me not to tell him, it was hard enough telling her, she said she suspected when pencil skirts and curly perms were all the rage and I started wearing men's Levis

she's sure it's a phase, which I'll throw back at her when I'm forty

Dad has no time for 'the fairies' and laughs at all the homophobic jokes comedians make on telly every Saturday night when they're not insulting their mother-in-law or black people

Amma spoke about going to her first black women's group in Brixton in her last year at school, she'd seen a flyer at her local library

the woman who opened the door, Elaine, sported a perfect halo of an afro and her smooth limbs were clad tightly in light blue denim jeans and tight denim shirt

Amma wanted her on sight, followed her into the main room where women sat on sofas, chairs, cushions, cross-legged on the floor, drinking cups of coffee and cider

she nervously accepted cigarettes as they were passed around, sat on the floor leaning against a cat-mauled tweedy armchair, feeling Elaine's warm leg against her arm she listened as they debated what it meant to be a black woman

what it meant to be a feminist when white feminist organizations made them feel unwelcome

how it felt when people called them nigger, or racist thugs beat them up

what it was like when white men opened doors or gave up their seats on public transport for white women (which was sexist), but not for them (which was racist)

Amma could relate to their experiences, began to join in with the refrains of, we hear you, sister, we've all been there, sister

it felt like she was coming in from the cold

at the end of her first evening, the other women said their good-byes and Amma offered to stay behind to wash up the cups and ashtrays with Elaine

they made out on one of the bumpy sofas in the glow of the street-light to the accompaniment of police sirens haring by

it was the closest she'd come to making love to herself

it was another coming home

the next week when she went to the meeting
Elaine was canoodling with another woman
and blanked her completely
she never went again

Amma and Dominique stayed until they were turfed out, had worked their way through numerous glasses of red wine

they decided they needed to start their own theatre company to have careers as actors, because neither was prepared to betray their politics to find jobs

or shut their mouths to keep them
it seemed the obvious way forward
they scribbled ideas for names on hard toilet paper snaffled from
the loo
Bush Women Theatre Company best captured their intentions
they would be a voice in theatre where there was silence
black and Asian women's stories would get out there
they would create theatre on their own terms
it became the company's motto
On Our Own Terms
or Not At All.

2

Living rooms became rehearsal spaces, old bangers transported props, costumes came from second-hand shops, sets were extracted from junk yards, they called on mates to help out, everyone learning on the job, ad hoc, throwing their lot in together

they wrote grant applications on old typewriters with missing keys, budgets felt as alien to Amma as quantum physics, she balked at becoming trapped behind a desk

she upset Dominique when she arrived for admin sessions late and left early claiming headaches or PMT

they rowed when she walked into a stationery shop and ran straight out again claiming it had brought on a panic attack

she had a go at Dominique when she didn't deliver the script she'd promised to write but was out late night clubbing instead, or forgot her lines mid-show

six months after its inception, they were constantly at loggerheads
they'd hit it off as friends, only to find they couldn't work together

Amma called a make-or-break meeting at hers

they sat down with wine and a Chinese takeaway and Dominique admitted she got more pleasure setting up tours for the company than putting herself in front of an audience, and preferred being herself to pretending to be other people

Amma admitted she loved writing, hated admin and was she really any good as an actor? she did anger brilliantly – which was the extent of her range

Dominique became the company manager, Amma the artistic director

they employed actresses, directors, designers, stage crews, set up national tours that lasted months

their plays, *The Importance of Being Female*, *FGM: The Musical*, *Dis-arranged Marriage*, *Cunning Stunts*, were performed in community centres, libraries, fringe theatres, at women's festivals and conferences

they leafleted outside venues as audiences left and arrived, illegally plastered posters on to billboards in the dead of night

they started getting reviews in the alternative media, and even produced a monthly *Bush Women* samizdat

but due to pathetically poor sales and, to be honest, pathetically poor writing, it lasted for two issues after its grand launch one summer's evening at Sisterwrite

where a group of women rolled up to enjoy the free plonk and spill out on to the pavement to light up and chat each other up

*

Amma supplemented her income working in a burger bar at Piccadilly Circus

where she sold hamburgers made of reconstituted cardboard topped with rehydrated onions and rubbery cheese

all of which she also ate for free in her breaks – which gave her spots

the orange nylon suit and hat she wore meant customers saw her as a uniformed servant to do their bidding

and not her wonderful, artistic, highly individualistic and rebellious self

she slipped free crusty pies filled with apple-flavoured lumps of sugar to the runaway rent boys she befriended who operated around the station

with no idea that in years to come she'd be attending their funerals

they didn't realize unprotected sex meant a dance with death

nobody did

home was a derelict factory in Deptford with concrete walls, a collapsing ceiling and a community of rats that defeated all attempts at extermination

thereafter she moved into a series of similarly squalid squats until she found herself living in the most desirable squat in the whole of London, a Soviet-sized former office block at the back of King's Cross

she was lucky enough to be one of the first to hear of it before it filled up

and stayed upstairs when bailiffs set a hydraulic excavator at the main door which triggered violent countermeasures and prison sentences for the head-bangers who thought a bailiff down deserved a good kicking

they called it the Battle of King's Cross

the building was thereafter known as the Republic of Freedomia

they were lucky, too, because the owner of the property, a certain Jack Staniforth, living tax-free in Monte Carlo, loaded from the profits of his family's business in Sheffield cutlery, turned out to be sympathetic to their cause once news reached him from his estate holding company

he'd fought for the International Brigade in the Spanish Civil War

and a bad-investment of a building in one of London's seediest districts was a forgettable footnote to his accounts

if they looked after the place, he wrote

they could stay for free

they stopped the illegal tapping of electricity and opened an account with the London Electricity Board

likewise with the gas, hitherto powered by a single fifty pence piece jammed into a meter

they needed to set up a management system and gathered one Saturday morning in the lobby to thrash it out

the Marxists demanded they set up a Central Committee of the Workers' Republic of Freedomia, which was a bit rich, Amma thought, seeing as most of them had taken 'a principled stand against the running dogs of capitalism' as an excuse to not work

the hippies suggested they form a commune and share everything, but they were so chilled and laid back, everybody talked over them

the environmentalists wanted to ban aerosols, plastic bags and deodorant, which turned everyone against them, even the punks who weren't exactly known for smelling minty the vegetarians demanded a non-meat policy, the vegans wanted it extended to non-dairy, the macrobiotics suggested everyone eat steamed white cabbage for breakfast

the Rastas wanted cannabis legalized, and a reserved plot on the land out back for their Nyabinghi gatherings

the Hari Krishnas wanted everyone to join them that very afternoon banging drums down Oxford Street

the punks wanted permission to play shouty music and were duly shouted down

the gay guys wanted anti-homophobic legislation enshrined into the building's constitution, to which everyone replied, what constitution?

the radical feminists wanted women-only quarters, self-governed by a co-op

the lesbian radical feminists wanted their own quarters away from the non-lesbian radical feminists, also self-governed by a co-op

the black radical lesbian feminists wanted the same except with the condition that no whiteys of any gender were allowed inside

the anarchists walked out because any form of governance was a betrayal of everything they believed in

Amma preferred running solo, and mixing with others who didn't try to impose their will on anyone else

in the end a straightforward rotating management committee was formed with various rules against drug-dealing, sexual harassment and voting Tory

the plot out back became a communal space featuring scrap metal sculptures

courtesy of the artists

*

Amma managed to lay claim to a typing pool so large she could jog around it

with its own private toilet and sink that she kept blissfully clean and suffused with floral scents

she coated the walls and ceiling with a striking blood-red paint, ripped up the corporate-grey carpet, threw a few raffia mats on the wooden floor, installed a second-hand cooker, fridge, bean bags, a futon, and a bath reclaimed from a junk yard

her room was big enough for parties and big enough for people to crash

the disco beats of Donna Summer, Sister Sledge, Minnie Riperton and Chaka Khan swirling on vinyl got her parties going

Roberta, Sarah, Edith, Etta and Mathilde Santing were the soundtracks to her end of night seductions

behind the eighteenth-century black lacquer Chinese screen, rescued from a skip outside the old Chinese Embassy

she worked her way through many of the women of Freedomia

she wanted one-night stands, most wanted more than that

it got to the point where she dreaded passing her former conquests in the corridors, like Maryse, a translator from Guadeloupe

if she wasn't knocking on Amma's door in the middle of the night begging to be let in, she was lurking outside it to harass whoever was getting what she wanted

this progressed to name-calling from her window whenever she saw Amma approach the building, all of it coming to a head when she tipped a bucket of vegetable peel over Amma one day as she passed beneath her window

infuriating both the environmentalists and the management committee who took it upon themselves to write to Amma that she 'stop shitting on her own doorstep'

Amma wrote back how it was interesting that quickly people turned into *totalitarian fascists* once they'd been given a little power

but she'd learned her lesson and wasn't short of attention; groupies queued up for Amma and Dominique as the main players of Bush Women Theatre

everyone from baby dykes in their late teens to women who could be their mothers

Amma didn't discriminate, she bragged to her friends that her tastes were truly egalitarian as they traversed culture, class, creed, race, religion and generation

which, happily, gave her a bigger playing field than most

(she kept her predilection for big tits quiet because it was un-feminist to isolate body parts for sexual objectification)

Dominique was more selective and monogamous, serially so, she went for actresses, usually blonde, whose microscopic talent was overshadowed by their macroscopic beauty

or models whose looks *were* their talent

women-only bars were their hangouts

Fallen Angel, Rackets, the Bell, the Drill Hall Theatre bar on a Monday where the lesbianarati hung out, and Pearl's shebeen in Brixton on a Friday night run by Pearl, a middle-aged Jamaican woman who stripped her basement of furniture, set up a sound system and charged at the door

Amma experienced commitment to one person as imprisonment, she hadn't left home for a life of freedom and adventure to end up chained to another person's desires if she slept with a woman more than two or three times, they usually went from attractively independent to increasingly needy

within the space of a *week*

she'd become their sole source of happiness as they moved to assert their authority over her autonomy, by any means necessary

sulks, tears, accusations of selfishness and heartlessness

Amma learnt to head all women off, to state her intentions upfront, to never sleep with the same person twice, or pushing it, thrice

even when she wanted to

sex was a simple, harmless, human pleasure and until her late thirties she got a lot of it

how many were there? one hundred, another fifty? surely not more than that?

a couple of friends suggested she try therapy to help her settle down, she replied she was practically a virgin compared to male rock stars who boasted conquests of thousands and were admired for it

did anyone tell them to go and get psychoanalysed?

unfortunately one or two of her earlier conquests have been harassing her on social media of late where the past is just waiting to smack you in the face

like the woman who posted that Amma had been her first when they slept together thirty-five years ago and had been so trashed she vomited all over her

it was so traumatic I never got over it, she wailed

or the woman who chased her up Regent Street shouting at her for not returning her calls from around the same time

who do you think you are, you pretentious show-off theatre luvvie? you're nothing, that's what you are, *nothing* you must be off your meds, love, Amma shouted back, before escaping into the subterranean warren of Topshop

Amma long ago lost interest in bed-hopping; over time she began to crave the intimacy that comes from being emotionally, although not exclusively, close to another person
non-monogamous relationships are her thing, or is it called poly-amory now? as Yazz describes it, which as far as she can tell is non-monogamy in all but name, *child*

there's Dolores, a graphic designer based in Brighton, and Jackie, an occupational therapist in Highgate
they've been in the picture seven and three years respectively and are both independent women who have full lives (and children) out-side of their relationship with her
they're not clingy or needy or jealous or possessive, and they actu-ally like each other so yes, sometimes they indulge in a little ménage à trois
upon occasion
(Yazz would be horrified if she knew this)

the middle-aged Amma sometimes feels nostalgic for her younger days, remembers the only time she and Dominique went on a pilgrim-age to the legendary Gateways
hidden down a Chelsea basement in the last years of its fifty-year existence
it was almost empty, two middle-aged women stood at the bar wearing men's haircuts and suits and looking as if they'd walked straight out of the pages of *The Well of Loneliness*
the dance floor was dimly lit, and two very old and very small

women, one in a black suit, the other in a forties-style dress, danced cheek-to-cheek to Dusty Springfield singing 'The Look of Love'

and there wasn't even a glittery disco ball spinning from the middle of the ceiling, sprinkling stardust on to them.

3

Amma throws her coffee in a bin and walks directly towards the theatre, past the concrete skateboarding area emblazoned with graffiti

it's way too early for the youngsters to begin their death-defying leaps and twists without helmets or protective knee pads

the young, who are so fearless

like Yazz, who goes out cycling without a helmet

who storms off when her mother tells her that wearing a helmet might be the difference between

a/ getting a headache

b/ learning to talk again

she enters the stage door, greets the security guard, Bob, who wishes her well for tonight, makes her way through the corridors and up the stairs and eventually on to the cavernous stage

she looks out at the empty, auditory wilderness of the fan-shaped auditorium, modelled on the Greek amphitheatres that ensured everyone in the audience had an uninterrupted view of the action

over a thousand people will fill the seats this very evening

so many people gathered to see her production is quite unbelievable

the entire run almost sold out before a single review has been filed

how's that for demand for something quite different?

*

The Last Amazon of Dahomey, written and directed by Amma Bonsu

where in the eighteenth and nineteenth centuries women warriors served the king

women who lived in the king's compound and were supplied with food and female slaves

who left the palace preceded by a slave girl ringing a bell warning men to look away or be killed

who became the palace guard because men couldn't be trusted not to chop off the king's head or castrate him with a cutlass while he slept

who were trained to climb naked over thorny acacia branches to toughen up

who were sent into the hazardous forest for nine days to survive on their own

who were crack shots with muskets and could behead and disembowel their enemies with ease

who fought the Yoruba next door and the French who came to colonize

who grew to an army of six thousand, all formally married to the king

who were not otherwise permitted sexual relations and any male child born to them was killed off

on first hearing about this Amma decided they must have been at it among themselves because wasn't that the case when the sexes are segregated?

and the idea of her play was born

the last Amazon is Nawi, who enters the stage as a vulnerable teenage bride presented to the king; unable to bear his child, she's

24

cast out of his bedchamber and forced to join his female combat troops where she survives the hazardous induction and rises up the ranks through her powerful physicality and cunning battle strategies to become a legendary Amazon general who shocked foreign observers with her fearless ferocity

Amma shows Nawi's loyalty to her many women lovers long after she tires of them, making sure the king assigns them lightweight domestic duties rather than kick them out of the compound to a life of destitution

at the end of the play, old and alone, Nawi reconnects with her past lovers, who fade in and out as spectres, courtesy of holograms

she relives the wars where she made her name, including the ones the king instigated to provide captors for the abolished slave trade in the Americas, with outlaw slave ships outrunning the blockades in order to do business with him

she's proud of her achievements

video projections show her battles in action, thunderous armies of charging Amazons brandishing muskets and machetes

hollering and swelling towards the audience

spine-chilling, terrifying

in the end
there is Nawi's death
lights slowly fading
to blackout

Amma wishes Dominique could have flown over to see a play she was the first to read ten years ago when Amma wrote it

a play that's taken this long to get staged because every company she sent it to turned it down as not being right for them and she couldn't bear the thought of resurrecting Bush Women Theatre to put it on

when Dominique left, she was left to steer the battleship alone

which she did for a few years, feeling abandoned, never finding someone to replace Dominique who had provided the practical solutions to Amma's creative ideas

she dismantled the company in the end

and went freelance

Shirley

her oldest friend will be here tonight, she's attended every one of Amma's shows since she was a teenager, has been a constant in her life since they met as eleven-year-olds at grammar school when Shirley, the only other brown girl in the school, made a beeline for her in the playground when Amma was standing alone one lunchtime amid the excitement of green-uniformed girls screeching and whooping and having fun skipping with ropes and playing hopscotch and games of tag

there was Shirley standing before her

Shirley, with perfectly straightened hair, her face so shiny (Vaseline, Amma later discovered), with her perfectly-knotted school tie, white socks pulled up to her knees

so composed, so neat, so nice-looking

unlike Amma's own messy hair, mainly because she was unable to stop unpicking the two braids her mother plaited for her every morning

or stop her socks slipping down to her ankles because she couldn't help rubbing one foot against the other leg

and her school cardigan was three sizes too big because her mother had made it to last three years

26

hello, she said, my name's Shirley, do you want me to be your friend?

Amma nodded, Shirley took her hand and led her to the group she'd just left who were playing rubber band skipping

they were inseparable after that, Shirley paid attention in class and could be relied on to help out with homework

Shirley listened for hours to Amma talking about the crushes she had on boys, and later, after a transitional bisexual period (with brief crushes on Shirley's brothers Errol and Tony), girls

Shirley never had a negative word to say about her sexuality, covered for her when she bunked off school and listened avidly to her tales from the youth theatre – the smoking, snogging, drinking, acting – in that order, even when their paths forked after school, Shirley into teaching, Amma into theatre, they maintained their friendship

and even when Amma's arty friends said Shirley was the dullest person on the planet and did she have to invite *her*? Amma stood up for Shirley's ordinariness

she's a good person, she protested

Shirley babysat Yazz whenever she was asked (Amma also babysat Shirley's girls once or twice, maybe?)

Shirley never once complained when Amma needed to borrow money to pay off her debts, which she sometimes wrote off as birthday presents

it felt one-way for a long time, until Amma reasoned she made Shirley's safe and predictable life more interesting and scintillating

and *that* was what she gave back

then there were the members of her group or *squad*, as Yazz corrects her, no one says group of friends, Mum, it's so, like, prehistoric?

she misses the people they used to be, when they were all discovering themselves with no idea how much they might change in the years to come

her group came to her opening nights, were at the end of a phone (landline, of course – how *did* that work back then?) for a spontaneous night out

were there to share and stir-up dramas

Mabel was a freelance photographer who went straight once she hit her thirties, ditched all her lesbian friends as part of her reinvention as probably the first black, Barbour-wearing, horse-riding housewife in the Shires

Olivine went from being un-castable in Britain because she was so dark to landing a major crime series in Hollywood and living the life of a star with ocean views and glossy magazine spreads

Katrina was a nurse who returned to Aberdeen where she belonged, she said, became a born-again Anglophile, married Kirsty, a doctor, and refuses to come down to London

Lakshmi will be here tonight, a saxophonist who composed for their shows, before deciding there was nothing worse than a song and a tune and began to put the niche into avant garde and play what Amma privately thinks of as bing-bang-bong music, usually headlining weird festivals in remote fields with more cows than punters in attendance

Lakshmi has also developed an improbable guru persona for the gullible students she tutors at music college

who gather around the hearth of her council flat sipping cheap cider from tea cups

while she sits cross-legged on the sofa in flowing robes, long hair streaked with silver

denouncing chord progressions in favour of micro-tonal improvi-
sation and poly-tempic, poly-rhythmic and multi-phonic structures
and effects
    while declaring that composition is dead, girls and boys
    I'm all about the contemporary extemporary

even though Lakshmi is approaching sixty, her chosen lover, male
or female, remains in the 25–35 age range, at the upper end of which
the relationship ends
    when Amma calls her on it, she comes up with a reason *other* than
that they're no longer quite so impressionable, fresh-faced and
taut-skinned

then there was Georgie, the only one who didn't survive into the
nineties
    a plumber's apprentice from Wales, she was abandoned by her
Jehovah's Witness family for being gay
    she became the lost orphan child they all took under their wing
    the only woman in a council's plumbing team, she had to endure
constant innuendo from her male colleagues with their jokes about
screw hole locators, blow bags, nipples and ballcocks
    as well as comments on what they'd like to do with her arse
when she was fixing something under a sink or peering down a
gutter

Georgie
drank two litres of Coca Cola a day and mixed it with spirits and
drugs at night
    she was the least lucky of their group in attracting women, and
sadly, stupidly, thought she'd be on her own forever

many a night out ended in tears with Georgie saying she was too ugly to pull, which wasn't true, they all endlessly reassured her how attractive she was, although Amma considered her more Artful Dodger than Oliver Twist

which in the lesbian world wasn't such a bad thing

Amma can never forget the last time she saw her, both of them sitting on the kerb outside the Bell as the revellers drifted drunkenly off while Amma forced a finger down Georgie's throat to make her regurgitate the pills she'd taken in the toilets

for the first time in their friendship, Amma actually showed her frustration with her friend for being such a hopeless case, for being so insecure, for not being able to cope with adulthood, for getting off her face all the time, it's time to grow up, Georgie, it's time to grow the fuck up!

a week later she went over the top floor balcony on the Pepys Estate in Deptford where she lived

to this day, Amma wonders how Georgie died

did she fall (accident), fly (tripping), throw herself off (suicide) or was she pushed (unlikely)

she still feels guilty, still wonders if it was her fault

Sylvester always shows up on first nights, if only for the free booze at the after-party

even though a few days ago he accused her of selling out when he cornered her outside Brixton tube station on her way home from rehearsal

and persuaded her to have a drink with him at the Ritzy where they sat in the upstairs bar surrounded by posters of the independent films they'd been going to see together since they first met as students at drama school

films like *Pink Flamingos*, starring the great drag queen, Divine, *Born in Flames*, *Daughters of the Dust*, *Farewell My Concubine*, Pratibha Parmar's *A Place of Rage* and *Handsworth Songs* by the Black Audio Film Collective

films that inspired her own aesthetics as a theatre-maker

although she's never admitted her equally lowbrow tastes to Sylvester, who's too much of a political purist to understand

such as her addictions to *Dynasty* and *Dallas*, the original series and their recent incarnations

or *America's Top Model* or *Millionaire Matchmaker* or *Big Brother*

and the rest . . .

Amma looked around the bar at the other alternatives who'd moved into Brixton when it was crime-addled but affordable

these people were her people, they'd lived through two riots and were proud of their multiracial social circles and bloodlines, like Sylvester, who'd gone on a pilgrimage here to visit the gay community centre that came and went and met the man who became his life partner, Curwen, newly arrived from St Lucia

they used to make such a striking couple

Sylvester, or Sylvie, was then blond and pretty, he spent most of the eighties wearing dresses, his long hair flowing down his back

he was out to challenge society's gender expectations, long before the current trend, he's taken to complaining, *I* was there first

Curwen, freckled and light brown, might wear a turban, kilt, lederhosen and full make-up

when he felt like it

to challenge various other expectations

he said

Sylvester's now grey, balding, bearded, and is never seen in anything other than a threadbare Chinese worker's suit

which he claims is an original from eBay

whereas Curwen wears a retro donkey jacket and denim dungarees

two young men sat at the table next to them, awkward and incongruous with their office haircuts, smooth cheeks, crisp suits, polished shoes

Amma and Sylvester exchanged looks, they hated the interlopers who were colonizing the neighbourhood, who patronized the chi-chi eateries and bars that now replaced a stretch of the indoor market previously known for stalls selling parrot fish, yam, ackee, Scotch bonnet peppers, African materials, weaves, Dutch pots, giant Nigerian land snails and pickled green eggs from China

these upmarket places also employed security guards to keep the locals out

because while their clientele loved slumming it in SW2 or SW9

they couldn't hide the fact that SW1 and SW3 were in their DNA

Sylvester was very active in the Keep Brixton Real Campaign

he'd lost none of his revolutionary zeal

which wasn't necessarily a good thing

Amma sipped her seventh coffee of the day, this one laced with Drambuie, while Sylvester slugged beer from a bottle, the only way a revolutionary should drink it, according to him

he still ran his socialist theatre company, The 97%, which toured to fringe venues and 'hard-to-reach communities', which she should also *still* be doing

Amma, you should be taking your plays to community centres and libraries, not to the middle-class bastards at the National

she replied that the last time she took a show to a library, the audience was mainly made up of homeless people who were sleeping at best, snoring at worst

it was about fifteen years ago, she vowed never to again

social inclusion is more important than success, or should it be called *sick-cess*? Sylvester replied, and Amma couldn't convince him she was right to move on to bigger things as he kept knocking back the beers *she* paid for (well, you must be earning a lot now you've hit the big time)

she argued it was her right to be directing at the National and it was the theatre's job to make sure they attracted audiences beyond the middle-class day-trippers from the Home Counties, reminding him this included his parents, a retired banker and homemaker from Berkshire, who came to London for its culture, parents who supported him, even when he came out as a teenager

he'd once let slip while drunk that he got a monthly allowance

(she was far too nice to ever remind him of this)

the thing is, she said, while troublemaking on the periphery's all well and good, we also have to make a difference inside the mainstream, we all pay taxes that fund these theatres, right?

Sylvester offered up the smug expression of a tax-dodging outlaw

at least I do *now*, she said, and you *should*

he sat back, his eyes watery from the beers, silently judging her, she knew that look, the drink was about to bring out a viciousness otherwise absent from her good friend

admit it, Ams, you've dropped your principles for ambition and you're now establishment with a capital E, he said, you're a turncoat

she stood up, gathered up her African print patchwork bag and left the premises a little further down the high street she looked back and saw him leaning against the wall of the Ritzy rolling up a cigarette

still rolling up

you stay there, Sylvie.

4

Amma walked to her house in the dark, still grateful she'd become a homeowner so late in life, at a time when she was practically homeless

first of all Jack Staniforth died and his son Jonathan, who'd been chomping at the bit for years at his father's simply scandalous decision not to financially capitalize on the King's Cross regeneration scheme that would one day run trains direct from London to Paris

gave the Citizens of Freedomia three months' notice

devastated, Amma nonetheless had to admit she'd had a spectacularly good run as she'd never paid a single copper penny in rent in what had become one of the most expensive cities on the planet

she cried when she left her former office with its jogging sized dimensions and windows overlooking the trains that rolled into the station from the north of England

she couldn't afford commercial rents and wasn't eligible for subsidized housing

Amma sofa surfed until she was offered someone's spare room

she'd come full circle

then her mother died, devoured from the inside by the ruthless, ravenous, carnivorous disease that started off with one organ before moving on to destroy the others

Amma saw it as symptomatic and symbolic of her mother's oppression

Mum never found herself, she told friends, she accepted her subservient position in the marriage and rotted from the inside

she could barely look at her father at the funeral

not long after, he too died of heart failure in his sleep; Amma believed he'd willed it upon himself because he couldn't live without her mother, who'd propped him up since his early days in England

she surprised herself at the strength of her grief

she then regretted never telling him she loved him, he was her father, a good man, of course she loved him, she knew that now he was gone, he was a patriarch but her mother was right when she said, he's of his time and culture, Amma

my father was devastated at having to flee Ghana so abruptly, she eulogized at his memorial, attended by his elderly socialist comrades

it must have been so traumatic, to lose his home, his family, his friends, his culture, his first language, and to come to a country that didn't want him

once he had children, he wanted us educated in England and that was it

my father believed in the higher purpose of left-wing politics and actively worked to make the world a better place

she didn't tell them she'd taken her father for granted and carried her blinkered, self-righteous perspective of him from childhood through to his death, when in fact he'd done nothing wrong except fail to live up to her feminist expectations of him

she had been a selfish, stupid brat, now it was too late

he'd told *her* he loved her, every year on her birthday when her mother was alive, when he signed the card she bought and sent for him

her successful older brothers kindly gave her the greatest share of the family home in Peckham
which paid for a substantial deposit on a small terraced house with a box garden in Railton Road, Brixton
a place to call her own.

5

Yazz
was born nineteen years ago in a birthing pool in Amma's candle-lit living room
surrounded by incense, the music of lapping waves, a doula *and* midwife, Shirley and Roland – her great friend, who'd agreed to father her child when the death of her parents triggered an unprecedented and all-consuming broodiness
luckily for her, Roland, five years into his partnership with Kenny, had also been thinking about fatherhood

he took Yazz every other weekend, as agreed, which Amma regretted when she found herself missing her newborn instead of feeling deliriously free from Friday afternoons to Sunday evenings
Yazz was the miracle she never thought she wanted, and having a child really did complete her, something she rarely confided because it somehow seemed anti-feminist
Yazz was going to be her countercultural experiment

she breastfed her wherever she happened to be, and didn't care who was offended at a mother's need to feed her child

she took her everywhere, strapped to her back or across her front in a sling, deposited her in the corner of rehearsal rooms, or on the table at meetings

she took her on tour on trains and planes in a travel cot that looked more like a carry-all, once almost sending her through the airport scanner, begging them not to arrest her over it

she created the position of seven godmothers and two godfathers to ensure there'd be a supply of babysitters for when her child was no longer quite so compliant and portable

Yazz was allowed to wear exactly what she liked so long as she wasn't endangering herself or her health

she wanted her to be self-expressed before they tried to crush her child's free spirit through the oppressive regimentation of the education system

she has a photo of her daughter walking down the street wearing a plastic Roman army breastplate over an orange tutu, white fairy wings, a pair of yellow shorts over red and white stripy leggings, a different shoe on each foot (a sandal and a welly), lipstick smudged on her lips, cheeks and forehead (a phase), and her hair tied into an assortment of bunches with miniature dolls hanging off the ends

Amma ignored the pitying or judgemental looks from passers-by and small-minded mothers at the playground or nursery

Yazz was never told off for speaking her mind, although she was told off for swearing because she needed to develop her vocabulary

(Yazz, say you find Marissa unpleasant or unlikeable rather than describing her as a shit-faced smelly bottom)

and although she didn't always get what she wanted, if she argued her case strongly enough, she was in with a chance

Amma wanted her daughter to be free, feminist and powerful

later she took her on personal development courses for children to give her the confidence and articulacy to flourish in any setting

big mistake

Mum, Yazz said at fourteen when she was pitching to go to Reading Music Festival with her friends, it would be to the detriment of my juvenile development if you curtailed my activities at this critical stage in my journey towards becoming the independent-minded and fully self-expressed adult you expect me to be, I mean, do you really want me rebelling against your old-fashioned rules by running away from the safety of my home to live on the streets and having to resort to prostitution to survive and thereafter drug addiction, crime, anorexia and abusive relationships with exploitative bastards twice my age before my early demise in a crack house?

Amma fretted the whole weekend her little girl was away

adult men had been ogling her daughter since before puberty

there are a lot more paedophiles out there than people realize

a year later Yazz was calling her a feminazi when she was on her way out to a party and Amma dared suggest she lower her skirt and heels and raise the scoop neck of her top so that at least 30% of her body mass was covered, as opposed to the 20% currently given a decency rating

not to mention *The Boyfriend*, glimpsed when he dropped her off in his car

as soon as Yazz was in the door, Amma was waiting in the hallway to ask her the sort of harmless question any parent would ask

who is he and what does he do? hoping Yazz would say he was in the sixth form, a relatively harmless schoolboy then

Yazz replied with dead-pan insolence, Mum, he's a thirty-year-old psychopath who abducts vulnerable women and locks them in a cellar for weeks on end while he has his wicked way with them before chopping them into pieces and sticking them in the freezer for his winter stews

before waltzing upstairs to her room leaving a whiff of whacky-backy

nor is the child she raised to be a feminist calling herself one lately

feminism is so herd-like, Yazz told her, to be honest, even being a woman is passé these days, we had a non-binary activist at uni called Morgan Malenga who opened my eyes, I reckon we're all going to be non-binary in the future, neither male nor female, which are gendered performances anyway, which means your *women's* politics, Mumsy, will become redundant, and by the way, I'm humanitarian, which is on a much higher plane than feminism

do you even know what that is?

Amma misses her daughter now she's away at university

not the spiteful snake that slithers out of her tongue to hurt her mother, because in Yazz's world young people are the only ones with feelings

but she misses the Yazz who stomps about the place

who rushes in as if a hurricane's just blown her into a room – where's my bag/phone/bus pass/books/ticket/head?

the familiar background sounds when she's around, the click of the bathroom door when she's in it, even though it's just the two of them in the house, a habit begun at puberty which Amma finds affronting

the exactly ten crunches of the pepper mill over the (canned!) tomato or mushroom soup that she prefers to Amma's lovely homemade ones

the murmur of music and radio chatter coming from her bedroom
in the morning

the sight of her daughter curled up on the sofa under a duvet in the
living room on Saturdays, watching television, until she's ready to go
out at midnight

Amma can just about remember that she too used to go out late
and return home on the morning bus

the house breathes differently when Yazz isn't there
waiting for her to return and create some noise and chaos
she hopes she comes home after university
most of them do these days, don't they?
they can't afford otherwise
Yazz can stay forever
really.

Yazz

I

Yazz

sits on the seat chosen by Mum in the middle of the stalls, one of the best in the house, although she'd rather be hidden away at the back in case the play is another embarrassment

she's tied her amazingly wild, energetic, strong and voluminous afro back because people sitting behind her in venues complain they can't see the stage

when her afro'd compatriots accuse people of racism or microaggressions for this very reason, Yazz asks them how they'd feel if an unruly topiary hedge blocked their view of the stage at a concert?

two members of her uni squad, the Unfuckwithables, are seated either side of her, Waris and Courtney, hard workers like her because they're all determined to get good degrees because without it they're
stuffed

they're all stuffed anyway, they agree

when they leave uni it's gonna be with a huge debt and crazy competition for jobs and the outrageous rental prices out there mean her generation will have to move back home *forever*, which will lead to even more of them despairing at the future and what with the planet about to go to shit with the United Kingdom soon to be disunited from Europe which itself is hurtling down the reactionary road and making fascism fashionable again and it's so crazy that the disgusting perma-tanned billionaire has set a new intellectual and moral low by being president of America and basically it all means that the older generation has RUINED EVERYTHING and her generation is doooooomed

unless they wrest intellectual control from their elders

sooner rather than later

Yazz is reading English Literature and plans to be a journalist with her own controversial column in a globally-read newspaper because she has a lot to say and it's about time the whole world heard her

Waris from Wolverhampton, seated to her right, is reading Politics and wants to become a Member of Parliament, to *re-pre-sent*, and will go down the community activism route first, à la Barack 'Major Role Model' Obama

Come Back Barack!

Courtney from Suffolk, seated to her left, is reading American Studies because she's really into African-American men, and she chose her course because of the option to study in the States for her third year where she hopes to pick up a husband

the theatre is predominated by the usual greyheads (average age one hundred)

Mum's friends and diehard fans are dotted all over, they should be grey but are more likely to shave it off, dye it or cover it up with head-wraps

she looks over at Sylvester, slumped in his seat, scruffy as hell in his tatty blue 'Communist China' overalls, his beard makes him look more like an Amish farmer than an urban hipster

way too old for it, Sylvie

his arms are crossed and he's scowling like he really wants to *not* enjoy the play before it's even begun, when he notices her ogling him, puts on a smiley face and waves, probably embarrassed that she's read his mind

she waves too, putting her nice-to-see-you-face back on

he's one of her godfathers, but was demoted to the C List when he sent her the same birthday card three years in a row – a cheap re-cycled charity one at that, as for birthday presents, he stopped them when she turned sixteen, as if she had no need for financial support once she could legally have sex

the A List goddies part with money, lots of it, every year on her birthday, they're the best as they really want to keep in with her as their conduit to the younger generation

a couple of goddies have disappeared altogether on account of fall-ing out with Mum over some pointless melodrama

Mum says Sylvester should stop sniping at other people's suc-cess (hers) and that as he won't change with the times, he's been left behind

you mean the way you felt not so long ago, Mum?

ever since she landed the National gig she's got very snooty about struggling theatre mates, as if she alone has discovered the secret to being successful

as if she hasn't spent way too many years of her life watching crap television while waiting for the phone to ring

this is the problem with having a daughter with X-ray vision
she can see through the parental bullshit

Uncle Curwen isn't with Sylvester tonight because he believes politics is way more dramatic than anything on stage at a theatre: 'Brexit & Trumpquake! – behold the comedy of errors of our time' being his latest mantra
as a Lambeth Labour councillor, he's usually at meetings fire-fighting, or as Sylvester counteracts, causing them, because he likes to drag the carpet from underneath Curwen's political self-importance
who needs enemies when your life partner undermines you on a regular basis?
Curwen uses antiquated expressions like 'right on' and likes to keep it real by frequenting the dingiest pub in Brixton where the old timers sit around still moaning about Maggie Thatcher and the Miners' strike, one of the few pubs that haven't been turned into a wine bar, gastro-pub or champagne bar, as Mum whinges
as if she herself wasn't part of the gentrification of Brixton years ago
as if she herself isn't a frequenter of the artsy hotspots like the Ritzy
as if she herself didn't take Yazz to one of the very champagne bars she supposedly scorns to celebrate passing her 'A' levels a year early
just this once, Mum whispered as they entered the part of the indoor market that's now frequented by posh banker types who looked at them as they walked down the lane between bars as if they were looking at natives on their cultural safari
yet who was it who was spotted at the Cereal Lovers Café in Stockwell by one of Yazz's mates not so long ago?
a café that specializes in selling over a hundred types of breakfast cereal at extortionate prices

a café that only those who've truly sold their souls to Hipster Hell would even think of venturing into

a café that's so outraged the locals they keep smashing the windows in

as for Dad

(you can call me Roland, no, you're my dad, *Dad*)

he's sitting a couple of rows in front of her, wearing one of his Ozwald Boateng suits – brilliant blue on the outside, purple satin on the inside

his head is shiny, thanks to cocoa butter first thing in the morning, last thing at night

he's straight-backed, thanks to monthly Alexander Technique sessions to counteract what he calls academic hunchback syndrome

every so often he casually glances around to see who's recognized him off the telly

Dad's budget in clothes could pay her university fees for a year, the very fees he *says* he can't afford

it's his thing, prioritizing fashion over the self-sacrifice of proper fatherhood

hers is rummaging through his stuff in search of the large denomination banknotes he leaves in his jacket pockets in his walk-in wardrobe in the (four-storey) house on Clapham Common with its white wooden flooring, yellow walls and the original Cartier-Bresson photographs he chanced upon in a car boot sale in Wembley when he was a teenager and bought for a pound each

as he boasts to all first-time visitors when they walk past them in the entrance hallway

it's also probably fair to say she was probably *too* young at thirteen to innocently open the drawer under his bed and come across a leather gas mask type thing with a leather dick attached where she presumed a nose should be, along with associated whips, gels, handcuffs and other unexplainable objects

unfortunately, once seen, never unseen and it was a lesson for her at a young age that you never know people until you've been through their drawers

and computer history

Dad

the author of the *New York Times* and *Sunday Times* bestselling trilogy: *How We Lived Then* (2000), *How We Live Now* (2008), and *How We Will Live in the Future* (2014)

Dr Roland Quartey, the country's first Professor of Modern Life at the University of London

really? *all* of it, Dad? she asked him when he told her proudly on the phone about his latest professorial number

isn't that, like, a bit of a tall order? don't you have to be an expert on everything in a world that encompasses over seven billion people and like about two hundred countries and thousands of languages and cultures

isn't that more like *God's* purview? tell me, are you God now, Dad? I mean *officially?*

he mumbled stuff about the Internet of Things and Pokémon, terrorism and global politics, *Breaking Bad* and *Game of Thrones* and then threw in quotes he attributed to Derrida and Heidegger for good measure, which he always does when he can't handle a tricky situation

what about bell hooks? she shot back, quickly scrolling down the reading list for her 'Gender, Race and Class' module on her phone what about Kwame Anthony Appiah, Judith Butler, Aimé Césaire, Angela Davis, Simone de Beauvoir, Frantz Fanon, Julia Kristeva, Audre Lorde, Edward Said, Gayatri Spivak, Gloria Steinem, V. Y. Mudimbe, Cornel West and the rest?

Dad didn't reply

he wasn't expecting this, the student outwitting the master (grass-hopper rocks!)

I mean, how on earth can you be a Professor of Modern Life when your terms of reference are all male, and actually all-white (even when you're not, she refrained from adding)

when he eventually spoke, his voice was choked, his car had arrived (not cab), he had to dash off

if true, the car (car = limo and cab = taxi) would be to chauffeur him to a television studio because he regularly pops up on the telly to have arguments with people even more arrogant than himself

he's become a media-whore, Mum opines disapprovingly, he was such a great guy before he became famous and was corrupted by celebrity, he used to believe in something, now he only believes in himself, your father is very establishment, Yazz, that's why they lionize him, he's not an outsider like me, trying to get a foot in the door and being given crumbs, Yazz, *crumbs*

funnily enough, when Mum watches him on the telly, she begrudgingly agrees with pretty much everything he says, and she can't say she's an outsider now she's on at the National

Dad did an epic sulk after Yazz's epic take-down

he couldn't have her to stay for that weekend or the next or the next

deadlines-deadlines-deadlines, you know how it is?

*

47

the thing is, if she and her father are going to have a healthy relationship into the future, it's up to her to keep him in check because no one else is going to do it, he surrounds himself with what Mum calls his 'court sycophants', the people Yazz meets at his parties, mainly famous white people off the telly who see him as an honorary one of them

she's almost got there with Mum, although it was a hard slog, especially when she was fourteen or fifteen and Mum was prone to hysteria when she didn't get her own way

now she knows better than to try to control or contradict her daughter

all Yazz needs to say these days is, don't sass me, Mumsy! and she shuts up

Dad's on that learning curve too

he'll thank her in the end

Kenny (Godfather Number Two, who wisely gives her birthday cheques starring *two* zeros) is sitting loyally next to Dad

Kenny's also bald and mustachioed in a 1970s way (*not* good), he's a landscape gardener and she and him get along mainly because he has no delusions about his own greatness, they'll watch *X Factor* together just for the sake of it, whereas Dad will pretend it's because he's going to write about its cultural significance

they go out riding their bikes very early on a Sunday morning before the city wakes up, across the common to Battersea, down the backstreets to Richmond and the river, for the pure enjoyment of it, not because it's enforced exercise to stay slim

which is the only reason Dad runs marathons

Kenny did ask her to be a bit less negative towards Dad the other day after he'd gone upstairs in a huff over a harmless comment she'd made

Yazz replied she was going through her cynical late teenage years, I just can't help it, Kenny, once I come out all lovable again on the other side, I'll let you know

Kenny cracked up at that, he likes to remind her he's known her since she was a sperm among millions in Dad's test tube and when Mum used to complain she was giving her a good kicking inside her womb

to which she quipped back that it was because she had an embryonic premonition she was going to be born into poverty

once she's graduated and working, she's going to persuade Mum to sell her house, correction, *their* house, which is now worth a fortune thanks to *Mum's* gentrification of Brixton

Mum can downsize to a bungalow, which will be very practical for a woman her age, probably in one of the unfashionable seaside towns where they'll be cheaper

with the money left over from the sale of the house, Yazz can buy a small flat

a one-bedroom will do for now

helping me on to the property ladder will be the defining act of your life, Mumsy

she didn't reply

Yazz wishes the play had already opened to five-star universal acclaim so that she can watch it stamped with pre-approval, it matters because *she'll* have to deal with the aftermath if it's slagged off by the critics and Mum'll go on an emotional rampage that might last weeks – about the critics sabotaging her career with their complete lack of insight into black women's lives and how this had been her big break after over forty years of hard graft blah di blah and how they didn't *get* the play because it's not about aid workers in

Africa or troubled teenaged boys or drug dealers or African warlords or African-American blues singers or white people rescuing black slaves

guess who'll have to be on the end of the phone to pick up the pieces?

she's Mum's emotional caretaker, always has been, always will be

it's the burden of being an only child, especially a girl

who will naturally be more caring.

2

Yazz has a massive poster of Hendrix in her room at uni with his crazy hair, hippy headband, rippled chest, bulging crotch and electric guitar

a cultural signifier for all those who enter her room to instantly know what kinda badass they dealin' wiv

although her eclectic and unpredictable taste extends beyond the electric rock riffs of prehistory to A$AP Rocky to Mozart to Stormzy to the Priests to Angélique Kidjo to Wizkid to Bey to Chopin to RiRi to Scott Joplin to Dolly Parton to Amr Diab and so on

she's even got a recording of the über basso profundo Oktavist singers of Russia who don't so much sing as make the earth rumble

so much radness and who's way ahead of da mob dem?

her room is the largest in her block on account of the 'extreme claustrophobia and social anxiety' stunt she pulled to get it

it overlooks the canal that runs along the border of the campus through to the wetlands beyond with its otters (or is it badgers?) and herons (or is it geese?) and other birdy, animalistic things she doesn't recognize and can't be bothered to look up she'd rather fill her head with stuff that will help her get on in life and naming the wildlife of eastern England don't come into it

the other side of her room overlooks the pathways that zig-zag through the campus, from which a stream of caners stagger past her window to their rooms most nights, usually drunk and selfishly loud, having been drinking in town or in the Student Union bar

she's only been in it once as it was crammed with the drunken dregs of humanity, i.e. the type of boys who get progressively mal-odorous as the term progresses because their mother isn't dunking them screaming into a bath every night

the kind of boys who wear increasingly injured expressions because they don't understand why no one will sit next to them in lectures and no one wants to tell them, yo, you stink, bro

Yazz thought she'd find romance at uni, a nice guy on her level who doesn't look like the back of a bus and is taller than her (prerequisite)

someone to snuggle up to on Saturday evenings and to laze away Sunday mornings in bed listening to music while she catches up with the *New Yorker*, *Observer*, *gal-dem*, *The Root*, *Atlantic* and *thegrio*

because one day she will write for them

sadly, Mum has more pulling power than her and is actually con-sidered hot in the lesbian world

her girlfriends *du jour*, as Dad puts it (hey, why speak English when you can speak French?), are two white women, Dolores and Jackie, although Mum has been with every ethnicity known to humankind (it's called multiracial whoredom)

they're all very cosy together which is quite heart-warming seeing as Mum's women have gone to war over her

it's strange, and suspicious, because with Dolores and Jackie there are no screaming matches, no ranting answerphone messages, no one trying to kick in the front door in the middle of the night, and no one skulking in a corner looking daggers at her rival at Mum's parties

it's like they actually like each other, Yazz suspects they have gruesome threesomes, and can't bring herself to ask

besides, she's lost count of the women who've come and gone to the point that the new ones barely register on her Richter scale of annoyance

there'll inevitably be a new face around the breakfast table trying to befriend the daughter of their new lover, running around making her toast, omelette with cheese and tomatoes, pouring her juice, washing up the dishes after her

the daughter who'll drop numerous unsubtle hints when her birthday/Christmas/Easter are approaching

(and why isn't the marmalade on the table?)

when Yazz talks about her unusual upbringing to people, the unworldly ones expect her to be emotionally damaged from it, like how can you not be when your mum's a polyamorous lesbian and your father's a gay narcissist (as she describes him), and you were shunted between both their homes and dumped with various god-parents while your parents pursued their careers?

this annoys Yazz who can't stand people saying anything negative about her parents

that's her prerogative

anyway, she's resigned herself to hanging out with the squad at uni rather than going out manhunting

it's unfortunate that she's coming of age as one of the Swipe-Like-Chat-Invite-Fuck Generation where men expect you to give it up on the first (and only) date, have no pubic hair *at all*, and do the disgusting things they've seen women do in porn movies on the internet

which she suspects the boys in her halls watch all day and all night, boys who are rarely seen outside their rooms (lectures? what lectures?)

she's only been on one date at uni, which involved sitting at a bar with a male specimen she'd thought was an interesting person, who was obviously swiping his phone to see if someone more fanciable was in the vicinity before making his pathetic excuses about having to do revision

she left shortly after he did, saw him chatting up a woman in a bar a few doors down when she passed on her way home

Yazz reckons that by the time guys her age want to settle down, her ovaries will be busted and they'll be on to women half their age who can still drop babies at the drop of a hat

so

even though she's considered reasonably attractive (as in not 100% ugly), with her own unique style (part 90s Goth, part post-hip hop, part slutty ho, part alien), she's having to compete with images of girls on fucksites with collagen pouts and their bloated silicone tits out

Yazz has considered dating older guys in their thirties (who are always up for banging teenagers), until she visualizes the nose hair, wrinkly cock and pot belly scenario

so until such time as someone suitable comes along (if he ever will) who can offer proper commitment with a view to a monogamous relationship in the long term (her mother she is not), she's got herself a booty call in Steve, an American who's studying for a PhD on 'the interrelationship and aesthetics of hip hop and racial politics in the eighties'

unfortunately, he's also got a girlfriend in Chicago, which provokes something of a moral conundrum when they're in bed together, and she calls and he lies about what he's doing

Yazz sometimes has sleepless nights worrying she'll be alone for the whole of her life
if she can't get a proper boyfriend at nineteen what hope is there for when she's older?
a couple of Mum's female friends have been single for decades, not the lesbians who have little problem getting off with each other, but the straight ones who've got good jobs and houses and no partner to share it with, who say they're not prepared to settle at this stage in their lives
Mum accuses them of 'Looking for Obama Syndrome'
behind their backs

Nenet, the third member of the squad, is engaged to Kadim who's studying in America, her parents chose him for her
she resisted at first until they threatened to cast her out, and the thought of having to actually find a job after uni and earn her own money, like the rest of them, brought her round
luckily, she hit it off with him once she actually met and got to know him, and is often off for long weekends (like Wednesday to Monday) in Connecticut where he's studying
even so she gets As for her coursework, she's that clever
she's also super-confident and the last person anyone should mess with
when a boy on campus starting sending her explicit texts, she reported him to the university and he narrowly avoided being thrown out

when a classmate was raped and broke down in front of her, Nenet paid for a lawyer who got the rapist imprisoned for six years

after which, they all agree, he'll be back on the streets raping more women

Waris is dating Einar, a Somali-Norwegian boy she's been with since they sat in History together at school

they're both big anime fans and go to London Comic Con every year

Waris draws cartoons as a hobby and is developing a female Somali superhero

who hunts down men who hurt women

and castrates them, slowly

without anaesthetics

while they lounge around, Yazz makes everyone hot chocolate from sachets and offers the shortbread biscuits Mum makes for her as she's weirdly taken up baking since Yazz went to uni, almost like she realizes she's not been the perfect picket-fence mum and is making amends

three-quarters of the squad don't drink much, if at all

Yazz's mind is her most valuable asset and she's not going to mess with it

Waris says yes to the hijab and sex outside marriage, no to booze and pork

Nenet says she expects to start drinking after a few years of marriage to Kadim when he takes on his first official mistress, which is what happened with her own mother, who starts the day with a G&T and ends it with a liqueur, having consumed a bottle of wine or three in between

Courtney's the only one whose social interactions are accompanied by red wine

Yazz was drawn to Waris on the second day of Fresher Week at the welcome party in the sports hall where they both skulked on the periphery; Yazz gravitated towards Waris's resting bitch face, as she later told her, which Waris took in good humour, asking Yazz if she'd looked in the mirror recently

they agreed that their peers were really immature, while sipping iced tea in a corner of a Starbucks on campus far away from the bedlam of the other freshers running around with their foam parties, disco paintballing, treasure hunts and group pub crawls that were bound to end up with A&E emergencies, Yazz predicted

whose idea was it? she wrote on the official Fresher Week feedback form

to introduce these poor young things to alcohol poisoning the first week they're away from home?

why don't you also book them into rehab now instead of waiting for the first signs of liver damage to show in their second year?

Waris
matches her headscarves with the colour of her flowing clothes
she has green days, brown days, blue days, floral days, fluorescent days – never black days (she's not a traditionalist)
she often sticks her phone just inside her hijab to carry out hands-free conversations, which Yazz tells her is an excellent blend of religiosity and practicality
to which Waris replies that she wears a hijab to make a statement about her Muslim identity, and while there are those who make out

it's a proper religious thing, there's nothing about women covering up in the *Koran*, you know?

Waris doesn't ever leave her room without applying a smooth paste of foundation on to her already perfect complexion

whole tubes of mascara to thicken already forested eyelashes

and her eyebrows are painted into a high arch that practically stretches all the way to her ears

Waris says she's ugly without her 'face on', even though Yazz re-assures her that Somali women are the most beautiful in the world, and that includes you too, Waris

Waris says she's fat, even though she's perfectly normal-sized, pinching her thighs so hard they go mottled then showing Yazz her 'cellulite', which is non-existent, Waris, it's just flesh being squeezed so tightly it nearly pops

she sometimes wears sunglasses when there's no sun – at night and inside buildings

she even tried it on in class, looking fierce and super-cool until one brave lecturer, Dr Sandra Reynolds (call me Sandy, guys and gals), showed she wasn't the pushover they thought she was when she ordered Waris to take them off unless she had a medical condition and certificate to prove it

or to leave her class

it's to make myself look fearless, Waris explained to Yazz after they'd treated themselves to a pizza one Saturday lunchtime and were making their way back to campus on the slippery and rainy cobbled streets of the university town where they stood out

or maybe it's to hide your fear, Yazz suggested, you're actually feeling fear-*ful*, the words are separated by a few letters, fear-*ful* or fear-*less*, similar but diametrically different, see?

Yazz felt a surge of preternatural wisdom beyond her years
it was one of those moments
Waris looked pensive as they walked on in silence, and then replied, equally sagaciously, perhaps it's both

in that moment Yazz understood why they got on so well, they were on the same intellectual wavelength

life was different before 9/11, Waris said, as they left the town behind and walked along a busy main road passing big old houses made of thick slabs of grey stone; she was too young to remember the 'before era', when her mother said people looked at hijabbed women with surprise, curiosity or pity

then there was the 'after era', when her mother said they began to be viewed with a blatant hostility that gets worse every time a jihadist blows white people up, or mows them down in a truck

at times like these Waris braces herself to get even more shoved, spat at and called names such as dirty Arab when I'm not even Arab, Yazz

Waris said it's crazy that people are so stupid to think over one and a half billion Muslims all think and act the same way, a Muslim man carries out a mass shooting or blows people up and he's called a terrorist, a white man does the exact same thing and he's called a madman

both sets are mad, Yazz

I know, Waris, I *know*

Yazz sees the dirty looks Waris gets when they're walking through town

she gives dirty looks back on her friend's behalf

Waris said her grandmother rarely left their council flat in Wolverhampton any more, it was too hard for her to walk the street and get such hostility, and she's never stopped mourning everything she's lost

she lived a well-off lifestyle in Mogadishu until 1991, in a family where all the adult men worked in the family dental practice, until they were killed and she fled here with her daughters

these days her grandmother pops prescription pills

she sits in the living room disappearing into herself

until one day she'll be lost to them for ever

Xaanan, her mother, is completely different, though, she drummed it into us kids that we could either decide to be crushed by the weight of history, and modern-day atrocities, or we could go into warrior pose

Dad works in a factory, Mum has two jobs, the first is working in a refuge for Muslim women and the second is teaching self-defence to women who cover up, so they can learn how to protect themselves from the 'hijab grab' and related assaults

she teaches a mixture of Krav Maga, Jiu Jitsu, Aikido and Pencak Silat at the local community centre, Waris said proudly; Waris herself learned mixed martial arts alongside her mother

Yazz and Waris arrive back at the campus and walk down the lane, rain abating, skies clearing, rainbow appearing

they pass the gym with students in sporty gear entering and leaving

they pass the laundry, students in a zombie daze watching the machines rotate or playing with their phones

they pass the arts centre with a gallery and a café inside it selling unaffordable coffee and unaffordable cakes for the posh people who come on to campus to use it they walk past the blocks of the accommodation quarter with music and weed drifting out, until they get to theirs

they go inside the building and climb the stairs as Waris continues talking, says she's learned to give as good as she gets if anyone says *any* of the following

that terrorism is synonymous with Islam

that she's oppressed and they feel her pain

if anyone asks her if she's related to Osama bin Laden

if anyone tells her she's responsible for them being unemployed

if anyone tells her she's a cockroach immigrant

if anyone tells her to go back to her jihadist boyfriend

if anyone asks her if she knows any suicide bombers

if anyone tells her she doesn't belong here and when are you leaving?

if anyone asks if she's going to have an arranged marriage

if anyone asks her why she dresses like a nun

if anyone speaks slowly to her like she can't speak English

if anyone tells her that her English is really good

if anyone asks her if she's had FGM, you poor thing

if anyone says they're going to kill her and her family

you've really suffered, Yazz says, I feel sorry for you, not in a patronizing way, it's empathy, actually

I haven't suffered, not really, my mother and grandmother suffered because they lost their loved ones and their homeland, whereas my suffering is mainly in my head

it's not in your head when people deliberately barge into you

it is compared to half a million people who died in the Somali civil war, I was born here and I'm going to succeed in this country, I can't afford not to work my butt off, I know it's going to be tough when I go on the job market but you know what, Yazz? I'm not a victim, don't ever treat me like a victim, my mother didn't raise me to be a victim.

3

That afternoon they ended up dancing to Amr Diab in Yazz's room

Yazz tells Waris it's important to counterbalance the state of being cerebral with the state of being corporeal

Waris asks her if she means they need to do physical activity because they spend too much time thinking?

yes, that's it, Yazz says, making elaborate movements with her arms as she dances

why didn't you just say that then?

they're still playing his songs very loudly later that evening with Nenet, who lives on the same corridor and first introduced the famous Egyptian singer to them; Yazz had instantly found herself transported as soon as the lyrics poured out of Diab's sexy lips on the screen

Waris loved him too, said Diab's music stirred her soul

Yazz said he made her feel love for the man who'll one day be on the receiving end of her passion

Waris said that man should be afraid, very afraid

Nenet said Diab was old school so for her it was more of a nostalgia thing, as she showed them how to dance Arabic-style with swaying hips and swirling arms, while high on jelly babies

it became their thing – Amr Diab evenings

*

Courtney, who lived next door, knocked on the door in her pyjamas, and asked them to turn it down because she's trying to sleep and it's, like, midnight?

Yazz told her to listen *very carefully* to the other people playing loud music in other parts of the building, can she hear them? above and below?

of course she can, it's a Saturday night, and as soon as the security guards who've been called drive off, the noise starts up again

everyone's at it, right? Yazz said, hands on hips, so why are you targeting *us* in particular, giving Courtney a look rich with subtext

it was a tense moment, diffused by Nenet, who said she knows how to handle conflict because her father was in the diplomatic service for the entire thirty years of Mubarak's presidency of Egypt

that's called a dictatorship, Waris challenged her

it's called political stability, Nenet swatted back

Nenet's grandfather had grown up with Mubarak in Kafr El-Meselha, he worked in the Ministry of Justice with him, their families were friends

as a diplomatic couple, her parents acquired the skills to talk to anyone as if they were deeply interested in them, even when they hated the bastards, they'd even be nice to you, Waris, Nenet once said, reassuringly

Waris knew what Nenet meant, Somalis were looked down on in Egypt

when Mubarak's government fell during the Egyptian revolution, Nenet's family fled to the UK where they had citizenship anyway because her dad had invested a million pounds here to get it

prior to that, her parents lived in lots of countries while she'd gone to boarding school in Sussex don't ask me where my family money comes from, she said, replying to Waris's enquiry

they've never told me

Nenet welcomed Courtney into Yazz's room, all diplomatic smiles to diffuse the situation, come in, what's your name? offering her Coca Cola, and when the music began again, showed her moves

just let yourself float, Courtney, imagine you're water, air, light, let the music move your body, don't overthink it, the aim is to dance with yourself for yourself

Courtney was soon swirling and floating with the rest of them, she liked this fa-la-la music and why hadn't she heard of it before?

don't you think that's a bit offensive? Yazz asked

why? I like it and belly dancing's fun, too

it's not called belly dancing, Yazz replied, that's so Orientalist and we don't tolerate that here, at which point Nenet told Yazz to cut it out and explained their dancing is inspired by what's now called Raqs Sharqi

okay, Courtney said, shrugging, doing a fancy spin and dancing as if she could divorce her hips from her waist, her waist from her chest, her arms from her torso and her hands from her arms

she was moving better than all of them

they all crashed on Yazz's floor that night, had breakfast together in the refectory

Courtney told them she grew up on a wheat and barley farm in Suffolk, they joked it explained her farm girl looks

sparkling eyes, Nenet said

translucent skin, Yazz said

milkmaid breasts, Waris added

Waris, who'd never left Wolverhampton before travelling for university open days, admitted she'd never stepped on a farm in her life

me neither, Yazz said, my soul is urbanista not ruralite

Nenet informed them that her parents have a farm in the Cotswolds which breeds llamas and a wine estate in the Franschhoek Valley in South Africa

Waris said it was all right for some, to which Nenet replied it's not my fault, Waris said fair-dos

Yazz said that while she liked the idea of fresh milk, the idea of cocks crowing when you want to sleep in put her off, similarly she liked the idea of fresh milk but not milking cows to get it, or killing them for your beef burgers

Waris said she liked the idea of going on daily bracing walks across the meadows, whereupon Courtney told her she hates walking and there are no meadows anywhere near her farm

as she ate her breakfast of eggs, bacon and baked beans, Courtney made the mistake of asking Waris why she wore a headscarf

Yazz looked up from her muesli expecting to see Waris kick off, instead, she dug her spoon in her thick porridge and said in a surprisingly mild voice that it's Number One – cultural, Number Two – political, and then, just as Yazz expected her to say Number Three – none of your damned business, she didn't

Waris simply said her mother told her she didn't need to explain herself to anyone

Nenet, on to her second espresso and nibbling on a boiled egg, was ready to step in – not necessary, Courtney apologized, although she sounded more petulant than sorry, I was only asking because I didn't know

cool, well now you do

*

64

Yazz decided that although Courtney was quite ignorant of other cultures, she'd shown strength of character and chutzpah, a precondition for joining the Unfuckwithables where they all tended to speak their minds and you had to fight back and not run off crying to the toilet like a wimp

she liked Courtney
and if she liked her
she was in the squad

one Monday morning a few months later, Yazz informed her, as they queued for the toilet after the Race, Class and Gender class, that she was in effect now an honorary sistah with an *h*, a term that originated with black women which was now being appropriated (typical!) by those who weren't

however, Courtney could never be a fully-fledged sistah, only honorarily so

she explained that being a sistah was a response to how we're seen as much as who we are, which actually defies simplistic reductionism, and that who we are is partly a response to how we're seen, babe

Yazz found herself calling people she liked 'babe' these days, it wasn't forced or pretentious, it just happened naturally

it's a conundrum, Yazz continued the conversation over lunch of bean soup for her (protein for the brain) and meat, mash and mushy peas for Courtney

people won't see you as just another woman any more, but as a white woman who hangs with brownies, and you'll lose a bit of your privilege, you should still check it, though, have you heard the expression, check your privilege, babe?

Courtney replied that seeing as Yazz is the daughter of a professor and a very well-known theatre director, she's hardly underprivileged

65

herself, whereas she, Courtney, comes from a really poor community where it's normal to be working in a factory at sixteen and have your first child as a single mother at seventeen, and that her father's farm is effectively owned by the bank

yes but I'm black, Courts, which makes me more oppressed than anyone who isn't, except Waris who is the most oppressed of all of them (although don't tell her that)

in five categories: black, Muslim, female, poor, hijabbed

she's the only one Yazz can't tell to check her privilege

Courtney replied that Roxane Gay warned against the idea of playing 'privilege Olympics' and wrote in *Bad Feminist* that privilege is relative and contextual, and I agree, Yazz, I mean, where does it all end? is Obama less privileged than a white hillbilly growing up in a trailer park with a junkie single mother and a jailbird father? is a severely disabled person more privileged than a Syrian asylum-seeker who's been tortured? Roxane argues that we have to find a new discourse for discussing inequality

Yazz doesn't know what to say, when did Court read Roxane Gay – who's amaaaazing?

was this a student outwitting the master moment?

#whitegirltrumpsblackgirl

Courtney added that as she only fancies black men and is likely going to have mixed-race children, her 'white privilege' is in any case going to be seriously dented, like at least 50% of it, and it's incredible in this day and age that she'd never met any black people in the flesh before she came to university from Dartingford which is entirely white except for three Asians

Yazz informed her that's a non sequitur, conversation-wise

Courtney replied that she herself is a big fan of the non sequitur which really only means that a conversation is free-flowing and intuitive, as opposed to following a predictable trajectory, so to speak

Yazz excused herself to go to the toilet.

4

Yazz invited Courtney to stay at hers at the end of their first year

she warned her that at least one of Mum's harem was likely to be walking about the house half-naked in the morning and trust me, that's not a pleasant sight with the oldies

Courtney'd only been to London once before, a day trip involving a bus tour to Buckingham Palace, Trafalgar Square, Big Ben, St Paul's Cathedral and the Tower of London, before getting the train straight back to Dartingford

they shared Yazz's double bed and chatted before they went to sleep that first night with the lights off and the moon shining straight on to the bed, which made the night feel special to Yazz, especially when the nights were warm and the window was open

as they lay there, Yazz asked Courtney why she hadn't visited the capital more often, you don't know what you've been missing, babe

it's because my parents don't like London, Courtney replied, they think it's a hellhole full of coloureds, suicide bombers, left-wingers, luvvies, gays and Polish immigrants, who deprive the hardworking men and women of this country of the chance to earn a good living; Dad gets all his political thoughts from the newspapers, quotes from them verbatim, although funnily enough he's friends with Raj, the mechanic in the village, they drink together down the pub

when I call him a hypocrite, he says, it's *Raj*, Courtney, he's *different*

you can tell your dad from me that the British economy would collapse without immigrants to set higher working standards, Mum says give me a Polish plumber or electrician over homegrown work-ers any day

it makes no difference to him, he says they're all the same, love, meaning all the people he hates

I can't wait to see his face when I bring home a mixed-race baby

Yazz showed Courtney Peckham, Stockwell, Brixton, Streatham

as they walked down Brixton High Street, Courtney said she was going to faint at all the beefsteak on show, couldn't help staring at the juicy buns on the boys whose jeans were so low they exposed almost their entire underpants

Yazz noticed that those 'buns' reciprocated Courtney's attention, her creamy softness pouring ostentatiously over the top of her denim blouse

they stared at Courtney, not at Yazz, who wasn't the one getting checked out as usual, and she usually got checked out a *lot*

not that she's interested in the kind of male who belts their trousers underneath their bum

today it's all about Courtney, who's not even particularly hot and it's like Yazz is invisible and her friend is an irresistible goddess

a white girl walking with a black girl is always seen as black-man-friendly

Yazz has been here before with other white mates

it makes her feel so

jaded

they arranged to meet up with Nenet at her family house behind Queensway

Nenet texted the directions, 'around the corner from Hyde Park LOL'

they arrived at a large house behind a security gate and had to ring the bell to be let into a drive made of crunchy gravel

a maid wearing a black uniform with white pinafore let them into a hallway of marble floors, fountain, colonnades and a winding Hollywood staircase that went all the way up to a domed roof

Nenet came bounding down the stairs to greet them holding a tiny ball of fluffy white fur in her arms, her shih-tzu, Lady Maisie

here, she said, thrusting it at them, have a cuddle

Courtney was happy to oblige, even let it snuggle up to her face, cooing about how cute it was, being used to far worse with farm animals, Yazz imagined, like pigs and sticking her hands up cows' anuses to release their constipated stools

she herself declined to touch it, not liking to get too close to things that licked their own bottoms clean

Nenet gave them a quick tour of the house, which Yazz thought was sick, as in obscenely rich *sick* not sick as in wonderful

Nenet apologized for her mother's ostentatious taste in home decor, not for her wealth

please be careful what you touch, squaddies!

Yazz noticed Courtney acting as if she was honoured to have been allowed into Nenet's life now that she'd seen how she lived

Nenet was now 'Nenet who lives in a huge house near Hyde Park', something Yazz couldn't mentally undo or un-factor into her opinion of her friend

she realized that knowing someone comes from money isn't the same as witnessing the extent of it in close proximity

*

they went for a walk in Hyde Park, strolled along the Serpentine in the sunshine

Yazz looked out at the blue lake and people enjoying themselves in pedalos and rowing boats

the path around it seemed to be a cruising strip for rich Arabs, the car park rammed with cars with doors that opened upwards and golden wheel hubs that could save the National Health Service

Nenet, who usually wore designer sportswear at uni, was clad in a tight top, short skirt, high heels, and looped over her shoulder was a Chanel bag with a gold chain

her body language changed whenever a group of young men approached to admiringly check her over, which they did without fail, what with her cascading black hair, gleaming brown skin and toned legs

this was her milieu, she was walking like a princess, a bit up herself

Nenet always insisted she was Mediterranean, much to Yazz's amusement and Waris's annoyance when she tried to convince them she wasn't black or even African as her family were from Alexandria on the Egyptian coast

you're African, Nenet, Waris lambasted her, go on, admit it, you're an African woman, and she'd jump on Nenet and pretend to beat her up, the pair of them squealing like six-year-olds

the Serpentine cruisers ignored Yazz who was way too dark for them (yeh and they can piss off)

they boldly slow-stripped Courtney with their eyes as if she was a chambermaid

Courtney got off on it, loving the attention

Yazz didn't want to break the news to her

*

the three of them discussed university in a way they didn't when they were on campus, but somehow today felt different, their first year had passed, the long summer stretched ahead

Yazz and Courtney were going to spend it prepping for their second year by getting on top of their reading lists, that and summer jobs would keep them busy

Waris had already started an internship at a Wolverhampton charity for ex-offenders

Courtney was about to start work in a lifestyle farm shop in Suffolk that sold cookers for ten thousand pounds

Yazz was waitressing in a hip West End restaurant frequented by oligarchs, celebrities and Premier League footballers with their trophy wives, mistresses and escorts

she made notes on her phone for her future memoir

and took surreptitious photos with her iPhone

Nenet, who was getting off on being in her natural habitat and the centre of attention, confided that she wasn't planning on doing any reading for her Art History course because – guess what?

she blurted out that she didn't need to

and this is confidential so pleeeeaaase don't tell a soul, especially not Waris, the truth is that I commission my essays from a retired academic

she turned to face them, expecting admiration, approval

Yazz was stunned, replied quietly, you're supposed to work for your degree like everyone else, I didn't know you were one of the cheats

it's not cheating when everyone else is doing it

that doesn't make it right and not everyone is at it

wake up, Yazz, people aren't going to tell you, are they? Kadim's MBA is costing him a fortune

Yazz wondered if their friendship could overcome Nenet's cheating on top of her extreme privilege, it explained why she could binge-watch an entire Netflix series the night before an exam and still get an A+ for her coursework

Nenet was a spoilt, lazy and immoral princess who didn't play by the rules and would do anything to hold on to her privilege, even marry someone picked by her parents

Yazz wondered if sharing the same corridor in halls and being one of the few brown girls on a white campus was really enough to keep the Unfuckwithables together post-university, or even into their second year, come to think of it

Yazz had to work hard, to lay the groundwork for the future because she's got to be at the top of her game, and Courtney (or rather Roxane Gay) really was right, she can see that now, privilege is about context and circumstance

and even if she was rich she wouldn't cheat, she's going to earn her first class degree and like Waris will bust a gut to get it, she's not going to be ejected into the big bad world with a poor degree and no master plan, last term she met third year students about to graduate who looked terrified when she asked them about their next steps

a Master's in Journalism beckons, in London, where she fits in and can live rent free with Mum

she's already a regular feature writer for the student newspaper, *Nu Vox*, and her column, *Why is My Professor Not Black?*, inspired by a student conference she attended in her first term, generated more online comments than any other that month, only half of them totally ignorant, of course, written anonymously by the inbred, pea-brained, racist, cowardly, fugly and utterly friendless *trolls* of this planet

the point is, the article boosted her rep and she's become a personality on campus, someone asked for her opinion by the Media Society and student radio

she's going to try and place articles in professional newspapers and über-blogs next year, and she's going to assume the editorship of *Nu Vox* in her third year, when she's eligible

she's going to get herself elected President of the Media Society

she's already thinking about her campaign strategy

woe betide any pipsqueak usurpers who get in her way

she knows it won't be easy, she's ready for the fight

*

Yazz reflects on the rest of the squad

Courtney's a really nice person, formerly naïve and uncomplicated, who's grown so much since she first arrived at uni and is now more worldly-wise through her membership of the squad, who aren't your typical students in the east of England, that is:

a badass humanitarian whose mother is a lesbian luvvie and whose father is a gay 'intellectual'

a super-rich (cheat) who's politically connected to the old Egyptian elite

a Muslim Somali woman who wears a hijab and is a mixed martial artist

Waris is the deepest of them all, because her family has such a painful history, even though she hates it when people feel sorry for her

Waris's life has been the most unfair and it's forced her to prematurely *maturate*

just as life's obstacles have forced her, Yazz, to prematurely *maturate*, too

and so it begins
The Last Amazon of Dahomey
the play.

Dominique

Dominique came across Nzinga at Victoria station in the rush hour
 as she was being knocked down by the steamrollering effect of
London's ruthless commuters determined to catch their trains at all
costs

her bag fell open and everything fell out: passport, *A–Z*, *Rough
Guide to London*, hemp purse, tampons, Zenith E camera, Palmer's
hand cream, evil eye charm, ivory-handled hunting knife

Nzinga was profusely grateful when a passing Dominique
approached to help, the pair of them scrambling about on the station
floor gathering up her belongings

when that was done, and Nzinga was once more upright and composed, Dominique found herself in front of an extraordinary vision

the woman was statuesque, her skin glowed, her robes flowed, her
features were sculptural, lips fulsome, thin ropes of dreadlocks fell
freely down to her hips, silver amulets and bright beads sewn into them

Dominique had never seen anyone like her before, offered to buy her coffee, confident she'd say yes because lesbians, and she suspected this one was, usually did

they sat opposite each other in the station café as Nzinga sipped on a glass of hot water with a slice of lemon in it, the only hot drink she allowed to pass her lips, she said, I don't abuse my body

meanwhile

Dominique, drinking a cup of granulated coffee into which she'd dissolved two sugars and was dunking a succession of digestive biscuits (a packet of Maltesers at the side for dessert), felt guilty about the rubbish she was unthinkingly putting into her body – abusing it, yes, abusing it

she'd never met an African-American before and Nzinga's accent evoked the sensory delights of warm cornbread, sticky ribs, gumbo, jambalaya, collard greens, cracklin', fried cabbage, peanut brittle – and other foods she's read about in novels by African-American women

Nzinga was visiting England for the first time since leaving as a small child, on her way back from a pilgrimage to Ghana where she'd spent two weeks, it was her first time in the Motherland, visiting Elmina Castle where captured Africans had been incarcerated before being shipped to the Americas as slaves

the guide led them into a dungeon, shut the door

in the hot, suffocating darkness he graphically described how up to a thousand people were crammed into a space meant for two hundred, with no facilities or sanitation and little food or water, for up to three months

in that moment all the painful history of four hundred years of slavery entered my body in a way it hadn't before and I broke down and sobbed, Dominique, I sobbed and realized more than ever that the white man has a lot to answer for

Dominique stopped herself replying that the African man had also sold Africans into slavery so it was a lot more complex than that

Nzinga was a builder of timber houses on 'wimmin's lands' in the 'Dis-United States of America' where she'd lived since she was five and her mother, tiring of Nzinga's father who flitted between various women in England and the Caribbean, fell for a handsome ex-Forces man via correspondence

she was only twenty-two when she stupidly moved Nzinga and her brother, Andy, from their flat in Luton into what turned out to be a mobile home in a trailer park in Texas

where she and her brother slept on the floor by the kitchenette, while her mother and the man shared the pull-down double bed and had loud sex a few feet away from them

he drank hooch from the minute he woke up to just before he fell into a drunken and drugged stupor at night, picking up odd jobs here and there

her mother found work in a chicken factory, was idiotically convinced she could cure him of his addictions and make a life for her children with him

her futile attempts to curtail his addictions resulted in being beaten up so often she gave up trying to change him and fell into the drug life herself

what began badly became worse as Nzinga found herself being badly raised by two junkies whose priority was not her and her brother

eventually the inevitable happened when she reached puberty, there'd been earlier signs, inappropriate touching and comments she'd been too young to decipher and later, too vulnerable to ward off

she had her virginity stolen while her mother and brother were out shopping and she'd stayed in to do her homework the next morning she managed to tell a teacher at school after she'd burst into tears, a man, as it happens, who'd always told her she was clever child – practically the only good man she's ever known

a social worker was assigned, she and her brother were fostered out to a family

who cared for them but did not love them

not deeply, not unconditionally

Andy went into the army at sixteen and turned his back on the sister who'd turned into a bull-dyke, as he called her when he discovered her in bed with her girlfriend

luckily, I really was bright and worked hard to get into the recently desegregated University of Texas at Austin, instead of the local community college

upon graduation, I set off to live in a women's commune to get away from people like my brother and the *beast*

when my mother died from an overdose

my brother and I didn't talk at the funeral

or since

Dominique sat there listening to the extraordinary vision before her, a woman who'd risen above the tragedy of her terrible childhood to become so magnificent, who exuded such warmth and experience

people saw Dominique as tough and self-sufficient, yet compared to Nzinga, she wasn't, Nzinga was powerful, unconquerable, her presence and energy dominated the café, her voice suffused a grey Monday afternoon with an exotic sensuous drawl

she was a zami, a sexy sistah, an inspiration, a phenomenon

Dominique wanted to curl into this woman and be looked after by her it was a new feeling because she'd been fully independent since leaving home, and here she was, feeling, what? excited? definitely

perhaps falling in love with a complete stranger

I think you might be right, Dominique replied later that day as they sat in Cranks wholefood restaurant in Leicester Square after Nzinga had suggested her relationship history of blonde girlfriends might be a sign of self-loathing; you have to ask yourself if you've been brainwashed by the white beauty ideal, sister, you have to work a lot harder on your black feminist politics, you know

Dominique wondered if she had a point, why did she go for stereotypical blondes? Amma had teased her about it without judging her, she herself was a product of various mixtures and often had partners of all colours

in contrast, Nzinga had grown up in the segregated South, although shouldn't that make her pro-integration rather than against it?

Dominique wondered if she really was still being brainwashed by white society, and whether she really was failing at the identity she most cherished – the black feminist one

she decided that Nzinga was a fairy angel sent to help her become a better version of herself

she became Nzinga's personal guide around the city, keen to show off how well she knew its history and hotspots, hopping on and off buses, taking shortcuts through the labyrinthine tunnels of the underground, slipping down ancient alleyways in the city's oldest parts, showing her the remnants of the Roman wall from nearly two thousand years ago, taking her on to the pebbly Thames beaches when the tide was out, where mud-larkers trawled for buried archaeological relics, through the numerous parks, greens, public gardens and wilder commons, on canal walks that lasted hours from Little Venice to the marshes of Walthamstow, on river cruises to Greenwich and Kew

at night, they slipped into tucked-away women's clubs
where they made out in darkened corners

they slept together the day they met and every night thereafter

it's so sublime, it's spiritual, Dominique raved at Amma when she turned up for work a fortnight later to a desk-full of incomplete tasks

I've fallen in love properly for the first time in my life with the most wonderful woman I've ever met, who desires me from a position of inner strength, Amma, and it might sound odd but that's so new to me and darned sexy, like she can rip my clothes off whenever she wants to (which she does) and I feel helpless and dominated (which I like), whereas my previous lovers desired me from a position of weakness, of adoration, which just isn't interesting to me any more

the tension between us is electrostatic, Ams, it's like I'm being charged up with electric volts, we can't bear to be apart, not even for five minutes, Nzinga is so wise and knowledgeable about how to be a liberated black woman in an oppressive white world that she's opening my eyes to, well, everything, it's like she's Alice and Audre and Angela and Aretha rolled into one, seriously, Ams

Amma replied that this Nzinga must be something else to turn the coolest dyke of us all into a lovestruck teenager, so when do I get to meet Alice-Audre-Angela-Aretha? what's her real name, by the way?

Cindy, if you must know, don't *ever* tell her I told you

80

Dominique agreed to bring her to lunch at the King's Cross squat, on Nzinga's strict proviso that only women of colour were invited, and the food had to be completely vegan, organic and fresh

or she couldn't be in the same room as it.

2

Nzinga really did look spectacular when she walked in the door of Amma's room in Freedomia

she was at least six foot tall with ornamented dreadlocks, large wooden Akuaba fertility doll earrings, red trousers, a cream embroidered caftan and strappy Roman sandals

she was somewhat older than them, yet somehow appeared ageless

Amma noted how the force of her presence had the effect of diminishing everyone else's

before she arrived, her guests wanted to like Nzinga because they liked Dominique, now she was here, they wanted to impress her

Amma wanted Nzinga to prove herself worthy of Dominique's love

Nzinga sat cross-legged in the circle of women on the floor where the meal was to take place (Amma found the idea of a dining table too suburban)

vegetable casserole with sweet potato, salads and brown loaves were spread out before them on a plastic tablecloth

(everything was from the budget supermarket, nothing was organic or fresh, who could tell once vegetables were cooked or chopped, and how dare Nzinga demand everyone eat according to her preferences)

the conversation was lively, everybody wanted to talk to Nzinga who'd been afforded a gravitas she hadn't earned, Amma thought, simply by looking like a swamp-diva-voodoo-queen

Nzinga lapped up the attention, was friendly, no *magnanimous*, with everyone, until she ruined it by exclaiming, somewhat scornfully, how weird it was to hear so many black women sounding so *Britissshhh*

Amma thought she was accusing them of being too white or at best, in-authentically black, she'd come across it before, foreigners equating an English accent with whiteness, she always felt the need to speak up when it was implied that black Brits were inferior to African-Americans or Africans or West Indians

in any case, it might explain why Dominique had adopted an American lilt in the short period of time she'd been with Nzinga (oh Dominique!)

that's because we are, Amma replied, British, *all* of us are, right? yet she was instinctively aware that to challenge Nzinga wasn't wise

Nzinga didn't miss a beat in replying that black women need to identify racism wherever we find it, especially our own internalized racism, when we're filled with such a deep self-loathing we turn against our own

it struck Amma that this woman could be a formidable opponent, the energy that had hitherto radiated warmth had quickly turned radioactive

Dominique, usually an opinionated loudmouth, was oblivious to the bilateral tensions in the room – two alpha females about to go nuclear

she sat purring at her beloved's side

we have to be vigilant, Nzinga said to the gathered women who seemed hypnotized by her, we must be careful who we allow into our lives, she said, now staring at Amma with open hostility, there are women among us who've been sent to destroy us, internalized racism is everywhere, my friends (*her* friends?)

we have to be vigilant about everything, and everyone

point made, she then proceeded to ignore Amma

we have to be vigilant with our language, too, she continued, have you noticed that the word black, for example, always has negative connotations?

heads nodded, to Amma's dismay, what was the matter with them?

Nzinga then launched into the racial implications of stepping on a black doormat rather than over it, of not wearing black socks (why would you step on your own people?), and don't ever use black garbage bags, she instructed, as for blackmail, blackball, black mood, black magic, black sheep, black-hearted, I never wear black underpants, for example, why crap on myself? I'm surprised you all don't know this already

there were more nods, Amma kept flashing Dominique looks, is she serious? are *you* serious? except Dominique was too preoccupied lapping up this codswallop

Amma had had enough, she alone would have to deal with this woman, seeing as everyone else's brains had turned to mush

that's not a problem for me, she said, because guess what, I've not crapped my pants since I stopped wearing nappies as a kid

there was a detectable ripple of suppressed laughter in the room, great! she was breaking Nzinga's spell, who was livid, this is no time for cheap jokes, Amma, I think you need to listen to Bob Marley's 'Redemption Song' and emancipate yourself from mental slavery

Amma considered thanking Nzinga for informing her she was mentally enslaved, and told her that African peoples were referred to

83

as black long after the word made its appearance in the English language, so it makes no sense to retroactively impose racist connotations on to its everyday usage, and if you do, you're going to drive yourself mad and, I'm sorry to say, everyone else with you

I'm surprised you don't know this already

it took Nzinga under a minute to make her excuses, Dominique in tow

Amma was pleased to see the back of the awful *Cindy*

the old Dominique would have done the same in her position

the new Dominique had become gullible to every piece of shit the voodoo queen spouted

how on earth had this happened?

Amma hoped the Nzinga phase would end when the woman returned to America

she *was* returning to America, wasn't she?

at the end of their summer of love, Dominique (cowardly) told Amma on the phone she'd been issued with an ultimatum by Nzinga, either she goes to the US with her, or we go our separate ways, I don't do long distance, daaarlin'

Amma told her she was crazy, don't go with that woman, Dominique, don't go

but having found real love, Dominique followed it to America.

3

Nzinga was a teetotal, vegan, non-smoking, radical feminist separatist lesbian housebuilder, living and working on wimmin's land all over America before moving on, a gypsy housebuilder

Dominique was a drinking, drug-dabbling, chain-smoking lesbian feminist carnivorous clubber who produced theatre by women
and lived in a London flat

she soon became a teetotal, vegan, non-smoking, radical feminist
lesbian housebuilder on wimmin's land called Spirit Moon, which
only allowed lesbians to reside there

other females could visit, adult males and boys over ten could not

their job was to help build affordable houses in order to tempt
younger women to revitalize an ageing community

the rural setting of Spirit Moon with its endless space and vistas
was invigorating to Dominique compared to the polluted air, dirty
streets, frenzied atmosphere and hard-edges of London where life
happened at such a fast pace she'd been swept up into its masculine
(as Nzinga pointed out) metropolitan maelstrom ever since first arriving from Bristol

the two of them were allocated a log cabin at the furthest reaches
of the estate, an idyllically isolated corner where they could snuggle
away from the world and toast crumpets over an open hearth

in front of them were fields, behind was a beech, birch and maple
forest

that first night Dominique was too excited to sleep, she went to sit
on the veranda in the darkness listening to the unfamiliar sounds of
the countryside

how could Amma have wanted to deny her this experience? was it
jealousy, as Nzinga suspected, saying that as she'd usurped Amma as
the most important person in Dominique's life, Amma couldn't handle it?

it was true that she and Amma had been soulmates without the sex and now Nzinga was her soulmate, a total, one-off goddess, why couldn't Amma see that? and her rudeness at the dinner was unforgivable, how could she have twisted Nzinga's words when she was only trying to help everyone understand how racism worked?

Nzinga was a good person with a big heart

who'd landed in Dominique's life when she was in between lovers and ready for something different

and just as she was tiring of running a theatre company where she spent too much time on the conveyor belt of writing grant applications with a measly 10% return

Amma hadn't really taken on board her complaints about this, had always reminded her what a great team they were, Dom, look at what we've achieved

yes, but deep down Dominique had wanted something new, an adventure, even though she hadn't articulated it and didn't know what form it would take

long summers on Lesbos where she camped on the beach with hundreds of other lesbians were no longer quite so enchanting after seven consecutive years

European city breaks were okay but hardly fulfilling, she'd been to Guyana a couple of times and knew she couldn't really live there easily as an out lesbian, and she wasn't interested in teaching English as a second language somewhere abroad, a popular option with other twenty-somethings

and then Planet Venus beamed Nzinga down to her at Victoria station to give her the Great Love that Changes Everything

that first week at Spirit Moon they were invited to a buffet at the house of Gaia, who owned the estate and bequeathed it to the trustees in her will, to ensure it remained wimmin's land in perpetuity her home was a sprawling ranch house with vaulted ceilings, patchwork throws, curvilinear sculptures of female bodies, pottery vases, bucolic paintings and tapestry wall hangings Gaia had made herself

there were no images of any men

anywhere

they poured outside to enjoy the warm night, the lawn lit by flaming torches staked into the ground

the clear soprano of Joan Baez, mournful alto of Joni Mitchell, and the richer, melodious contraltos of Joan Armatrading and Tracy Chapman emanated from the deck of the record player on the veranda

Dominique heard crickets, the distant sounds of owls, the hum of women enjoying each other's company, she was fascinated and felt like a time-traveller who'd voyaged into a quite magical alternate society

the women's faces were tanned, healthy, seemingly untroubled, as if they were at ease with themselves and each other

all this happy-happiness felt weird to Dominique as she moved among this group of strangers who greeted her with genuine enthusiasm

was this a cult?

she was used to cool Londoners who checked you out with a critical eye before deciding if you were worthy of their time and conversation

Gaia's grey hair was whipped up into a bun, others wore plaits or crew cuts, a couple of the black women favoured the simplicity of cornrows

they wore jeans and slacks, tee-shirts and baggy shirts, gilets or waistcoats, jumpsuits and baggy dresses, nobody wore make-up or high heels

they brewed their own beer, had a vineyard, a few smoked cigarettes and marijuana, Dominique longed for a relaxing draw, but she'd promised Nzinga she was done with it, agreeing that a poisoned body was a sign of a poisoned mind

the women who lived in the community came from every profession, as well as former housewives, they were craftswomen, chefs, teachers, farmers, shopkeepers, musicians, many were retired

Dominique was curious to know more

Gaia told her she'd been through the wars for social and legislative acceptance in the fifties and sixties, eventually deciding to turn her back on men, she was done with the patriarchy

when she inherited her parents' Long Island mansion, she bought this farm

did she miss men?

never, the women of Spirit Moon try to live in harmony, even when arguments break out, we have a talking circle and try to sort it out, women can also choose to live hundreds of acres apart until things cool down, a feud might take years to heal, in time there's forgiveness, even if scars remain

occasionally a resident is forced to leave over unsanctionable behaviour such as violence or theft, if a woman goes straight and wants relationships with men, she has to leave, if she's celibate, she can stay, once we had a woman who turned and was caught sneaking men on to the property at night

she had to go

Dominique said the women seemed very laid back, not the ballbreakers of her imagination, although there was nothing wrong with ball-breakers, she'd even been accused of it herself there's no need to be breaking balls here, Dominique (what a pretty name you have), because there are no men here, which is why we come across as serene to you, we can just be ourselves, reclaiming the Feminine Divine, connecting to and protecting Mother Earth, sharing our resources, making decisions communally but maintaining our privacy and autonomy, self-healing the female body and psyche with yoga, martial arts, walking, running, meditation, spiritual practice

whatever works for each one of us

Dominique chatted freely, moving at ease between the women, as fascinated with them as they were with her, a black British woman, a rarity in these parts, they commented, visibly appraising her favourably

she was used to that, and enjoyed it

Nzinga stayed in her seat on the veranda all night, grim-faced, people approached her warily as a result, whenever Dominique looked over, she noticed Nzinga monitoring her every movement, although it didn't stop her mingling, enjoying a conversation with a stunning Native American woman called Esther, who wore a figure-hugging jumpsuit, who taught Ashtanga yoga to women in town, who hoped Dominique would come to her sixty-fifth birthday party

I'd love to, Dominique replied, complimenting Esther on looking so great for her age, just as Nzinga unexpectedly tapped her on the shoulder

we have to go

really?

they walked back to their house in the dark on paths that cut through the fields either side of them, Nzinga beamed the torch ahead, Dominique felt happily removed from her customary life in London in this quite special place, was she going to go all hippy-dippy, too?

Nzinga was quiet for a while, then declared it's better if we don't socialize any more, once is enough, I'm here to be with you, not them, and I can only take so much of the fake friendship of white women and their flunkies, if they invite you to their talking circle say no, it's a ruse to find out your private business and use it against you at a later date

remember we're here to work, it'll only mess things up if we blur the boundaries, and trust me, don't believe all that Mother Earth bullshit, I've been around enough of these women's communities to know these witches are as malevolent as any other person out there

why are we here if you're so critical of them? Dominique asked

because I don't want to live in a man's world

they continued talking and walking, feet crunching on stony ground

with me, you're safe, Nzinga said, although Dominique wasn't feeling particularly unsafe

with me, you're complete, although Dominique wasn't feeling incomplete

with me, you're home, because home is a person and not a place

Nzinga said she'd been thinking about renaming Dominique as Sojourner, a feminist re-baptism, after Sojourner Truth, the anti-slavery activist, proceeding to deliver a potted history, although Dominique knew exactly who the legendary abolitionist was, as every self-respecting black feminist did, and said so

she still got the lecture

it will be a feminist awakening of your new self, Nzinga explained, having a name more appropriate than a feminized Dominic

I like my name

so keep it, I'll call you Sojourner anyway, daaarlin'

Dominique decided Nzinga could call her what she liked, she wasn't going to answer to bloody Sojourner or any other name, Nzinga was showing signs of being a bit odd, perhaps Amma was right when she'd warned her, don't go to America with that woman, Dom, you'll regret it

the veranda light of their log cabin emerged out of the darkness, Nzinga said the dark wasn't something to be feared when staying on land occupied only by women

Dominique thought rapists and serial killers didn't need to be brain surgeons to surmount a high fence to get to their prey

they lit candles in the bedroom, made love, Nzinga said it was how they shared their deepest connection, Dominique agreed to that, sex with Nzinga was a wholly enjoyable experience in that Nzinga mainly serviced her, which she discovered she liked, as opposed to the more egalitarian actualities of her sexual past, which now seemed unfulfilling, although not at the time

as they lay awake afterwards in each other's arms, Dominique did feel complete, or at least more complete

Nzinga stared up at the low beams of the timber ceiling and told Dominique she'd earned the right to hear more about her life, starting with Roz, her first partner, now it was clear they were going to spend the rest of their lives together

Dominique thought that was premature

a lifetime was a vast distance into the unknowable future

when you're still only in your twenties
it's early days yet, Nzinga
she wanted to say

it was on wimmin's land in Oregon where Nzinga met Roz who
she thought was the love of her life, an older white woman who
showed her that women were much happier without men

Roz was a builder of everything from garden sheds to tree houses
to cabins to large houses and barns, Nzinga was apprenticed to her

for the first few years she felt cherished, blessed

it was a pretty idyllic existence working together during the day, loving together at night, until she discovered Roz was a lapsed alcoholic
who kept it secret, it came out when Nzinga found Roz's secret stash of
gin which she was working her way through while Nzinga slept

after the first confrontation, nothing Nzinga could do was right

they fought, first verbally, then physically, ornaments were
smashed, furniture upturned, curtains ripped off, window panes
cracked, one night Roz was rushed to hospital, a broken bone, minor
head contusions, nothing major, nothing life-threatening

the (all white, of course) women's community blamed Nzinga,
said they'd had enough and it was time for her to go, which was
deeply unfair

she was callously evicted, packed her belongings into a single
rucksack, was escorted to the gates and ejected into the outside world

it took her years to get over the injustice of it

Nzinga hit the road, hired herself out to women's communities on
the Eastern seaboard, recovered emotionally, had a couple of relationships that ended badly when people revealed their true selves,
decided to go searching for a true soul sister, which took years

I had to travel all the way to London to find her

you – Sojourner

Nzinga turned to face Dominique, pillow to pillow, cupped her cheeks in her large, strong hands

now that I've opened up to you, let's agree not to keep any secrets between us from now on, I want to know everything about you and you will know everything about me

agree?

Dominique nodded, aware, however, that turning her head from side to side was practically impossible because it was held in the iron clamp of Nzinga's hands, no longer just warm and romantic but mechanical

do you still love me?

more than ever, Dominique replied honestly, even more admiring of Nzinga for her honesty and strength in surmounting such trials

she was grateful that such a woman had chosen her

or rather

as Nzinga said, love chose them.

4

A few months in and the love that chose them was too often tumultuous

they were arguing more than Dominique ever had in her life, to the point where she wondered about the truth of Nzinga's break-up with Roz

Nzinga never saw herself as less than faultless

the problem with you, Sojourner, is that you're used to leading instead of being led, she'd say, remember you're my apprentice – in housebuilding, in living a truly radical separatist feminist lesbian life, in steering clear of the enemy, in living free of chemical toxins, in living off the soil and on the soil, it really won't work if you insist on fighting me at every turn

so when did our love affair turn into an apprenticeship? I'm a leader myself, aren't I?

ah, but is that really you? Nzinga challenged, often in the middle of the night when Dominique was desperate to sleep and they'd been arguing for hours and just when she nodded off, Nzinga would shake her awake and start making the same points again

what if you drop the tough girl act and just *be*?

what if you discover who you truly are deep down?

what if you allow yourself the luxury of being cared for – completely?

Dominique's feelings were conflicted, Nzinga was still glorious, still magnificent, still the object of her passion, still someone she believed wanted the best for her, who'd rescued her from London

as she was often reminded

when things were good, Dominique felt the headiness of a love that really might last for ever

when they weren't, she wondered what she was doing with someone who wanted to micro-manage her entire life, including her mind

why did Nzinga think being in love with her meant she had to give up her independence and submit completely?

wasn't that being like a male chauvinist?

Dominique felt like an altered version of herself after a while, her mind foggy, emotions primal, senses heightened

she enjoyed the sex and affection – outside in the fields when

94

summer arrived, wantonly naked in the heat, unworried about anyone coming across them, what Nzinga called Dominique's sexual
healing, as if she'd been suffering terribly when she met her

Dominique let it pass

she wanted to talk this through with friends, Amma most of all, or
the women at Spirit Moon, she needed a sounding board, it wasn't
going to happen, Nzinga kept them at a distance, kicked up a fuss
when Dominique made overtures of friendship to the women they
worked with

she decided it wasn't worth the hassle, and although she sent three
letters to Amma, she never heard back when she did receive replies
from her parents and siblings

was Amma still angry with her for leaving her and the company?

when she once suggested phoning her long distance from the post
office in town, Nzinga sank into a terrible funk for days

it was a sign Dominique was rejecting her

who never mentioned it again.

5

Before arriving at Spirit Moon, Dominique had naïvely thought of
housebuilding in purely romantic terms; she'd imagined her lean, long,
much admired body becoming even more toned, supple and strong
through using it as nature intended – working in the great outdoors,
doing strenuous physical exercise, enjoying camaraderie with her co-
workers, getting sweaty and dusty and looking forward to showering
it off at the end of the day before sitting down to a hearty meal

work would be simple, vigorous and life-enhancing

well, it didn't quite work out like that

having never lifted anything heavier than stage weights, she found eight-hour days of manual labour unbelievably gruelling, her joints ached and never had time to recover, her smooth, elegant hands blistered, lacerated and coarsened, even underneath protective gloves, and she had to wear a helmet that didn't shield her face from the sun

she imagined herself down the line: practically crippled, calloused, with a face as craggy as an ancient fisherman

Dominique decided she wasn't cut out for such work, unlike her co-workers who were built like brick-houses, including Nzinga

they were the butch ones, she was not, and even if she was (she'd never felt the need to categorize herself) it was clear American butches totally outclassed British butches in the Butch Universe

Dominique felt quite femme beside them

at the start of her second week on the job, she refused to get out of bed because her back felt like it was broken, yes, broken, she told Nzinga, looking tragic, doleful, tearful, until Nzinga promised her lighter duties cos I gotta look after my baby, don't I?

thereafter Dominique's duties involved minor jobs such as hammering nails, stapling insulation to timber frames, painting, decorating, and providing coffee and snacks several times a day

at home, Nzinga insisted on cleaning the log cabin herself, because she wanted to make sure it was as dust-mite free as possible

Dominique didn't object, seeing as her idea of housework had always involved waving a feather duster-wand over various surfaces as she skipped around a room

Nzinga also insisted on doing all the cooking because she alone understood how to formulate the right nutritional balance for them to sustain perfect health, which Dominique wouldn't have minded except Nzinga cooked without salt, which was banned from the house, and spices, which Nzinga said agitated both the stomach and the emotions eating became both an unpleasant ordeal and a performance of enjoyment

Nzinga also washed Dominique's clothes, by hand, because I am enslaved by my love for you, she said, in jest or perhaps not, in spite of Dominique's protestations that she wanted to wash her own undies, especially the ones stained with menstrual blood

Dominique began to regret allowing Nzinga to do everything and make decisions for her

she started to yearn to do the housework herself, yearn to cook, to clean, to do a job that was more intellectually demanding

her life was becoming empty of purpose other than to love Nzinga unconditionally, and, increasingly, obey her

even the simplest things became a source of difficulty

was it really her fault men ogled her in town when she wore (knee-length) shorts and a (sleeveless) baggy tee-shirt

should she really have to cover up instead of being 'provocatively dressed' as Nzinga accused her

why should she wear her hair (usually a thick, wavy mixture of Afro and Indo) almost shaved to her scalp, cut by Nzinga herself with the barber's clippers she bought for this very purpose?

why shouldn't she have a chat with the gentle community baker, Tilley, when she went to collect bread in the mornings?

because the women who appear the nicest are the most passive aggressive and ultimately the most dangerous because they will come between us, don't you realize that people want to sabotage our great love affair?

and why shouldn't she read books by men that she'd picked up in the library in town?

you can't live a womanist life and have male voices in your head, Sojourner that doesn't make sense, it's taking things too far

why don't you shut your goddam mouth

they were sitting up in bed, it was the early hours, again, Nzinga had been on her case about her past girlfriends for hours, she brought them up every so often, this time trying to convince Dominique they had been playthings who meant absolutely nothing to her

Dominique was fed up of convincing her that past girlfriends weren't a threat to their present relationship, she'd already told her many times that the love she felt for a couple of them was nothing compared to what she felt for Nzinga, not realizing that to admit any kind of love for her exes was unacceptable

she wanted to leave the room, to sleep elsewhere in the cabin, or on the porch, anything to escape Nzinga's droning voice; not possible, Nzinga would follow her out of the room and keep it up, sometimes until dawn

they were all white women, they were never going to stick around

I'm the one who left them, it was true, she was the dumper, never the dumpee

what I'm saying is, only a black woman can ever truly love a black woman

okay, I give in, I agree, let's turn off the light and go to sleep

I don't want you to give in, I want you to change, to understand my reasoning at a deeper level and accept it as the truth.

6

Almost a year to the day Dominique had arrived at Spirit Moon, there was a knock on the cabin door late one afternoon

Nzinga was cooking, Dominique had been lying on the sofa staring emptily at the clouds moving in the sky

it was Amma standing before her, delighted to see her

fucking hell, Dominique shouted, it was so good to see her, they collided in a hug

I was so worried about you, Dom, one postcard when you arrived and that was it, you never answered my letters

what letters? Dominique was about to say when Nzinga appeared behind her and asked why she'd invited *this person* to stay?

she hadn't, Dominique answered, cringing, isn't it great Amma's here?

Nzinga said nothing, returned to the kitchen, resumed cooking

undeterred by Nzinga's rudeness, Amma marched into the main area of the open plan living room cum kitchen and inspected it as if expecting to see corpses hanging from the beams by meat hooks

she flung her knapsack on the floor, threw herself on to the sofa, I'm parched, Dom, gimme a tonic water with ice and you can throw vodka in it as well, you know the drill

Dominique had to explain the house was an alcohol-free zone, as she poured Amma water from the filtered jug

since when, Amma asked (with her face)

Nzinga created an atmosphere glutinous with tension as she silently prepared a thick, garlicky bean and mushroom stew which she served with wholemeal bread

on the wooden dining table – a bench either side

Nzinga looked down at her food as she ate, Dominique could tell Amma found the meal unpalatably bland, she'd asked for salt, there was none

by now Dominique was almost used to a salt and spice-free diet, the initial cravings had gone, her appetite had adjusted its expectations she asked her friend about everyone back home, eager to know the goss, careful not to show any affection for those she'd left behind, or regret at leaving them

Amma volleyed back a few questions about life at Spirit Moon

Dominique told her they work on the building site five days week, sometimes six, spend evenings back here, often exhausted, Nzinga cooks up a storm in the evenings, early nights usually, weekends they go shopping and for walks, they have a vegetable garden which needs tending, read books – by women, it goes without saying, preferably feminist, sometimes they see a film in town, walk out if it's offensive

she wanted to add – it's a bit like you and I in our early theatre days, Amma, except we never left a show that offended us without heckling, she didn't say this, Nzinga would feel undermined, Dominique would be accused of elevating her bolshie history of heckling with Amma over their relatively passive cinema walk-outs

Dominique answered Amma's questions, no, they didn't mix with the other women in the community, preferring not to get involved, and yes, life was quiet, how they liked it, it was perfect, that's what it was, perfect

as she spoke, Dominique was embarrassed by how pathetic and puritanical her life sounded, how devoid it was of the happenings of back home, the never-ending dramas of relationships and the women's scene, the highs and lows of running a theatre company, the city itself, the politics, the demonstrations against Maggie Thatcher, protests against Clause 28, marches to Reclaim the Night, weekends spent at Greenham Common, their outlaw friends who were involved in 'lost' cheque-book scams, who lined their shopping bags with silver foil to avoid alarm detection in department stores, who jumped over ticket barriers at tube stations and jumped traffic lights as a rule

it felt so long ago, so far away

the year spent with Nzinga had been without regular updates to Amma, who would have questioned and challenged her on everything

she was her sounding board, her truthsayer, her Number One supporter

Nzinga only looked up when she'd finished eating, gonna hit the sack, she took the pottery bowl to the metal sink and before she reached it, hurled it in with such force, it smashed and shards flew out

she brushed past Amma as she stormed across the floor to the bedroom, Sojourner, you coming?

who's Sojourner? Amma asked as Dominique leapt up

Dominique didn't answer as she left the room

it was seven p.m.

the next morning Dominique found a chance to sit with her friend on the steps outside while Nzinga was in the shower

she takes ten minutes, Dominique said, glancing nervously behind her, it's a ritual she won't forgo, even with you here

Amma suggested they take a walk away from the madhouse, Dominique said the stoop would have to do otherwise Nzinga would get suspicious

suspicious of what?

7

The field opposite the cabin that morning was of the most vivid-green ryegrass as it extended all the way out of sight to the end of the property a pine forest was visible in the distance, the sky was a heavenly, cloudless blue

Dominique was proud to show off the view to Amma who knew her London flat so well, with windows that backed on to a pub's blackened walls and belching water pipes

surely Amma would be convinced she'd made the right move in at least one respect – this is paradise, right?

Amma mumbled something about the right place with the wrong person and complained about the godawful cup of dandelion 'coffee' she'd been forced to drink as the real thing wasn't allowed, and she now had a banging caffeine withdrawal headache barely numbed by the painkillers Nzinga had caught her popping out of their plastic casing at breakfast, who then proceeded to tell Amma off for bringing drugs into her home

the only words she's spoken to me so far, Dom

they sat there for a moment, soaking it up, Dominique wondering when Amma was going to kick off

she didn't disappoint, launched into one about her friend being under the Evil Cindy's spell and did she know that cult gurus controlled their followers by cutting them off from their family, friends, colleagues, neighbours, anyone who might intervene and say, hey, what's happening here?

I'm going to organize a rescue attempt, Dom, a group of mates from London who'll descend like an SAS squad and rescue you from Batshit Crazy Cindy

she laughed, Dominique didn't

I'm in the middle of something, Ams, I'm trying out a new way of living, a new way of being, Nzinga is showing me how to live a truly womanist life, male energy is disruptive, Amma, the patriarchy is divisive, violent and authoritarian, misogyny is so unthinkingly entrenched I can see why women give up on them for ever, it's so special here, so liberating to be removed from having to deal with male oppression every day

I've always known you to like men, Dom, we even love those who are close to us, we might understand the patriarchy (thanks for telling me how it works by the way), but we see men as individuals, don't we? you were never separatist or misandrist, what's happened to you?

nothing's happened to her, Nzinga's voice boomed over their heads, she'd been standing behind them

she wedged one damp, muscular leg between the women, and then the other, effectively separating them physically – they'd been link-ing arms

Nzinga plonked herself down in the space she'd created, was wearing a towel, still dripping wet, launched into a speech about all men ultimately being complicit in a patriarchal system that enabled female genital mutilation and seeing as women's genitalia are being butchered all over the globe in the name of culture or religion or whatever, why not do the same to men who perpetrate most of the world's sexual violence? bank their sperm when they're virile teen-agers then castrate the bastards

Nzinga pressed herself up against Dominique, an arm around her neck

it felt less like a sign of affection
more like a strangling

Amma stood up, went into the house, packed her carry-all, returned to stand in front of them

I'm off, back home, *your* home too, Dom, come with me

Dominique didn't need rescuing, she shook her head

Nzinga pulled her closer, kissed her noisily on the cheek, good girl.

8

After Dominique and Nzinga had completed ten new properties at Spirit Moon, Nzinga wangled a deal with Gaia to stay in their home until they could secure a contract elsewhere

there was nothing to do except be with each other all day

Dominique should have sloped off then because the relationship was already irreparable, but she found herself unable to make such a big decision when she'd lost the ability to make even the smallest ones, such as what she ate and wore, and who she was allowed to speak to

she became wrapped up in the nightmare cocoon of Nzinga's increasing paranoia

these women are out to destroy our great love affair, Sojourner

when she came across the other women, Nzinga was at her side so she couldn't really speak freely to them or she'd be told off later for saying the wrong thing

even her morning trips to fetch bread from Tilley provoked another all-night rant after Nzinga followed her, analysed their body language from a distance and decided they were flirting

Nzinga announced she'd fetch the bread herself from now on, she also went into town on her own to do the weekly shop because of Dominique's imagined behaviour around men and no, not getting you any chocolate as a special treat, it's bad for you, and did she *really* need to see the dentist (who was a man), or was it a ruse?

the day Nzinga punched Dominique on the arm was the day she thought she'd leave, reasoned it was a one-off, discovered it wasn't when a single punch progressed into multiple ones

Dominique didn't want to escalate Nzinga's aggression by fighting back, until she confessed to herself she didn't really have it in her to do so, she was genuinely non-violent

when she tried to storm out of the house to get away during rows, Nzinga blocked the door with her imposing size, legs astride, ordered her to sit down on a chair and breathe deeply, Sojourner, breathe deeply, rid yourself of this negative energy, the world is dangerous out there

all day Nzinga's voice megaphoned into Dominique's consciousness, resounding, pounding, she spent such little time alone, she forgot how to spend time alone, she took to sleeping in late and going to bed early, she hated being outside in the unrelenting brilliance of sunshine

when she wasn't sleeping, she was staring into space

it was a Saturday morning, Nzinga had headed into town in the truck to do the weekly shop, saying she'd be gone all day – a test, she usually returned after a couple of hours and snuck up to the cabin on foot to see what Dominique was getting up to

this time, as soon as she left, Gaia appeared outside their home on her moped, as if she'd been parked up somewhere waiting for Nzinga to leave; Dominique heard the engine first, nobody ever came by, who was this?

she watched Gaia walk towards the cabin

Gaia said, we're concerned about what's happening here, you're not the woman you were when you arrived, you haven't been spotted for over a month, is everything okay?

everything's fine, Dominique replied, standing at the door, not daring to open it too widely

Gaia stared at her with the knowledge and wisdom of having spent her entire adult life surrounded only by women, she sat on the steps

Dominique, come sit with me

we know what she's like, Gaia said, we've all experienced her wrath, her unreasonableness, her general animosity towards the world, to us, you can talk to me

Dominique resisted saying anything, it would be such a betrayal of Nzinga who insisted on complete loyalty all the while pinching her arm so hard it bruised so that she'd remember to never and I mean *never* talk to anyone about me or our relationship

you can talk to me, Gaia repeated, laying a light hand on Dominique's own, transmitting compassionate strength to her, until Dominique felt herself softening and admitted to Gaia, as much as to herself, that yes, she was trapped in a relationship with a violent woman of unsound mind with no foreseeable way out

in betraying Nzinga, she was at last being true to herself

Gaia comforted her, we will help you get away, okay?

really?

do you have any funds?

she never got round to adding my name to what was supposed to be a joint bank account, and asking for my share of our savings will be tantamount to telling her I'm leaving her and I don't know what will happen then

I can loan you enough money to get yourself sorted, where do you want to go, back to England?

not really, at least not yet, I can't face the humiliation and I'd like to see more of America

I have friends in West Hollywood who will put you up until you
have plans, pay me back when you can, do you have your passport?
    Nzinga keeps it safe for me – I know her hiding place
    we'll come by this time next Saturday
    to drive you to the airport.

9

It took years for Dominique to stop beating herself up for staying
with Nzinga for as long as she did – nearly three years, *three* years
    how could she have been so weak when she'd been so strong, and
was again after she left her?
    grateful to go back to the self she had lost

    after Spirit Moon, she stayed with Gaia's lawyer friends, Maya and
Jessica, who welcomed her the afternoon she arrived with a meal of
fresh salads and a peaceful little yellow room at the back of their
expensive property overlooking their orange and lemon grove
    that first night Dominique felt disoriented, Nzinga was still in her
head, in fact she squatted it illegally for a very long time
    she often had nightmares of her coming at her through the bed-
room window brandishing the hunting knife she'd had when they
met, which she'd kept under the mattress

    the next day Maya and Jessica asked her what she'd like for dinner,
Dominique wasn't used to having a choice, spent ages deliberating;
in the end they indulged her wishes and barbecued a meat medley of
burger, turkey drumsticks, sausages, pork, lamb chops and steak –
with salad

after a few bites she ended up running to the loo to throw up, returned and picked at the salad

that evening she stayed up late with the two women who'd met each other at art school, swapped their careers as impoverished artists to pursue corporate law, forwent job satisfaction in order to earn big bucks and work eighteen hour days that killed their creativity

they planned to retire at fifty, resurrect their artistic selves, if it's not too late

they were enthralled to hear about her theatre and clubbing life in London, admired the fact that she and Amma had chosen a creative path even when it was financially unstable and they'd probably never be homeowners or have a pension

Dominique sat with them in their warm grove drinking delicious wine late into the night

it was like a sedative was wearing off and she felt herself surging with energy

she was hyper, she was high, she was coming back to life.

10

Dominique fell in love with the West Coast, entered into a marriage of convenience with a gay man, assisted by Maya and Jessica who loaned her the cost

her English accent was a huge selling point in her dealings with Americans, it elevated her, as did her model looks (she was told often enough) and cool biker style, lesbians in particular wanted to help her, to open doors for her, to be part of what they thought she represented

Maya and Jessica allowed her to live cheaply at theirs for a couple of years until she found her feet

her first job was working in admin for a film company, a stepping stone to producing live arts events

she felt blessed that she could quickly establish herself, and once she was, invited Amma to visit

who never said an outright, I told you so

Dominique also attended a weekly counselling group for female survivors of domestic abuse

as the weeks passed she heard people share their life stories and reach life-changing epiphanies

when she took the plunge, she discovered it was indeed cathartic

she came to appreciate that as the oldest girl in a family of ten, she'd had to mother the younger ones when she'd been deprived of being properly mothered herself

as soon as she was born, her mother was pregnant with another child, and each newborn baby had to have her mother's full attention

Dominique worked out she'd been drawn to Nzinga because she was subconsciously looking to be mothered

then mothering had turned into smothering, and Mummy turned out to be Daddy, as she told Amma, who disagreed and said it was about bad luck rather than unresolved childhood issues, you're becoming too American, Dom

Dominique kept in touch with Gaia until she passed away, she'd written that Nzinga had been evicted from the community soon after Dominique left, had raged across the property trying to find out where 'Sojourner' had gone, threatening people and smashing windows

the police were called, the women didn't press charges
rest easy, she doesn't know where you are

Dominique still spent years having nightmares about Nzinga coming at her through a crowd or driving into her as she crossed a street or appeared in a public place, even during her opening speech for the Women's Arts Festival she founded after a few years in L A

Nzinga would be berating her for leaving her when she'd so kindly taken her on as an apprentice, shown her how to be fully womanist in a misogynist world

I gave you everything, *everything*, you'd be nothing without me, Sojourner, *nothing*

many years later, Dominique was told that Nzinga had died some twelve years after she left her

her last girlfriend, Sahara, introduced herself at the festival, she'd become lovers with Nzinga at a women of colour spirituality retreat in Arizona

she talked about you a lot, Dominique, she'd heard about the success of this festival and totally took credit for it, she was your mentor and had made you, she said, you'd used her, no thanks, no public acknowledgement, no belated payments for her extensive investment in your personal development, she was planning to come to L A to confront you, but it was never the right time

I now think she was scared that the person she'd thought of as weak had become powerful

I totally bought her story about you until a few months into our relationship she started treating me like a disciple instead of a lover, and became possessive, aggressive and played mind control games

I was in my twenties, she was in her fifties

she wouldn't let me out of her sight, said I should be grateful that she'd rescued me, from what? who knows, I never got an answer that made any sense

I was ready to leave her within the year when she had a major stroke, became immobilized, and I couldn't

she was so utterly alone in the world except for me – no home, friends, no family to call on, she said everyone always left her

when she died, I felt released

hearing of her former lover's death, Dominique also felt released, sad, too, that Nzinga's life really had been one of abandonment

and she'd not been capable of seeing that the fault, as an adult, lay with her

Dominique met Laverne in her counselling group, as the only two lesbians they gravitated towards each other

Laverne was an African-American woman who liked to blend into the background, who spoke softly and thought deeply

originally from Oakland, now based in LA as a sound technician, her previous girlfriend had been violent

she left her the third time she ended up in A&E

Dominique found Laverne pleasant and easy company, she'd studied international relations, was well-read and passionately interested in global current affairs

Dominique began to expand her reading beyond women's literature into non-fiction books about the world at large

they could spend hours discussing the consequences of the fall of the Berlin Wall and the break-up of the Soviet Union or the marriage war played out in the media between Princess Diana and Prince Charles

or the wars in the Middle East, or the Brixton and L A riots

or the relationship between climate change and capitalism

or the histories of postcolonial Africa, India, the Caribbean and Ireland

their friendship deepened over time and eventually became physical

they respected the free will of each other and made no demands

they were lovers for four years before moving in together, even then Dominique worried that the equilibrium of their relationship, from seeing each other several times a week to seeing each other every day, would throw their relationship off-balance

it didn't

they wanted children, adopted baby twins, Thalia and Rory, whose parents had been killed in a gangland shooting

they became a family, married each other when it became legal

Dominique moved to America nearly thirty years ago

she considers it her home.

Chapter Two
Carole

I

Carole
walks through Liverpool Street station with its inter-galactic glass
and steel ceiling propped up by towering Corinthian columns
   she's headed for the escalators and the soaring windows that let in
a holy glow of morning light
   she passes underneath the timetable board listing departures and
arrivals
   articulated through the medium of glowing alphanumeric, text
flipping and updating as announcements bellow from the clustered
boom boxes informing passengers about platform numbers and item-
izing all stations on routes to final destinations
   where this train will end
   and the numerous delays due to vandalism on the tracks or leaves
on the line or sun on the line or a body under a train

how *very* inconsiderate, not to her

to choose to throw yourself in front of a mechanical iron beast weighing thousands of tons and racing at a top speed of one hundred and forty miles per hour?

to choose such a brutal and dramatic finale

Carole knows what drives people to such despair, knows what it's like to appear normal but to feel herself swaying

just one leap away

from

the amassed crowds on the platforms who carry enough hope in their hearts to stay alive

swaying

just one leap away from

eternal

peace

these days, however, she feels very much alive, very much 'looking forward' as they say at work, to the next 'window of opportunity'

these days she's a willing orchestral player in the cacophony of London's busiest station with a footfall of nearly 150 million pairs of living feet every year, the anonymous convergence of commuters who are 99.9% genetically identical regardless of their visual packaging, regardless of their psychological wiring – warped, tangled, shorted, electrocuted

all of them so perfectly composed, so poised and in control, socialized to be out in public as reasonable members of society this Monday morning where all dramas are interiorized

look at her

in her perfectly-tailored city clothes, the balletic slope of her shoulders, straightened hair scraped back into a martial topknot, eyebrows plucked with calligraphic flair, her discreet, no-nonsense jewellery of platinum and pearls

Carole
whose daily lexicon revolves around the orbit of equities, futures and financial modelling
who loves to immerse herself in a universe where fiscal cells split off to create gazillions of replicas of themselves spinning off into beautiful infinity
the glittering stars of wealth that make the world go around
her idea of bedtime reading is to scrutinize the profitability of businesses and oversee investment plans for the commodities of the African and Asian markets
the darkness of night pouring into her study through its old-fashioned sash window
her face bathed in the blue light of her hypnotically addictive 24-inch iMac
the computer screen where she alone, it seems, ignores the parallel universe of social media and what she considers its time-suck temptations
at least *her* addiction to the electronic motherboard is productive, she tries to convince herself, clicking on the never-ending monetary websites of cyberspace that pop up, NASDAQ, Wall Street Journal, London Stock Exchange
while also monitoring the international news that affects market conditions, the weather conditions that affect crops, the terrorism that destabilizes countries, the elections that affect trading agreements, the natural disasters that can wipe out whole industries, agricultures and communities
and if it isn't related to work, it's not worth reading

*

but with the news now available on the minute every minute, she can't ever keep up and can't stop the hyperactive habit of clicking on just another hyperlink

even when she can't take anything in any more, can't remember the last website she visited, doesn't know why on earth she doesn't just call it a day when she knows she'll fall asleep at her desk, usually in the post-midnight hours, only to awaken hours later and drag herself bleary-eyed to bed

the terror of the Gods of Theta and Delta

who rob her of the consciousness that protects her

sleep

when bad things happen

to bad little girls

who

ask

for

it.

2

Carole steps on to the silver steps of the escalators with the rest of the commuting populace in their sombre office palettes as it elevates them skywards from below ground to the street level of Bishopsgate

she's headed for an early morning meeting with a new client based in Hong Kong, whose net worth is multiple times the GDP of the world's poorest countries

she's thinking he'd better not do a double-take when she enters the executive meeting room one long glass wall looking out on to the City

the other bearing a massive splash of tax-deductible artwork that cost the price of a Zone 2 town house

she's thinking he'd better not look at her as if she should be attached to a trolley bearing flasks of coffee, assortments of teas (herbal, green, grey, Ceylon) and those individually packaged corporate biscuits

she's used to clients and new colleagues looking past her to the person they are clearly expecting to meet

she will stride up to the client, shake his hand firmly (yet femininely), while looking him warmly (yet confidently) in the eye and smiling innocently, and delivering her name unto him with perfectly clipped Received Pronunciation, showing off her pretty (thank-god-they're-not-too-thick) lips coated in a discreet shade of pink, baring her perfect teeth as he adjusts to the collision between reality and expectation, and tries not to show it while she assumes control of the situation and the conversation

it's all about having the upper hand with Carole, who takes these little conquests, as she imagines them, when she can

perhaps he'll find himself unexpectedly attracted to her, which the more sophisticated try to hide, unlike the Nigerian petrochemical billionaire a few years ago who wanted to expand his investment portfolio into copper

who invited her to a working lunch at the Savoy, only for her to discover it was in his private dining room in the Royal Suite

where he gave her a tour of its eight rooms designed with stately home largesse: Greco-Roman colonnades, Lalique chandeliers, antique busts on plinths, silk papered walls and pastoral English paintings he pointed out that the mattress in the master boudoir was hand-sprung with each spring wrapped in cashmere

it's like sleeping on air, Miss Williams, he said as he showed her the suite's 'menu of pillows' on a silver-embossed card

as if she was the kind of woman who'd amputate her aspirations to become one of his decorative appendages

she had to politely extricate herself from his intentions without jeopardizing the business

letting him know she was engaged, to Frederick Marchmont, she said for emphasis

furious that he wanted to undermine her hard-won professionalism

today she will force herself to project a positive approach to her meeting, after all, her shelves are stacked with motivational books ordered from America telling her to *visualize the future you want to create, believe you can and you're halfway there*, and *if you project a powerful person, you will attract respect*

so what will her meeting be?

fan-bloody-tastic!

except she can't help remembering all the little hurts, the business associates who compliment her on being so articulate, unable to hide the surprise in their voices, so that she has to pretend not to be offended and to smile graciously, as if the compliment is indeed just that

she can't help thinking about the customs officers who pull her over when she's jetting the world looking as brief-cased and be-suited as all the other business people sailing through customs — *un-harassed*

oh to be one of the privileged of this world who take it for granted that it's their right to surf the globe unhindered, unsuspected, respected

damn, damn, damn, as the escalator goes up, up, up

c'mon, delete all negative thoughts, Carole, release the past and look to the future with positivity and the lightness of a child unencumbered by emotional baggage

life is an adventure to be embraced with an open mind and loving heart

but there was that one time, at the start of her career, in a country known for its terrible record on human rights, even though she'd told them she was there to meet a team from their national bank, and presented the documentation to show them, which they refused to look at

even her body was

invaded

as if she were an impoverished mule with half a kilo of white powder stuffed up her fanny, or waiting to be evacuated out of her bowels in the little plastic bags she *obviously* must have had for breakfast that morning

the invasion of alien hands in a window-less, dungeon-like room cut off from the flow of the airport, while another grubby immigration official in a sweat-stained blue uniform

looked on

it brought back such memories

such memories she'd locked away, it was all she could do not to collapse on the floor of the interrogation room

that had lain dormant for years after *it* happened, when Carole was thirteen and a half and at her first party with no adults hovering like prison warders ruining the fun for everyone at LaTisha's place, whose mum was on a special training weekend for work and whose older sister, Jayla, had abandoned her 'babysitting' duties to spend the night at her boyfriend's

not before ordering LaTisha to be-have and not have no mates round upon pain of death or we'll both get busted

so what did LaTisha do now she had the place to herself for like the first time in her life? texted her crew to bring a bottle and galdem bring mandem to even things out, only those wiv a six pack, lol, and they better be buff or you won't be allowed in, ya gets?

Carole hadn't hitherto been interested in boys, was labelled the Super Geek of Year 9, preferred the mind-bending pleasures of mathematical problem-solving, inspired by her mother, Bummi, who was raising her alone after her father died

it is the night before LaTisha's party and Carole and her mother are sitting at the washed-out Formica kitchen table, Carole's homework piled up on one side

Carole wears flannelette shorts and her favourite vest with a teddy bear on it

dinner of pounded yam and bitter-leaf soup steams in a shared wooden bowl

they are perched thirty-two floors up in a tower block among hundreds of others packed together like rows of crates spread wide and stacked high

they are over six hundred feet away from the concrete slabs and green trees of ground level

and closer than they should be to the planes in the flight path of City Airport

*

Mama

wears a house-wrappa with faded orange blooms knotted above her breasts

her arms are bare, hair free to stick up at crazy angles

her spine is straight because she was taught to sit upright and cross-legged on the floor, as she tells her daughter when she slouches, sit up straight and speak properly, why do you talk like the tearaway children of the street

Mama

whose feet are strong and scarred from walking barefoot over forested ground

Mama

scoops up pounded yam with her hands, dipping it into the stew, speaking in between mouthfuls

let us wonder, Carole, at the genius of hyperbolic geometry, where the sum of the angles adds up to less than 180 degrees

let us wonder at how the ancient Egyptians worked out how to measure an irregularly-shaped field

let us wonder at how X was just a rare letter until algebra came along and made it something special that can be unravelled to reveal its inner value

you see, maths is a process of discovery, Carole, it is like the exploration of space, the planets were always there, it just took us a long time to find them

clever Mama, who taught her to send X and Y off into complicated calculations and to trust them to present her with the right conclusions how she loved memorizing the quadratic equation, when her classmates didn't even know what it was

how she loved being the best at something, standing out

as she did for sure the next day at LaTisha's, having convinced Mama (who was dozy about everything except maths) that she was at a sleepover

when she was at a party heaving with teenagers crowding the corridor, curtains closed, furniture pushed to the sides in the living room, two side-table lamps covered with red dishcloths creating a nightclub vibe

while the girls stood in groups dancing self-consciously in the centre of the room and the guys loitered against the walls and Busta Rhymes was played low enough not to bring the neighbours knocking

and LaTisha yelled at people not to get waved or misbehave and no one was allowed into the bedrooms upon pain of death and definitely no smoking and at the first whiff of whacky-backy she was gonna evict the perpetrators because on my life, this ain't no joke

except Carole was drinking for the first time in her life, and quickly got totally waved on vodka and lime so sweet she barely noticed the 40% alcohol in it, drained several glasses through a fluorescent squiggle straw like it was lemonade on a hot summer's afternoon

when Trey, Alicia's older brother, who was studying Sports Science at university, and his crew arrived

here at last were real mandem, pure buff-ness, who swaggered into the living room, much better than the boys Carole's age who were still pulling girls' hair in the playground and running away giggling

she began amping it up in front of them

glad that LaTisha had forced her to dress up and get your head out of those useless books and grow up, Carole

hoping the lipstick she was wearing for the first time hadn't rubbed off as she bunched her lips into a sexy pout

as she flicked the glossy Cleopatra wig that hung down to her shoulders

as she twerked her hips like the girls in the music videos, wearing the PVC hot pants she'd borrowed from Chloe, the heels she'd borrowed from Lauren that made her legs look really long and shapely all of a sudden

when she noticed he was staring at her, like she was The One, even though he'd never noticed her before when he walked down the high street

no one had ever looked at her the way Trey was looking at her tonight, at the tiny halter top that showed off her assets that had grown from nothing to something mega-major in the past year

where did *they* come from?

she and LaTisha agreed human biology was so weird and random, man

with such an audience she found herself spinning around and around in the middle of the living room, arms out, just for the hell of it, spinning around and around because the drink made her feel so free, and her emotions so bubbly, and she was simply so attractive as she spun around to Busta's growls with the vibrations coming out of the speakers charging around her body until the spinning went from her feet to her head and she keeled over and almost regurgitated the chips she'd had earlier and heard laughter and serves her right for showing off only to be rescued from total embarrassment by Trey, who dived into the crowd, helped her up, said he'd look after her and you're so hot you should be arrested, Lady

he put his arms around her, she'd not been hugged by anyone since she was ten and began to escape Mum's claustrophobic squeezes

Mum was warm and squashy, Trey's chest was hard but when she peered up at him, his grey eyes were soft as he stared deep into her soul

love, was this love? even though they'd just met and she still felt a bit sick?

Trey – she tried it out in her mouth, Carole & Trey, or was it T-R-A-Y? oh no, that wouldn't work, she couldn't be married to a kitchen accessory, lol, marriage? whoa, where did that come from? OMG, hubz, was this her future hubz?

his hand stroked the back of her head, she wished he wouldn't, the wig might come off

he told her she needed fresh air, you're so delicate I got to protect you, Lady

she couldn't wait to tell LaTisha, who'd be soooo jealous yet pleased for her too, you've grown up, Carole

he led her through the crush of the hallway, ushered her out the front door, it was dark outside except for the lights from the street lamps and chilly

once outside, he bundled her up under his arm as if her head was a package he was carrying and when she tried to lift it, she couldn't and it was going round and round and she felt overpowered by his cologne or was it deodorant? actually, it smelt like air freshener

would they stop and kiss? her *first* kiss, not with tongues, which

124

was revolting, but gently on the lips like in the old black and white films Mum liked to watch

except she couldn't move her head out of his armpit as he walked her out of the estate

it was as if she was being lifted off her feet, floating on the wings of love, was that a song? they went towards the short alley that led to Roxleigh Park where she and LaTisha had spent their childhood on the swings talking about the meaning of life and pondering the imminent new millennium that was going to be like totally-epic and weirdly-sci-fi as they kicked their legs in the air and felt the wind blow through the furrows of their cornrows

he took her over the little bridge that crossed the stream and through the gate that used to be shut until the council gave up replacing the padlock

they were not alone

she heard other voices

she tried to look up again, it was like her head was in a vice and she wasn't walking no more, she was being frogmarched

then she was flat on her back on the ground, damp grass against her bare back, legs and arms, she wanted to sleep, just five blissful minutes, felt her eyes close, when she opened them, she couldn't see, she'd been blindfolded, her arms were pinned above her head

how had her clothes come off?

then
her
body
wasn't
her
own

no
more

it
belonged
to
them

and she, who loved numbers, became innumerate
couldn't count, didn't want to
feeling alien body parts on and in parts of her body that were so
private, so gross, she hadn't even felt them herself
it was hurtinghurtinghurting
onandonandonandon into infinity, which was something without
end like 0.333333 or 0.999999, except that it would end, because the
purpose of life was to journey towards its conclusion, otherwise it
wasn't life, the two went together, as Mum once told her, looking
sadly at her old wedding photos

Carole forces herself to think of her favourite number, 1729
the only number that can be the sum of two numbers to the 3rd
degree in different ways
one to the power of three is one
twelve to the power of three is 1728
add them to get 1729
there's also ten and nine, each to the power of three, which is then
1000+729

after minutes or hours or days or years or several lifetimes had
passed, it stopped

you were gagging for it, and by the way, you were great
then they were gone
and
so
was
she.

3

Carole never told a soul
definitely not Mama who'd tell her off for lying
or LaTisha and the others because everyone said it was Sheryl's
fault for wearing slutty clothes when it happened to her in the same
park in Year 8
was it Carole's fault?
she suspected it was, shut herself in her bedroom, buried herself under
her bedclothes, turned up late for school or bunked off because what was
the point in learning when something like this had happened to her?
what was the point in learning about the relationship between the
deforestation of the rainforest and climate change?
or the Russian, French, Chinese and American revolutions?
or why a forty-thousand-year-old baby mammoth discovered in
Siberian mountains in 1997 did not decay?
or why frequency modulation is not used for commercial radio
transmissions in the medium and long wave bands?
I mean, what – was – the – point?

until
one day

it was like she woke up from like a bad dream, and she looked down the concrete bunker corridors of her inner-city comp on the anniversary of *it*

observed her mates joshing about, as usual, getting ready to sit at the back and have a laugh in class

at LaTisha, who believed studying was for mugs, man, mugs

at Chloe, who had a side line at school as a supplier of ecstasy

at Lauren, who was only interested in the next shag

and Carole felt like she was seeing them on a screen in a documentary about a bad London comp, their skirts hitched up, ties undone and every school rule about hair, make-up and jewellery broken

she saw their futures and hers, as baby-mothers pushing prams, pushing fatherless timebombs

forever scrambling down the side of sofas for change to feed the meter, like Mum

shopping in Poundland, like Mum

scrambling around markets at closing time for scrag-ends, like Mum

not me, not me, not me, she told herself, I shall fly above and beyond

be gone   from tower blocks with lifts stinking of piss

be gone   from rotten low-paid jobs or the dead-end dole
            queue

be gone   from raising my children alone

be gone   from never being able to afford my own home, like
            Mum

            or take my children on holiday or to the zoo, like
            Mum

or to the movies or the funfair or anywhere except
church

she decided to prove the teachers who'd given up on her wrong,
the teachers who usually
walked down the penitentiary-style corridors in a daze, their eyes
glazed, insulated from the racket made by two thousand teenagers
talking at once
especially Mrs Shirley King, the head of Green House, to which Carole
belonged, who'd marked her out as very promising after her Year 7 and 8
exams showed she was one of the brightest kids we've ever had, Carole
who blanked her once she started bunking off

Mrs King
was an old bat, Fuck Face, the School Dragon, she wouldn't let
anyone get away with anything, who put them in detention for turning up only five minutes late to class, which was just plain evil, and
then she'd *dare* say it was for their own good, to learn discipline,
which was *outrageous*, they all agreed
but who else to ask for help now Carole knew she wanted to do
better?
she took the plunge, approached the dragon and her head wasn't
bitten off, as expected, when she asked her for advice about which
subjects she'd need to study for the best careers and which universities to apply to when the time came
was surprised to be obliged on all counts, on strict condition she
never skipped another day, never turned up late, did her homework
on time, sat at the front of class with the children who are here to
learn and want to go places, Carole

and you must change your social circle (social circle, what the hell *was* that, even?)

Mrs King

who proceeded to hassle her for the rest of her time at school, filling her with dread every time her hawk eyes spotted Carole amid hundreds of kids doing something she didn't approve of like laughing too loud, or walking too fast down the corridors (which *isn't* the same as running), she picked her out and told her off, especially when she saw her with LaTisha, Chloe or Lauren, lecturing her on how those girls will hold you back, Carole

Mrs King

who harassed her for *four* years, even when she was back on track and didn't need her

poking her nose in, and phoning her mother if her grades dropped even slightly

Mrs King

who unfairly took all the credit when Carole scored a starry set of alpha grades in all her GCSEs and was called to interview a year later to study maths at Oxford University

where the Admissions Tutor in her book-lined study marvelled at Carole's class sizes of a *surely unlawful* three score and five, which makes your academic achievements all the more impressive, young lady

only for Mrs King to give a speech in assembly on the last day of Carole's schooling that her protégé, after much dedicated and hard work on Mrs King's part, was the first child in the school's history to make it to such a prestigious university

robbing Carole of her moment of glory.

4

Carole arrived at the ancient university via bus, tube, train and a long walk from the station through crowds, dragging her suitcase on wheels, and moved herself in, climbed the winding, creaking wooden staircase to her room in the eaves that overlooked the quadrangle with sheets of ivy clinging to ancient masonry

on her own

her mother couldn't get the day off work and anyway, it was just as well because she'd wear her most outlandish Nigerian outfit consisting of thousands of yards of bright material, and a headscarf ten storeys high, and she'd start bawling when she had to leave her only child for the first time

Carole would forever be known as the student with the mad African mother

that first week she counted on one hand the number of brown-skinned people in her college, and none as dark as her

in the baronial dining hall she could barely look up from her plate of revolting Stone Age food, let alone converse with anyone

she overheard loud reminiscences about the dorms and drugs of boarding school, Christmas holidays in Goa, the Bahamas, gap years spent climbing Machu Picchu, or building a school for the poor in Kenya, about haring down the M4 for weekends in London, house parties in the countryside, long weekenders in Paris, Copenhagen, Prague, Dublin or Vilnius (where *was* that, even?)

most students weren't like that but the really posh ones were the loudest and the most confident and they were the only voices she heard

they made her feel crushed, worthless and a nobody
without saying a word to her
without even noticing her

nobody talked loudly about growing up in a council flat on a skyscraper estate with a single mother who worked as a cleaner
nobody talked loudly about never having gone on a single holiday,
like *ever*
nobody talked loudly about never having been on a plane, seen a
play or the sea, or eaten in a restaurant, with waiters
nobody talked loudly about feeling too uglystupidfatpoor or just
plain out of place, out of sorts, out of their depth
nobody talked loudly about being gang-banged at thirteen and
a half

when she heard another student refer to her in passing as 'so
ghetto', she wanted to spin on her heels and shout after her, excuse
me? ex-cuuuuuse me? say that to my face, byatch!
(people were killed for less where she came from)
or had she misheard it? were they actually saying *get to* – the
library? supermarket?
she couldn't even make eye contact when she walked along the
narrow corridors built for the smaller men of long ago, centuries
before women were permitted entry, as she'd been told at the first
induction where everyone seemed to be making instant friends and
she spoke to no one
people walked around her or looked through her, or was she imagining it? did she exist or was she an illusion? if I strip off and streak
across the quadrangle will anyone notice me other than the porters

132

who will no doubt call the fedz, an excuse they've been waiting for ever since they first set eyes on her

when a student sidled up after a lecture to ask for some ecstasy, Carole almost texted her mother to say she was on the next train home

at the end of her first term she returned to Peckham informing her mother she didn't want to return to university because although she liked her studies and was managing to stay on top of most of it, she didn't belong there and wasn't going back

I'm done, Mama, I'm done

eh! eh! which kain nonsense be this? Bummi shouted, am I hearing you correctly or you wan make I clean my ear with matches?

listen to me good, Carole Williams

firstly – do you think Oprah Winfrey (VIP) would have become the Queen of Television worldwide if she had not risen above the setbacks of her early life?

secondly – do you think Diane Abbott (VIP) would have become Britain's first black woman MP if she did not believe it was her right to enter politics and represent her community?

thirdly – do you think Valerie Amos (VIP) would have become the first black woman baroness in this country if she had burst into tears when she walked into the House of Lords and seen it was full of elderly white gentlemen?

lastly, did me and Papa come to this country for a better life only to see our daughter giving up on her opportunities and end up distributing paper hand towels for tips in nightclub toilets or concert venues, as is the fate of too many of our countrywomen?

you must go back to this university in January and stop thinking everybody hates you without giving them a chance, did you even ask them? did you go up to them and say, excuse me, do you hate me?

you must find the people who will want to be your friends even if they are all white people

there is someone for everyone in this world

you must go back and fight the battles that are your British birthright, Carole, as a true Nigerian

Carole returned to her college resolved to conquer the place where she would spend the next two and half years of her life

she would fit in, she decided, she would find her people, as her mother had advised

not with the misfits who skulked about the place with scowls on their faces, their hair gelled up into purple Mohicans

or those with multi-coloured dreadlock extensions, people who were going nowhere fast, as far as Carole was concerned, as she watched them walk through town with placards and loudspeakers, people who would horrify her mother if she brought them home

to have come this far? did your Papa sacrifice his health so that you could become a punky Rasta person who smells?

nor was she interested in the boring ordinaries, as Carole began to think of them, students who were so bland they disappeared, even to her

certainly not the cliques of the elite, now that she knew they existed, who were unreachable, who went to public schools renowned for producing prime ministers, Nobel laureates, CEOs, Arctic explorers, famous theatre directors and notorious spies

who clearly belonged more than anyone when they had to sit fully-gowned in the dining hall every evening overlooked by the faculty who lived in, who'd probably never left since they were undergraduates there themselves, who passed on rituals the students found ridiculous such as 'donning your sub-fusc and walking backwards around the Fellows' Quad with a glass of port in your hand at two a.m. to stabilize the space-time continuum at the changing of the clock back to Greenwich Mean Time'

faculty who probably found the idea of *not* eating dinner while facing a room full of future prime ministers and Nobel laureates *rather discombobulating*

Carole's school was renowned for producing teenage mothers and early career criminals

she preferred the pot noodles in her room route

she studied the inmates to find the best match for her, approached those with the most friendly demeanours, was surprised when people responded warmly

once she actually started talking to them

by the end of her second term she had made friends and even got herself a boyfriend, Marcus, a white Kenyan whose family owned a cattle ranch there, who unashamedly had a thing for black girls, which she didn't mind because she was delighted to be desired and he treated her considerately

she knew she could never tell her mother about him, who'd made it clear she had to marry a Nigerian, not that Carol was even thinking of marrying Marcus, they were only nineteen, her mother would then ask her why she was courting someone who did not respect her enough to marry her

it would be lose-lose

before Marcus, Carole had been scared of men, throughout the rest of her school years she didn't want to be anywhere near them she imagined herself never finding anyone she could trust, who wouldn't violate her when she least expected it; she was surprised when her friendship with Marcus turned into something romantic after they began to study together in the library and go for walks afterwards

soon she was sneaking him in for the night

Marcus made her more socially acceptable than she could ever achieve on her own

he was proud to show her off, linking arms or holding hands when out in public

he hired a private room in a restaurant for her nineteenth birthday meal

he was the first person to make love to her with her permission

Carole listened and learned from her new social circle

what would you like? instead of *whatdyawant?*

to whom were you speaking? instead of *who was you talking to?*

I'm just popping to the loo instead of *I'm gonna go piss*

she watched what they ate, and followed suit

learnt that Spanish omelette with eggs and stuff was much classier than English omelette (with eggs and stuff)

twenty-for-a-pound frozen bread rolls were no match for spongy, delicate, tearable fresh brioche

polenta chips dipped in olive oil and herbs were *much preferred* to greasy potato ones dipped in the cheapest heart-attack-trans-fat

and who knew that rice flour could be used to make bread, that bread could be stuffed with olives, that olives could be stuffed with bits of dried tomatoes, that baked tomatoes could be stuffed with cheese and that cheese could be made with bits of apricot and almonds, and almonds used to make milk

she was introduced to sushi (preferably homemade with a sushi kit given as a Christmas present) and guacamole (pronounced *gwacamolay*)

she discovered something called asparagus that made your pee smell funny, learnt that anything green was good to eat so long as it was served cold, lightly steamed and/or crisp

Carole amended herself to become not quite them, just a little more like them

she scraped off the concrete foundation plastered on to her face, removed the giraffe-esque eyelashes that weighed down her eyelids, ripped off the glued-on talons that made most daily activities difficult

such as getting dressed, picking things up, most food preparation and using toilet paper

she ditched the weaves sewn into her scalp for months at a time, many months longer than advised because, having saved up to wear the expensive black tresses of women from India or Brazil, she wanted her money's worth, even when her scalp festered underneath the stinky patch of cloth from which her fake hair flowed

she felt freed when it was unstitched for the very last time, and her scalp made contact with air

she felt the deliciousness of warm water running directly over it again without the intermediary of a man-made fabric

she then had her tight curls straightened, Marcus said he preferred her hair natural, she told him she'd never get a job if she did that

she was invited into family homes that were privately owned

homes without carpet on the floors (out of choice), with no nets at the windows so any old nosy parker could see inside (bizarre)

137

homes with a preference for the old and decrepit such as grandfather clocks that rattled loudly in hallways and antique wardrobes that suffered from woodworm

tatty old sofas were covered with blankets (*throws*) and were *much preferred* to shiny leather ones that squeaked when you sat on them

wooden dining tables proudly displayed knife wounds from generations of graffiti vandalism such as

The Rule of Man v. The Rule of Law: Discuss

Is Grey the New Black?

Esme loves Jonty who loves Poppy who loves Monty who loves Jasper who loves Clarissa who loves Marissa who loves Priscilla who loves Clemency

or something like that

her new pal Rosie's home even had sections called wings and parapets, in case the Vikings invaded again, as Rosie joked when she showed Carole around

the gardens were called grounds with no neighbours for miles around, because they were in the middle of nowhere and could make as much noise as they liked, which in Rosie's case meant hiring a garage band to play on the lawn for her twentieth birthday party

among the guests were those Carole also now called her friends, Melanie, Toby, Patricia, Priya, Lucy and Gerry

in the morning she heard the squeaky toy screech of tropical green parakeets as they flew past the bedroom window, which she mistook for parrots

she looked out on to a lawn, a lake, peacocks roamed free

later that day she was introduced to the concept of walking

just for pleasure.

This morning, Carole steps off the escalator, exits Liverpool Street station

begins to move down Bishopsgate with the inner force of a swinging wrecking ball through the choreographic chaos of the rushing hour

as she takes the long way around to her place of work in order to get just a little more exercise in because she'll probably spend most of the next fourteen hours sitting down

even though she went for her daily jog as she does every day

while Freddy is still snug in bed until he'll spring out of it twenty minutes before he's due to leave, shower, shave, dive into a bowl of Rice Krispies and put on the suit he rotates with seven others

ditto the shoes

she runs from Fulham to Hammersmith every morning

along with all the other fitness freaks in their bright designer jogging gear and pedometer wrist straps that measure everything from their blood pressure and heart rate to see how far and fast they're running

a few like her even pound the pavement in the freezing dawn of winter

when icy particles hang off the illuminated green and gold of Hammersmith Bridge with its eerily glowing towers and heraldry

she runs for her life because to slip up is to begin descending the slippery slope to giving in to failure, to inertia, to feeling sorry for herself about that moment in her life which still creeps to the front of her memory when she least expects it she was a child at the time, how could those beasts have done that to her? how could she have blamed herself when she was so blameless?

the only morning she doesn't run is when she's doubled over with period pains for which she takes extra-strength painkillers in order to haul herself to work or risk being accused of pulling a monthly sickie

busted! yes, you *are* a woman

she even contemplated having her womb taken out to eliminate periods altogether, which would surely be her greatest possible career move, a tactical hysterectomy for ambitious women with menstruation problems

Carole arrives at the bank's headquarters overlooking the river, where it was clear from her first day on the job she was expected to be as groomed as her counterparts on American television dramas about female lawyers, politicians, and detectives

women who miraculously spend their working day wearing bondage-tight skirts and vertiginous, destabilizing heels which make their feet look bound

the erogenous zones of crushed muscles and cramped bones, encased in upmarket strippers' heels

and if she has to cripple herself to signal her education, talent, intellect, skills and leadership potential then so be it

her morning mantra in the bathroom mirror

I am highly presentable, likeable, clubbable, relatable, promotable and successful

I am highly presentable, likeable, clubbable, relatable, promotable and successful

I am highly presentable, likeable, clubbable, relatable, promotable and successful

forget the fact she's got Vivaldi's *Four Seasons* as her ring tone, the public face of her musical taste

sometimes

Carole loves dancing like a warrior queen to frenzied beats of the war-painted shamanistic godfather, Fela Kuti

loves the way he rips apart her emotions with his polyrhythmic percussions and unashamedly flatulent horns blasting away all pretence at nicety-niceness with his anti-corruption-lyrical-political broadsides

and the futuristic psychedelics of Parliament Funkadelic

who teleport their freakilicious mothership logic into her brain, activating its neglected right side with their crazed imagination

and outrageously costumed performances she loves to watch on YouTube

while dancing

for herself

out of it

out of her head

out of her body

feeling it

freeing it

nobody watching

nobody judging

moving on to James Brown, the Godfather of Soul

get on up, Carole, get on up

which is exactly what she's doing as she disappears between the glass revolving doors of the tall office building

steps on to the oceanic green and grey whorls of 900-million-year-old Connemara marble (proudly inscribed on a plaque)

walks past the cheery school leaver receptionist wearing a cheap

plastic weave (she really should tell her) who's so grateful when Carole stops for a motivational chat – what are your plans, Tess? you
can't stay here for ever, you've got to move on up

she swipes her card on the turnstile, enters the inner sanctum
glides into the sleek lift when its glass doors slide silently apart,
behind Brian, her boss
who took her out for a drink a year after she'd joined the firm
she spent hours trapped in a brick alcove with him in a basement wine
bar, listening to him going on about how he's never got over the fact that
while his father, grandfather and great-grandfather were fishmongers at
Billingsgate who came home stinking of rancid fish, he himself had
walked into a job as a trader at the Stock Exchange straight out of a crap
secondary modern school (in the days when you could), with no qualifications other than a savant ability with numbers and the gift of the gab
and worked his way up
he was committed to opening doors for others such as herself,
he said, because the idea of the meritocratic culture of banking was
a myth, and you're never going to be invited to join any gentlemen's
clubs or golfing clubs and get fast tracked that way
even though her line manager had told him she was greatly admired
for her research skills, scarily analytical thinking, concise yet comprehensive reports, confident presentation skills, unfailing adherence
to deadlines, ability to grasp financial data at a speed not known to
normal humans, as well as fascistic attention to detail – rumour has
it that a stray or absent comma has yet to be detected
so he was going to make sure the firm promoted her to Associate
sooner than most
because she deserved it
so what if she was only interested in spreadsheets and not

spreading her legs, although those days have long passed as a way for a woman to get on, quite right too, he said, plunging into tales of the heady hedonism of his stock trading career in the eighties, when boozy lunches ran into 'gin & tea time' and from thereon spilled tip-sily into the 'cocktail hour' before a pack of them trawled West End bars eventually ending up at strip joints

he'd been tamed by middle age, he said

she saw no signs of it as he became progressively inebriated, leery and confessional about his increasingly plasticized wife, who was at risk of becoming more man-made than organic

who put up with his affairs in order to hold on to the lifestyle he offered her, recently buying a fish tank for their conservatory filled with the rarest, ugliest, most expensive fish in the world

what else was she going to spend his money on when she had everything?

and until recently he's had an indecently juvenile mistress from Lithuania ensconced in his *pied à terre* in the Barbican, who'd since graduated with a degree in computer science

freeing up space for a third woman in his life, if you're ever tempted, I mean that body with those brains, he has fantasies, he said, before rush-ing off to the loo to throw up before he had a chance to divulge them

Carole and Brian greet and exchange pleasantries as they stand opposite each other in the see-through lift that shoots six people at a time in six seconds up to the top floor offices

whereupon Brian turns towards his suite to sit facing a glass wall that overlooks the spires of the City's gothic churches and the baroque guild halls of the livery companies, including his own

The Worshipful Company of International Bankers

*

he still wants her, she can tell, the filthy old lech, how dare he talk to her like that, she still got promoted to Associate prematurely, she almost respects him for that, and she recently became a Vice President, one of several hundred in this bank, as opposed to the thousands in others

her mother tells everyone about her daughter the Vice President

as if she's VP of the United States of America

Carole stops a while and looks out of the glass wall on to the undulating wave of the Millennium Bridge

elegantly slim-line and initially so unstable it closed for two years shortly after opening because no one suspected that so many people crossing it at the same time would begin to walk in lockstep

and the effect, like armies of marching soldiers stamping the ground in sync, created vibrations that caused the bridge to sway

it's how she sees herself, walking in silent lockstep with the people who are going places

she watches the stream of people crossing the bridge this morning, most of whom are more engaged with their phones, taking selfies, tourist pics, posting, texting, than actually taking in the views either side of the bridge

people have to share everything they do these days, from meals, to nights out, to selfies of themselves half naked in a mirror

the borders between public and private are dissolving

Carole finds it fascinating and appalling, she's read that one day humans will have a network of nano-electronics integrated into their neural pathways, implanted at the cellular level a month after conception, self-growing, self-repairing

we'll all be cyborgs, she thinks, primed to behave in socially acceptable ways, instead of primal beings who cannot be so easily controlled

perhaps it will stop vile men raping drunken little girls
(and getting away with it)
perhaps it will stop little girls feeling it's their fault
(and never telling a soul)

far off in the distance, Carole sees a plane begin its descent into City Airport, probably passing over her childhood estate in Peckham

she wonders what happened to LaTisha, last seen by Carole sticking two fingers up at the school as she exited the doors of the former workhouse at sixteen, they'd been such great friends once – *I swear, on my life, this ain't no joke*

LaTisha's probably a babymother now, or a gang leader, or banged up, or all three

all of Carole's closest circle of friends are from university, most are high flyers

Marcus, now a great friend after their relationship ended when he returned to Kenya after university, works in wildlife conservation, has a Kenyan wife and mixed-race children, Carole is godmother to their eldest

Rosie is a barrister for Slaughter & May, a Magic Circle law firm; Toby is a management consultant with KPMG, a Big Four auditor; Patricia is completing a PhD in Theoretical Physics; Melanie is an executive at Google UK; and Priya is in training to become a GP

only two of them are straggling behind, Lucy, who doesn't know what she wants in the long term so takes short-term temping contracts, saves, goes off backpacking like a teenager, returns to England full of stories but her career hasn't moved on poor Gerry became a learning mentor in a Middlesbrough school to research the great novel he was going to write about northern working-class boys

seven years later, he's still there and the novel hasn't been written

they catch up when they can, individually, as a group, at dinner parties, the occasional wedding, or they decamp for the weekend to Rosie's parents' manor where she has the run of the place now since the parents retired to their second home in Barbados

Carole, who took up horse riding there while still a student, considers herself an equestrian these days

she also counts clay-pigeon shooting as a hobby

she looks over at the Tate on the opposite side of the river, where she occasionally wanders the galleries to clear her head during lunchtime (when she takes one), to marvel at the ability of artists to make such mind-blowing creations out of their imagination

imagination

what was that?

does she even have one?

she allows her gaze to travel south along the river path that leads towards the National Theatre, opening an all-female production this very night about black lesbian warriors, according to Freddy, who was probably exaggerating for comic effect

he has tickets, insists she attend, is going to drop by to drag her away to see hot lesbian action on stage and hopefully be turned on enough to entertain the idea of the mythical threesome: two women, one man, you know you want to, Honeycakes

no I flipping well don't, she replies, laughing

he never fails to amuse her, never fails to be there for her when she wants him, to love her as she wants to be loved

to leave her alone when she needs solitude

Carole has only had two boyfriends, Marcus and Freddy, it's not that she consciously rejected black men, it was the other way round, they were in short supply at university and those that made it there didn't generally go for the few dark-skinned black women around

nor in the City brasseries she frequented when single and on the lookout

not that she's blaming them, it's what they have to do to get on, to reduce the threat they're supposed to be to society

one thing she's learnt is that falling hopelessly, helplessly in love is actually a highly selective process

she was never going to marry a street cleaner, was she?

she met Freddy at a party a couple of years into her job when she was living back home with her mother to save money

she was flattered that this handsome, preppy and genuinely plummy man was interested in her when the room was full of stunning debutante types eyeing him up

she said yes to the Curzon Soho cinema date to see a Venezuelan film on a Sunday afternoon

yes to the leisurely walk through the backstreets of the West End to Hyde Park

yes to dinner in a Lebanese restaurant on Edgware Road and thereafter late-night drinks at his father's club in Pall Mall

yes to his knockout humour and genuine interest in her life and opinions yes to his intelligence, conversational skills and easy-going personality

yes to his romantic hand-holding and all-round good manners

yes to his obvious infatuation with her

he told her he was raised in a villa in Richmond with a lawn that swept down to the Thames with its own jetty where a motorboat was moored for excursions

he was enthralled by her own childhood on a Peckham housing estate, impressed that she'd made it against so many obstacles

he said he had merely stepped rather casually into the grooves of a pre-ordained track laid down by his family, beginning with an eccentric boarding school in Wiltshire attended by almost every male in his family since 1880, a school that taught Latin and Ancient Greek for twenty-one out of the thirty-one classes a week when his father was there

thankfully cut back to *only* seven classes in Freddy's time

after a whirlwind world tour during his gap year, he flew to a private New England liberal arts college, most generously endowed by his alumnus father the year his Straight C son applied

the son who graduated four years later with an embarrassingly low Grade Point Average on account of being side-tracked by about thirty other teenage boys left to their own devices for the first time in a frat house where he partied most nights and ingested various mind-altering substances which often left him out of it for days

barely able to speak, let alone write

not that it mattered

in his final semester he was offered a well-remunerated starter position in the City as a result of his mother calling in a favour from a school friend who'd been one of her bridesmaids she said Freddy could start the day he landed back in Old England from New England

no interview necessary, he'll just need to do a bit of boring old form-filling, darling

ever since, he's found the corporate lifestyle so stultifying and soul-destroying, he dreams of living in a wigwam in a field and growing his own food

Carole moved directly from her mother's flat where she stayed rent free for a couple of years after graduation to save for a mortgage

into Freddy's house in Fulham where the relationship moved into the engagement phase

I'll be the househusband in the relationship, he promised, hang prettily off your arm when required, mow the lawn, make jam, supervise the housekeeper and raise our lovely tawny offspring

she loved that he was prepared to be subservient to her ambition

she knew she'd go further faster with him at her side

he said his parents wanted him to marry someone whose lineage, like theirs, could be traced back to William the Conqueror

you should have seen their faces when I told them.

Bummi

I

Bummi

did not foresee the long-term negative impact of her daughter
going to the famous university for rich people

especially when she returned home after her first term wailing that
she could not go back because she did not belong there

whereupon Bummi applied a tissue or two to her daughter's eyes and
cheeks and asked her outright and forthrightly, Carole, have I raised a
fighter or a quitter? you must return to the university and get your degree
by hook or by crook or I cannot vouch for the consequences of my actions

Bummi did not subsequently expect Carole to return home after
her second term speaking out of her nose like there was a sneeze
trapped up it instead of using the powerful vibrations of her Nigerian
vocal power, all the while looking haughtily around their cosy little
flat as if it was now a fleapit

did she think her mama did not notice the external manifestation of her internal mind? eh! eh!, you do not raise a child without becoming an expert in the non-verbal signals they think you are too stupid to see

that first summer holiday Carole worked in Marks & Spencer in Lewisham, not to start paying off her student debt like a responsible adult, but to buy clothes from those expensive fashion shops called Oasis and Zara, instead of getting bargains at New Look and Peacock

in her second year she barely came home at all and by her final year she was spending weekends and holidays at her friend Rosie's family manor in the countryside, which had more rooms than a housing estate, she said, it's simply divine, *Mother*, simply divine

(*Mother* – was she being ironical?)

when Bummi watched her daughter collect her degree at graduation, tears streamed down her face so heavily it was like rain lashing a car window

without the windscreen wipers

she wished Augustine was there to witness their little girl making it, she also wished Carole had come home to continue celebrations with the pot of bush stew Bummi had cooked specially, hoping that now her daughter had graduated, she would return to her real culture and even eat with her hands again instead of side-glancing her mama for doing so, as if she was a savage from the jungle

before she got on the train back to London, Bummi impressed upon Carole for the umpteenth time that now she had to acquire a high-flying job and then a respectable Nigerian husband in order to give her grandchildren

Carole had introduced no boyfriends to her mother thus far, which meant they were of little importance to her daughter

*

nearly a week later, Carole returned to the flat red-eyed and 'exhausted' because she had been out 'partying', Mother

what is this partying? Bummi asked, you are too old for such things, are you sleeping around? is that it?

no, I'm a *virgin* (was she being ironical again?)

Bummi gave her the benefit of the doubt, and you must stay that way, remember you are Nigerian and not one of these tarty English girls, I will now defrost the bush meat stew for you and we can have it for dinner tonight

I'm not hungry, don't bother, Carole replied before going into her room, shutting the door and only reappearing the next morning

when Carole quickly found a good job at an investment bank, Bummi was happy that she decided to stay at home to save for a mortgage

where Bummi tried to coax and cajole her into going to church to meet the three young Nigerian men she had picked out for her, all with good degrees and varying degrees of handsomeness (she did not want ugly grandchildren)

I'm really not interested at the moment, Carole replied

do not leave it too long, Bummi warned her, by the time you are thirty you are past it

and so everything was going along quite nicely for a couple of years, although Carole worked very late and stayed with friends most nights, she said, who lived nearer to the City

then one morning at breakfast (a cup of sugarless coffee for Carole) while Bummi tucked into the delicious yam porridge her daughter loved before she went to the university, and then began to say it was as inedible as warm cement

Carole said, I have something to share (typical English, all this *sharing* preamble instead of just speaking directly about the matter at hand)

I've got engaged to be married, Mother

her daughter spoke to the faded lino on the kitchen floor as if she had never seen it before, except it had been there since before she was born

to a wonderful man called Freddy

Bummi felt fireworks going off in her brain (Catherine wheels and rockets)

what is this? she thought, this girl tells me she is going to marry a man she has not yet even introduced to her mama? how long has this been going on? Bummi asked, unable to swallow the lump of porridge in her mouth that really did feel like warm cement

a while, Carol replied, oh and he's white, English, she mumbled, we've been dating for ages and I'm really in love with him, so there you have it

so there you have it

Carole stared directly at Bummi with an expression that said, and there's nothing you can do to stop me, Mother

Bummi tried to count to ten, she only got to 9.2 before jumping off her chair so fast Carole sprang up too

why you like to dey like cause so much wahala for me, eh? na play you dey play, abi? you don spit ontop your papa life! you don spit ontop your people! which kain shame you wan bring on this family? you don disgrace me! I no sabi you at all, at all at all

Bummi paced up and down the tiny kitchen forcing Carole to squeeze herself into a corner

she resisted the urge to slap her daughter about the head, because no matter how naughty she was, even as a small girl, she could never

153

beat the only person in the world who had come into creation for nine months inside her very own womb

the child who was delivered perfectly formed and crying for her mama's comforting milk at Guy's Hospital

Great Maze Pond

Waterloo

London, SE1

United Kingdom of Great Britain

Bummi wished Augustine was still alive to talk sense into their girl

she was not meant to raise a child alone in a high-rise building in a foreign country

she felt as helpless now as she had when Carole went through her sulky period at thirteen years of age and started skipping school, her high grades plummeted to low ones, and she shut herself in her bedroom for entire weekends except to come out and wash, eat and go to the toilet

what are you doing in there?

sleeping, I'm tired, Mama, she'd reply through the door

why are you tired all the time when all you have to do is go to school and work your brain, whereas I have to be on my hands and knees cleaning every day? who should be tired? you or me?

when Bummi asked the women at church for advice, they reassured her it was teenage hormone problems that would pass

which it did

a year or so later

her clever little girl was no longer sleeping her childhood away and had returned to the top of the class in most subjects

one of her teachers, Mrs King, a very considerate lady who took a special interest in helping her daughter, said Carole had the ability to go far if she sustains her current work ethic, Mrs Williams

Bummi was so proud when Carole got into the famous university for rich people that she photocopied her university acceptance letter not once, not twice, but *thrice*

framed and mounted them – one on the wall in the hallway, one on the door inside the toilet and one above the television where she herself could glance up at it while watching the box

she could not have predicted it would lead to Carole rejecting her true culture

Bummi regarded her daughter standing in the corner of the kitchen like a trapped animal who did not think it was safe to move

she did not want her child to fear her

Carole, she said, sitting back down, come, listen to me, you hardly know this Freddy-come-lately character whereas I have known you your entire life, who is he to you when you are every-thing to me? there is no point getting on in this country if you lose who you really are, you are not English or did you give birth to yourself?

you are a Nigerian, first, foremost and last-most

Carole you must marry a Nigerian for your poor papa's sake, abi?

when that did not produce the required results, Bummi decided to henceforth ignore Carole, starting that very evening when Carole came into the kitchen hoping to prepare their Sunday dinner together as usual

the fridge was empty, with not even bread, milk or margarine, all of which Bummi had thrown into a garbage bag

*

Bummi continued to ignore her daughter

on the three-seater settee in the sitting room where they usually jostled up against each other while commenting raucously
on whatever Nollywood DVD with shaky camerawork was playing on the flat-screen TV in the corner, she refused to let Carole
massage her tired feet with cocoa butter as usual, and played deaf
when she gingerly asked if she could make her a hot mug of Milo,
Mother?

Bummi sat at the other end of the sofa in stony-faced silence, sniff-
ing at regular intervals and wiping her eyes until the girl left the
room

thereafter Carole stayed out of her way and when she shouted out
good night through the door when she came home late, Bummi did
not reply, kept on reading *The Joys of Motherhood* by her country-
woman, Buchi Emecheta, a novel Sister Flora, her friend from
church, had recommended when Bummi had unburdened her woes
to her

Sister Flora told her that the mother in the novel, Nnu Ego, was a
sufferer too, read it and you will feel better about yourself, Sister
Bummi

later, she heard Carole's feet pad out of the kitchen into the
bathroom and then into her own bedroom, shutting the door
noiselessly

Bummi hoped she was crying herself to sleep every night

then one morning

as Bummi sat in the kitchen plucking out the bad grains from a super-
size sack of Basmati rice she'd bought in the Bangladeshi minimart on
the high street that was twenty times cheaper than the small-small pack-
ets of rice sold in the rich people's supermarket at the corner

Carole came in before going to work looking all *English*, as usual, her navy blue raincoat tied tightly to show off her reduced waist, her hair slicked back into a bun, pearls around her neck

you'll be pleased to hear I'm moving out and in with Freddy, Mother, you'll never have to see me again

she stood there, expecting Bummi to ignore her, except something shifted in that moment and Bummi felt it was right to give her a ticket back from Coventry, it had been hard not talking to her, as the weeks progressed into two months and nearly three, her hurt had deepened and she was afraid of what might come out of her mouth

I dey vex so tey I no fit talk
and she did not want to disown her daughter
the only person left in her life who she loved

you see here, Bummi said, gesturing at the sack of rice, English people like to waste their money in expensive supermarkets on over-priced goods in fancy packaging, and then dare to complain in the bus queue about the economy going down the drain while giving *me* filthy looks, when it is them, yes, *them* who are going down the drain with their susceptibility to fancy advertising that causes a slump in their personal finances as a consequence

you English people, I want to tell those dirty-lookers, should ask *me* how to shop in this country because we immigrants are much cleverer at it than you, we refuse to pay ridiculous amounts for spices simply because they are in pretty little glass jars with 'a scattering of cardamom pods' or 'fine strands of saffron' on the label

what is a 'scattering'? tell me now? or 'a generous pinch'? is it a pound or a kilo? no, it is a *pinch*, you *fools*, then they have the cheek to turn their noses up at our good-quality money-saving immigrant shops into which they dare not venture in case they are kidnapped by terrorists or catch malaria

moreover, we people know how to haggle for a good price in the market instead of paying the extortionate amounts on display with 'rob me, I am a fool' written across our foreheads

why pay a pound for a pound of apples when you can get them for less if you stand your ground and out-talk the market trader until they are so vanquished they will practically give them to you for free just to get rid of you?

with such savings accumulated over time, you can purchase a whole chicken if you similarly haggle with the butcher

one chicken can last several meals if you make soup

and are watching your waistline

my point is that you are a Nigerian

no matter how high and mighty you think you are

no matter how English-English your future husband

no matter how English-English you yourself pretend to be

what is more, if you address me as Mother ever again I will beat you until you are dripping wet with blood and then I will hang you upside down over the balcony with the washing to dry

I be your mama

now and forever

never forget that, abi?

by the time she had finished, Carole had tracks of black mascara running down her cheeks and Bummi was grateful to once again feel the warmth of her child's body when they held each other

the child who left the flat in tears that morning thanking *Mama* for talking to her again because, she said, when your own mother pretends you don't exist, it is like you are dead

Bummi watched Carole as she stepped into the urine-smelling lift to take her to ground level
her daughter would soon belong completely to them.

2

Bummi remembers how her own mama gathered up her wrappa to flee Opolo in the Niger Delta
after Bummi's papa, Moses, had been blown up while illegally refining diesel
heating barrels of crude oil in the swamps while standing too close to the flames of this cottage industry was dangerous
producing diesel from oil that was only two barrels away from an open fire was dangerous
the whole Delta knew, yet how else to survive in that devastated place where millions of barrels of oil are suctioned up by the gargantuan drills of the oil companies from thousands of metres down into the earth to provide precious energy for the rest of the planet
while the land that produces it is left to rot

when Bummi's papa passed, the plot of land he owned where they farmed cassava and yam was taken by his relatives in broad daylight
you were his traditional wife, not his legal one, they shouted at Iyatunde, as they all descended on her hut directly after his funeral

commot for dis place now-now, dis na our property now, we no wan see your leg here again, you no get anything to do for this place!

Bummi remembers the long walk with Mama through the forest to her grandparents' home

carrying their possessions in two baskets upon their heads

back in the small-small hut where Mama's life began, her grandfather informed them he was going to marry Bummi off as soon as she reached puberty

she go don ready soon, I fit manage that dowry moni, it go solve plenty problem for me, this one wey pocket dry everywhere

that night Mama told her that she was not going to allow her father to force his traditional way of life on to her child, just as he had chosen her own husband for herself when she was fourteen

the next morning, with the little money she and Moses had saved tied up in the folds of her wrappa, she took Bummi by the hand before her father woke up

and they fled the orange gas flares of the refineries burning twenty-four hours a day into the humid skyline for hundreds of miles

they fled the toxic fumes that made breathing the very air difficult because to inhale deeply was to die slowly

they fled the acid rain that made the water undrinkable

they fled the oil spills poisoning the crops, the diseased fisheries in the soupy creeks, the fishing baskets lifted out of the water congealed with gummy black oil

crayfish, crab, lobster – don die

swordfish, cat-fish, croakers – don die

barracuda, bongashad, pampano – don die

*

they started the journey to Lagos where they moved into Makoko-on-Water and shared a bamboo hut on stilts with another family, with a platform for sitting outside and a shared canoe to steer through the dark and dirty waters

Mama asked for work everywhere in the crowded city of Lagos, with Bummi trailing behind her feeling so ashamed of her dirty old clothes and blackened flip-flops

she hated the big city with its noise and the filthy exhausts of the city cars that tried to run her over

at first Mama tried to peddle roast corn and puff-puff on the streets until the other traders chased her away, this na our market, commot!

Bummi watched her mama humiliate herself begging for work, they arrived at a local sawmill where trees that had been felled in the interior were lashed together to form floating forests that were towed downstream to the city

her mama found the supervisor, Labi, walked boldly up to him, told him she was as strong as any man, could he not see her powerful arms from farming?

Oga, I get pikin wey mus' chop, I fit do this work, I no dey go anywhere, just give me work, abeg

Mama worked six days a week in the deafening din and dust of the sawmill where she said the men got used to her once they saw she worked harder than they did

then one day Labi said she did not need to carry planks of wood on her head any more, it was donkey work for idiots, and she was not an idiot, she could help operate the buzz saw

at first Mama was happy until she came home shaking her head, saying, dat man, im tell me say no free lunch-o

I go give us betta life and commot us for this suffer
we go still survive, my pikin

weekdays Bummi was collected by canoe to take her to the floating school on the lagoon, where the teacher collected the fees for his
salary as soon as each child arrived, or they were sent home

it never happened to her because Mama would rather go without
food than have her miss a single class

she told Bummi she was being ferried towards an education,
towards an educated husband and an educated job sitting down at a
desk that paid good money so that if her future husband died, she
could support herself and her children

until the unthinkable happened when Bummi was fifteen

Mama slipped while trying to fix a cranky, steam-powered saw at
the end of a shift and did not move quickly enough when its teeth
whirred viciously back into action

Labi came to school to tell Bummi the bad news

she remembers collapsing on to the bamboo slats of the school's
floor and crying into the waves churning below, she remembers getting into the canoe and being taken back to her hut where she curled
into a ball

she remembers being told by Labi that he had paid her rent and
schooling for one month while he sought out relatives, na because of
your mama, I dey do this thing for you-o

he located a distant cousin, Aunty Ekio, who offered housework and
childcare duties in exchange for accommodation and an education

Bummi was relieved she'd no longer have to survive on her own
back in Lagos

men were coming for her when she went shopping alone in the
market

including one big oga with one big belly in one big car who offered
to set her up as his concubine
while blowing cigar smoke in her face
exclusive contract only

Aunty Ekio came to the front door of her concrete house when
Bummi knocked on it, raw with grief, and flung herself prostrate on
the ground in respectful greeting, upset that her aunty did not in turn
greet her as a long-lost relative
you should be grateful I took you in, Aunty Ekio said, showing
Bummi her three-level concrete house, the first time Bummi had been
inside a home not made of bamboo, with rooms that led into other rooms
such as one called a nursery for the children to play with their toys
and a 'walk-in wardrobe' for Mrs Ekio

Bummi soon discovered her aunty spent her days reading fashion
magazines, going to the beauty salon, 'lunching with the ladies',
cooking when she had to, and watching videos
Bummi had to be on call before and after school
Boomeee!!! Aunty Ekio shouted for her morning tea in bed, or if
the furniture was not polished enough, or the children had messed up
their clothes, or she wanted help in the kitchen, or for Bummi to
change the television channel for her, or she needed something from
the market
Boomeee!!! Aunty Ekio shouted when she had a broken nail, bring
me the file *now-now*, even though Bummi might be eating, or constipated on the toilet, or doing her schoolwork, or making sure the two
boys took their bath without killing each other
she herself had to wash-down with the garden hose

*

Boomeee!!!, she heard when she was spitting into Aunty's cup of tea and muttering, I go injure you, lady, I go injure you, before taking it to her on a pretty plastic doily on a small tray

Boomeee!!! she heard when she went to market, realizing it was an echo within the corridors of her mind, arriving back home to Aunty asking what took her so long? do you take me for a fool-fool? were you making chit-chat with the boys?

Boomeee!!! was shrieked into her sleep amid nightmares of losing this home too, just as she had in Lagos and Opolo before that

Boomeee!!! she heard while sitting on the bus to the University of Ibadan when she began her studies in mathematics in the overcrowded lecture theatre

students sitting on the floor and in the aisles

where she dropped off to sleep at the back during her first lecture

only to be woken up by a graduate teaching assistant who had entered the empty room to set up for the next lecture

a young man called Augustine Williams

Augustine

who invited her to lunch that day, telling her she was a very pretty girl when she knew for a fact she was not

Augustine

who thereafter sought her out at lunchtime to sit in the shade of a tree in the grounds to eat ugba and abacha or peppered snails, suya or moi moi

the two of them soon existed in a force field that cut them off from the bustle of the rest of the campus, how did this happen? two people meeting by chance and feeling as if they had known each other for ever

he said he could see sadness in her face when it was in repose, which made her appear mysterious and beguiling she was surprised he was trying to see inside her, that anybody would, was she now mysterious and beguiling? she looked at herself in the mirror from every angle that evening trying to see herself as he saw her

unlike the boys at college who treated women like toilets, he waited a long time before he tried to kiss her – a quick peck on her left cheek which she refused to wash off for three days

with Augustine in her life, Bummi did not feel so alone

they were two halves of a circle moving towards completion

Augustine had grown up with his social worker father and typist mother who had resided in the same house since they were first married, whose own parents lived locally, as did his brother and sisters, aunts and uncles, who all descended on Sunday afternoons for a buffet of okra soup with fu fu, buku stew, sesame spinach stew with palm-nut oil, vegetable yam, noodles, pasta, fried chicken and salad

when he asked Bummi to be his wife, he reassured her that his parents would accept her, even though she had no close family to vouch for her, his parents believed marriage should be about love and compatibility above all other considerations

they prided themselves on being progressive

Bummi's hair was newly hot-ironed when she walked through the door of Augustine's home in a lacy white dress which came modestly below her knees and wearing her freshly whitened Bata sandals

you are welcome, Mrs Williams said, as she ushered her into the living room, flowery curtains shutting out the midday sun

Mrs Williams wore an elegant bubu of blue birds in flight

she joined Bummi who sat stiffly on the wicker sofa looking up at the many framed black and white ancestral photographs dotted on the ledge that ran around the top of the walls

Mrs Williams took Bummi's hand in both of hers and held them, Bummi marvelled at their soft warmth, her own mother's had been hard and scratchy

Mrs Williams said she wanted her son to be an honourable and responsible person, that was all a mother should ask for

we do not want a dowry, you have our blessing, you will be our daughter now

Bummi thought she was a very lucky girl

Augustine did not feel so lucky, he complained when they went for their long Sunday afternoon walks past miles of maize fields in the hazy sunshine

his family was not connected enough to get him a job in government or business as befitting his PhD in Economics

if he left for England, he was sure to find a job that would take him around the world as a globetrotting businessman or consultant

he would eventually own properties in New York, LA, Geneva, Cape Town, Ibadan, Lagos and of course, London

he would do it, yes, he would do it

by the grace of God.

3

By the grace of God

Bummi and Augustine migrated to Britain where he again could not find work befitting his qualifications he settled into the seat of a minicab until he had saved enough money to set himself up in business (import-export)

and researched trade possibilities between Britain and West Africa via the sweatshops of Turkey, Indonesia and Bangladesh

sadly, London was more expensive than he had imagined, saving was impossible and when the Nigerian economy went on a downturn, he had to send cash transfers back home

Bummi and Augustine agreed they were wrong to believe that in England, at least, working hard and dreaming big was one step away from achieving it

Augustine joked he was acquiring a second doctorate in shortcuts, bottlenecks, one-way streets and dead ends

while transporting passengers who thought themselves far too superior to talk to him as an equal

Bummi complained that people viewed her through what she did (a cleaner) and not what she was (an educated woman)

they did not know that curled up inside her was a parchment certificate proclaiming her a graduate of the Department of Mathematics, University of Ibadan

just as she did not know that when she strode on to the graduation podium in front of hundreds of people to receive her ribboned scroll, and shake hands with the Chancellor of the University, that her first class degree from a Third World country would mean nothing in her new country

especially with her name and nationality attached to it

and that job rejections would arrive in the post with such regularity she would ritualistically burn them in the kitchen sink

and watch them turn to ash to be washed down the plughole

which is why when their daughter was born, they named her Carole without a Nigerian middle name

Augustine worked nights, collapsed fully clothed on to their bed, smelling of the cigarettes he smoked all day and the can of extra stout he drank when he got home

just as Bummi dragged herself out of bed

to join her tribe of bleary-eyed workers who emerged into the dimmed streetlights of her new city to clamber aboard the red double-decker buses that ploughed the empty streets

she sat in sleepy silence with others who had hoped for a better life in this country, huddled in her eiderdown jacket in winter, her feet in padded boots, longing to sleep, afraid to miss the stop for the office building where she scraped away hardened faecal matter in toilet bowls and disinfected everything that came into contact with human waste

where she hoovered up dead skin cells into vacuumed fluff, mopped and polished floors, emptied paper baskets and rubbish bins, cleaned keyboards and wiped down monitors, polished desks and shelves and generally made sure everything was spotless and dust free

striving to do her best, even if her job was not

Augustine said the least he could do was be a good father to Carole, as his mother continued to advise him by letter

do not be distant, authoritarian and uncommunicative, my son, be close to your daughter when young and you will remain so when she is older

Bummi loved seeing her husband play rough-and-tumble with Carole, pretending he was a horse as she rode on his back for hours giddy-up, Papa, giddy-up

she loved it when he made Carole a doll's house from market crates, painting it, furnishing it with cardboard furniture, making dolls from pegs – what an exceptional man he was

she felt sad when he said to her one day, if we cannot make it here, perhaps our child will

Augustine

dear Augustine, who died of a heart attack while driving over Westminster Bridge transporting drunken partygoers in the early hours of New Year's Day

after too many unbroken nights with junk food on the go

doubling his salary in the busiest period of the year while halving his already unknowingly, genetically, chronically heart-diseased life

Bummi lost her Faith the minute she walked into the Chapel of Rest and saw her beloved Augustine lying there in body only

his brown complexion was drained of life and tinged with grey

his mouth was forcibly closed, his jaw clenched shut, as if pinned together

he did not open his eyes when she entered to look lovingly at her

he did not hear her when she spoke to him, he did not hold or soothe her when she sobbed

she decided there was no great spiritual being watching over her, protecting her and the people she loved

Bummi went through the motions of going to her church, the Ministry of God, it was expected, she found solace with her friends there

but she no longer believed any of the words that came out of her mouth in prayer or psalms or hymns the space once occupied by God was now hollow, and with no god to promise everlasting salvation, it hit her hard how much she was on her own

and how she and Augustine had been trapped in a despair that had paralysed their ability to snap out of it, devastated by the weight of a rejection that had not been part of their dreams of migration

and she asked herself — how can I rise above my situation in order to raise my child as the sole wage-earner in a parenting situation of one?

she asked herself — do I not have a degree in Mathematics? further, do I not possess the intelligence to acquire a first class degree in Mathematics, without even sleeping with the professor?

do I not enjoy the challenge of problem solving?

the more she asked, the more she understood she must do what Augustine was himself too weak to do

she was going to become someone who employed others, rather than someone waiting to be employed

she was going to become the proprietor of her own cleaning company, which would be an Equal Opportunities Employer, like all other cleaning companies

she wished Augustine was around to share the joke

that night she dreamed of employing an army of women cleaners who would set forth across the planet on a mission to clean up all the damage done to the environment

they came from all over Africa and from North and South America, they came from India and China and all over Asia, they came from Europe and the Middle East, from Oceania, and from the Arctic, too

she imagined them all descending in their millions on the Niger Delta and driving out the oil companies with their mop and broom handles transformed into spears and poison-tipped swords and machine-guns

she imagined them demolishing all the equipment used for oil production, including the flare stacks that rose into the skies to burn the natural gas, her cleaners setting charges underneath each one, detonating from a safe distance and watching them being blown up

she imagined the local people cheering and celebrating with dancing, drumming and roasted fish

she imagined the international media filming it – CNN, BBC, NBC

she imagined the government unable to mobilize the poorly paid local militia because they were terrified by the sheer numbers of her Worldwide Army of Women Cleaners

who could vaporize them with their superhuman powers

afterwards, she imagined legions of singing women sifting the rivers and creeks to remove the thick slicks of grease that had polluted them, and digging up the land until they'd removed the toxic sublayers of soil

she imagined the skies opening when the job was done and the pouring of pure water from the now hygienic clouds for as long as it took for the region to be thoroughly cleansed and replenished

she imagined her father, Moses, a simple fisherman, steering his canoe through the transparent waters of the creeks, a man who was still supporting his family in the dignified tradition of their ancestors

she imagined her mama, in good health, taking it easy while farm-hands looked after their land

which had not been stolen by his relatives because Moses had not died

she imagined Augustine, a Green Finance Economist coming up the garden path of their house wearing a business suit and with a smart briefcase returning from chairing his latest Economics and the Environment conference at the United Nations in Geneva or New York

Bummi needed an injection of cash for driving lessons and other start-up costs; what to do when everybody she knew was living hand to mouth
except for Bishop Aderami Obi of her church
who started to behave differently towards her after Augustine died
who began to visually gorge upon her body whenever he saw her, like she was the first course, main course and dessert merged into one
when he talked, it was to the bountiful breasts Augustine had worshipped
when he put a reassuring arm around her after church, he slid his hand lightly down her back, sweeping it over her buttocks so slyly nobody else would notice
when she tried to move out of his way, he pressed closer to her
Bishop Obi was a rich man, a powerful man, his congregation of two thousand bestowed upon him the gift of omnipotence in his bidding to do God's work on earth
and he behaved as if it was his right to pester his female parishioners, in which case, it was her right to ask him to loan her the money to start her business
had they not paid a tithe of 10% of their monthly conjoined income into his begging bowl for many years? money they could ill afford
Augustine had believed the pastor's sermons, that to commit financially to his church was to commit to God, and to commit to God would lead to prosperity untold and a reserved front row seat in heaven
she saw it for what it was, a very lucrative business for a very clever man
her husband had also been a clever man, except his brains were

fried with garlic when it came to believing every word that came out of Bishop Obi's mouth

he would not be swayed otherwise, even when the bishop bought a private jet and a private island in the Philippines

with his parishioners' money

one Monday evening when there was no service scheduled, the pastor arranged to meet her about her loan in the parlour of the old bingo hall that was now his mega church

she let him undress her with his greedy hands in the vestry

she let him excitedly caress her released C-cup breasts – as if it was Christmas

she let him pull down her lacy new undies (ten for the price of one)

she gasped and groaned as if in ecstasy when he entered her, taking too long to expel his little devils into the plastic black sheath that pumped her until he cried out, blessed be his holiness! blessed be his holy name! God O continue de place everybody for dis world and belle go continue to dey sweet everybody, hallelujah! Sister Bummi, hallelujah!

Bummi smiled demurely at the pastor when his goal had been achieved, and swiftly reassembled herself

she wrapped herself back up in her blue and purple outfit and re-tied her headscarf while he re-zipped his flies and re-buckled his belt

she was now a businesswoman

this was her first transaction

she looked discreetly away when he withdrew an envelope of cash from his jacket pocket, a low-interest loan to be repaid over two years

it would have taken twice as long to save a quarter of it on her salary thank you, sah, she said, curtsying, humble, God don butta my bread

she walked home, filled her bath with salts, lay in it for hours, topping it up at regular intervals, trying to sweat him out of her

she would never tell anyone how low she had gone to elevate herself and her daughter

every time she closed her eyes, she could feel his hot, voracious, harsh tongue licking her ears, his lips telling her she was his dutty whore, his fat cheeks against her, his big hands squeezing her buttocks, his huge stomach pushing against hers

as he speared the most sacred part of her body.

4

As Chief Executive of BW Cleaning Services International Plc, Bummi advertised in the spendthrift people's supermarket, lined up a couple of cleaners and clients, domestic and business, only to quickly discover that they could all let her down at the last minute

this was not going to be a walk in the park, but life was not a walk in the park, abi? there was only one person to be relied upon, herself

she would start small and grow big, and allowed Sister Flora from church, who could not have children herself and wanted them, to look after Carole when necessary, and sent herself out on jobs

her first client was a lady called Penelope Halifax

who lived in one of those big houses in Camberwell with attic rooms for the servants of olden times

these days all these people could afford was a weekly cleaner

when Bummi walked into the house with stained-glass windows on the front door, old-fashioned tiles on the hallway floor, high ceilings, large windows and many flights of stairs winding up, she realized how small her world had been thus far in England

nobody she knew lived like this, not even her Nigerian friends from church who owned their own homes

did not live like this

Penelope was tall, a retired schoolteacher who was quite pleasant-looking with the kind of dyed hair that's neither blonde, grey nor white

she wore ill-fitting clothes to hide her substantial womanliness

Bummi never understood why English women did not show off the outline of their fulsomeness, the more fulsome the better, so long as it was done with decorum

in her culture a substantial woman was a desirable one

Penelope had been a schoolteacher at Carole's school, Bummi noticed a framed farewell card in the hallway

she wanted to mention this to Penelope, to develop a friendly working relationship with her client because if people like you they are more likely to keep employing you

but the lady told her, you're here to work, not to indulge in social discourse, she then instructed her never to open any drawers, cupboards or wardrobes

or go into pockets or bags

Bummi wanted to bite the woman's head off, but bit her tongue instead

Penelope soon broke her own rule and talked non-stop to Bummi as she followed her around the house moaning about her awful first husband, Giles, an engineer, who was a sexist twat stuck in the dark ages, she said, and her godawful second husband, Phillip, a psychologist, who she discovered was a flea-bitten dog who chased any mangy, randy tart behind her back

Bummi thought the woman was sophisticated on the outside,
uncouth on the inside

yet she was also obviously lonely, her children had long ago left
home

Bummi felt sorry for her and every week discreetly cleared away
the large supply of empty wine bottles left by the kitchen bin

once she had several regular clients, Bummi started to recruit
staff and produced a job description to show applicants she was
serious

1/ highly skilled in cleaning and emptying waste containers and
eliminating debris from designated areas

2/ good knowledge of tools and chemicals in cleaning process

3/ safe use of detergents and chemicals, good ability at vacuum-
ing, proven record of sweeping, hand dusting, buffing and wiping

4/ demonstrated ability of sterilization of water coolers

5/ competency in dusting lighting fixtures and polishing metal
hardware

6/ complete dedication to accuracy and attention to detail

7/ knowledge of the importance of protective clothing and
self-care

she soon had four Nigerians, two Polish and one Pakistani on her
books

who went through a training programme on the job to meet her
professional standards

she went to an evening class at the library to familiarize herself
with computers and the internet, and found an accountant because
she did not want to end up in Holloway Prison for tax avoidance

by the time Carole began her banking career in the City, Bummi had a staff of ten

one of them, Sister Omofe from church, was the most pleasant and diligent worker of them all

her husband, Jimoh, had taken a second wife back in Port Harcourt where he ran his mobile phone business and left her to raise their two sons, Tayo and Wole, alone

the two women became fast-fast friends as they mopped floors and polished desks

you see that man? Omofe said, I hope his snake gets diseased, shrivels up and poisons him from the inside

I think you did not marry him to become wife Number One? Bummi replied

I did not, I am a modern woman and I will put rat poison in his stew next time he comes to Britain, expects to stay with me, and as soon as he has dropped his bags and eaten my food, goes out drinking Guinness in those nightclubs filled with young girls wearing next to no clothes

Sister Omofe, I have seen them with my own eyes on the tube-train late on Friday and Saturday night when I am going to work and they are going to party, the young girls in this country dress like prostitutes

that is because they are, Sister Bummi, they have no self-respect, just like my two sons have no self-respect, they are running wild without their father to discipline them, they are making merry hell, only yesterday I had the police bobbies at my door saying my boys were suspects in the robbery of a woman on the top of the bus along with the other hooligans on the way home from school, did I not tell them to sit at the bottom of the bus with the law-abiding people?

when I hit them, my hands bounce off

when I threaten them with curfew, they break it

and when I hid their computers in my bedroom, they kicked down the door

they will either end up dead in a hoodie gangland shootout, or locked up, and I will spend the rest of my life either visiting their graves or visiting them once a week in the clink

is this my fate?

Sister Omofe, send them home to Nigeria, is that not the tried and tested solution?

you are a woman of solutions, Sister Bummi, Omofe replied, taking Bummi's hand, squeezing it

a few months later, Omofe told her sons they were going on holiday to Nigeria and upon arrival they were driven to a strict boarding school in Abuja, paid for with a loan from the bank

now I too am alone, Omofe said to Bummi after they had left, as the two women sat on an expensive red leather sofa in an empty office reception room in an empty office building that was many storeys high, on an empty city street at three o'clock in the morning

eating the chicken, rice and salad Bummi had prepared

Bummi looked forward to seeing Omofe at work and at church, where they sat together, she began to miss her when they were apart, found herself longing to touch her new friend in ways that were not acceptable

she imagined them lying together as man and wife

and instead of it feeling bad, it felt right

Omofe invited Bummi to sleep at her flat in a tower block in New Cross one morning when they had finished work and were about to board the bus home their feet were sore, their eyes sleepy and bloodshot, their armpits sweaty

the bus arrived and after the hordes of office workers, smelling of strong perfume and cologne, shampoo, coffee and even toothpaste had disembarked, they climbed on and sat comfortably pressed up together on the seat

Bummi felt tingles down the side of her body that blended into Omofe

my home is an empty nest, Omofe said, we can be company for each other

after they had each bathed and were ready to sleep, Omofe went to the doorway of her bedroom and said, I have made up a bed for you in Tayo and Wole's room although as it is a bunk bed, it is not fitting for a woman such as yourself

you are welcome to sleep in my double bed, which is more spacious

it is up to you

Omofe padded barefoot over the thick carpet of her bedroom wrapped up in a creamy bath towel, her plump brown upper back and backs of her legs shone, her wig was off and her natural brown hair was short and glistened

it is up to you, she repeated over her shoulder, and when she reached her bed, with her back to Bummi, she let her towel drop

Bummi followed her into the room as if in a trance, just as she could not help but allow Omofe to explore her relaxed and warm bath body

they both had generous folds of flesh and luxurious breasts

Omofe felt like home to Bummi and her expert activities culminated in the most intense pleasure

as their activities progressed, she also found pleasure in recipro-
cating, as her mouth travelled wherever it wanted to go until Omofe
cried out

Bummi stayed over at Omofe's as often as she could
    she admitted to herself she had been hungry for a long time, had
ignored it because she would never consider taking on another husband
    to replace someone irreplaceable was impossible
    this was different, Omofe was a woman

— Tayo and Wole returned from Nigeria after several years, transformed into civilized teenagers who were angry with their father for
only visiting them twice and at their mother for her betrayal
    although the two women carried on their communion at Bummi's
flat, it was strange being with Omofe in the bedroom she had once
shared with Augustine, and in the flat she shared with her daughter, the daughter she could never tell of this unmentionable thing that
she did
    the shame she had tried to suppress began walking towards her
    she did not want to be that sort of person
    it was not who she was

Bummi could no longer relax enough to enjoy herself, she turned
over and went to sleep, stopped responding to Omofe's increasingly
tentative touches
    tell me, what can I do to please you, Bummi? I will correct my
actions accordingly
    Bummi did not know what to suggest when the problem lay not
with Omofe

*

180

she stopped inviting her friend to come and stay, and when Omofe invited herself, Bummi declined

she also stopped taking the same shifts as her, stopped going shopping with her in the market, and started to avoid her in church

Omofe, tired of asking Bummi what was wrong without getting an answer, cut herself off from her and eventually left to work for another cleaning company

later she appeared at church with Sister Moto – *of all people*

Sister Moto had been a plus-size model and liked herself too much, she wore traditional dress and posed as if she was the Queen of Peckham

she had her own hairdressers' shop on the high road, her old catalogue photographs were plastered all over its walls, and she referred to it as the Nigerian Ladies' Community Centre, South East London Chapter

which Bummi thought arrogant and preposterous

Sister Moto raised either suspicion or pity because she had never had a boyfriend to anyone's knowledge, or got engaged, married, had affairs with other women's husbands or even flirted with the men who wanted her

and most of them did

Bummi made sure to sit behind the two women

Sister Moto with her back characteristically straight and proud, her light green bubu flattering her lighter skin

Omofe, in contrast, was shorter, darker, with pleasantly rounded shoulders and attractively fleshy arms Bummi wanted to reach out and stroke, as well as her thick, dimpled thighs and her ample, delectable hips with the stretchmarks Bummi thought looked like art and felt like Braille

Bummi noticed how the two women sat silently as the church filled up, as if they were not acquainted
yet there was something intimate between them, she wondered if others had thought the same when she and Omofe had sat together
when everybody stood to sing, she noticed their bodies instinctively lean towards each other

Bummi was surprised at how quickly Omofe had moved on
she was surprised at how upset she felt about this.

5

Kofi
was another cleaner on her payroll, a retired Ghanaian tailor who wanted to supplement his pension
he was also older than most of her staff, yet he worked harder and never complained
he had one deceased wife, five adult children, many grandchildren and a three-bedroom house in Herne Hill that he rented from the council for years, before they allowed him to buy it
he was also holding on to the remnants of bushy grey hair above his ears and on the crown of his head
she wanted to tell him to shave it off
he was bald, he should accept it

*

Kofi

invited her to a 'Ghanaian fusion music night' in a bar in a cinema called the Ritzy in Brixton

other than church, this was her first time listening to live music in England

she did not like the sound of the group who had a singer, drummer and guitarist, but she liked the mood lighting and the small-small tables where she and he could eat snacks, drink lemonade (for her), lager (for him) privately

the other people were scruffy bohemian types who had not bothered to dress up

she noticed all the races were mixing willy-nilly and two gay gentlemen were holding hands, and nobody seemed to mind, strangely

Kofi looked at ease in this peculiar environment, he tapped his feet to the music, nodded and grinned back at strangers, in spite of the fact that his grey suit and tie was as out of place as her bright orange traditional dress and head-tie

she liked the way Kofi looked at her across the table, as if she was the most beautiful woman in the world

he asked her about her life, she just shrugged, what was there to say?

a daughter, a business, a deceased husband

when you are ready to talk, I am here to listen, he said

he invited her to attend his Pentecostal church – she refused

he invited her to watch his grandson play in a school football match – she accepted

he invited her to his youngest daughter's wedding – it was too soon he invited her to a meal in his home, which she accepted, and enjoyed his palm-nut soup, fermented corn dough balls, lamb chops and cabbage

she liked the fact that this was a man who could cook

further, a man who wanted to cook for her

Kofi implied, after a respectable period of courtship, that he'd like to enjoy relations with her in his bed, which meant she had to decide if they were going to be more than friends and if so, what she was doing with a Ghana man?

she asked herself if it was what she wanted

she came to the conclusion it was what was offered

Carole met him and said, he's a keeper, Mama, don't you think it's about time you removed your wedding ring?

it took fifteen minutes to free herself, with washing-up liquid

he invited her on holiday to his timeshare apartment on Gran Canaria, I will sleep on the sofa, he said, you can take the bed

every morning she sat on the top floor balcony with a view of sandy, rippled roofs, and looked down on to the swimming pool where Kofi did forty laps surrounded by the kind of palm trees she recognized from home

Bummi tried cocktails for the first time and liked them, especially Margaritas, which felt like a soft drink until she realized she was giggling like a girl

they walked along the promenade in the evenings, arm in arm, under the parade of palm trees with the sea lapping the black rocks

she told him the story of her early life – the water and oil of the Delta, the water and timber of the lagoon

Kofi offered to escort her back to Opolo, to visit her people, she could not face it, she said, the situation had not improved there, it had worsened, whichever relatives remained were unknown to her

she told him too many people in her life had died young

she confided that every time he left her sight, she expected him to not return – a car accident, a bomb gone off, a stroke in the pool, a heart attack in the bathroom while she slept

he reassured her he was not going to die for many a year yet, his own father was ninety-four years of age

he himself took multivitamins and cod liver oil every morning

she told him more about Carole, who worked in a bank in the City, and about Freddy, who was from English high society

she said how upset she had been when Carole told her she was marrying a white man, it was the beginning of the end of the pure Nigerian family line

their children will be mixed, and their children will look white

to be wiped out in two generations

is this why we came to England?

Bummi had been prepared to hate Freddy on sight

the first time Carole brought him into the flat he practically leapt through the door with his blond hair flopping about, his gangly legs all over the place, he was full of good cheer, not snootily side-glancing her humble home, he said how cosy it was

I'm so pleased to meet you at last, he said, you don't look old enough to be Carole's mother, I can see where she gets her looks from

Freddy likes to watch Nollywood movies with her, jokes he's an honorary Nigerian and he *simply adores* eating her food, especially the yam porridge she makes for breakfast when they stay over, and Carole was even eating it again, which was a miracle

she told Kofi that Freddy has turned Carole into a more relaxed and jolly person

Freddy arranged for Bummi to meet his parents in a London restaurant, which she was looking forward to

except he warned her that although they'd warmed to the idea of Carole, once they saw how classy, well-spoken and successful she was (most importantly for his mother, how slim and pretty, too)

they're still old-fashioned snobs

Freddy's father, Mark, looked uncomfortable, said little at the dinner, Carole sat there with a fake smile plastered on her face the whole time

Pamela, his mother, smiled at Bummi as if she was a famine victim, when she started explaining the meaning of *hors d'oeuvres* to her, Freddy told her to stop it, Mummy, just stop it

she gave Bummi a 'vintage' bottle of wine from their vault, which 'really needs to be divested of its crumbling cork before it's more sediment than liquid'

Bummi accepted the gift graciously and did not understand why English people thought old wine, probably poisonous, was so special let alone drinkable

she herself had a nice gift for Pamela, five yards of indigo *aso oke* fabric

Bummi hoped she would only have to see these people once more in her lifetime – at the wedding

but Carole and Freddy married in a registry office without telling

anyone because they said the thought of planning a proper wedding felt like a mountain lain with land mines
Bummi should have been angry
instead she was relieved.

6

Bummi is lying on the green lounge chair in the garden of the Herne Hill house she shares with Kofi
the sun is importing its vitamin D directly on to her skin
Kofi is in the kitchen behind her cooking their evening meal
they too married in a registry office, and went on a two-week honeymoon to the Scilly Isles, which they loved, the people so nice and friendly

Bummi misses Omofe more now than she did when they split up
ideally she would like to have both her and Kofi in her life – a pipe dream because only men are allowed to be polygamous
these days Omofe works in Sister Moto's salon and, according to rumour, is living with her
as Bummi had long abandoned the Ministry of God, their paths do not cross, except for one time when she was back in Peckham and walked past Sister Moto's salon and peered in the window
Omofe was at the reception by the window, and glared at her as if to say, what are *you* doing here?

lilac wisteria spreads across the shed at the end of the garden
in front of this is a patch of different types of long grasses, what she calls their meadow, which rolls into their long lawn

the apple trees that line the left side are their orchard
the small pond Kofi dug out is little more than a big puddle, she teases him
he insists on naming it Lake Kofi

Freddy and Carole visit most Sundays for lunch
Freddy brings her flowers and chocolates and says, hello Mum, it's good to see you, you're looking marvellous as usual, and gives her a big hug and a kiss
sometimes Kofi's children and grandchildren join them

Bummi sits back and sips on the lemonade Kofi has made from fresh lemons and brought out to her
she wishes her mother was alive to enjoy her new life
see me now, Mama, see me now.

LaTisha

I

LaTisha KaNisha Jones
walks through the Fruit & Veg section of the supermarket, where she
works as a supervisor, fifteen minutes before the doors are due to open
she's Chief Fucking Bitch on the prowl
or Major General Mum
as her kids call her

she's already consulted with the personal shoppers who've been
trawling the aisles during the night for online orders, to synchronize
on replacement stock
she's checked the warehouse to make sure her section's deliveries
are in order and she'll shortly be recording 600 kilos of King Edward
potatoes as undelivered, even though the supplier has charged the
store for them (criminals!)
she for one isn't going into negative inventory today, which will

show up tomorrow as an unexplained deficit on her otherwise (almost) spotless report card

she's done data rotation with the scanner, made sure the shelves are properly stacked with older stock on top

she's made sure the displays of fruit are neatly arranged, all of them perfectly shaped and unblemished as per customers' wishes, who don't realize that most fruit in its original, unadulterated state looks anything but standardized in shape, texture, size and colour

as she learned at the supermarket training academy

or that carrots were purple, yellow or white until seventeenth-century Dutch farmers cultivated the mutant orange ones of today

as she likes to impart to her kids, Jason, Jantelle and Jordan, to make learning more interesting for them because they have no choice other than to do well in their exams

unless they want to be chained up in the cellar without food, water or toilet facilities

for twenty-four hours

as she threatens

frequently

LaTisha

is wearing her uniform of navy blue trousers with a crease down the front, navy blue cardigan, fresh white shirt, hair gelled down and side-parted

very smart and professional, because that's what she is now, after she crawled her way out of the horror movie of her teenage years

to begin climbing the giddy heights of retail supremacy

winner of Colleague of the Month six times in three years

Supervisor of the Month three times in six months

the money's crap, only one pound per hour extra for a helluva lot more responsibility and she's still on shifts and still has to work weekends

at least it means she's on the move, who knows, she might make general store manager one day if she works hard, sucks up to her superiors, doesn't piss off her colleagues (too much) and stays focused on her goal, which means remaining single

LaTisha started working for the supermarket when she left school a head-banging argumentative gobshite with no qualifications who wouldn't take no orders from no one

just like school when it tried to impose its senseless rules

she didn't see the point in studying when it didn't make you happy (swots were miserable and had no dress sense) and too much studying wears your brain out (scientific fact)

as she told her teachers

especially Fuck Face Mrs King who used to accost her in the corridors, you're not stupid, LaTisha, if only you'd apply yourself

LaTisha replied that it made common sense to conserve your mind power, Mrs King, all the while emoting pure insolence, a special skill of hers, according to the teachers

our brain cells are dying all the time and I'll deplete my resources – like our endangered planet, Mrs King, if I use too many of them in my youth, I might even end up going ga-ga in old age, she said, while emitting a look that said, yeh, just like you, F F

Mrs King struggled to reply and just when she looked like she'd found the right words in her mind and was about to speak them

LaTisha walked off

(result!)

*

the same with sports, which she got out of as often as possible with periods lasting from the beginning of the month to the end of it

were they going to ask to see her used tampons?

she even thought of starting a No School Sports campaign because enforced exercise was going to wear their bodies out and nobody was telling them the truth

as she told *Ms* Robertson, her sports teacher, who also accosted her in 'the corridor of teachers with nothing better to do than harass innocent people' to tell her she needed to do sports to keep fit and stay healthy

it's like this, *Mzzzzzzzz*, LaTisha replied, what about ballet dancers who end up crippled when they're old? or gymnasts who end up with replacement hips? and runners who do their knees in?

and you're telling *me* sport is good for me?

Mzzzzzzzz Robertson likewise struggled to reply

(result!)

she'd have said all of this in the rally speeches of her imagination, standing on a podium, speaking into a megaphone preaching the word of common sense to her generation of teenagers, inciting rebellion on a grand scale from the children of the world, creating utter havoc

which is what she felt inside after Daddy left

Daddy worked in Pest Control for the council, which gave him great job satisfaction, no two days are ever the same, he'd say, as they sat around the kitchen table eating their tea of fish fingers and salad, it's my role to kill the devilish vermin who plague people's properties and give them nightmares, and then to heal their trauma with reassuring words

it's a vocation, a calling, my contribution to the world, y'unnerstan?

Mummy's eyes disappeared into her forehead, and LaTisha and Jayla would giggle, even though they'd heard it all before, he was still funny in a silly way

weekends he topped up his income as a bouncer in a swanky night-club, like a UN peacekeeper except on a smaller scale, y'unnerstan?

prompting more eye-rolling from Mummy

Daddy had long black dreadlocks and was six foot five and just as wide

it's all muscle, not fat, here, feel this, he'd say to LaTisha, flexing his enormous biceps from his bodybuilding sessions at the gym

have a squeeze, she couldn't even make a dent in them, or circle them with her two hands when he asked her to have a go at that too

by the time Jayla asked if she could have a go, he was too busy eating, he said, not now, later, Jayla, later

except later never came

he liked rubbing shoulders with famous footballers, who were good tippers and secret gamblers because they earned too much too soon for too little, so them doan know the value of money

there was a back room in the club where they lost more cash than most people earn in a lifetime; they begged to have their photographs taken with him, the legendary Glenmore Jones, king of the bounc-ers, as he boasted around the kitchen table

the other way round more like, Mummy said

Daddy would look fake-outraged

footballers offered him jobs as their private security man; he declined because he liked to be home at teatime

I want to be with you guys, my children plus my wife equals my life because L is for *love*, I is for *immortal*, F is for *family*, E is for *eternal*

193

he did night shifts at the club every other weekend
came home Saturday and Sunday morning

her parents used to take her and Jayla to all the free museums in
London
Mummy said children who did well in life had parents who took
them to museums, and you don't need to be rich to do that
once inside, they let her and Jayla lead the way, although it was
LaTisha who got her own way more than her sister, who was shyer
and held back
if LaTisha wanted to spend forever looking at the scary dinosaurs
before anything else, it was allowed
she did just that for years, wishing she could climb inside their
skeletons
until she got bored of their prehistoric weirdness and Mummy
said, I'm glad that phase is over
same with the sharks in the London Aquarium who were really dangerous, although close enough to almost touch behind the glass tank
surrounded by all the smaller fishes with their creepy shapes and
ogling eyes
it was like being in a fantasy world when she watched them
she couldn't really believe they were real

once a year they went to Butlin's at Skegness
they couldn't afford to go to the Caribbean as a family which should
have been their Number One holiday destination to visit relatives
one day we'll take an ocean liner there, Mum said, with a swimming
pool and cinema on board
we'll start saving this very week, Daddy agreed

*

Mummy came from St Lucia when she was two years old

she grew up in Liverpool, went to a church school with a good reputation, and got on to a social worker course as soon as she left it

Daddy came from Montserrat when he was thirteen speaking funny and looking foreign, as he told his kids a hundred million times

when he complained of the cold, the teachers said he had behavioural problems

when he spoke patois, they thought he was thick and put him in a class the year below, even though he was top of his class back home

when he was naughty with his white schoolmates, he alone was singled out and sent to the Sin Bin

when he got angry at the injustice of it all, they said he was being abusive

when he stomped out of the classroom to let off steam, they said he was being aggressive

so he decided to be, threw a chair at a teacher, narrowly missing him the first time

but not the second

he was sent to Borstal for the crime of chair-throwing, LaTisha, it was like a prison for young offenders, where he served time with junior murderers, rapists and arsonists

I didn't want to be like them so I kept mi head down, luckily I was a big bwoy so they didn't bother me

once I was free again, I picked myself up and made a life for myself inna dis country, LaTisha, addressing her alone, even though Jayla was at the table too

Jayla accused her of being Daddy's favourite

it was true and she liked it

not gonna deny it

*

I put all-a my pent-up rage into bodybuilding, never lost mi temper with nobody ever again, that's why the daddy you know is such a peaceable and agreeable person, ain't that right, Pauline?

yes it is, I find your father very agreeable indeed, girls, and they'd both laugh like it was a private joke between them

so one minute it was all happy families with jokes, then the September she started secondary school, he left

didn't even let them know he was going, like there was no preparation for it, he went when the girls were at school and Mum was at work, left a note on the table saying he was sorry

it was like, how can this even happen? is this for real or one of his practical jokes?

Mummy went into meltdown, tried to contact him – when his phone rang, they realized it was in the house, he'd left it under his pillow

she called everyone who knew him and found out he'd gone abroad somewhere

LaTisha sat by the living room window waiting for him to come home, Jayla stayed in her room

the whole of that Monday night, LaTisha sat there, dozing off, waking up when foxes started fighting, or a neighbour's car pulled up or people walked past talking loudly

the whole of Tuesday, and that night, too, the whole of Wednesday

Mummy didn't force her and Jayla to go to school because she was in a right state herself, took compassionate leave, her sister Aunty Angie came round and took over the cooking and consoling duties, forced LaTisha to have a bath, eat, clean her teeth, forced her to go to bed the fourth night she went to sit by the window that night LaTisha took Daddy's dressing gown from the back of the bathroom door and slept inside it, smelling his sweat and deodorant, feeling his arms around her

weeks later, Mummy reached him on the phone and screamed down it

he couldn't provide a viable excuse, LaTisha heard her tell Aunty Angie, who said he was obviously with another woman, usually the reason men left their families

he'd said he wasn't coming back, Angie, not now, not ever, I thought he was a big softie, I realize I don't know him

Angie dug around and discovered he'd gone to live in New Jersey with Marva, one of Mummy's friends from work, who'd grown up there

Tiannah, her cute four-year-old daughter, was his

Mummy took down all photos of him, burned his remaining clothes, threw away his favourite things like his mug, Imperial Leather soap, old flannel

LaTisha and Jayla were never to speak of him again, he doesn't exist any more

except the ghost of him did, LaTisha could see and feel him everywhere

at the kitchen table telling them the stories her mother said were exaggerations if not downright fabrications

in the downstairs hallway when he came in and called out, Daddy's home! knowing her and Jayla would drop whatever they were doing to be the first to rush up and hug him hello

in the living room in his special armchair with the electronic leg rest, hearing him snore and wake up with a start when they tickled him all of them dancing to soul and Motown albums at birthday parties and at Christmas, and to reggae on Sunday evenings

his bulk filling the corridor upstairs, the game she and Jayla played when little of running under his legs to get past him before he could clamp them shut

hearing his voice booming downstairs when she was upstairs

she even missed him banging on the bathroom door to hurry up and why do I have to live with three ooman who take so rahtid long to do their tings?

her mother started to overeat, crept downstairs in the middle of the night to raid the fridge, snuck gin into her water from breakfast onwards, thinking they didn't notice, or the bottle going down

or a new one in her shopping bag

every two days

then Mummy sat them down either side of her on the sofa in the living room and told her and Jayla that it was time for them to know the truth

Jayla, your father is a previous boyfriend of mine called Jimmi who turned violent, when he tried to throw me down the stairs, I caught the train from Liverpool to London that evening

he never knew I was carrying his child and I've not seen him since

she fell for Glenmore in the last weeks of her pregnancy

he said he'd love the child as his own

Jayla wouldn't talk to LaTisha about it, stayed inside her room even more, played computer games when she wasn't at school and when LaTisha went in to sit on her bed and chat like they used to, she was told to shut the door when you leave without Jayla even looking up from her computer

one morning when they were all having breakfast together, Jayla said she wanted to meet her dad, the man you've kept from me my entire life, Mummy – who rooted out the address of his parents, you shouldn't go, Jayla, he's bad news

Aunty Angie took Jayla to Liverpool, they turned up on the doorstep of the house where he grew up, his mother was taken aback when she revealed who she was, had to admit she was the spitting of Jimmi

Jayla could tell she wasn't pleased to see her

she called Jimmi on the phone in the hallway, told him to come and meet his daughter, *another* one, she heard her whisper

he cyan't meet you, she said when she walked back into the room, he's got enough children, don't need no more

you're better off without him in your life

when Jayla returned home distraught, LaTisha told her to forget him, he's another bastard, like Daddy

when Daddy phoned LaTisha on her birthday, nearly a year later, he cried down the phone, he'd done it because he realized he loved Marva more than Pauline

that don't mean I doan love you and Jayla, y'unnerstan?

she put the phone down on him.

2

Losing her dad the way she did was something LaTisha never talked about; whenever people asked, she told them he'd died of a heart attack it was easier than explaining what had happened, people thinking there must be something wrong with her and her family

else why would he leave?

she ran wild, hated school, couldn't concentrate, even Mummy couldn't control her and she was a social worker, I'm sending you home to Jamaica where they'll beat sense into you, LaTisha

yeh, whatevs, I could do with a Caribbean holiday

then she threw the legendary party when she was thirteen, except her mother came home too early the next morning when she was *supposed* to return home that evening

when the house would've been cleaned up, so whose fault was it really?

LaTisha was asleep with a boy in her bed (name? can't remember)

furniture was upturned, drink and sick stains, smoke burns, a ripped curtain, a broken lamp, plastic cups, scattered ash and cigarette butts because as the party had progressed deep into the night, with a load of strangers piling in, she'd given up trying to make people behave and not get waved

what the flamin' heck

she joined them

bwoy! she got the beats of her life that day

her mother, who supposedly didn't believe in corporal punishment, went at her like a nut job with a belt *and* a saucepan *and* a shoe and an *iron* that nicked her under the chin, at this point LaTisha realized she was in the danger zone and rushed out of the house

she went and sat on the swings in the park for the rest of the day had to tolerate people poking their nose in, are you all right, dear? including the man who lived alone down the road and never spoke to nobody

who invited her into his flat for a cup of tea and cake

as if she was a gormless mug

it was what her mum later called a 'turning point' in their relationship

LaTisha called it GBH, but wisely kept her mouth shut, promised to behave from then on, which she did, at home, didn't want to be maimed for life, or even lose it

not at school, though, which was as shit as ever, where she made the most of a bad job with Chloe and Lauren who were also there for the laughs

Carole, too, until she went cold on her crew

who didn't want to hang out with them as much, until she just didn't hang out with them full stop, as if someone had told her that the whole point of school was to work hard and be miserable

the opposite of her crew's manifesto

Carole became the swottiest of the paperpushers, won prizes, went completely up her own arse, as well as up Fuck Face's

when Lauren saw Carole on the tube a few years ago in the rush hour, she pretended not to see her, I swear to God, LaTisha, I was eyeballing her inches from her face and she looked right through me

LaTisha found Carole online just the other day, Vice President of a bank (*shut* UP!)

she looked really professional and pleased with herself

it wasn't the Carole she once knew

it was someone else

*

LaTisha has long wanted to show Carole she's not the roughneck she used to be, the roughneck who wasn't good enough to be her friend.

3

As the Hot Foods section manager is late today, she makes her way over to the rotisserie to give it the once over

it's all present and correct and Rupa, who's usually on the fish counter, is covering for Tammy who was fired last week, caught when security put a hidden camera in the back room because her till wasn't tallying

caught in the act of eating spicy chicken wings, irrefutable evidence, had to go, sacked over snaffling chicken wings after seven years on the job

what was she thinking?

everyone was told about it as a warning, even though the store regularly suffers close to a million pounds' shrinkage every year on account of employee theft, shoplifting, cashier and admin errors and whatever

it's a hazard of large-scale retail in spite of all the enhanced technology and security LaTisha keeps abreast of in preparation for her next promotion

working hard?

reading boring documents?

love it!

she's grateful she wasn't caught herself in the early days when she was stacking shelves, did a lot worse than Tammy but her excuse was more valid it went like this

she'd had Jason, her first child, for Dwight, an accident, he didn't want to use a condom, said he'd withdraw, clearly not in time (many times not in time)

she didn't show until it was too late

Dwight was a security guard at the store, it's how they first met in the canteen as she sat there shooting her mouth off about something deep and meaningful

when he leaned over and whispered, you're so fit, LaTisha

that's all it took

plus buying a Big Mac and strawberry milkshake after work that day, sweet-talking her all the way, LaTisha-bae this and LaTisha-bae that

like he was pouring honey over her naked body and licking it off

which is what he said he wanted to do to her, you make me hard just looking at you

he snuck her into the garage conversion flat at the bottom of the garden of his family home

while his mum watched telly in the main house

snuck her out again in the morning, before his mum woke up, she'd warned him not to bring girls back

LaTisha wondered if there'd been others, it didn't matter, he was hers now, and she began to feel close to him, especially as he liked to talk afterwards

previous boys only wanted an orgasm and not a conversation, let alone a relationship

which is what they were having after seven months together, going cinema and concerts, doing normal boy-girl things

he was the first person she told the truth to about her dad's disappearance, told him how upset and rejected she'd felt, even let him see her cry a few times, which had never happened with anyone

your dad shouldn't have done that, Dwight said, stroking her back, it don't make him a bad man, though, only a weak one, nuff mans be like that

she hadn't thought of that

so Daddy was weak?

so was Dwight, it turned out

when a new girl started at work who the boys rated a ten (the girls rated her a three), she came on to him in a sluttish way and suddenly it was like, LaTisha who?

she tried to talk to him, he said he'd moved on

moved on from what? there was nothing wrong with us, Dwight

you made me feel claustrophobic, bae, you're too intense, too much too soon, I'm not ready to settle down, ya gets?

what do you mean too much too soon? I haven't asked you for *anything*

LaTisha badmouthed him to her friends on the phone late into the night, only to end up bawling because she still wanted him and how could he do this to her?

I confided in him and he shat on my trust

they commiserated, he's a dog, LaTisha, you can do better than him, he doesn't deserve you, forget him, which she tried to do until she discovered her expanding belly wasn't puppy fat

she was pregnant

and seven months gone, like one of those teenagers who go for a dump in the toilets at school only to find out they're giving birth instead and it's like OMG and WTF and I didn't even know I was pregnant and

you're the father of this baby, Dwight, the one inside here, she patted her stomach

they were outside the store just before his shift, she was so angry he'd got her into this mess in the first place

are you gonna man-up about it, D?

she said it was his fault

he said it wasn't

like

how can it not be when he'd refused to put on protection when they'd done it, saying real men don't wear condoms, it don't feel right

you should have known better, she told him

so should you

Mummy went through the roof, literally exploded like a rocket through the kitchen ceiling first, then the bathroom ceiling above it, then through the roof and high into the sky until she calmed down enough to come back to earth with a thud

how can this happen to me, she wailed

it's not happening to you, LaTisha shot back

that got her a slap so hard it almost sent her flying across the room and she almost ended up stuck into the wall – arms and legs splayed

like in those comic cartoons

Mummy was so angry she'd said LaTisha had to pay for the child herself, threw her out after another row, ranting about LaTisha bringing shame on the family, I don't believe it, she prattled on, I've got a *babymother* for a daughter *you* can talk, LaTisha replied

Mummy pushed her out of the house so hard she fell on the pavement almost cracking her skull open

LaTisha screamed back at the slammed door, found a brick from the loose ones on their garden wall, pelted it through the living room window

by accident

it was only supposed to crack the window, not smash it to bits

anyway, Jason was safe in the kitchen

even so Mum screamed she was calling the police

LaTisha knew she'd never do that, would she?

instead she brought her things out, including Jason

I work with girls like you all day, I can't come home to one as well

she gave her an emergency number

didn't even call it for her

LaTisha ended up in emergency accommodation for young mothers, how could her mum do this to her when she had a baby to look after, and it meant she'd lost the one person who could show her how to raise him

at least Dwight manned up for a few seconds

made sure their shifts overlapped so she could get as many things as she needed for the baby without detection

she didn't like stealing but convinced herself it wasn't like the supermarket couldn't afford it with their billions in profits and exploitation of poor workers

it was their fault for not paying her enough, and anyway, how else was she gonna support the baby on her own?

a week later Mummy turned up to take her home, not before calling her a bloody fool and I had to teach you a lesson and that baby will die if you're left alone to look after it and you can't pick your family, can you?

LaTisha gave her the biggest hug, told her how much she loved her and thankyouthankyouthankyoumummy

luckily Jayla had been unemployed since she left school at sixteen so she looked after Jason during the day when LaTisha went to work

Jayla loved children, couldn't wait to have her own

LaTisha wondered how that was going to happen when she played computer games all day and only went out to take Jason around the park and go on Tinder dates that didn't work out

she'd come home early saying he wasn't the one

now that LaTisha had two people to help raise Jason, she felt the burden roll off her and on to them

even though Mummy said, I don't know if I've got any love left to give

when LaTisha watched her with Jason, it was obvious her love for him was infinite

he made her smile more than she had since Daddy left

so there she was, LaTisha KaNisha Jones, aged eighteen, supermarket cashier, single, and boys wasn't exactly lining up to get serious with her as a single mother of one

when she met Mark in the nightclub she went to once a month with Lauren and Chloe

he was an electrician, had his own flat in Streatham, was *fresh* to *death*, and didn't press his hardness into her when they danced

they arranged a date that involved a film, pizza and even a wine bar – her first time inside one, where he treated her to champagne and opened doors for her all the way

she couldn't believe her luck and what with his bedroom eyes making her feel sexy and the drink making her feel romantic, she gave it up without protection in the back of his car in an empty parking lot that very evening

as they made out, he whispered, I knew the minute I set eyes on you that we were meant to be together, I can't wait for us to become one

it was the most incredible moment, and she was so ready to have a man in her life who could be a father to Jason

when the only thing it led to was Jantelle, who still hasn't met her father because when LaTisha tried to call the number Mark gave her

it didn't exist

so now she's nineteen, got two kids, no man, and feeling over-whelmed by the absolute mess she'd made of her life

so grateful for Mummy and Jayla's help because her other friends were still free people and had backed off because she wasn't

it was clear they didn't want to be burdened with a single mother as a close friend who was gonna be tied to her two kids for another sixteen years

meaning they'd have to be

as well.

4

Trey was the father of child Number Three

the older brother of a former classmate and an upgrade on the others because he worked as a sports teacher, at her old school (what were the chances??!!!)

she remembered him from her party when him and his mandem caused a stir when they turned up

as soon as he stepped in through the front door, LaTisha set her eyes on him; before she could make her move, Carole was spotted leaving the party with him so waved she could hardly stand up

the next Monday at school, when LaTisha asked her outright if she'd banged him, Carole said no way, fam, and wouldn't look her in the eye, a sure sign someone's lying (*believe*)

Trey asked her out on Facebook, maybe he remembered her, maybe not, he obviously wasn't put off by the loads of photos she'd uploaded of her two kids

which probably made her a saddo in most guys' eyes

he was topless in his profile pic, tried to look propa gangsta, except LaTisha could tell it was all show because his eyes were soft

all the other photos were of him and his crew, no girls at all, a sign he wasn't a player and was waiting for the right girl to come along before he committed

she dressed up for their date in a clingy, spangled dress and strappy heels, determined not to give it up until their *tenth* date

and would insist on a condom

he picked her up in his car from her house which was very gentlemanly, instead of meeting her at the Caribbean restaurant on the high street as planned

conversation was easy as they cruised through the streets, they had Peckham School for Boys and Girls in common, had a laugh about Mrs King, still there, still hated by everyone, still called FF but instead of taking her to the restaurant, they headed to his place for *a private* romantic meal, he said, instead of a noisy restaurant with loads of guys ogling her

what could she say to that?

she discovered he lived in a room in a shared house with a bed, a wardrobe and a sink, she thought of walking straight out again but he said, I've been dreaming of a dance with you, let's dance, LaTisha, let's dance

then I'll order an Indian

he played John Legend, pulled her towards him, and she thought, okay, dancing is harmless, except he got very handsy and it quickly got steamy between them

it had been a year since she'd given birth and all of this time
there had been like
NO SEX

she wasn't going to go all the way, just wanted to mess around a little until Trey unzipped his jeans while they were dancing and stuffed her hand down his trousers

okay, Trey, so I'm going to leave now? can you drop me off home please or, tell you what, I'll take the bus, I really have to go home and be with my kids and make sure I don't get myself into any more trouble
she said
in her head
while giving him a hand job on the bed and before she could object he was inside her and it wasn't even a first date let alone a tenth and she wasn't expecting it and he was really pumping hard and making her sore and she struggled to move out from under what felt like a block of concrete and I don't want to, not yet, get off me, please, Trey, she said

out loud to deaf ears
so she gave up
couldn't stop him
had led him on
anyway, she let him get on with it
until he groaned
as he finished
lay half on top of her
crushing her ribs
fell asleep
didn't want to disturb him by moving
wanted to go home
she really needed to go home to Jason and Jantelle and Jayla and Mum
when he rolled off her enough to escape she left quietly in case he woke up and ordered the Indian
she walked the streets until she found a bus stop, waited ages for it, it was cold and she wasn't dressed for it, had to change buses twice, it took her three hours to reach home
where she spent a long time in the shower
wondering if he'd done anything wrong or was it her fault
she should have stayed and talked to him about it
he might have said he hadn't heard her saying no
or that she drove him so crazy with desire
which was kind of flattering
and he couldn't stop
himself

she half expected him to call up the next week, hey, you left before I could tell you what a great time I had with you, fancy going to see a film at the weekend?

she waited for the call that never came, the only thing that did was Jordan

so now she had three kids, Jason, Jantelle and Jordan, all before her twenty-first birthday

three kids who'd grow up with no fathers in their lives

LaTisha began to take herself off on long walks through the back-streets in her lunch break at work, heading away from the nightmare of the Old Kent Road with its thundering vehicles and fumes

she tried to make sense of it all, of herself

she beat herself up for being so stupid, yes, stupid

Mum veered between blaming LaTisha for being such a useless article, and blaming herself for raising a child who'd become one.

4

LaTisha has finished her morning patrol of the supermarket

she's about to let in the earlies who prefer empty aisles to whiz their trolleys down without worrying about knocking over old ladies or young children

once it's opened, she's off upstairs to the office to check her emails and see who's pretending to be sick, a system open to exploitation as they don't have to provide a doctor's note until their seventh day of skiving

as someone who abused the system more than most, she *knows*

now she's a good citizen determined to catch out those who aren't, like Carter, who asked for holiday leave two weeks before Christmas and when she refused, called in sick

from Thailand

produced a sick note *ten days* later, from a dodgy foreign doctor, no doubt, and kicked up a fuss because she wouldn't accept it, it's too late, Carter, and Thailand isn't even in the EU last time anyone looked so it's not eligible at any time, she said calmly while he bellowed long distance that he was going to take out a grievance against her

you can do what you like, Carter, it's your prerogative

feeling proud of herself for suppressing the old LaTisha who'd've bellowed back — and see where it gets you, you fucking cunt

this is the New LaTisha

the one who got herself two 'A' levels at evening school

which really did her head in, her brain throbbed with headaches from too much thinking and memorizing, her eyes hurt from so much reading

she lost half her brain cells doing those courses, she did

the other half she's using for an online retail management degree with the Open University

in her second year, part-time, four more to go

this is the New LaTisha

who's nearly thirty and settled on being single for as long as it takes to meet a man who's right for her and her kids

apparently Tyrone, Section Manager of Electronics and Appliances, has a thing for her, she's been studying his behaviour to ascertain whether he's a player around women, so far so good

he's single, unmarried, no kids

she'll keep her eye on him, won't rush into anything

if ever, maybe never

*

her longest relationship was Kamal, who lasted nine months, they went on proper dates, she met his friends and family, he spent time at hers

Mum thought he was okay, Jayla liked him because he played computer games with her, the kids took to him because he spoilt them with sweets

the five of them looked like a family on his Instagram page

the relationship ended because although he liked her kids, he wanted his own

and although she liked him, she was done with being a baby machine

time to move on, they agreed, maturely, face to face

no lying or cheating or badness on his part

after him she dated a couple of guys she met at parties and discovered one of them was two-timing her with another woman who confronted her when she left his flat one morning

the other one seemed to have several women on the go, according to his texts, Tinder, WhatsApp and Facebook

which she read while he slept

both men were unceremoniously dumped

with immediate effect

this is the New LaTisha

who still lives with Mum and Jayla in the family home with Jason (twelve), Jantelle (eleven) and Jordan (ten)

her and Jantelle double up, the boys have the converted attic, Jayla and Mum have their own rooms

Jason is the oldest and cleverest, he likes studying more than the others, maybe because he's more responsible as the oldest as such she has the softest spot for him, can't believe he spent so many months growing inside her without her knowing

which makes her feel sad, he might have felt lonely without her talking to him and stroking her belly, which is what she did with the other two

Jantelle's special as the only girl, she looks most like her, a mini-me, and is the most thoughtful, whenever LaTisha is at her desk yawning, she'll come up to her and say, time to take a nap, Mummy, shall I bring you hot milk with honey in it?

Jordan looks like Trey and she suspects he's inherited his characteristics

Jordan's already been suspended from school, causes the most problems at home, refuses to go to bed, or stay in it when he's forced to, steals money, starts fights with his older siblings, and sneaks out to play when he's been grounded

she caught him watching porn on the family computer recently

the kids have three mothers

LaTisha is the strictest and most fascistic: homework, obedience, manners

Mum is the sweetest and more forgiving of her grandchildren's naughtiness than she was with her

Jayla is the maddest, won't leave the house at all now, won't see a psychiatrist, is really pale due to Vitamin D deficiency and is glued to her computer doing godknowswhat

then Daddy turned up unannounced a few weeks ago

LaTisha came home to find him sitting on his old armchair in the living room, as if he'd never left it

he was just as huge, his dreadlocks were more grey than black, and he had a big stomach he looked at her admiringly, lovingly, when she walked in the room

it didn't work out with Marva, he missed his real family

Mum didn't look like she was going to kick him out any time soon, it was as if her love for him was flowing back in uncontrollable waves

Jason and Jantelle sat there perched on the edge of the sofa unsure what to make of this giant who was their grandfather

Jordan had already decided, edged towards his grandfather who reached out and put an arm around him when he was close enough to be cuddled

Jordan beamed up at his grandfather, with such an angelic look on his face

she realized her youngest son needed her father in his life.

Chapter Three
Shirley

Shirley
(not yet Mrs King)
arrives at Peckham School for Boys and Girls
a former Victorian workhouse with two rectangular blocks of
concrete attached incongruously to both ends of it
approached by what was once called the Paupers' Path
leading up to its castle-sized doors

she's wearing a light grey pencil skirt and jacket, powder-blue
blouse, grey neck-tie, black patent leather court shoes, and her pride
as she passes through the formidable doors into the wood-panelled
entrance
wide staircases sweep up either side of the lobby ascending to the
upper floors
long corridors extend in two directions either side of her

she's way too early, wanders through the empty school, explores its light-filled classrooms, imagines its essence pouring into her soul, yes, her very soul

she isn't going to be a good teacher but a great one

one who'll be remembered by generations of working-class children as the person who made them feel capable of achieving anything in life

a local girl made good, come back to generously pass on

her parents, Winsome and Clovis, are proud of her for making it to university to read History and thereafter gaining a Certificate in Education

she's the one who's made it, not her older brothers

who didn't have to do any housework or even wash their own clothes, whereas she had to spend her Saturdays mornings doing both

who were given first helpings at meals they never had to cook, and extra portions because they were growing lads, including mega-helpings of the most desirable desserts

who weren't punished for speaking their mind, whereas she was sent to her room at the slightest sign of insurrection, keep your thoughts to yourself, Shirl

and while it's true they got the strap and she didn't – for going out without permission or not coming home on time from school – it was only because she never broke the rules

everyone thought Tony and Errol were destined to be football stars, Pelés in the making, one step away from World Cup glory

until they reached sixteen and their early talent didn't burgeon into a professional one, and their junior club memberships were terminated

they left secondary school early, became clerks pushing pens

instead of kicking a ball around Wembley
she's the Family Success Story

Shirley walks past laboratories filled with petri dishes and desicca-
tors, microscopes and pipettes
she walks past colourful art rooms with a few quite good paintings and an airy woodworking studio with work benches (for boys
only)
past a Domestic Science classroom with steel preparation counters
and gas cookers, ready to nurture the next generation of housewives, full-time housewife *and* full-time job, a downside of the
Women's Liberation Movement
it won't be the case for her
once she marries Lennox, they've agreed he'll do the cooking,
she'll do the cleaning, he'll do the shopping, she'll do the ironing
she didn't even have to fight for this
she's lucky to have him

classroom walls are decorated with flow charts and diagrams,
anatomy drawings, planets orbiting the sun, posters of extinct mam-
mals and a map of the world that makes Britain rival Africa in size,
testament to the colonial cartographers who got away with it for centuries, even now, it seems, as she approaches her very own classroom
on the second floor, the obligatory line-up of the kings and queens of
England on its walls
as well as a poster of Tutankhamun's golden death mask from the
British Museum exhibition she'd queued for hours to attend with her
school
the beautiful boy Pharaoh who lived thirteen hundred years before
Christ

whom every girl in her class fell in love with, swooning over their ancient Egyptian crush

there's also a poster of the monoliths of Stonehenge, mysterious against the Wiltshire plains as the sun goes down in the background, another unforgettable school trip

while between the lofty windows looking out on to the playing fields, Neil Armstrong walks on the moon with the caption: one small step for man, one giant leap for mankind

like her

every step she takes will raise these children up, she will leave no child behind

as she smooths down her skirt, fluffs up her neck-tie and curly perm, wooden desks lined up, blackboard wiped clean, white chalk on its wooden tray ready for her to inspire the mixed-ability classes of this comprehensive in this multicultural neighbourhood

as the little angels pour into the sunny classroom on the first day of the new school year, their babbling-stream voices full of excitement at meeting their new history teacher, not much older than them, who in that moment feels her heart burst with joy

as the sun emerges from the clouds to hit her in the face and powers her up with its energy and goodness

as she calls out the register when each class comes into her room that day, determined to quickly memorize their names, knowing the importance of a teacher's personal touch to establish rapport

Danny, Dawna, Decima, Devonne, Doreene, David
Janet, Jenny, Jackie, Jazil, Chris, Mark, Monica, Matthew
Rosemary, Lenny, Lloyd, Keith, Kevin, Helen, Ian
Sharon, Yasmin, Jasmine, Jasvin, Marlene, Merline, Ekow
Glenford, Garry, Gerry, Tim, Tom, Trevor, Tony, Terry
Kweku, Kwaku, Kwame, Winston, Smita, Leah, Akua

Julia, Jules, Julie, Juliette, Beverley, Brenda, Chaz, Maz, Rory
Remi, Yemi, Abi, Aarti, Eddie, Carlton, Kingley, Shabnam

God bless them all, her mission has begun – to make history *fun*
and *relevant* because we need to avoid repeating the mistakes of the
past and to deepen our understanding of who we are as the human
race, don't we, class?

sit quietly, don't fidget now, we don't exist in a vacuum, children, no
talking at the back, please, thank you, we are all part of a continuum,
repeat after me, the future is in the past and the past is in the present

their bright, shining faces looking up at her, a bit spotty, a bit
greasy, way too much forbidden make-up on some of the older girls,
yet they're obedient, doing as instructed, encouraged, no doubt, by
her passion and relatable personality

even little blighters like Kevin, Keith and Terry who turned up
with swastika motifs stuck on to their pencil cases and National Front
badges brazenly brandished on their blazers

which she deals with by educating them about Hitler's Final Solution, shows them photos of the Bergen-Belsen concentration camp
when the Americans liberated it at the end of the war

the shock of it triggering a hundred questions

miss! miss! miss!

no, they are *not* walking skeletons, but prisoners of war and they
are alive, just, and these were the gas chambers, and this here is a
mass burial pit full of real skeletons, and this is a drawing of women
worked so hard in the camps their wombs fell out, as you can see

pass them around and take a good look

or when race wars broke out in the classroom

look at this photograph of a lynching in Mississippi in 1965, yes,
those children are indeed clapping and cheering as this black man

hangs dead from a tree, his neck broken, his crime was to apparently stare suggestively at a white woman

miss! miss! miss!

no, there were never any trials, suspects were grabbed off the street and hung, shot, beaten or burnt to death

this, class, is what happens when prejudice gets out of hand

she had their attention and by the end of each term, their devotion, expressed through so many gifts of homemade cards and cakes, chocolate Easter eggs, Christmas presents and baskets of fruit that she was embarrassed to carry them over-spilling her arms into the crowded staff room (a sure way to make enemies) and took them directly to the boot of her car instead

Shirley

was praised by the headmaster, Mr Waverly, as a natural teacher, with an easy rapport with the children, who goes above and beyond the call of duty, achieves excellent exam results with her exemplary teaching skills and who is a credit to her people

in her first annual job assessment

Shirley felt the pressure was now on to be a great teacher *and* an ambassador

for every black person in the world.

2

The staff room is stuffed with sofas, tables, armchairs, coat racks and cork noticeboards studded with rotas for monitoring the breaks, postcards, fire evacuation instructions and a poster of a topless girl, barely sixteen, if that

teachers are coming and going, children are knocking on the door for this or that, answered by one or other annoyed member of staff, what is it *now*, Moira-Billy-Mona-Ruthine-Leroy?

can't we have our lunch in peace *for once*?

Shirley endures the fug of foul-smelling smoke without complaint, even though her eyes smart and her hair stinks so badly she has to wash it every night

such a scruffy lot, these teachers, she thinks, sitting neatly in her prim skirts and court shoes, watching them eat their cheese and tomato sandwiches or pork pies or Cornish pasties, instead of the disgusting slush served up in the school canteen

while she eats her salt-fish, sliced plantain and sourdough bun concoctions

hoping no one will notice, hates having to explain herself

to her left is Margo (Geography) who wears flowery-flowing dresses and her hippy hair long with two thin plaits wrapped halo-like around her forehead

she's teaching for as long as it takes to fund an overland spiritual voyage to an ashram in Goa, where she's going to find herself (first) and a husband (second) and leave this, *this*, she gesticulates

they started together, were allies against the Oldies, most of whom don't even know what pedagogical means

Shirley likes Margo because Flower-Power Margo likes and accepts her

on Shirley's other side is Kate (English Literature), her other friend, determined to make headmistress before she turns thirty-five, delivered with such conviction, both Shirley and Margo can only nod their heads, *of course* Kate is going make head teacher, having been raised by politician parents who said *everything* with conviction, according to Kate, who either had to match their confidence or be crushed by it

the bear-like John Clayton (Maths) sits opposite, sporting a beard that could house a legion of lice, a dirty-looking denim jacket, threadbare corduroy trousers and scuffed Jesus-creepers on his enormous feet

hardly setting an example to the kids, although she does like him – shambolic, apologetic, nice to her, which, she admits, is all it takes

he's reading a newspaper, its front page emblazoned with a police mug-shot of a black youth looking wild-eyed and menacing from across the ashtrays and tea-stained mugs on the coffee table

she wishes he'd put it away, it feels personal, embarrassing

she wants to talk to Kate and Margo about it, would they be interested, sympathetic or even understand? they didn't seem to notice her colour, or at least never mention it

she wants to tell them it's like she's personally being attacked by the media

that women clutch their bags nervously when they pass her in the street or she sits next to them on the bus, when she's never stolen so much as a penny from her mother's purse, a rite of passage for most kids, or even a pencil from the school's stationery cupboard, let alone toilet paper from public places, a common crime at university, whole rolls of it stuffed up jumpers or into bags by flatmates who were, she remonstrated, as they offloaded their spoils on to the kitchen table, common-or-garden *thieves*

Shirley tries not to succumb to the paranoia that comes from thinking every negative reaction is due to her skin colour

her mother told her she'll never know for sure why people take against her unless they spell it out, don't assume people don't like you because of your race, Shirl, maybe they're having a rough day or they're bad-tempered people

Shirley maintains a charm offensive of politeness, even to those colleagues who take against her like Tina Lowry (PE), who removes herself whenever Shirley sits next to her

and Roy Stevenson (Physics) who let the door slam in her face three times for her to be sure it really was intentional

and Penelope Halifax (Biology, Head of Sixth) who ignores Shirley's (dwindling) attempts at greeting in the school corridors where Penelope sweeps imperiously past her like a Dowager Grand Duchess from Imperial Russia passing a lowly peasant

Penelope
is the only woman to speak up at staff meetings where everyone sits in a large circle in the assembly hall that doubles as a gym and canteen, and smells of fresh sweat and stale cabbage

whose superior voice slices through the booming alpha-male teachers

who like to bat balls at each other across the circular court with the ferocity of tennis professionals and when Shirley and the other women try to interject, their less assertive voices struggle to be heard, are cut off by the alphas before they've even finished making their points

even Kate, who is otherwise garrulous, is shut up

Shirley abhors the fact that they're all pathetically resigned to letting the men, and Penelope

make decisions for the rest of them

this late May afternoon
after the sound of a thousand pairs of feet have stampeded out of

the building and down the drive leaving the school in a post-traumatic silence

Penelope addresses the issue of the school's poor exam performance, declaring that half the kids are so thick and badly behaved they should be suspended or even expelled from school

everyone knows which half she means

Penelope is known to give the misbehaving Pete Bennetts of this world detention, whereas the Winston Blackstocks are suspended

the first step towards expulsion

she should be forcibly retired, in Shirley's opinion

out with the Oldies

in with the New Order

the young guns

her

Shirley decides it's time to step up and speak out

I disagree, Penelope, we mustn't write them off, she says, feeling her mouth dry up as the alpha males start to shuffle in their seats

I believe in making society more equal for our kids, she ploughs on, ignoring pointed coughs telling her to get on with it or shut up

our kids, she emphasizes (the possibility of shared ownership), have been told they're failures, thick, as you put it, before they've proven otherwise

exams are all well and good but not everyone performs well under pressure or manifests their intelligence at a young age, it can be acquired later, you know, nurtured by us, we have to be more than teachers, we have to look after them, believe in them

if we don't help them, who will

Penelope?

*

a thrilled, hushed stillness animates the room

Penelope doesn't disappoint, I, for one, am not a social worker, she replies in a tone that affects great weariness at Shirley's obvious naïveté and dim-wittedness, and I really think you need more than two terms on the job before you challenge someone with fifteen years' experience to a duel

someone who actually knows what she's talking about

now

as

I

was

saying.

3

Shirley's rants about Penelope dominate her conversation with Lennox that evening, as they will many others

while he's cooking a Thai chicken coconut curry in the kitchen, she sits at the tiny fold-up table next to the door that opens on to their small yard overlooked by the back windows of similarly poky ter-raced flats

the smell of sliced shallots and minced garlic sizzles in the pan

when they moved into the rented flat the couple upstairs complained they'd never smelt anything so disgusting in over seventy years

well now you have, Shirley thought, shutting the door on them

intelligence is not innate, Lennox, it's acquired, in spite of what Penelope thinks, having a go at me in front of everyone, and she dares to call herself a feminist?

Shirley takes a sip of her cold Lucozade this unduly warm May evening

I'm not a snob, as well you know, I went to grammar school, come from working-class stock and believe in *egalitarianism über alles*, not to be confused with being a communist, of course, I know enough about Stalin and Mao to be disabused of any fantasies in that direction

at the same time, the truth is that hierarchies of power and privilege won't disappear, every historian knows this, it's innate to human nature and inherent in all societies in all eras and equally manifests in the animal kingdom, so I can't pretend otherwise

my job as a teacher is to help those who are disadvantaged

Lennox stirs in the red curry paste and grated ginger

she admires his straight back, his blue office shirt, collar undone, stomach nicely contained within the parameters of his belt, the rest of his body contoured in all the right places: shoulders, biceps, bum, thighs, calves, courtesy of regular gym visits

she'd wanted a man who looked like he could carry her, physically, not metaphorically

she'd wanted a man who'd treat her as equal, who was responsible with a sensible career plan (solicitor) and didn't drink (much), smoke (never), do drugs (only once) or gamble (not even the pools)

Lennox coats the skinless chicken pieces in the sauce of lemongrass, lime leaves and coconut milk, the meal will be delicious, it usually is as Lennox follows recipes to a T

he doesn't believe in taking risks, neither does she

*

at least grammar schools attempted to level the playing field, Lennox, she continues, and made it possible for brighter children to receive a better education

or else those public school boys would still be running the show as if it was the 1890s and not the 1980s

Lennox scoops basmati rice out of the value sack they keep in the larder, deposits it in a chipped enamel saucepan of boiling water on the two-ring stove

a case in point is our nation's current *Commander-in-chief*, who'd never have made it to the top of the political pile otherwise, love her or loathe her, it's the principle of social mobility I'm arguing here

Lennox chops coriander stalks and sprinkles them on top of their steaming plates, tries out a different international dish most nights, which is the only travelling they can afford while saving for a mortgage

they've journeyed through the Mediterranean and the Middle East, and recently leapfrogged over to South East Asia

she can't wait to savour the rich creaminess of the curry as it slides down her throat

they'll make love tonight, and once they're homeowners, they'll make babies

their hips found each other's dancing to Ken Boothe and John Holt spinning on the turntable of a basement blues in Chapeltown with wall-to-wall speakers, a pot of curry goat in the kitchen, and rammed with all the other Afro-Caribbean youngsters who couldn't get past the bouncers of the clubs elsewhere in the city

even if they did, were unlikely to hear the music they loved played

they got to know each other over the next few months of dating

he told her he'd been sent by his Guyanese parents to live in Harlem as a young child, while his newly migrated parents found their feet in Leeds

he was raised by his Great Aunt Myrtle, a magazine journalist, who urged him to work hard at school, even if it made him unpopular with his classmates

study now and reap the benefits for the rest of your life, she told him

meanwhile his mother progressed from Barney's biscuit and toffee factory at the back of Vicar Lane bus station where it was her job to clean out the vats, to Morrison's mail order warehouse on Marshall Street where she was a packer

his father progressed from Robinson's steel works where he worked evenings and weekends to earn a living wage, to Leeds Post Office which offered better hours and pay

once they were earning enough, they sent for him

and had three more children

Lennox returned to Leeds with the belief he could do better than his parents

he was a good student at secondary school but soon understood he was seen as a bad person outside it

an enemy of the nation on account of his skin colour

to be stopped and frisked by the cops, which began when he was twelve and looked fifteen, terrified when these grown men manhandled him in the street in front of everyone, tried hard not to cry, sometimes did

their parting shot, on your way, Sunshine, you're lucky this time

it was scary, creepy and emasculating, he told Shirley the first time he let his guard down and confided in her, every time it

happened I was relieved that I wasn't beaten up or killed in a police van or cell

I was a good boy who didn't mix with ruffians or get into fights

I started wearing suits outside of school, even though my mates laughed at me and others thought I'd become a Jehovah's Witness

I was a good boy who walked to Leeds Central Library every Saturday afternoon to pick up my supply of books for the week because I wanted to be well-read

Great Aunt Myrtle drilled it into me to be a person with knowledge, not just opinions

I decided to be a solicitor, maybe even a criminal barrister

these days when the police try it on, I let them know I'm a lawyer and they think twice about putting their filthy hands where they don't belong

Shirley had long felt angry on behalf of her brothers who'd also been harassed by the police since they were young

all black men had to learn to handle it, all black men had to be tough

and when the police killed or beat someone, they were allowed to investigate themselves, and exonerated the accused

weekly dating with Lennox escalated to cohabitation in their final year; once graduated, they moved to London together

Miss Shirley Coleman eventually became Mrs Shirley King

Saturday evenings they might catch a film, around midnight a party or club where they danced into the early hours to lover's rock, reggae, soul, funk

twice a year they shopped for essentials in the sales, she met up

with her group of girlfriends from university about once every two weeks

her best friend, Amma, was separate to this arrangement

they'd become friends at New Cross Grammar School for Girls

with its pipeline to the professional classes of Blackheath and the smarter postcodes of Greenwich, Brockley and Telegraph Hill, rather than the sink estates of Peckham

as eleven-year-olds they were subject to the gravitational pull of being the only black girls in their year and standing out because of it

Amma was the shyer of the two and Shirley felt protective of her; by their teens, Amma, whose parents were educated socialists (unlike hers who were neither educated nor political), got involved in the local youth theatre, became confident, went down the maverick route, railed against the system

Amma came out as lesbian to Shirley at sixteen

which was initially quite disgusting

it felt like a betrayal of their friendship although Shirley never let on her true feelings because she didn't want to hurt Amma

luckily, Amma didn't start wearing men's underpants, or ogling classmates in the showers, nor did she try it on with Shirley, who began to feel self-conscious of her body around her friend, and for a while was wary of sharing a bed when they stayed over in each other's houses

in due course she made the decision that so long as Amma didn't fancy her (there were no signs that she did), and so long as she didn't tell anyone, besmirching Shirley's own reputation as lesbian-by-association, it was sort of okay

fat chance

when Amma left school she started shouting it from the rooftops as if it was something to be proud of

her entire *raison d'être* was to rail against whatever prevailing orthodoxy she objected to and try to smash it to bits

which was impossible, so what was the point?

Shirley had to put up with her badge-wearing friend or lose the friendship, she can't not have Amma in her life

she loves her

as a *friend*

also

Shirley doesn't meet many new people, her social circles are from university and fellow teachers, whereas Amma makes new friends from the arty world practically every day, who also become Shirley's friends, of sorts

mostly gay, and while she doesn't get it or like it, she finds their unconventionality interesting enough to enjoy their company

so long as they're nice to her, and most of them are

they're a fascinating, artistic and radical counterpoint to my more practical and responsible existence, she tells Lennox

who accuses her of being over-analytical

Lennox and Amma have a mutual lovefest, he thinks she's a right character, which makes Shirley feel that she isn't

he comes more alive around her, sparring, more jokey and extrovert

they tease Shirley for being goody two shoes (as if Lennox isn't

himself), nor does he give a fig about Amma's sexuality, his Great Aunt Myrtle was in the closet, according to him

she lived for years with Gabrielle, her special friend who died, she kept her photograph on her bedside table

he remembers as a child finding a box in a cupboard when he was snooping, which contained photographs of Great Aunt Myrtle and Gabrielle from the thirties – wearing monocles, bow ties, riding jackets, plus fours, smoking cigars

he thought they were at fancy dress parties

he wishes Great Aunt Myrtle had felt free to be herself, she died not long after he returned to England, if she were alive now, he'd visit and get the truth out of her, tell her he approves, if that's the right word

Shirley likes his open-mindedness, even if she can't agree with him

it's not that she's backwards or anti-gay, it's more of a gut response to something that doesn't feel natural

even when she tries to reason with her opposition to it.

4

over time Shirley became an experienced schoolteacher who remained committed to giving the kids a fighting chance

realizing everything else was against them with such large classes and lack of resources and parents who didn't have a clue how to help them with their homework

parents who'd left school early to work in a factory or learn a trade or be assigned a bunk bed in a Borstal

she was quite unlike the cruisers in her profession, as she frequently complained to Lennox, who do as little as possible and openly

despise their charges as if they're an inconvenience rather than the reason they have a bloody job

it was bad and got worse when the Thatcher government began to implement its Master Plan for Education

teachers went into meltdown with pay battles and three-day strikes

and when the public lost patience with them the *Third Reich* took advantage and steam-rollered in the dreaded National Curriculum which imposed a syllabus that curbed her own pedagogical freedoms that produced excellent results

thank you very much

hot on its heels were the League Tables and with that came a whole raft of computerized data entry, form-filling, stats, inspections and pointless, mandatory after-school staff meetings *twice a week*, even when there was nothing to discuss

then Gestapo HQ enforced lesson plans, a new swear word in Shirley's ever-expanding canon: National Curriculum! league tables! lesson plans!

all of which left no room for responding to the fluctuating needs of a classroom of living, breathing, individualized children

nor could she freely write school reports any more, which she'd actually enjoyed, commenting on her pupils' progress, letting their parents know she was looking out for their child

instead she had to tick boxes according to a list of generic statements

she could no longer say, for example, that a child's handwriting had improved, making their work more legible and therefore higher gradable because she had encouraged the child to sit straight, concentrate and write slower

or that a child was no longer disruptive as the class clown but had channelled their comic ability into the drama group, at her suggestion,

and had shone in a school production of *Snow White and the Seven Dwarfs*
    unless such a question existed
    which it never did

then the Gestapo demanded each pupil produce a Folder of Good Work every year, carefully handwritten from their classwork or homework, which took up hours of valuable teaching time and stressed the kids out no end, to be kept in a file in case a parent or a child's new school asked to see it
    guess what?
    no one ever did
    what was she?
    a Cog in the Wheel of Bureaucratic Madness

when Shirley drove up to the school in the mornings
    moments before the inmates charged up the Paupers' Path to destroy any sense of equilibrium
    its monstrous proportions settled in her stomach
    like concrete

and as the eighties became history the nineties couldn't wait to charge in and bring more problems than solutions
    more   children at school coming from families struggling
                   to cope
    more   unemployment, poverty, addiction, domestic violence
                   at home
    more   kids with parents who were 'inside', or should have
                   been
    more   kids who needed free school meals

more   kids who were on the Social Services register or
                radar

more   kids who went feral – (she *wasn't* an animal tamer)

by the time the new millennium pitched up, knives large enough to disembowel rhinos were discovered in school rucksacks during what became regular spot-check inspections

pistols were hidden down socks

gang recruitment agencies, or as good as, loitered outside the school gates

a bustling drugs market in the school grounds replaced the tuck shop

there were increased sexual assaults on girls and more girls becoming mothers when they were still children themselves

the school installed a metal detector at the gate and security guards, passcodes were introduced for all doors and cameras appeared in the corridors

to each graduating class, she resisted the urge to offer advice on prison visiting times for their families, as opposed to encouraging them go on to further education

especially to the low-lifes, weirdos, sub-70 IQs (eugenics? love it!), potential serial killers and other deranged psychos who sat at the back of her classes and made such a racket that she, of all people, had to shout to be heard

she, who once had such exceptional class control she was asked to mentor junior teachers in the art of cultivating a quiet authority

an authority where her word was once God, now if kids fucked with her, she fucked with them back

because of *your* behaviour, the entire class will have to stay behind after school now she worried that one of the 'Category A' contingent would stab or shoot her as she walked alone past the hedges in the car park on a dark winter's afternoon

worst of all was the school's most promising Lifer-in-Waiting in Year 11, Johnny Ronson, whose sole purpose was to undermine her authority whenever she told him off for disrupting class

one time rubbing his crotch so that his prick stood up under his trousers

it was her word against his

no evidence, no witnesses

the little bastard

if only she could send these brats back to when the school was a workhouse, make them spend a day or two crushing stones to make roads or bones to make fertilizer

slave labour twelve hours a day for bread and gruel and a hard, blanketless floor to sleep on

the number of times she told them how generations of reformers and campaigners, unionists and clergy, do-gooders, writers, politicians in the Houses of Parliament and peers in the House of Lords had fought for their right to better themselves through education

she told them until she was bored of repeating herself

it

never

went

in

furthermore, after decades of religiously marking homework five nights a week, she now loathed doing it with a venom piles of *crap* piled up on her study desk produced by mostly semi-literates who made her life hell in the classroom

mixed ability classrooms? to think she once approved, it didn't raise standards, it lowered them

on this she and Penelope Halifax agreed

the strangest thing was that after many years avoiding each other, they bonded at being overlooked by the new crowd of teachers who now ran the show

they'd sit in the staff room together as youngsters of all races bounded about full of themselves, ignoring both of them as irrelevant antiquities

in spite of the fact that Penny was *considerably older* than Shirley

they particularly hated the naïve young graduates who bounced in at the start of every term with their PhDs and espousing their show-off 'constructivist' teaching theories

all ideology and no experience – *wankers*

wankers-wankers-wankers, she and Penny would mutter to each other under their breath, gloating as over the years the newbies either left or had the life sucked out of them

they loved it when a twenty-two-year-old rookie teacher who'd arrived as a fashionista size six began to trudge around wearing trousers with elasticated waists

join the club, dearie! Penny whispered to Shirley, and they'd collapse, ignoring the curious glances of their fellow teachers

who wondered why these two relics were having such fun

Shirley and Penny sat there with their sandwiches and moaned about the good old days when teaching wasn't over-bureaucratized and the kids weren't murdering each other in turf wars

when Penelope retired, her greatest ally was gone

Shirley wanted to leave for the private sector, a girls' independent populated by polite middle-class girls (preferably under thirteen) who knew how to say please and thank you and knew better than to get in teacher's bad books

she wanted teacher-pleasers, that's the truth of it

not gun-wielding, gum-chewing, coke-sniffing, up-the-duff, scumbag gangster thugs

she wanted girls whose parents 'helped' them so much with their homework they appeared to be child prodigies, the great middle-class scam she and Lennox had themselves perpetrated with their own two daughters

that's what she was now, middle-class herself

in which case, middle classes *über alles*!

the sticking point was the hard-won Education Act of 1944 that made school free for all children had been been the subject of her thesis at university

when push came to shove, she couldn't sell out on it

unlike the colleagues who absconded to fee-paying vistas and returned to boast about their outstanding inspection reports and dizzying position in the private school league tables

schools with rowing and equestrian clubs, lacrosse, rugby and squash teams

with Olympic-sized swimming pools and Olympic-trained sports coaches and fully-equipped theatres

who went on school trips to the Himalayas, the Pyrenees, Chile, even the Maldives to 'study the marine life' (oh *please*)

who boasted about the pleasure of teaching in a beautiful listed building that smelled of pine furniture polish rather than the overpowering blend of teenage odours, leaking urinals and

industrial disinfectant (health & bloody safety!) that burned the
throat and eyes

thank goodness they'd escaped the worst school in London, they'd
say, making eye contact, emitting pure pity

so when are *you* leaving this dump, Shirley?

she did think of applying to a better-performing state school,
the day after she had such a lovely dream of being a high school
shooter who mowed down the entire student body at assembly (worryingly, it wasn't a nightmare) and walked off with her machine-gun
trailing the dust like a latter-day bow-legged black female Clint
Eastwood

yet when she sat down in her study with an application form one
night, she couldn't get past filling in her name

Shirley King

the thought of being interviewed by a panel of strangers scrutiniz-
ing her intellect, skills, teaching philosophy (*everyone* had to have one
these days), her personality (ha ha ha), her clothes, body language,
looks (what looks?)

she imagined their rejection letters

'Dear Mrs King,

We had an exceptionally strong field of candidates for this position
and unfortunately for you we decided to make an offer to someone
younger, prettier, slimmer, less experienced, more enthusiastic, gullible and pliable

as opposed to a bitter old workhorse such as yourself who should
be sent out to pasture henceforth!

Yours Very Truthfully'

*

Shirley realized that everything she'd ever wanted, she'd achieved, which hadn't prepared her for rejection

she got into university at a time when only the brightest kids did

she got the first teaching job she ever applied to, and enjoyed the school before it went downhill

they'd bought a family house in Peckham Rye when the area was an affordable dump, now it's pricey and the mortgage is paid off

she'd found the husband she'd wanted when very young, sparing herself years of wondering if she'd ever find Mr Right

her parents adored Lennox from the minute he walked into their house when they were students

they said Shirley could bring him over as often as possible

her mother barely noticed her when he was present, and her history degree, which had previously elevated her status above her brothers, paled in comparison to his *law* degree

Lennox could do no wrong in her mother's eyes

nor in hers, a husband as suitable now as he was when they first met, as loyal and faithful

he still did the shopping, but only cooked at weekends, they ate takeaways or readymade meals in the week, the cleaner did the housework

she still met up with friends for a meal or to see a film or for cocktails

Lennox went out on Friday nights after work to trendy Covent Garden wine bars with his younger colleagues, returned home happy and late, reeking of smoke and red wine, a greasy chin from the kebab he'd picked up on the way home from the station

he was still a solicitor, specializing in personal injury and clinical negligence, had never even tried to become a criminal barrister, too stressful and underpaid

he made the right choice

they had sex on Sunday mornings after he'd brought her coffee in bed and before they read the newspapers

it had deepened, was tender when once it was craven and athletic

they still fancied each other, after thirty-something years of lovemaking

lately he'd taken up bird-watching, filled their garden with multiple feeders suited for the small birds he loved the most – the goldfinches, blue tits, wrens and the fearless robins who hopped about low on the ground

unfortunately, dropped seeds from the feeders also attracted pigeons who liked to shit on their garden furniture and strutted about the garden like Nazi bully boys

and the mice also behaved as if they'd been invited to dine

Lennox trapped and released them in the woods a few miles away because he couldn't bring himself to poison them

she'd warned him that at first sighting of a rat

she was going to get a hunting rifle

Lennox was a football nut, went to matches with his friends, his only real vice was watching way too much of it on TV

it was the main outlet for his feelings, it seemed to her, as she sat in the next room listening to him holler and exclaim and cheer and boo and groan at the behaviour on the pitch, especially when Leeds United were playing he'd been a hands-on father to their two daughters Karen and Rachel who were born two years apart and became the stars of the movie of their lives

it was hard juggling work and babies, her mother, in particular, pitched in, Lennox rolled up his sleeves in the evenings and weekends, and while he wasn't averse to changing nappies, he refused to do the bottle feed in the middle of the night

he slept undisturbed in the spare room

once the girls were weaned, he took them away for weekends at the seaside with her mother to give Shirley a much-needed break

she'd sleep a whole weekend away, grateful for her mother's support

Amma babysat Karen and Rachel once or twice, she was usually too busy, plus Winsome was wary she'd drink or smoke around her little girls

on the other hand, when Yazz was born, Shirley became her number one babysitter, Amma took it for granted that adding a baby to Shirley's family wouldn't be too burdensome

it's true that Karen and Rachel treated her like a kid sister

Yazz was a delight when she was pre-verbal, less so when she discovered the power of words

she and Lennox dutifully attended church every Sunday for *five years* to get their girls into the Church of England's Grey Coat Hospital School in Westminster

an ordeal because while both of them are Christians, they're not churchgoers

Karen is now a pharmacist, Rachel's a computer scientist

Shirley has come far enough for a Second Generationer

her girls have already gone further.

Shirley's on holiday with her parents in the retirement bungalow they built on a small patch of family land where they now live royally on British pensions

she feels another *annus horribilis* of a school year drain away as she sits on her favourite cane chair on the veranda

she has the latest Dorothy Koomson novel to devour by lamplight

meanwhile the moon shines over the Caribbean Sea

everyone's asleep including Lennox on the large double bed with crisp white linen that her mother replaces twice a week

it's good for her mother to have the family visit, it keeps her active and makes her feel wanted doing what she does best, looking after people, especially her only daughter

Shirley lives for that moment every summer when the taxi arrives at the coast and they walk down the narrow lane to her parents' house, dragging their suitcases behind them

there it is in all its loveliness, painted rose pink and surrounded by the blossoms Winsome tends so lovingly

just as she will lovingly tend to Shirley

she has six blissful weeks ahead of her before returning to the Hellhole High School for Losers, where she'll hand-pick more pupils to mentor

as she's done every year since Carole left

Carole

who came from a single parent family (didn't they all?)

she had such an exceptional grasp of maths in her first two years at the school they'd been hothousing her to sit her GCSE Maths two years early prematurely, it transpired

she got derailed by three girls who were the bane of every teachers' existence

LaTisha Jones, as bright as any child, leader of the pack and the queen of backchat, who answered every directive with an insolent, why should I?

who always left class early because I've got my period/I feel sick/my grandmother's just died, Mrs King

the same grandmother dying multiple times was something Shirley had put up with since she started teaching

she resisted the urge to ask, didn't your grandmother die last term? now get on with writing that essay, you nasty little child

next in line was Chloe Humphries

descended from a long line of career criminals and already taking up the family baton, according to her social worker

the third member of the gang was Lauren McDonaldson who had an STD, according to a very good (confidential) authority (the school nurse), on account of her promiscuity with the (older) boys in the school, including one of the (younger) caretakers, if rumours (toilet walls) were to be believed

anyway

lo

and

behold

a miracle did occur because one lunchtime, Carole, then fourteen, came looking for her (brave child as Shirley knew her nickname was School Dragon at best, Fuck Face, at worst)

both had been scrawled on blackboards enough times

awaiting her arrival

*

apparently the child had been told by an idiot colleague in the staff room to find Mrs King in her car, where she ate lunch – *undisturbed*

the passenger seat of her comfy Mitsubishi was reclined back as she worked her way through her ham, pickle and tomato sandwiches and listened to the soothing sounds of Smooth FM

when the child rapped on her window

Shirley wound it down while simultaneously feeling herself wind up

yes, what is it?

'scuse me, I need to talk to you

about what?

I wanna do better, miss, I mean Mrs King, I wanna work harder and everything and go university and get a good job and stuff

Shirley never found out what brought about this change of heart, it wasn't important, what mattered was that an erstwhile brilliant student was asking Fuck Face to improve her performance

applause! lights! hallelujah!

she thereafter made sure that the child was given everything she needed to do well in every subject she was taking

including securing grants from charities to buy extra textbooks, notebooks, stationery, even a computer

on the condition she attended a tutorial with her every month for the remaining four years of her schooling in order to monitor her progress and ensure she stayed focused on her studies

it worked and because of her the child went to one of the top universities in the world

in the end, Carole was the talented, fallen child who reignited in Shirley the reason why she went into teaching in the first place

the power of education to transform lives

*

thereafter she took a few promising children under her wing every year, pupils of obvious intelligence who were unsupported by their families and might otherwise end up as prostitutes or crack addicts or something

even when the results are variable, she does improve their chances, and nearly all of them go on to higher education

of those that don't, for example one became a bricklayer, another a plumber, they probably earn more than the graduates, if the papers are to be believed

the nicest returned to thank her, with presents

her mentoring project makes teaching slightly more bearable, although not so much that she looks forward to the start of every weekday

or feels satisfied at the end of it

Carole, her first and greatest achievement, never reported back as instructed, not once, not so much as a phone call or a thank you post-card since the day she left school over a decade ago now

it makes Shirley feel

well, used.

Winsome

I

Winsome
is preparing a family favourite of roast breadfruit, fried flying fish
seasoned with onion and thyme, with a side dish of grilled yellow
squash, eggplant, zucchini and pan-roasted mushrooms with a herb-
lemon sauce
as the sea air breezes into the kitchen through the mosquito meshes
that stop the flies invading in the daytime and the mozzies at night
she appreciates healthy eating now she's back home and eating
food grown in her vegetable garden and fish caught fresh
from the sea to her kitchen
direct

Shirley, Lennox, their daughter Rachel and her daughter Madison
are here
Tony, Errol, Karen and their families will arrive later this summer

Winsome likes having her family around her, and their friends; Amma has visited twice, she's been fond of her since she met Shirley at secondary school

every mother wants their child to have a best friend

Amma was a quiet child until she started attending the youth theatre and became a more extravagant personality who liked to wear eccentric clothes

Winsome told Shirley not to copy her, to dress to blend in or she'd become a target

Winsome was wrong, Amma never became nobody's target

when Amma came out as lesbian as a teenager, Winsome was worried the poor child's life would be blighted, and feared Shirley would catch the bug and be resigned to a life of misery too

she was wrong about that too

the French doors overlook the veranda where Shirley is winding down with a glass of wine while gazing dreamily at the sea like it's the most beautiful thing she's ever seen

she behaves like a tourist when she's here, expects everything to be perfect and wears all white: blouse, trousers, comfy sandals

I only wear white on holiday, Mum, it's symbolic of the psychological cleansing I have to undergo

Winsome is tempted to reply, you mean it's symbolic of you not helping out around here

she won't ever tell Shirley off, though, if her daughter gets upset she'll never hear the end of it

Shirley looks ashen and drawn when she first arrives from England, give her a couple of weeks and she's going to look radiant, her body will free-up itself from the up-tightness of city life and she's going to walk with more lyricalness

it happens to everybody if they stay in Barbados long enough

by the end of Shirley's vacation, she's going to look and walk as if she is truly a child of the soil, not one raised in a cold climate who feels everything is against her

as Shirley does

who's an emotional dumper

as Shirley is

complaining about her terrible job in that terrible school, and when Winsome advises her to leave and maybe become an educational consultant, Shirley replies, I don't want suggestions, Mum, I just need you to listen

Shirley

who's never satisfied with what she has: excellent health, cushy job, hunky husband, lovely daughters and granddaughter, good house and car, no debts, *free* luxury holiday in the tropics every year

tough life, Shirl

compared to Winsome who spent her working life standing on the open platform of a Routemaster bus

bombarded with rain or snow or hailstones

climbing stairs a million times a day with a heavy ticket machine hanging from her neck and big money bag around her waist that got heavier as the journey progressed giving her round shoulders and back problems to this very day

having to deal with non-payers and under-payers who refused to *get off de dam bus* who cussed her for being a silly cow or a nig nog or a bloody foreigner the hordes of schoolchildren fighting each other to get on the bus, same with the stampedes of suited cattle in the rush hour

the fights upstairs when she had to ring the bell for Clovis to stop the bus by a phone box so she could call the police because mobile phones hadn't been invented

the night shifts was worse what with drunks raging about and throwing up and assaults and someone was knifed to death

on her shift

not that she's complaining, she appreciated not having a boss keeping an eye on her and when the route was quiet she liked having a laugh with the regulars

Winsome takes the fish out of the fridge, scales, fillets, slices it with her sharpest knife, runs it under cold water, dips it in white vinegar, rinses it off again

she makes a marinade of myrtle pepper, garlic, coriander, thyme and oil in a bowl, coats the fish in it, wraps it in foil, puts it in the fridge

she picks up the breadfruit from the counter, cuts out the stem as she's not got the strength to twist it out with her bare hands no more

she cuts a cross into the top of the fruit, rubs vegetable oil all over its large, green, pimpled contours

pops it in the oven where it's going to bake for about ninety minutes

should emerge perfectly cooked to provide nourishment and pleasure for her family

she herself is a grateful person

grateful she had Barbados to return home to when her English friends had to stay over there and spend their old age worrying about the cost of heating and whether they'd survive a bad winter

grateful that as soon as she stepped off the plane to walk into the blast of heat, her arthritic joints stopped playing up

haven't so much as muttered a word of protest since

grateful that the sale of the house in London allowed them to buy this one by the beach

grateful that she and Clovis, now in their eighties, have a reasonable pension, and won't have to worry about money for the rest of their lives so long as they stay parsimonious, which is true of her generation anyway, who only buy what they need, not what they want

you got into debt to buy a house, not a new dress

Winsome counts her blessings every day and thanks Jesus for bringing her home to a more comfortable life

she thanks Jesus she made new friends with women who'd also returned from America, Canada and Britain and asked her to join their reading group

she was honoured, she'd been a bus conductor, they didn't mind

Bernadette had been a secretary in the civil service in Toronto and never married, her boyfriend visits her on the nights he doesn't visit his other women

Celestine's hot on conspiracy theories, was a clerk at the CIA in Virginia, lives with Josephine from Iowa, which she doesn't have to hide from them, but does

Hazel ran the first black hairdresser's in Bristol until her husband, Trevor, got early dementia and died, whereupon she sold up, came home, lives alone

Dora's thrice married, once widowed, once divorced, and now married to Jason, a management consultant, she's the most intellectual in the group and was one of Britain's first black schoolteachers back in the sixties

*

every month they read a new book, started off with *The Lonely Londoners* by the Trini writer Selvon, about young Caribbean men in England who get up to mischief and treat women badly, women who don't even get a chance to speak in the book

everyone agreed those fellas needed a slap upside their heads and they agreed to focus on women writers of the Caribbean, who would be more mature and responsible, and move on to the fellas later

Winsome feels quite a literary person these days and has got used to reading books, when for most of her life she only read the newspapers

her favourite writers are Olive Senior from Jamaica, Rosa Guy from Trinidad, Paule Marshall from Barbados, Jamaica Kincaid from Antigua, and Maryse Condé from Guadeloupe

her favourite poetry book is called *I is a Long Memoried Woman* by a Guyanese lady called Grace Nichols

we the women/whose praises go unsung/whose voices go unheard

she and the reading group had a big argument, no, it wasn't no argument, it was a *debate*, the other day, about whether a poem was good because they related to it, or whether it was good in and of itself

Bernadette said it was up to the literature specialists to decide what was good, they only knew whether they liked something or not

Winsome agreed, she wasn't no expert

Celestine said poetry was made deliberately difficult so that only a few clever people could understand it as a way to keep everyone else in the dark

Hazel said novels was better value than poetry books because they had more words in them, poetry books was a rip-off

(Winsome doesn't think Hazel should be in their reading group)

*

Dora said there was no such thing as objective truth and if you think something's good because it speaks to you

it is

why should Wordsworth or Whitman, T. S. Eliot or Ted Hughes mean anything special to we people of the Caribbean?

Winsome made a note to go to the library to look those names up

when she walked home from their weekly gathering

as the sun rose higher in the sky and the tourists peeled off the beaches back to their hotels and restaurants

her mind buzzed with their debates and she thought of how she could improve her arguments in the future

today

she looks out on to the beach to see Lennox and Clovis disappear around the bend to where Clovis moored the fishing boat he'd recently bought second hand

and was patching up

he almost drowned in the last one when it let in water, he only saved himself by bailing it out with a bucket all the way home

dragging himself exhausted up the beach

and letting the old boat drift away to its watery graveyard

both men are wearing knee-length shorts and short-sleeved cotton shirts, neither has much hair left, both have broad backs, strong legs (although Lennox is a bit bow-legged, which she still finds very sexy)

both have easy barefoot strides in the sand and are even a similar height and shape these days

Clovis has shrunk a little height-wise, Lennox has expanded a little width-wise

Winsome still wants him, not Clovis, but Lennox, she tells Shirley
she's lucky to have such a husband
   Shirley replies he's lucky to have her as his wife
   which is typical of her

Lennox will spend the summer helping Clovis out with the boat
   they'll replace planks, fit a new engine, install seating and windows, seal and paint it
   he's better in that respect than Tony and Errol who are more like
their sister
   we work forty-eight weeks a year, Mum, this is our recuperation
time, they protest as they pig out and drink too many beers
   her boys started off in junior jobs before rising up the ranks
   Tony is a crime decision maker for the Police Service
   Errol is a support manager for Children's Services
   they might still resent Clovis for giving them beats as children and
have scars on their backs and buttocks as evidence, but it was hard
raising sons in the seventies
   Clovis had to protect them from the malevolent spirits that would
bring them down: the police, skinheads – and themselves
   their parents had to give them a solid foundation with which to
face themselves and the world
   she didn't need to do that with Shirley
   girls have it easier

Rachel comes into the kitchen with Madison, all sleepy-headed,
who shuffles over for a hug, I love you, great-granny, she says, as
Winsome picks her up and inhales her good hair that's almost straight
and smelling of the shampoo Rachel used on it yesterday before leaving for the airport

she taught Shirley who in turn taught Rachel to ensure they was all clean and well-dressed when they got on a plane

you never know what might happen

you want sasparilla? she asks them

Rachel goes to the fridge and brings the jug over to the table, unlike Shirley who'll say yes and wait for it to be brought to her by the *maid*

would you like some, Nana? Rachel asks politely, she's the most considerate of her grandchildren

Winsome sets to slicing the vegetables and gathers the ingredients for the dressing of thyme, salt, ground black pepper, hot pepper flakes, grated lemon and sunflower oil

tell me about how you and Grandad met, Rachel asks her out of the blue, stroking Madison's back who's perched sleepily, precariously on her lap

Winsome must look taken aback because Rachel adds, I want to know your stories to pass on to Madison when she's older, Nana, I want to know what it was like when you were a person in your own right

Winsome has listened to her grandchildren's lives since they could speak, and they've never asked about her

she understands that young people are consumed by themselves, and her role is to comfort and reassure and be caring towards them when their parents are cross with them

Winsome likes the fact that Rachel is curious enough to know who her grandmother was before she was a mother, when she was a person in her own right, as she described it

except she never has been, first she was a daughter, then a wife and mother, and now also a grandmother and great-grandmother.

2

I met your grandfather soon after I arrived in England in the fifties, Rachel, at a West Indian gathering in a pub in Ladbroke Grove where I found myself sitting next to none other than Clovis Robinson from Six Men's Fishing Bay

our fathers were fishermen, but we only knew of each other at a distance

it took travelling thousands of miles for us to properly connect, he'd already been in England two years

he told me, it hard here, girl, it hard

we courted over the forthcoming winter months when I was adjusting to the weather and the culture

I was grateful to have him to support and steer me, even though he wasn't particularly good-looking or with a dashing personality, both attributes I'd imagined for a husband before I was mature enough to accept that it was easier to dream

than it was to make the dream come true

Clovis never once left me shivering outside our regular haunts, the Odeon Astoria on a Saturday evening or Stockwell Park on a Sunday afternoon

he was nothing like some of the wide boys from home who went crazy and jumped from one woman to another

who left half-caste babies all over England

who'd grow up without their daddies

*

we married and moved into a room in Tooting where we shared a sink curtained off in the hallway, and toilet in a cardboard cubicle, with a house full of other tenants

we started saving for a house because ordinary people could afford to buy houses in London in those days if they saved for long enough

then Clovis went and had the *dam chupid* idea that we use our savings and head off for the south-west of England

he'd heard it was warmer there and he could find work as a fisherman

what he was put on earth to do, he said, not slave away in a factory making fertilizers and inhaling toxic chemicals

as we both did for twelve-hour shifts

Clovis said he longed for the sea where he could breathe again

the last thing I wanted was to be a fisherman's wife, being a fisherman's daughter had been hard enough

I used to wake up at four to go out on the boat with my father and brothers, I worked in the market as a fish boner and fish scaler, spent summers selling the sea eggs my brothers dived for on the coral reefs and brought back for me in nets – their black spikes still moving creepily about

I had to take each one and crack it open with a spoon, scoop the golden roe out, and sell it as a delicacy at the market

what could I say to Clovis? a woman had to obey her husband in those days, Rachel

divorce was shameful and only granted on the grounds of adultery, if a marriage didn't work out, it was a life sentence

we took the train from Paddington to Plymouth where he looked for work in the shipping offices, and among the trawlers down at the harbour

he thought he'd walk into a job with his experience

I watched him approach the fishermen at the wharves or on shore, English cloth cap on his head, big English boots on his feet, see him doff his cap at the whiskery men of over sixty years ago who looked like they was something out of the Old Testament

he didn't have to say a word when he returned, I could tell by the way he walked, and felt sorry for him – and for myself

it was obvious most people in this part of the world were poor

why should they give work to a stranger, let alone him?

one evening we sat on a windy harbour wall eating fish and chips out of filthy newspaper, which is how English people used to eat it, yes, you can screw up your face, it was a disgusting custom

I tried to persuade him to give up on his silly pipe dream and return to London

he said, Winnie, I want to try the small islands of the Scilly Isles further south where it's warmer, and there must be lots of work for fishermen

Clovis, if that's what you want, why don't we return home where we belong?

Winnie, I mek up mi mind, I got to try this place, I have a hunch

if it was twenty years later, Rachel, I'd have left him there and then

if it had been thirty years later, I'd have lived with him before marrying him, you see it occurred to me that I didn't really know this man who wanted me to follow him around like a mindless idiot

oh well, I said, the Scilly Isles is a pretty name, mebbe it's a pretty place

I looped my arms through his to reassure him I was on his side

we go find out, love, he replied

*

we took buses and trains along the coast, and when we missed those, we walked

imagine us, Rachel, over sixty years ago, a coloured man and woman, Clovis six foot four with me a foot shorter, wearing my smart dress, coat and heels because we had to look respectable, a suitcase each, walking down country lanes where it seemed most people had never seen coloured people before, by the way the cars slowed down to gawp or hurl insults

we slept in train stations when nobody let us kip in lodgings

we travelled through places with beautiful names I wrote down and memorized: Looe, Polperro, Fowey, Mevagissey, St Mawes, Falmouth, St Keverne, the Lizard, Mullion, Porthleven

we reached Penzance, took the weekly boat to St Mary's

'The largest island of the archipelago of the Isles of Scilly'

soon as we landed, people wasn't just unfriendly, they was downright hostile, who were these two monkey people arriving on their likkle island?

the whole town came to a standstill when we walked down the main street, I grabbed hold of Clovis's arm and could feel him trembling

I needed him to be strong for me

you can't work here, they said, when Clovis asked down at the quay

you can't eat here, they said when we entered a little caff

you can't drink here, the barman said when we entered a pub, all eyes on us

you can't sleep here because your colour will come off on the sheets, said the woman who had a sign for lodgings in her window, people was that rude and ignorant back then, they spoke their mind and didn't care that they hurt you because there was no anti-discrimination laws to stop them

the only thing you can do is leave here and never come back, the policeman advised us when we went to complain

we boarded the ferry to Penzance, slept in the doorway of a church where we'd knocked the night before on the door of the rectory and curtains moved, nobody answered

Clovis, I said, I told you it wasn't worth the bother, now you and me are going straight back to the capital where people are more used to seeing coloureds

don't tell me what to do, Winnie, I will mek up my own mind, I want to give Plymouth another chance, it's on the coast, weather's still warmer than London, the countryside ain't that far away, and when we have pickney they can roam free like on Barbados, trust me

I have a hunch it'll all work out.

3

Clovis did get work, donkey work as a stevedore in Plymouth

carried huge barrels and heavy sacks from the ships to the warehouses and from the warehouses to the trucks

he got on with the other stevedores, many was seasoned former seamen who didn't think he'd dropped from Mars

they'd go for drinks after work, he came home tipsy on good nights, drunk on bad ones

after I'd put the children to bed, the three I had

in as many years

*

I was left alone with the children all day and all evening

I heard people cuss as they passed me, very few were friendly

I was served last in whatever shop I went into, even when I was first in the queue

cars deliberately drove into puddles when I was pushing Shirley in her black bassinet and the two boys was attached to harnesses either side of me

I was the one to find a dead rat on our doorstep

I was the one to live with GO HOME daubed in white paint on our front door until Clovis painted over it

I was the one who had to spend my evenings alone and scared they was going to throw a petrol-soaked rag through the window

however, Rachel, one thing I learnt from my time down there, is that if you stay somewhere long enough, and behave in a civilized manner, people will get used to you

Mrs Beresford, an elderly widow, who lived a few doors down, was the first to have a proper chat

she used to stoop down into the pram to stroke Shirley's cheek, who grasped her fingers and wouldn't let go

babies are innocent, Mrs Beresford said, this is an agreeable place to live, Mrs Robinson, once people get to know you

she handed the boys sherbet fountains and they eagerly snatched them before I could object because I didn't let them eat sweets, another bad English custom

I did allow them a small slice of the pound cake Mrs Beresford brought around on her first visit

she introduced me to Mrs Wright and Mrs Missingham, both from the local church, at a special tea she laid on for me and the children after school one day it was my first time in an English person's home, I remember it clear as daylight and wanting a home like this for my family

there was a rug of flowers over wooden floorboards in the sitting room, rose wallpaper, lots of pictures hung up, a heavy dresser with plates displayed in rows as if they were ornaments, which I found odd, heavy drapes at the window and a luxurious settee, or so it seemed to me, as well as to Tony and Errol who bounced up and down on it until I had to tell them to stop because Mrs Beresford was too polite to do so herself

she showed me how to toast crumpets over the coal fire
how to make tea using proper milk and not condensed
how to put the milk in last and not first

Mrs Beresford
invited us to church and when my family of five entered the drive, her and Mrs Wright and Mrs Missingham greeted us as if we was long-lost friends
they each took a child protectively by the hand
and walked us in

even at the park the mothers got tired of calling their own children away from ours as if they might catch leprosy
very small children don't care about skin colour, Rachel, until they're brainwashed by their parents
when Tony started at Everdene Primary School, followed by Errol, they came home in tears because the kids called them Sooty
they was getting caned and made to stand in a corner of the class-room with their faces turned to the wall by teachers who picked on them
it wasn't us, Mummy, they'd complain, it wasn't us

me and Clovis drummed it into our boys to behave well at all times

we knew our boys was lively but they wasn't bad

one time I was waiting to collect them at the school gate and saw two older boys jump Tony who fought back, my brave little boy

as I rushed towards him Mr Moray the headmaster got there first, grabbed Tony by the scruff of his blazer and marched him back into the building

the two bully boys laughed, dusted themselves off, picked up their satchels, walked scot-free out of the gates

when Shirley started primary school, she too came home crying at being called Sooty no matter how many times Clovis marched up to the school to tell Mr Watson to tell the children to stop picking on his pickney

then another coloured girl joined the school, a likkle half-caste called Estelle who was light-skinned with light hair that fell in Shirley Temple ringlets

Estelle was the type of red-skinned child people call pretty on account of it

her mother was one of those long-haired beatnik-types who wore black slacks, a beret, and a scruffy leather jacket like Marlon Brando

I was properly attired: below-the-knee dress, cardigan, coat, tights, shoes, headscarf tied under my chin

Vivienne tried to talk to me at the school gate, she was a painter, Estelle's father was a Cape Coloured in exile from apartheid in South Africa

what was apartheid or a Cape Coloured?

don't look so shocked, Rachel, apartheid wasn't general knowledge in those days, anyway Vivienne soon gave up trying to be my friend, which was fine because we had nothing in common – not even our daughters

Estelle was treated nicely by the teachers, who greeted the children when they arrived each morning, most of them ignored Shirley, who was too young to notice

Estelle, who couldn't hold a tune, was cast as Mary in the school nativity play and sung solos

Shirley, who had a lovely voice, was cast as a palm tree and made to stand at the back of the stage

along with the boy with a hare lip

and the girl with a club foot

the next day I told Clovis, you can stay here but the mother of your children is returning to London

with them.

4

Winsome is distracted by the men who come back into view through the kitchen window and amble up the beach in the blazing heat, neither wearing sun cream nor a sun hat, in spite of her nagging

years ago brown-skinned people thought they was immune from sun damage and ended up with skin cancer

even today most men don't bother with sun protection

as if it makes them less manly

Lennox is more like Clovis than she likes to think, physically and temperamentally

Winsome reckons this is why Shirley chose him, subconsciously he was familiar to her

maybe that's why Winsome herself took to her son-in-law

a younger, sexier version of the man she married

in a few weeks' time, after the men have made the boat sea-worthy

after

they've replaced the missing planks from the hull and installed the new engine and propeller

after

they've stood back and admired their handicraft

after

they've launched the boat with a bottle of rum smashed against her hull

they'll go out before daylight to capture flying fish, drop lines to pick up dorado and billfish along the way, once they're far out, they'll throw cane trash and palm fronds on to the sea to act as a screen, drop baskets underneath them that release bait slowly, once the flying fish have gathered for this meal, they'll be scooped into nets, although hauling in nets is harder when you're older, Clovis says, when he returns with an aching back that she massages for him

fishing is an important part of who he is, it makes him feel like a real man, a man who goes out to work, who provides, even in retirement

Madison wakes up on Rachel's lap, looks groggily around to orientate herself, tumbles from her mother's lap, waddles out of the door and runs to greet the men when she sees them walk towards the house on the coral-coloured sand

she positions herself between them, they each take a hand and swing her it's a charming picture

Rachel thanks Winsome for confiding in her, it's quite a story, Nana, you were a trailblazer

we was just two people who went foreign, Rachel, nothing trailblazing about that

well I think you're amazing, and now I'm going to sit with Mum, the only time I don't have to worry about her is when she's here, the rest of the time I dread she's going to have a stroke from the stress of her job

don't you be worrying about our Shirl, Rachel, she enjoys having something to complain about

once the family was back London in the sixties, they settled in Peckham, bought a bomb-damaged house, did it up over the decades

there was no more talk about haring off to places where they wasn't wanted

Clovis had three main preoccupations: going to work, raising the children, doing up the house

he discovered he liked DIY, like most men of his generation who spent their weekends being handymen

wore dark blue overalls and learned from manuals how to plaster, plumb and do electrics, bricklaying, carpentry

at first Winsome liked that she could almost predict how a year would pan out from the start of it to the end of it

barring aberrations like a roof leaking or a child rushed to hospital with appendicitis

in time they were able to joke about their adventures in the southwest, when Clovis was young and foolhardy (he admitted), and she was so vexed with him what she couldn't predict was that once her husband was domesti-cated, she began to wish he had more get up and go

Winsome had wanted safety and stability when she was new to England and Clovis represented familiarity, he paid her attention, was nice to her, she fell for him when she needed someone

it had matured into love, there being much to like and admire about her husband – he was never cruel, never strayed into other women's beds, was accommodating and sensitive to her needs

the problem was what he wasn't – exciting

when Shirley brought Lennox home for tea that first time when they were students, it was like one of the older Jackson Five lads was standing in her hallway

he was so vigorous and bulged with youthfulness, literally, his flared trousers were very tight

Winsome found herself feeling something she'd never felt for Clovis – a bursting sexual desire, passion, whatever they call it

she tried hard not to stare at his chocolatey skin that was so lickable, or into the pure whites of his intelligent eyes, whereas Clovis had yel-lowed eye whites from a childhood spent in the glare of the sun at sea

he had a neatly-clipped small afro, a figure-hugging shirt showed off his perfect torso

she wanted to run her hands all over him, massage his balls, feel him harden at her touch

Clovis ushered everyone into the sitting room where they gawped at this young man over their cups of cocoa tea

the two lovebirds sat holding hands on the sofa, while her and Clovis sat on armchairs making polite chit-chat

Clovis deepened his voice, she noticed, wanting to impress this university student it was obvious Shirley was smitten with Lennox, who was going to become a solicitor, she'd already told them proudly, and then he'd become a barrister and maybe even a judge one day

what a catch he was

lucky Shirley

before you knew it, they was all back in the hallway with the customary nice to meet yous and thank yous and you must come agains

her and Clovis waved them off as they made their way across Peckham Rye towards the station, and thereafter King's Cross and then the train back to Leeds

Winsome shut the door and began to climb the stairs to their bedroom, I got a likkle headache, she called out to Clovis, who didn't hear as he was already in the kitchen tuning into a pirate reggae radio station

she lay down on their bed

what on earth was going on?

maybe it was the onset of the change that made women more emotional, it would pass just as the menopause would

leaving her with her depleted oestrogen

and dying ovaries

except she didn't want it to, encouraged Shirley to come home more often for the weekend, of course you can bring Lennox with you

who kissed her on two cheeks in greeting

who put his arms around her affectionately when he was in the house, delighting Shirley that her mother and boyfriend had such a rapport

she liked the way his arms slipped around her waist when they walked in couple formation back from a trip to the cinema or a meal out, Clovis and Shirley striding ahead through the night streets of Peckham, her and Lennox trailing behind

she initiated sex more often with Clovis to get the frustration out of her system

Clovis, whose schooling ended when he was fourteen, didn't hold up well in comparison to Lennox who used long words like account-ability, restitution and *quid pro quo*

words she had to look up in the dictionary

Clovis wasn't interested in socializing beyond family get-togethers, he'd stopped drinking when they returned to London, he wasn't interested in going to see films or going to parties and having fun into the early hours the way Shirley and Lennox did lying in bed late on Sunday mornings drinking real coffee from a percolator while reading the newspapers, as Shirley reported back, before going out for brunch, Mum

Winsome had never even heard of brunch

she wished her body was as shapely as her young daughter's

she wished she'd had the education and choices Shirley had that meant Shirley could attract a man who was both a dish and ambitious

who married her and became the father of Rachel and Karen

who she babysat a lot more than she needed to because Lennox would drive her home afterwards

who sometimes put his hand on her knee for emphasis when he spoke to her in the car

whose goodbye kisses lingered a little too long, his soft lips full on or was she imagining it?

she reassured herself her attraction to Lennox wasn't a betrayal of Clovis or Shirley because it wasn't acted upon if it was, that would be different

if he turned up on her doorstep one day when Clovis was out and pounced on her

she would not have been able to resist

nor did she

when he rang her bell one afternoon, knowing she was on the late shift and at home, and Clovis was on the early shift

he'd taken the afternoon off, shut the door behind him and kissed her the way Clovis never did because when they first met he'd said full-on kissing was unhygienic

she made sure her tongue stayed in her mouth after that

it had never made contact with another human until now

Lennox untied the pinafore she wore to do the housework (polishing the banisters) and unbuttoned the summer dress she wore underneath it

he dragged off her nylon slip and the stockings held up with suspenders because she was old-fashioned and hated the discomfort of tights rubbing between her thighs giving her a rash that needed to be soothed with Vaseline

he seemed to like what he saw, as she discovered herself through his hands, his body through hers

she got so wet it trickled down her legs

who was this woman letting her son-in-law do her every which way?

who was this woman who took him into her mouth and enjoyed it? when the only time she did it to Clovis she had thrown up afterwards?

who was this woman who kept up with this young man who exploded multiple times inside her because he was virile and could go

on forever and so could she until they died from exhaustion because she was completely out of her mind and inside her body?
    until
    the alarm in the kitchen went
    she had to collect Karen and Rachel from the nursery
    they showered and dressed themselves
    left the house
    separately
    him
    first

    that night she couldn't sleep
    she went to war with her morals on behalf of her feelings
    guess which side won?
    she was nearly fifty
    she deserved to have this
    him

    that Sunday after family lunch, she made sure they were alone in the kitchen doing the dishes and arranged to meet him that week
    and so it continued for over a year
    once a week, sometimes twice
    and on the weekends they took Rachel and Karen to the seaside to give Shirley a break
    while the toddlers slept, they took advantage of the double bed
    they never spoke of what they did
    Lennox had urges, it was better she satisfy him than he left her daughter
    for another woman

*

and then he left her, or rather he stopped it

no explanation, no discussion, no excuses, no compassion

did he come to his senses at sleeping with a middle-aged woman? was he guilty at sleeping with his mother-in-law? was Shirley making love with him again? had she even stopped?

or had he found someone else?

Winsome never got an answer because she couldn't bring herself to ask

for a long time afterwards Lennox didn't look her in the eye, if he could help it, he didn't even look at her in the face

Shirley noticed she wasn't as pally with Lennox as before

don't be silly, you know how fond I am of him, Shirl

Winsome wished he hadn't awakened a longing in her that he wouldn't satisfy

he'd given her a taste of himself and then withdrawn it

she didn't hate him for it, she wanted him more because of it

he became fantasy material: they spent erotic afternoons in exotic hotels, she wore sexy underwear, looked younger than her age

in a fantasy anything was possible

even now, so many decades later, she feels the old attraction stir when he arrives for the summer, and when she catches him in a certain light

Lennox and Clovis are sitting on the white bench on the veranda with Madison nestled between them

Rachel sways on the stripy hammock Clovis hung up for his afternoon naps, they've all burst out laughing at something, not at what Shirley's said, her daughter has no sense of humour, probably at something Madison has said, something cute, because she is

*

Lennox glances up, catches Winsome's attention on him, waves
warmly, innocently
     not a flicker of acknowledgement in all of these years
     Shirley boasts that Lennox will never cheat on her
     Winsome always replies she found one of the good guys
     you lucky, Shirl, you lucky.

Penelope

I

Penelope's parents were dull and dispassionate automatons crawling towards their deaths
she wrote in her diary at the age of fourteen
it was unfortunate
because she herself was brimming with vivacity and racing towards a marvellous life that stretched gloriously ahead of her
as she also wrote
in her diary

her father, Edwin, was a surveyor, born and raised in York and, Penelope wrote, a slave to routine: rising on the dot, leaving on the dot, returning on the dot, dinner on the dot, bed on the dot, life on the dot
my father has never said anything remotely of *import*, she wrote, that has not been regurgitated from the *Daily Telegraph* he reads every evening when he comes home from work

the only interesting thing about him, she noted, was also the most seedy: a thick envelope of pornographic postcards hidden inside his tool trunk in the shed, never imagining that his daughter didn't need a penis to nail her own picture frames to her bedroom wall

Penelope's mother, Margaret, was also a dreadful dullard, although her background was somewhat more exotic

she'd been born in the newly created Union of South Africa after her English parents sold up their failing barley farm at Hutton Conyers in Yorkshire to take advantage of the Natives Land Act of 1913

which allocated over 80% of land ownership to the only people capable of looking after it, her mother told her

the white race

us

her mother said the natives had to surrender their land to the inevitable charge of economic progress for the betterment of society as a whole

and as they were now desperate for employment, labour was cheap

my father bought a barley farm there, Penelope, but failed to make a success of it because his farm workers were idle, resentful and thieving

he was advised by his fellow farmers to tie the worst offenders to a tree and flog them

thereby setting an example

it seemed to do the trick when he began to carry out the same punishment for crop theft

the workers seemed to settle down and get on with it after that

until one day when he was doing the rounds on horseback, a group of wayward field hands appeared out of the woods like a pack of frothing animals and set upon him

before he knew it, he was on the ground, his whip was in their hands, and they were using it against him

the poor man didn't stand a chance

your grandfather's mind never recovered, Penelope, he sold the farm for a song, brought the family back to England, we moved in with relatives and he never worked again

I was relieved to relocate to England away from the hatefulness of the natives who'd done such a terrible thing to my father

nor was it a place for a white girl to grow into womanhood

I didn't like the way native men looked at me

Penelope's mother came of age in civilized England, she said, enjoyed dances, made friends, cycled into the countryside on Sundays with a group of them, including a few bounders who were nevertheless such fun, had picnics, got merry on gin from their hip flasks

she'd sneak out at midnight to bathe naked in the River Foss with them

hitched her skirts above the knee when she was far away enough from home

flagrantly smoked in public when women who did so were considered vulgar

only decadent *sapphics* who cut their hair short and wore male clothing got away with it in those days, Penelope

I met your father at a hop, he was somewhat older than me, very handsome before he lost all his hair, called for me every Saturday evening at seven o'clock on the dot of the grandfather clock in my grandparents' hallway he started attending my church on Sundays, met me outside the haberdashery where I worked

I'd wanted to go to a training college to become an elementary school teacher, one of the few professions open to women in my day, except there was the marriage bar, Penelope, which meant I'd have to stop teaching as soon as I became a wife

there was really little point in training for something I'd have to give up

unlike the cads I'd known, your father was sober and sensible, which is what I needed in a marriage

my father had by then tragically died in an asylum

it was another terrible time for my family and your father easily slipped into my life as a source of companionship and comfort, he took me rowing on the River Foss, although never swimming or dancing, never drinking

all of which he regarded as unattractive pursuits for ladies

after three years' courtship, we wed

I do miss dancing, Penelope, the great pleasure it gave me, I often think of the past, of the person I used to be

I don't know where she went

Penelope's mother stopped talking, returned to her knitting, sewing, cooking, cleaning, ironing or any of the other activities that filled her days

leaving the conversation dangling

Penelope found it hard to imagine her mother had once been so rebellious and gregarious

she felt sorry for her having to choose between a career or a family which seemed terribly unfair and just as her mother couldn't wait to escape the savages of South Africa, she couldn't wait to go to college, have a career and leave her parents' straitjacketed lives behind

then came the moment they told her she was a lie and any compassion she felt for her mother sank without trace

to be replaced by a groundswell of bitterness

the lie was bad enough, although in years to come she came to understand their reasoning, rather, it was the cruelty in their telling of it

a cruelty that exposed the fault lines in who they were and who she was going to be in the world

you are not our daughter in the biological sense, her father told her at lunch on her sixteenth birthday (great timing)

she'd been left in a cot on the steps of a church

they'd waited until she was old enough to understand

she'd been mysteriously deposited without certification, no note, no clues, nothing

they'd tried for their own child for years, failed, found her in an orphanage, it was quite easy to adopt back then, they signed papers, took her home

what they didn't add, in that moment, was that they loved her, something they'd never told her

what she needed in that moment was a declaration of unconditional love from the people who'd raised her as their own

instead

they carried on as normal, even though tears were streaming down her face

they remained seated on the high-backed chairs in their allotted places around the oval dining table covered with a fringed tablecloth they unravelled the napkins rolled up in wooden rings with their names etched into them

they ate the lamb chops, minted potatoes and buttered peas they had for Saturday lunch

passing the gravy

passing the pepper

passing the salt

Penelope, unable to dislodge a potato stuck in her throat, left the table without permission, ran choking upstairs to her bedroom where she collapsed in a sobbing heap on her bed, desperately hoping that at least her mother might check up on her, she listened for the pad of slippered feet on the stairs, a tentative knock, the door opening, a pat on her back

a cuddle was too much to hope for

instead

she heard the man she'd thought her father until a short while ago leave the house to play golf with his brother (no longer her uncle), as he did every Saturday afternoon

the woman who used to be her mother would be sitting in front of the fire crocheting white booties for her youngest niece, Linda (no longer Penelope's baby cousin)

Penelope could hear comedy and laughter playing on the radio downstairs

to them it was a normal Saturday afternoon

Penelope broke down into tears for months afterwards, in private, away from the two people she lived with, who wouldn't approve of such demonstrative behaviour

away from her school friends who couldn't be let in on such a shameful secret

she was an orphan
a bastard
unwanted
rejected

now the disparity between them made sense
her parents were not her parents, her birth date was not her birth day
she was not of their blood or history

she kept torturing herself with terrible thoughts
how could her real parents have given her away so heartlessly?
discarded on the steps of a church like a sack of rubbish
what if rats had got to her first? or foxes? or a freezing night?
how could they have been so heartless? and just who were they,
anyhow? if she didn't know who they were
how could she know who she was?

there was no paper trail
she was a foundling
anonymous
unidentified
mysterious

later
when Penelope studied herself more closely in her dressing table
mirror, it became absurdly clear to her that she looked nothing like
Edwin and *Margaret*, as she would now think of them
Edwin was short, anaemic, blue-eyed and aquiline, features that
suited a man whose emotions rarely rose to any occasion, even his

occasional bursts of laughter sounded as if he were breaking a self-imposed rule not to enjoy himself

Margaret was even shorter, barely scraping five foot, thinning hair, grey-eyed, grey pallor

according to her wedding photograph she'd once been pretty

now she just looked

washed

out

Penelope, on the other hand, was tall for a girl at almost five-nine, with the full natural pout and hazel eyes that sealed her reputation as a glamorous beauty at school, she wore her curly, strawberry-blonde hair in a style à la Marilyn Monroe, had a 'light dusting of freckles' around her nose, and acquired an easily-won suntan in summer, considered *très chic* because it gave her a St Tropez glow

à la jet set

Penelope decided she would go to college, marry a man who idolized her, become a teacher and have children

all of which would fill the gaping, aching chasm she now carried inside her

the feeling of being

un

moored

un

wanted

un

loved

un

done

a

no

one.

2

Penelope homed in on Giles soon after her identity had been exploded into scattered fragments

she needed someone to put her back together again

he was the eighteen-year-old rugby captain of the boys' grammar school, and what a catch he was with his Heathcliff looks and championship confidence that swept lesser boys aside

who *wouldn't* want to be floating in the orbit of Giles the Great, Tsar Giles, King Giles the 1st of York

as she wrote in her diary

every girl in the school had a crush on him except those who were rumoured to be *sapphics*

Penelope became obsessed with ensnaring Giles

she lurked at his bus stop every morning in order to accidentally bump into him when he disembarked, daringly slipping into long strides beside him

luckily, conversation came easily between them and she became adept at cutting off other girls who tried to edge their way in, although she loved it when his rugby mates swelled their number and they all swept in a surging wave down the hill

she was the only girl among a group of sports heroes who were so full of a dashing machismo and braggadocio
   everyone else was cowed in their presence
   moved out of the way
   or were elbowed out
   by her

she and Giles began to brazenly hold hands, hidden amid the multitudes of their peers in their green and white uniforms
   he began to kiss her *au revoir* when they parted at her school gate, which was thrilling before such an audience
   either of those crimes could have got her hauled in front of the headmistress and expelled
   what did she care? she was in love, she would have Giles's babies, she would create her own bloodline, she was engaged at eighteen
   meanwhile the other girls in her class, fretting over pimples and puppy fat, were terrified of being left on the shelf
   she felt sorry for them, how awful to be fat and ugly and very likely alone for the rest of their lives
   whereas she was the golden girl
   and to be honest
   it suited her

Penelope married Giles soon after she graduated teachers' training college, he was already working as a civil engineer
   it was all pretty perfect, as she'd dreamed, Giles was so caring of her, enquiring as to her welfare, affectionate touches, a stroke on her cheek, a kiss at the nape of her neck, making her feel important, desired
   his well-paid job moved them to London, to Camberwell, to a grand house on Camberwell Grove in an otherwise poor area

he gave her a free hand with the decor: William Morris wallpaper, Uniflex dining table and chairs, De Sede Modular Sofa System, padded brown leatherette kitchen walls, orange shag rugs, avocado plastic bathroom

he tolerated her cooking experiments, never complained when the results were too salty or sweet, too burnt or undercooked, too soggy or congealed, too runny or stringy, too crumbly or lumpy, or required a hammer and chisel to break up pastry bases, homemade bread, roasted meat

she fell pregnant with Adam straight away, which delayed going into teaching, but there was plenty of time to build her career

a year later, Sarah wriggled out after a twelve-hour labour

Penelope didn't mind staying at home with the babies, not when they were newborns, she couldn't believe the love she felt for her children

Giles had filled the hole in her heart with his love, yet the love she felt for her children was overwhelming, limitless

she loved feeling in love with them

however

after three years of having two suckling children gorging on her engorged breasts, she began to feel sucked dry by them

it was all beginning to feel a tad *vampiric*, if she was honest

Sarah was still at the gurgling-dribbling stage of human evolution, while Adam had discovered (sigh) speech, and by the end of each day she was run ragged by his indecipherable chatter

she felt terrible feeling this and was eager to start teaching to counterbalance her now rather unwilling role as an earth mother, especially as she was beginning to feel quite side-lined from the greater scheme of things, what with the papers going on about the various cultural revolutions erupting globally, including the women's liberation one

meanwhile, she was knee-deep in kiddie poo and vomit

when Giles came home from work wanting to discuss the affairs of the world, inflated with intellectual self-importance now he was reading *The Times* on his commute, she was so ga-ga he gave up, ate his meal in silence, retired to his study

while she put the children to bed

she raised the issue of returning to her job as a teacher with him, it's not like we can't afford a childminder

he replied that it was impractical to have two masters: a boss at work and a husband

was he joking? not by the look on his face

at the mothers and toddlers' coffee mornings Penelope forced herself to attend merely to get out of the house, she and the other young women, bonded by motherhood and little else, exchanged advice on how to manage their children, husbands and cook the latest *must-have* new dishes doing the rounds such as quiche lorraine and spaghetti bolognese, all the while trying to control their offspring who wriggled about so incessantly everyone's arms were frantically whirling, and their eyes were likewise darting everywhere trying to ensure their lawless charges didn't climb the stairs and bounce back down head first or dismantle the fireguard to see what touching hot coals felt like

Penelope wrote in her diary that her brain cells were popping like stars dying off into irretrievable oblivion

when Mildred from Number 63 came up with the brainwave they organize a 'National Vol-au-Vent Day' to encourage more drinks parties in the neighbourhood, Penelope wanted to let out a howl to match her children's

thankfully

she discovered Gloria, the local librarian, in the nick of time, with whom she could pass a few words of *sensible* conversation when borrowing and returning children's books

Gloria had secretly, cleverly, gleefully got away with ordering six copies of Betty Friedan's *The Feminine Mystique*

she confided conspiratorially over the oak counter

was recommending it to all the well-spoken young mothers who visited the library during the weekdays, either pushing children in prams in front of them or dragging them, usually screaming, behind them

a sign, Gloria said, that these bright women are frustrated with their lot

Penelope couldn't get enough of Ms Friedan, whom she hid in the cupboard with the brooms, hoover and ironing board – safe in the knowledge that Giles had never actually opened the door to her 'den', as he put it

it blew her mind to hear how America's educated housewives were supposed to be satisfied with their roles as mothers and homemakers, but who were, in reality, simmering with a discontent they were not allowed to express, all those poor women imprisoned inside their suburban houses and consigned to cooking and cleaning instead of discovering a cure for blindness or something equally as noble

she realized then that what she'd hitherto thought personal to her was, in fact, applicable to many women, masses of them, women whose husbands forced them to stay at home when they were more than willing to put their intellect to good use in the skilled workforce, women, such as herself, who were going bonkers with boredom and banality

Penelope embarked on a campaign to lobby Giles for her return to work, who still insisted she remain at home as it was the natural order of things going back to time immemorial:

me hunter – you homemaker
me breadwinner – you bread-maker
me child maker – you child raiser

Giles scoffed when she expressed her resentment at the working-class women of England who were allowed to go out to work and the hundreds of millions of women in the Third World who enjoyed the fulfilment of both motherhood *and* job satisfaction, *Giles*

if it's okay for them, why not me? she said, resuming her lobbying when she brought him his cup of tea in bed every morning, following him around the house as he got ready for work, talking at him through the door when he spent far too long on the lavatory (what *are* you doing in there?), continuing her freedom crusade as she prepared his breakfast of eggs on toast, *and* while he ate it, *and* while he was putting on his overcoat for work because somehow, *somehow*, she was going to make him change his mind

until one morning he put his fist though the glass window of the front door, shouting that she was lucky it wasn't her face

before slamming it behind him

she got to keep the house (she'll give him that)
easily had custody of Adam and Sarah (they were a burden for him)
she found a childminder and employment at Peckham School for Boys and Girls, a new comprehensive down the road

*

289

she met husband Number Two, Phillip, at a college friend's wedding six weeks after the decree nisi was brought in an envelope up the garden path by the postman
   signalling her official status
   as available.

3

   Phillip was something else, a *real* catch, a brilliant psychologist who charmed the French satin knickers off her at a friend's wedding reception
   where they ended up snogging on the dance floor once the music turned smoochy
   continuing the party in her hotel room that night

   almost as soon as she met him, the turbulent emotions Penelope felt at the dissolution of her marriage (regret, sadness, loneliness, self-loathing, fury that Giles had turned out to be such a male chauvinist pig)
   dissipated
   Phillip, she quickly discovered, was a Clitoris Man, and sex between them was a revelation
   unlike Giles: left a bit, right a bit, up a bit, down a bit, bingo, Giles, how clever you are!
   Phillip knew what it was and how to find it without her directions and what to do with it
   furthermore, he was a caring, sensitive soul who wanted to help people feel better about themselves

*

they had a quickie wedding with only two witnesses in attendance, she didn't want to jinx it by going the whole nine yards

Phillip rented out his large Highgate home and moved into her equally capacious four-storey house, using the front reception room for his private practice

in a sense it was quite satisfying that *she* was now the one leaving the house to go to work while The Husband stayed at home, albeit working

nontheless, it was *symbolic*

it was also a great relief when the children eventually took to him, after a few difficult months including broken nights when she rocked Sarah, in particular, who missed her father awfully, back to sleep

Phillip won them over by being tactile and affectionate (unlike Giles), talking and listening to them (unlike Giles), reading to them (unlike Giles), and helping them with their homework (unlike Giles) while she marked schoolwork

another refreshing thing about Phillip was the extent of his interest in her, he wanted to know who she was deep down inside, the real Penny beyond the pleasant, people-pleasing façade, as was her fate as a woman and mother

she was flattered he should care so much

nor did he try to impose old-fashioned values on her like horrid Giles, a Tyrannosaurus Brute who believed in the superiority of the male species

Phillip was a man in touch with modernity

a New Man

as she wrote in her diary

so far so good

until she noticed Phillip's benevolent probing had a tendency to

291

turn into intrusive interrogations when she did things he didn't like or when he couldn't get his own way

especially when she expressed herself frankly which, as a liberated woman to a liberated man, should have been quite acceptable

let's find out what's prompting this negative behaviour, shall we? he'd ask, leaning forward in his chair, the half-eaten dinner on the dining table between them, staring so deeply into her eyes she felt, how to describe it? psychologically *raped*, yes, that was it

what happened to you as a child, Penny? he'd ask, it's clear you have abandonment issues, let's unearth your subconscious memory, shall we?

I'd rather my subconscious memory remain just that, she replied

then let's uncover your repressed sexual desires to see what's holding you back from being a better person?

or

I want you to dig deep, Penny, in order to understand why you obsessively clean the toilet three times a day?

I do it because you piss on the seat, darling, she snapped back

when he asked her why she was equally obsessive about sweeping the kitchen floor?

I do it because you drop toast and biscuit crumbs on it that are trailed through the rest of the house

when he asked her why she didn't rinse off the wine glasses before stacking them on the draining board?

she responded by flinging them on the floor

when he asked why she didn't like his friends (with their black-framed glasses, black rollneck jumpers and smug intellects), she replied, to be honest, Phil, they're not my type, resisting the urge to add, like you, I think, like you

when he asked why she objected to his *Playboy* subscription when he thought she approved of the Sexual Revolution, didn't she want a liberated man after all? was she really such an old-fashioned fuddy-duddy?

she responded by taking a pile of them into the garden and feeding them to a burning mound of crackling autumn leaves and trimmed bracken

then he accused her of drinking too much, there were two Pennys: the Sober One was logical, whereas the Drunk Sister was irrational

she told him he was being absolutely ludicrous and a bottle of wine a night is *not* overdoing it, Phil, what about the Scandinavians with their vodkas for breakfast or the Mediterraneans with their wine with lunch and dinner? and another thing, why was it all right for you to drink in the pub with your friends of an evening but not all right for me to go continental in the privacy of my own home? you should be grateful to have a wife with such sophisticated European habits

now pass the walnut loaf, Camembert and fig chutney, *darling*

Penelope came to the conclusion that marrying someone when you're in love with them was perhaps not such a good idea, better to wait a few years (ten, twenty, thirty, never?) to see if you're still compatible after the passion has subsided and reality set in

she admitted to herself that things had gone sour with Giles once their sexual chemistry failed to ignite, which happened after their first child was born

Giles wasn't much turned on by lactating breasts or her fuller figure; he never said so, but she could tell by the way he looked at her (repulsed), and his behaviour (not wanting to touch her)

after childbirth she mourned the waist that wouldn't return to its

293

original measurement, and she mourned the lost bouncy ball quality of her breasts

he stopped telling her how devastatingly beautiful she was when previously he said it several times a day

she realized how addictive it had become

without it she craved it

and felt ugly

however

she was resolved not to give up on Number Two, hoping he wouldn't give up on her (like Giles), even when he began to forget the A–Z of her sexual desire

or maybe he just couldn't be bothered, whatever the reason, he resorted to the same unimaginative missionary pumping as her ex

she decided she'd rather be unhappy than endure the public humiliation of another failed marriage and become a social outcast

Rule Number One: couples do not invite single women to their dinner parties

the children learnt to tiptoe around both of them, were still nice to Phillip, whom they loved as their stepfather, Penelope felt bad for putting them through two ruined marriages in their young lives

by the time they'd grown and flown, their mother and stepfather were, in reality, living separate lives with nothing to say to each other any more, not even to have blazing rows

they continued to share the house, had separate quarters, two televisions, two telephone lines, a his and hers end of the kitchen

until, unimaginatively, he traded her in for a younger version of herself, one of his clients, nineteen-year-old Melissa, a Nordic blonde type

Penelope found used condoms in the kitchen dustbin when she went on her weekly investigatory rummage

that evening she cornered him against the fridge, a pan of boiling water poised in her hand

he admitted he'd been seeing this Melissa for a while, had been afraid to tell her; it wasn't the cheating that mattered so much to Penelope (she convinced herself), it was sneaking around behind her back in their home, with a woman younger than her own daughter

he said it was nothing to do with age and that as Melissa's childhood was relatively recent, it was easier for him to help her uncover repressed memories, you know, help her sort herself out

she missed Giles then, at least *he* wasn't a creepy psychological predator like Phillip

sadly, he was on to (*Indian*) Wife Number Two in Hong Kong where he built bridges and lived on one of the tropical outlying islands in a pad with its own menagerie of birds in the grounds

as Adam and Sarah reported back

once he started inviting them over for the summer holidays, which only happened when they were teenagers with whom he could hold adult conversations

they adored their much younger half-Indian half-brothers, Ravi-Paul and Jimmy-Dev

and accused her of racism if she ever said a word against them

her kids were examples of political correctness gone mad.

4

Penelope was left alone after Phillip Le Creep had gone back to his Highgate pad – he kept his, she kept hers – and after the kids had grown and flown

she had the house to herself for a few years, found a wonderful African cleaner called Boomi, who gave the place the once over, which seemed a terrible waste of money when most of the rooms were empty

Penelope decided to become a landlord, converted the upper floors into bedsits, rented out to Japanese students

who were so clean, quiet, orderly and respectful

so nice to be bowed to when she collected the rent

she didn't like being single, discovered it wasn't easy to find a mate in middle age

men didn't notice her any more and she didn't know how to engage in subtle flirtation to get attention when suitable sorts were around, because she'd never had to

as a younger woman men had gravitated towards her and she had merely responded, graciously, flirtatiously, or (she could now see) rudely

the big question that plagued her was this: how do you get a man to take you out when it's the last thing on his mind?

on her first and last blind date via an agency, the prospective candidate for marriage (on paper, at least) stood up and walked out as soon as she walked in and sat down

for the first time in her life, she almost wished she was 'the other way'

she'd read an article that said while older and middle-aged men typically went for younger women, both older women and younger women often fell for middle-aged women

sadly, there wasn't a sapphic bone in her body

the women's magazines Penelope now read argued that women should not define themselves by a male partner, that to depend on a man was a sign of weakness

all quite different to the magazines she'd read as a young woman, which advised the opposite

she tried to be happy food shopping for one, happy to go to sleep alone, happy to wake up in an empty bed, happy that building site workers no longer wolf-whistled after her (to think she'd once objected)

happy to look at her middle-aged body in the mirror without pulling a face, because the female form should be accepted in all its different shapes and sizes, shouldn't it?

Penelope wanted to embrace self-love and self-acceptance

getting rid of the full-length mirrors in her home was a good start

she should also be happy at work seeing as she'd lost her first marriage over her right to do it

at first she'd enjoyed teaching the disadvantaged children of the area whose parents had an inter-generational history of paying taxes in this country, even though she knew most of them wouldn't go on to great things

a supermarket till for the ones who were numerate, a typing pool for those who were numerate *and* literate, further education for those who could pass exams sufficiently well

she felt a sense of responsibility towards her own kind, and didn't like it at all when the school's demography began to change with the immigrants and their offspring pouring in in the space of a decade the school went from predominantly English children of the working classes to a multicultural zoo of kids coming from countries where there weren't even words for please and thank you

which explained *a lot*

she loathed that feminism was on the descent, and the vociferous multi-culti brigade was on the ascent, and felt angry all the time, usually at the older boys who were disrespectful and the bullish male teachers who still behaved as if they owned the planet

the type who used to patronize her when she'd started the job years ago, to the point of tears

who never included her in their conversations except to look at her tits

she'd have to sit there silently being objectified along with the other young female teachers and the posters of topless models plastered on the noticeboard in the staff room

just as some of the female pupils were harassed by male teachers who groped them, and honestly, did anybody take it seriously when girls complained that *this* male teacher had stroked her breasts, or *that* male teacher had smacked her on the bottom, or *another* male teacher had put his hand up her skirt?

she knew of two males who'd had 'liaisons' with female pupils

and got away with it, they all got away with it

the male teachers

would head off for a pint in the Green Dragon after work, never thinking to invite her or any of the other teachers who had a *womb*

the male teachers

who made decisions before the staff meeting began so that the rest of them were presented with a *fait accompli*, without a hope in hell of catching up on decision-making conversations begun at lunch or in the corridors or over the telephone the previous evening

it took her years to realize she wasn't being slow and stupid, she learned the hard way to shoehorn herself into debates, to force them to explain *exactly* what the hell they were talking about, to hold them to account

she learned the hard way to crush any opposition to the ground, especially young upstarts like Saint Shirley the Puritanical of the Caribbean

as she described her in her diary

Shirley was barely out of her teaching probation when she took a pot shot at Penelope at that staff meeting all those years ago – at the only woman in the school who dared stand up to the men

why didn't Saint Shirley attack one of the male chauvinist pigs who pontificated *ad infinitum* instead of a strong woman who'd brought petitions into work for both the Equal Pay Act and the Sex Discrimination Act, both of which were eventually passed into law

improving the situation for all working women

she should be admired and respected by her female colleagues

it took her a long time to forgive Saint Shirley but when she did, the became friends, work friends.

5

Penelope
went home from school each evening to her Golden Retriever, Humperdinck

always there for her, always eager for a cuddle, who'll listen to her for hours without interruption, who whimpers when she leaves the house, greets her as soon as she steps back in the door, jumping up for a hug

Humperdinck was named after her favourite crooner from the seventies, Engelbert Humperdinck, the tanned sex-bomb still oozing so much charisma she can barely contain herself when he appears on television, his teeth glittering like polished pearls

so much sexier, in her opinion, than his nearest rival, Tom Jones, the famous pelvis-thruster with the big voice from the Welsh valleys

she also reconnected with the Sisterhood, her college friends who were sympathetic enough to overlook the fact she'd barely had anything to do with them when she was married

Giles only liked to surround himself with fellow boring engineers and their (house) wives, she told them, while Phillip's milieu was pseudo-intellectuals and their drippy Save the Planet spouses

she admitted she'd lost the *me* of myself and was subsumed within the *we* of marriage, relinquishing even her surname

Penelope Halifax who became Penelope Owsteby who became Penelope Hutchinson before reverting back to her maiden name

which wasn't really hers in the first place

(she kept the shame of that to herself)

they went to their favourite health spa in Cheltenham twice a year for what they called their Detox/Retox Weekends

to indulge in sisterly conviviality while getting massages, facials, saunas and delightfully tanked with the wine they smuggled in

for their drinking sessions in the suite furthest away from the uptight spa staff in reception

who thoroughly disapproved of people *actually having fun*

*

Penelope

was secretly relieved when a gal pal's marriage collapsed too, because then she didn't feel so awfully, terribly alone

they could go to the theatre and cinema together, enjoy meals out and art exhibitions, holidays at her *authentically* rustic cottage in Provence, spa trips to the Alps and Thailand

her daughter became a great support to her after the end of Marriage Number Two

her best friend, as Penelope often reminded her, and not only when she'd had a drink or two and phoned her in the early hours

Sarah never hung up on her, not once, I'm here for you, Mum, and please don't do anything stupid, *please*

Penelope didn't have the suicidal gene, and it upset her that her daughter thought otherwise

Sarah had boyfriends, but not fallen in love yet, perhaps because she'd seen how *that* played out with her mother

she talked about having children and said, Mum, the day I have kids is the day I give up work, I don't want to be a working mother

that's fine, Penelope reassured her, and meant it

all she wanted was for her daughter to be self-fulfilled

at this point in her life, feminist politics can sod off

look where it got her?

Giles paid the children's university living expenses, and thus became their favourite parent

it saddened her when they didn't give her preferential love when she'd been the parent who raised them

after his degree, Adam scarpered off to work in Texas as a

petroleum engineer, at least it was better than the job in the Middle East that had also been on the table

Sarah became an actor's agent in a big agency in the West End, complained about stars who treated her like the hired help

it's a lot less glamorous than you think, Mum

she came home for lunch every other Saturday from her house-share in Whitechapel (why she chose to live in the grotty East End was beyond Penelope, who still associated it with Victorian slums and Jack the Ripper)

Sarah's housemates were young professionals, half of whom were Asian

well-educated and well-spoken

so hardly Asian at all

in winter Penelope usually made Sarah's favourite broccoli and parsnip soup

with crusty rolls

in summer, it was her favourite salad of greens, tomatoes, figs, edible flowers and goat's cheese

with crusty rolls

Penelope preferred heavy food such as pasta and potatoes, thick stews, rich curries and the most gooey of saccharine desserts like sticky toffee pudding

she liked to feel completely stuffed after a meal

her stomach stretched to bursting

or she felt emotionally empty

Sarah would gossip indiscreetly about her clients, which Penelope loved it was as close as she'd ever get to the people who appeared in the celebrity magazines she read that transported her from the miserable reality of her own existence into a fantasy world of glossy people with their perfect lives

even though she knew it was a feel-good panacea for the gullible masses, it still soothed rather than induced envy

Sarah said the more successful actors blamed her if they didn't get seen for a coveted part, or if they did and it all backfired and their career went tits-up, she got blamed for that too

while the non-famous actors blamed her for not being famous

most of her gay actor clients pretended to be otherwise, while the married ones got up to all sorts of stuff, you won't believe what I hear, Mum, like the famous married actor whose *thing* is to crouch on top of a glass table and crap on it while a pretty young woman is lying underneath it

trust me, showbiz folk are more fucked up than most people, you'd pale in comparison, I mean I didn't actually mean it that way, I'm not saying you're fucked up, hey, we're all fucked up, aren't we?

she said

dipping her bread so far into her soup it drowned
and couldn't easily be rescued.

6

A few years later and the front door bell rings
Penelope can see the blurry outline of Sarah and Craig
and hear the excited giggles of Matty and Molly, their small twins

*

she opens the door, they pile in, the children jumping up at her, Humperdinck jumping up at everyone, Sarah pecking her on the cheek, Craig gives her his usual *Australian* hug

he works in cinematic sound production, met Sarah at a premiere where he was in control of the acoustics and she was chaperoning a newly-signed starlet

for lunch Penelope has made a crusty pizza piled high with pastrami, tomatoes, cheese (no olives or peppers, which the little ones hate)

and a green salad, which they won't touch either (nor will she)

she loves it when Sarah and her gang arrive, for the duration of their visit she forgets all her usual self-pitying (be honest, Pen) preoccupations

after lunch, the children become even more rumbustious as carbohydrates turn into sugar and they start racing around her living room

Craig, whose father was a mine geologist, grew up running barefoot in Queensland with his aboriginal friends, believes children should be raised as free spirits, including in her lounge, apparently, where they knock over a cup of coffee, throw cushions at each other, jump on to the window ledge to try and swing from the curtains and it's only when Molly almost plugs a finger into an electrical socket that Craig bellows at her to get away from there, Molly!

Sarah smiles apologetically at her mother, but doesn't tell them off for fear of being called a spoilsport by Craig

her grandchildren need a few slaps when they get out of control, which Penelope is quite willing to administer – it's child abuse, according to Craig

instead

she cajoles them on to the sofa by holding two lollipops in her hands and once they've fallen for it, snuggles them under an arm each (without *obviously* throttling them), and proceeds to read them a story about a talking train

Sarah's gang live in a second-floor flat in Brixton, which Penelope only visits when it's unavoidable, such as the twins' (unfortunately *annual*) birthday party

the white walls are covered with the children's cave drawings and the furnishings are stained with their paints, felt-tip pens and remnants of food, regurgitated or otherwise, including squashed peas and melted chocolate

Penelope tries to sit on the edge of her seat while avoiding touching *anything* as she ends up with sticky or, more worryingly, wet hands

once Penelope has lulled the twins to sleep with her special soporific storytelling voice, and they're dozing off under an armpit each, Sarah decides to tell her, because there never *will* be a right time for this, Mum, that they're moving to Sydney where Craig has been offered a job to head Dolby Audio

Penelope's response is immediate, emotional, extreme and uncontrollable

soon after, she's face down on her double bed, hears her bedroom door creak open and Sarah's voice urging the twins to *go on, go on*

their warm (and *heavy*) little bodies are soon crawling all over her, digging their knees into her back, sitting on her head, wiping her wet cheeks with their sticky little paws

s'all right, grammy, s'all right, don't be sad, grammy

one of them decides it's more fun to blow raspberries down her ear, while the other treats her ample posterior as a trampoline

it dawns on her how much she's going to miss seeing these two little monkeys grow up.

Chapter Four
Megan/Morgan

It's absurd that Megan's mother Julie treated her like it was the nineteenth century and not the nineteen-nineties into which she'd been born

as Megan reflected with hindsight when she could articulate the unfairness of her problematic childhood to herself

and analyse it once her eyes were opened by Bibi who came into her life to make it all right

her mother was unthinkingly repeating patterns of oppression based on gender, one example was that Megan preferred wearing trousers as a child, which she found more comfortable than dresses, she liked the look of them, liked having pockets to put her hands and other things into, liked looking like her brother Mark who was three years older wearing trousers really shouldn't have been an issue for a girl born in her time, but her mother wanted her to look cuter than she already was

like the cutest of the cutest cutie-pies

she was determined to dress Megan up for the approval of society at large, usually other females who commented on her looks from as early as she can remember

it was the defining aspect of Megan's early childhood, she didn't actually have to do or say anything except be cute – an end in itself

which reflected well on Mum, who could bask in the glory of the compliments that poured forth as a validation of her love of an African man

between them they'd produced such an admired kid

and made the world a better place

Megan should have been grateful and accepted her cute status, what girl doesn't want to be told how lovely she is, how special?

except it felt wrong, even at a young age, something in her realized that her prettiness was supposed to make her compliant, and when she wasn't, when she rebelled, she was letting down all those invested in her being adorable

Mum being her primary cute investor

who she let down a lot, one Sunday Megan threw herself on to the floor in hysterics when forced to wear another vile, pink, puffed-up dress

and she kept it up until her mother was vanquished

Megan was her otherwise liberal mother's blind spot

there's something not quite right about Megan, she overheard her telling Aunty Sue one Sunday after lunch

as they sat drinking tea in the tiny sitting room with just enough space for one small sofa, two armchairs and a telly

she's such a beautiful child but there's not a feminine bone in her
body
   I hope she grows out of it, I worry about her
   where will it all end?

   meanwhile
Dad was in the garage with Uncle Roger, her two boy cousins,
and brother Mark, tinkering with the prehistoric Cortina Dad still
drove
Dad came from Malawi where he boasted everything was repair-
able: watches, pens, furniture, clothes, lamps, broken crockery
superglued together jigsaw-style, and yes, his daughter
   he was her mother's enforcer, and after the dress protest that day
(victoriously, she got to wear red jeans), he'd ordered her upstairs to
play with her Barbies

   the Barbies with their stick legs and rocket breasts were another
problem Megan had to endure
   she was supposed to spend hours dressing up or playing house
with them, including the darker ones she was supposed to find more
relatable
   in a fit she'd once tried to commit Barbicide, defaced them with
coloured marker pens, chopped off hair, extracted eyes with scissors
and de-limbed a few
   it resulted in the punishment of bed without any tea
   the Barbie invasion proliferated on birthdays and at Christmas,
relatives talked about her incredible collection, as if she'd actually
chosen to have them in her life
   on her bed, on shelves, sitting on the mantelpiece, on the window-
sill, each one creepily staring her out wherever she was in the room,

like in a horror film, mind-talking her with their perfectly-pouty mouths saying, yeh, we know you hate us but we're here to stay

when she stuffed them under her bed at night, her mother took them out again the next morning and repositioned them in the room

going on about how much they cost

and what's wrong with you, Megan?

GG, her great-grandma on Mum's side, was the only one who accepted Megan just as she was

GG allowed her to roam the countryside around her farm with Mark for the five weeks they spent with her every summer

they'd go riding down the back of the house to the lake, circum-navigate it, and gallop across the fields

until the year she turned thirteen and her periods started, and Mum turned up for the last week, as usual, and said she was running too wild and would have problems later on in life

you have to keep her where you can see her, Mum said to GG, we've got to nip her tomboy tendencies in the bud

Megan was eavesdropping at the kitchen door (bad habit), heard GG tell Mum not to be so silly, Julie, I myself roamed wild as a child

Mum still threatened to stop Megan's annual holidays on the farm

Megan watched through the ancient kitchen window as Mark rode out of the yard on a pony for a day of freedom, knapsack on his back containing a flask of orange juice, sandwiches, fruit and a mobile phone

he looked back and shrugged, there was nothing he could do

GG spent the rest of the week teaching Megan how to make Victoria sponge, gateau of peaches, vanilla slices and orange cheesecake oh well, there's no harm in learning how to bake, she said when her mother was present

when she wasn't, she said, let's play along with this for now, Megan, next summer you'll be free to play out again

we've got to make sure Mark doesn't tell

which he didn't

Mum was a nurse, Geordie born and bred

a bit Ethiopian because GG's mum was half Ethiopian, and a bit African-American, because of her grandfather, Slim, who married GG

she looks almost white in a family that's proudly got lighter with every generation

until she went and ruined it by marrying Dad, an African, fellow nurse at the Royal Victoria Infirmary, who loved her until she loved him back

so the story went every time they told it

Mum said she was colour-blind, when she looked at Chimango she saw not the darkness of his skin but the lightness of his spirit shining through

it put him streets ahead of all rivals, and trust me, Megan, I was spoilt for choice

Megan wondered how Mum couldn't see Dad's colour when that was *all* most people saw, including many of Mum's own family

who refused to smile in the wedding photograph

stood there like a row of undertakers

Megan was part Ethiopian, part African-American, part Malawian, and part English

which felt weird when you broke it down like that because essentially she was just a complete human being most people assumed she was mixed-race, it was easier to let them think it

the girls at school cooed over Megan's 'natural suntan', which they tried to emulate by spending their pocket money lying on sunbeds

likewise with their curly perms trying to unsuccessfully reproduce her blonde corkscrew curls

she had it made, really, according to her classmates, the boys liked her too

then her body started to show womanly curves and it didn't feel right, it wasn't what she felt herself to be

so much so that she hated catching herself in mirrors, hated the breasts that appeared without her permission

two amphibian mounds taunted her with their nipple eyes

she thought she'd grow into her body, but it began to repulse her, at sixteen she shaved off her hair to see what it felt like, loved running her hands over her new, low-maintenance bristle

she felt free, weightless, herself

except it had the drastic effect of turning everyone against her, her classmates implored her to grow it back

why would you even do this to yourself? are you crazeee?

the girls she thought were friends dropped away, embarrassed to be seen with her, G G reassured her there was something wrong with a friendship based on having the right haircut

hurt but resolute, Megan abandoned all pretence at conforming

she wore men's shoes, black lace-ups, liked how comfortable they were, how powerful she felt when she walked in them, loved that men didn't eye her up any more

which was liberating

*

at the end of that school year when her class was voting on titles, she won two: the butchest girl in the class, and the ugliest – scrawled in chalk on the class blackboard and with a black marker pen on the white toilet walls

it felt like the whole school was laughing at her

Megan walked out of school that day for the last time, she left behind two thousand kids sitting at their desks working towards a future with at least a few qualifications

she'd been headed for university where Mark was already making a success of his life

she walked into a job in McDonald's, the first one she applied to

devoured the free Chicken Legends, Quarter-pounders with Cheese, and Belgian Chocolate Honeycomb Iced Frappés in her breaks

she pumped herself with additives until she looked ready to pop like an inflated balloon

this was her life now
McStupid
McFuckedUp
McStuck
McForever.

2

Megan spent her evenings hanging about on the Quayside with the men and women who accepted her as she was

an outsider, just like them, she snorted, injected, smoked, swallowed whatever came her way cocaine, crack cocaine, ketamine, cannabis, LSD, ecstasy, whatever took her to a higher, happier plane

at first she was experimenting with it, until she found herself craving her next fix and sleeping with the men who could provide it for her

up against damp alley walls, behind warehouses on the wharves, inside hallways, behind bushes, on dirty mattresses

the relief when blood stained her pants, when tests came back negative

she slept with the women who took a liking to her

discovered she preferred them

her parents charged rent seeing as she'd ruined her life by dropping out of school

she made sure to get up for work every morning, even when she'd come in at dawn completely off her face and her head vibrated to a concert of amplified heavy metal sounds and her brain cells were fused with vomit

she snuck downstairs as her parents busied themselves in the kitchen

she made sure to slam the front door so hard the house reverberated with after-shock

as she headed for a McBreakfast of McSausageBacon&CheeseBagel at her McJob

one night, unable to sleep, Megan made the mistake of returning to social media to spy on her former classmates

the academic achievers were celebrating their 'A' level results, posting about the universities they were going to attend

others were showing off the jobs they'd got, the boyfriends who'd proposed, the babies on the way, the countless nights on the lash where they'd had the best time of their lives clubbing-partying-festivalling-getting-drunk-high and being happyhappyhappyhappy happyhappyhappyhappy, with complexions filtered to perfection, waist-lines digitally slimmed, their smiley friendships and relationships, and even though she knew a few of these girls were annies, bulimics, had been bullied, were depressed, had social anxiety

you wouldn't know it from their posts
it was still a wake-up call

she decided not to head off to the riverfront that evening to hang with her *homies*, her *bezzies*, who accepted her as one of them, who lived for their next hit, with their scabby dogs and petty crime life-styles, who annoyed the hell out of the regular people who walked along the Quayside to visit its venues, restaurants and bars

Megan went cold turkey when her parents went on holiday to Majorca

Mark was at Camp America (of course he was), she stayed home, turned off her phone, watched her parents' videos to distract her, showered several times a day to rid herself of the sweaty tox-ins that made her stink, flushed herself out with water, got the shakes, scratched herself raw when legions of ants bit into her flesh, took enough painkillers to subdue the headaches but not enough to kill her

went to sleep on Day Nine and slept (blissfully) through the night
for the first time in as many months
she woke up
born
again.

On her eighteenth birthday Megan walked into Tattooz 4 U on Nelson Street, its walls smothered with photos of tattoos etched into every body part imaginable (and unimaginable)

her birthday money was stuffed into her jeans pocket to give to Rex, the bald tattooist, who had a second (younger, handsomer) version of his face tattooed on to the back of his head

she wanted a design that reflected the story of her life: flames, she instructed him, to show that she was living a life consumed by the fires of hell

Rex said her tempestuous feelings as a teenager wouldn't last, was she really sure she wanted to create a tattoo that would?

she wanted to snap that he was patronizing her, reminded herself that this man was going to be scraping an electric needle over her skin for the next few hours

as slowly her pain transmuted into bloody body art

to show the world how upset she was with it

and to really piss her parents off

which it did

when she returned home flashing her first full sleeve of raw tats

at which point Mum

having prepared a birthday tea of homemade chicken pie, chips, mushy peas, trifle, cake and candles

pulled it all off the kitchen table via her best tablecloth in one dramatic bullfighter moment

the entire contents ended up scattered and smashed on the kitchen floor

whereupon Dad threatened to throw her out for upsetting her mother

she shouted back that *she* was the one who was upset, it was *her* birthday and *they'd* ruined it, and in one equally dramatic moment stormed out of the house without any money or keys
only to turn around and ask to be let back in again
which they did, without hesitation
to apologies all round

cosmetic, as it turned out
her mother couldn't get over the tats, which she saw as symbolic of the beginning of the end of her daughter's life as a normal person
Megan came to the conclusion she was never going to find herself if she remained living with her parents
she dragged a black rubbish bag of her possessions down the stairs, refused her father's offer to drive her to wherever she was going, ignored her mother's pleas that she stay: we can work things out, we love you, we really love you, Megan, talk to us
too little too late, Megan said (she'd heard that somewhere)
she moved into a hostel with other teenagers
determined to live a life
no longer defined
by her parents

she spent the first few hours in her newly independent republic staring out of a window that framed a small square of pure sky
all hers

over the next few months she felt herself shedding layers of what had been imposed, hoping to reach the core of herself
she wondered if she should really have been born a man because she sure as hell didn't feel like a woman

perhaps that was the root of her problems

she came home from work to the noise of fellow youngsters having fun through the partition walls

exacerbating her aloneness

yet she knew this was exactly what she needed

solitude

to register what she was feeling

forcing herself to become deaf to all sound except her own

it felt like meditation as she concentrated on the concertina of her own breathing

for moments or was it minutes?

at a time

finding

peace

momentarily

enough to consider her next move

which was to explore the internet, that held the answer to all questions

while lying in her single bed in the chilly early morning hours, wrapped up inside the dark insulation of her duvet, lit by the glare of her laptop

she found sanctuary in chat rooms with other young outsiders as pissed-off as she was, discovered the trans world, engaged in conversations with people on the trans spectrum

sometimes saying the wrong thing online, encountering someone called Bibi who wrote back, I'm going to hit the next person who confuses transsexual with transgender, I swear! people won't tolerate ignorance on here, love, transgender people are only transsexual when they medically transition, okay?

right

fine

Megan clearly had to walk on eggshells or risk setting off a land mine, none of it really made sense to her, weren't manhood and womanhood set in stone? she asked Bibi

wrong again! Bibi replied, gender's a social construction, most of us are born male or female but the concepts of masculinity and femininity are society's inventions, none of it is innate, are you following?

no, not really

hey, it's actually 'Feminism 101', where you been, Megan? head in the clouds?

yeh, 'spose so, living on Planet Parents, don't bite, btw, just curious

ah, a sensitive one, I'll go easy on you from now on, do your research, seriously

Megan discovered that feminism was massive right now, how could it have passed her by?

she thought of her mother who'd disparaged feminists as man-haters, not for me, she'd say whenever it came up, I like men, I like being domesticated and I love your father, so how can I be a feminist?

Dad would nod his head and say something like, you've seen what happens when I try to hang up the washing or make the beds

Megan told Bibi she'd thought feminists were synonymous with manhaters, although as she typed the words she realized she'd never actually made up her own mind about it

O here we go! Bibi fired off, of course feminism isn't about man-hating! it's about women's liberation, equal rights and freedom from limiting expectations, you need to think for yourself instead of par-roting the patriarchy, time to grow up, Megan!

I thought you were gonna go easy on me

er, yeh, okay, can't help myself, I promise to be sweet as candy from now on

I just want to be myself, Bibi

wow, talk about low ambitions, don't you want to change the world?

I wanna change my world first, Bibi, one step at a time

like like like like like ☺

now you're taking the piss

nope, I honestly agree with you, we all just wanna be ourselves and make sure we're okay in the world, hey, I'm a supercalifragilisticexpialidocious person, really

I'll be the judge of that

ooooh, now you're giving as good as you get, lol

Megan studied the photo of Bibi more closely, she was Asian, twenties, maybe? thick, square black glasses, thick black hair about her shoulders, serious expression

attractive

very

Megan already knew it was time to grow up, the whole point of leaving home was to find out where she began and her parents ended

tell me more about what you know about feminism and gender, and I know I should already know but I *don't*, OK?

gotcha, so here goes: women are designed to have babies, not to play with dolls, and why shouldn't women sit with their legs wide open (if they're wearing trousers, obv) and what does mannish or manly mean anyway? walking with long strides? being assertive? taking charge? wearing 'male' clothes? not wearing make-up? unshaved legs? shaved head (lol), drinking pints instead of wine? preferring

320

football to online make-up tutorials (yawn), and traditionally men wear make-up and skirts in parts of the world so why not in ours without being accused of being 'effeminate'? what does effeminate actually mean when you break it down?

the thing is, Megan, much as I reject conformist gender bullshit as above, I still feel female, I've known it since like forever, for me it's not about wanting to play with dolls, it goes much deeper than that

it's what I've become these past seven years as I transitioned from Gopal to Bibi

oestrogen, breasts, vagina

now you know

so Bibi had been born a man and was now a woman, Megan had wondered, daren't ask, she might bite her head off

and Megan was a woman who wondered if she should have been born a man, who was attracted to a woman who'd once been a man, who was now saying gender was full of misguided expectations anyway, even though she had herself transitioned from male to female

this was such head fuckery

she shut the lid of her computer to go to sleep, when she opened it again Bibi would be there

they were now messaging deep into the night and early the next morning, hardly sleeping in between, both admitting they daren't Skype or meet just yet, in case when they came out from behind the deceptive smokescreen of social media, the chemistry wouldn't be there

let's keep the fantasy alive a while longer, Bibi wrote, I've been here before and when I met the person face to face we had nothing to say to each other

*

Bibi lived in Hebden Bridge, had grown up in Leeds

she worked as an administrator in a care home after getting a degree in Cultural Studies in Sussex, chosen to be as far away from her parents as possible who really didn't *get* that she was a girl in a boy's body

it wasn't part of their master plan, Megan, which was to marry me off to a suitable girl from the right caste and produce the next generation of my family

instead they got a cross-dressing son who kept his alter ego inside his bedroom, until he started to venture to the local shops in dresses and make-up

in a Hindu community where everybody knew everybody

I was kicked out, don't contact us again, you are sick in the head, you are no longer our son, and let's get one thing straight

you will *never* be our daughter

Bibi said the old people at the care home accepted her as a human being, you're our Bibi and we love you, they'd witnessed her transition to female

Bibi felt she'd finally got the body denied her at birth, which was also an eye-opener, Megan, once I started presenting fully as female, I realized I'd taken a lot of things for granted as a man

I miss sitting alone in bars late at night nursing a quiet pint, without feeling self-conscious or being hit on

and I can't stand watching the plague of telly dramas where young women are butchered by psycho serial killers and end up on a slab with their torso slit open down the middle with a coroner holding their bloodied heart in their hands

I used to love those shows, now I feel they're ultimately a way to wield power over women, to frighten them – *us*

I'm also wary of walking home late at night on my own, I miss being respectfully called sir when I'm in a shop or restaurant, and I'm definitely taken less seriously when I open my mouth

you see, Megan, I learnt first hand how women are discriminated against, which is why I became a feminist after I'd transitioned, an intersectional feminist, because it's not just about gender but race, sexuality, class and other intersections which we mostly unthinkingly live anyway

right that's enough of me talking (till the cows come home), hope I didn't sound too preachy but I can't help myself

what about you? Megan, where do you stand with all of this? time to spill the beans, love

Megan replied that she was working it out, taking her time, she'd recently been taken aback when she came across hundreds of genders on the internet, that, annoyingly, complicated the matter

she'd spent hours trawling, assessing, evaluating

genders like trans female or trans male and non-binary made sense to her, and she came across non-binaries in other countries like the Hirjas of India and the Two Spirits of Native Americans, others were total head fucks like quivergender – a gender whose intensity fluctuates, polygender – identifying as multiple genders, or staticgender – like fuzzy television static and how can your gender change multiple times a day as the synchgenders claim? Bibi, by the time I finished travelling into the batshit-crazy end of the Transgenderverse I was stressed with a capital S, I call it the Transloonyverse, lock 'em up and throw away the keys LOL!!

Bibi messaged right back, how dare you disrespect trans people's right toself-define, weird to you not to them, you sound like an ignorant oppressor, don't come into our world and make fun of us, fuck off!

Megan shot right back with fuck off yourself
hitting send in the heat of the moment

there was total silence for nearly four whole days, Megan worried
she'd lost her, she didn't want to be the first to make contact
   Bibi did
three simple words
we should meet.

4

Megan and Bibi had their historic first meeting in Caffè Nero on a
Saturday afternoon in Newcastle station, planned so that either party
could make an easy getaway if they loathed the sight of each other,
while thousands of agitated football fans poured back into the station
through the barriers, escorted by rozzers in riot gear, at the ready if
anything kicked off

Megan thought Bibi was as exquisite as she looked in her
photograph – lustrous black hair tied back, no make-up, flawless
skin, small-boned, jeans, off the shoulder fluffy jumper, trainers
   she was like a dancer, compact, toned, it was hard to tell she'd once
been male
   Bibi explained over mocha that as tarting up in high heels, tight
skirts and wearing a thick layer of face paint is all about gender and
not biological sex, she wears what she likes and feels comfortable doing so, although other trans females might think that being a
woman is all about adhering to a stereotyped version of womanhood,
when clearly most women can't be arsed with it all?

she gestured at the women walking around the station, look at them

Megan felt rattled at Bibi in effect mansplaining, she was a woman with male confidence, who went on to say that dressing like a woman means wearing every variety of clothing you can imagine, including baggies like these, she pulled at her blue jeans

you don't have to tell *me*, Megan said when she could get a word in edgeways, pointing out her own baggy jeans and outsized red and white check shirt, sleeves rolled up (the tats cost enough), don't forget *I'm* the expert here

of course you are, Bibi exclaimed, look at *me* telling *you*, you have to stop me from becoming one of those trans females who think they know more about being a woman than those who've lived their entire lives as one

trust me, Megan replied, I will, relieved that they weren't going to fall out within ten minutes of meeting

as the conversation proceeded to race along with no pit stops

they talked until their nerves jangled with the caffeine they kept ordering and later in a wine bar when their emotions swelled with the lagers they were drinking

they held hands over the table, amused when others did a double take – was that a man and woman or two women?

Megan told Bibi that after considering the options in depth, what makes most sense to me is the concept of gender-free, being born female isn't the problem, society's expectations are, I get this now and I'm so glad I didn't go down the sex change route

gender confirmation, love, Bibi snapped

all right, keep your hair on, I'm allowed to make mistakes so be patient with me, or I'll think you're totally up yourself

Bibi looked suitably chastised

the truth is, Bibi, I could never get my head around taking testosterone, and I really didn't want to thicken my skin, deepen my voice, bulk up, get hairy and phalloplasty was never on the cards, not for me

I would like to get rid of *these*, though, Megan pointed to her flat chest, breasts bound underneath her shirt

that would improve the quality of my life no end, she said, opening up more as the conversation continued on the journey back to Bibi's tiny rented cottage in Hebden Bridge later that evening

with its sagging seventeenth-century beams and subsided floors

where Bibi said Megan was welcome to stay

as they went in for their first kiss on the double bed

Hebden Bridge

was a small haven of organic-friendly and environmentalist residents and shops

of Tai Chi, Pilates, meditation, yoga and holistic healing classes

of writers, theatre-makers, filmmakers, visual artists, dancers and activists

of old-fashioned hippies and new-fashioned non-conformists

as well as people whose families had lived there for generations, and were used to the bohemians who'd begun arriving in the sixties

Megan loved its cobbled streets and short walks to the Calder Valley and Hardcastle Crags where they rambled for hours, physically and verbally, wearing bright rain macs and walking boots

Megan wondered aloud how she could put her gender-free identity into practice when they were living in a gender-binary world, and that with so many definitions (sane *and* insane, she refrained from saying), the very idea of gender might eventually lose any meaning, who can remember them all? maybe that was the point, a completely gender-free world, or was that a naïve utopian dream?

Bibi replied that dreaming wasn't naïve but essential for survival, dreaming was the equivalent of hoping on a large scale, utopias were an unachievable ideal by definition, and yeh, she really couldn't see billions of people accepting the abolition of the idea of gender completely in her lifetime

Megan said in which case demanding gender-neutral pronouns for herself from people who'd no idea what she was going on about also seemed utopian

Bibi said it was a first step towards changing people's minds, although yes, like all radical movements, there'd be much resistance and Megan would have to be resilient

they pounded the muddy grass in rain, and after it, mist coming out of their mouths before words did

Bibi's Labrador, Joy, raced ahead, so happy to be outside, as they were, country lovers, both of them

happy to be away from the human race

they started on an incline, navigated slippery rocks and moss, left the mist behind them, entered a cloudless part of the valley, the sun reappeared behind the grey sky, the land fell away behind them

they put their hoods down, surveyed the glossy green landscape

Megan said maybe she should become a missionary of the gender non-conforming crusade going forth to spread the gospel that gender is one of the biggest lies of our civilization

it's to keep men and women in their place, she shouted out to the landscape, as if evangelizing from a pulpit

her voice echoed back from the valley walls
can you hear me can you hear me can you hear me?

they discussed the best gender-neutral alternatives such as ae, e, ey, per, they, and tested each word to see if the words tripped off the tongue or tripped over it, ditto with the alternatives to his and hers: hirs, aers, eirs, pers, theirs and xyrs

Megan decided to try out *they* and *theirs*, what matters most to me, is that I know how I feel, and the rest of the world might catch up one day, even if it'll be a quiet revolution over longer than my lifetime, if it happens at all

you're right, Megan, Bibi replied, in the meantime, don't get antsy with people when they screw up your preferred pronouns, even when they want to remember, people will get it repeatedly wrong, they have to rewire their brains to adjust and that's not easy, it takes time

Megan laughed, look who's talking
they held hands
where they felt most safe doing it
in the middle of nowhere.

5

Morgan (no longer Megan)
has self-identified as gender-free for six years now, they've learnt to be cool with it when people don't use or understand their preferred pronouns
initially they wanted to punch their lights out

they're leaning on the wall overlooking the River Thames outside the crowded after-party of *The Last Amazon of Dahomey* at the National Theatre, written and directed by none other than Amma Bonsu

the legendary black dyke theatre director

their head is still shaven, once a week their bald pate is made smooth and shiny courtesy of a razor run once in one direction over shaving foam and once in the other

that's it – 'hair' done

their white shirt sleeves are rolled up high to show off tattoos of red and yellow flames rising up their arms, black jeans are slung low, fold up at the end to show off white ankle socks, brogues

Morgan's relieved to have escaped the schmoozing egotarians of London's cliques

a couple of them had been forced to say hello when they stood in their flight path, but instead of stopping for a chat had quickly moved on, Morgan wanted to have at least a couple of meaningful convos with the natives before they left, how ridiculous to come all the way down to London and spend it alone

yet this is exactly what's happened because unlike their social media persona which is confident and witty when there's time to redraft posts at leisure and Google long words before using them, it's another matter in the flesh

so far they've not said a complete single sentence to anyone

Morgan had escaped outside, lit a roll-up, a glass of pretentious fake champagne in hand (no down-to-earth beers or lagers)

they look over at the overblown buildings on the other side of the river

the usual clashing mish-mash of the capital's monstrosities

Morgan gets lost in this city, their senses assaulted to the point of disorientation by the jumble of high roads and side roads and relent-less traffic and the pressure of millions of people walking too fast

who'll mow them down like convoys of unstoppable army tanks crushing their spidery self

they can't get their head around city-dwellers who complain the countryside looks all the same to them when it's this city that's cha-otically confusing

Morgan has no problem navigating the Yorkshire Dales, Peak Dis-trict or the wilder reaches of Northumberland

with an uninterrupted view of the sky to keep one's line of vision empty

and psyche

healthy

they've only been here a few hours and are already missing the North, where people are more genuine, friendlier, and don't put on airs and graces

Londoners think they're the centre of the bloody universe, ignore the rest of the country and keep up their relentlessly unfunny jokes aimed at the *peasants* who live *ooop* North, eat fried Mars bars for breakfast, get so hammered at weekends they end up pissing their pants in the gutter, and are generally inter-generational, unemployed scroungers

as Morgan encountered from two Londoners on the train down from Newcastle this very afternoon

who'd amused themselves by spoofing the stereotype, not for a minute thinking the black person sitting opposite them was a born and bred Geordie

*

Morgan's badly missing Bibi, too, they only said goodbye to her this morning, caught the train down, and will see her again tomorrow

they feel vulnerable being so far away, after six years together the two of them are in synch with each other's rhythms

their lifestyle is quiet, peaceful, compatible

they'll happily spend their evenings sitting side by side with Bibi on the sofa reading, something Bibi insisted Morgan take up in order to broaden their mind, imagination and intellect, I can't be with someone who doesn't read books

Bibi reads non-fiction, her latest hero is Gloria Steinem, Morgan reads thrillers

sex is interesting, they enjoy sharing their reinvented bodies with each other, giving and receiving pleasure

according to what works for them

every other weekend they visit G G from Friday night to Sunday morning, help out with stuff around the house and farm, go on long walks

G G can't get a handle on Morgan's gender identity – understandable when she's spent ninety-three years living on the same farm in one of the remotest parts of the country

G G's incredibly fit for her age, and incredibly stubborn, she won't move out of the farm and into a home, Morgan and Bibi worry about her, have given up trying to persuade her it's the best course of action

I was born here and I'll bloody well die here, she said last time they tried, and anyone who says otherwise can sod off

the last time they visited, G G said she'd changed her will and left it to Morgan on the understanding it's kept in the family, invite all your non-binding people to come and stay and be themselves if you like, and when you die, you can pass it on to the family member most likely to look after it: why should I give it to my bairns when they abandoned it as soon as they were legally able to abscond and will have estate agents poking around before I'm cold in the grave

after they'd got over the shock, Morgan thought it was the most exciting thing that had ever happened to them, so long as they survived the inevitable shitstorm from the rest of the family, who'll accuse them of sucking up to G G to get hold of her estate and might even contest the will, say G G was of unsound mind

Bibi was totally game, they'd since discussed the idea of reinventing the farm for people who have reinvented themselves

astonished that G G had come up with such a radical idea

Morgan recently arranged an Ancestry D N A test for G G which links people with blood relatives who've also had it done

G G had talked a lot recently about her own mother, Grace, who'd not known her father, a seaman called Wolde from Ethiopia, it bugged her right until her death

it was the big mystery of Ma's life, she said, and G G felt sad that Wolde would forever remain a mystery

Wolde, who stopped off in South Shields in 1895 and impregnated Daisy, her grandmother, before buggering off

which is what Morgan will shortly do from this awful after-party

they were asked to review the play for a fee for the lifestyle magazine, *Rogue Nation*, on account of their Twitter following of over a million followers

which apparently turned them into an 'influencer'

as opposed to a high school dropout who wasted too much time online and had no discernible career to speak of

as they joked to Bibi who didn't disagree with them

@transwarrior was initially used to chart their journey from tomboy to non-binary, these days they use it more widely for general trans issues, gender, feminism, politics

it's good for lobbying and adding their outraged voice to protests

their Twitter account brings them invites to everything: concerts, first nights, film premieres, book launches, private views, hotels, edgy fashion shows

Morgan doesn't have a clue how to analyse or contextualize a play, book or film, it doesn't matter, it's their following that counts, not the quality of their critique or prose

soon there'll be no need for proper critics, the so-called 'experts' who've been running the show since forever, most of them here in London, it's all about the democratization of critical opinion, the papers say, and that includes someone like Morgan whose tweets get more readers than the proper critics

it can go to a person's head if they're not careful

as Bibi reminds them

Bibi keeps them grounded, says the so-called democratization of reviews means the lowering of standards, and that subject knowledge, history and critical context are at risk of being lost in favour of people who only know how to write in attention-seeking soundbites, I don't mean you, Morgan, Bibi reassures them, you're a true trans warrior who's making people pay attention to important issues

sometimes Morgan thinks Bibi does mean them

Morgan
turned down an invitation to write their autobiography, told the

publisher they couldn't imagine writing more than 280 characters at a time, and anyway, they really didn't want to write hurtful things about their family, the angle the publishers were after, a 'how I triumphed over my painful childhood' number

on that note, things have improved with the folks at home to the point where Morgan is on good terms with them these days

Mum dotes on Bibi, of course she does, she's *feminine*

Morgan has already posted their first comment on the play

Just seen #TheLastAmazonofDahomey @NationalTheatre. OMG, warrior women kicking ass on stage! Pure African Amazon blackness. Feeeeerce! Heart-breaking & ball-breaking! All hail #AmmaBonsu #allblackhistorymatters Book now or cry later, peepalls!!! @RogueNation

it's been liked 14,006 times and retweeted 7,447 times and the numbers keep ratcheting up

there'll be more to come on that score: Unmissable! A tour de force! Go see, transgirls, transboys, ladyboys & butchies, all the queers & all the queens & the intersectional warriors out there and all my fellow non-binary darlings #africanwomenshistory4everyone

Morgan

throws the wine glass into the Thames where it'll sink to the bottom to join other objects like leather shoes and goblets preserved deep in the river bed from before the Roman invasion

as Londoners are proud to brag in those documentaries fronted by posh gits who've been to public school

they take a last drag of their third roll-up, stub it out, will slope off to the expensive hotel room in King's Cross in order to get the first train out of The Smoke in the morning, when they see someone familiar standing talking to a black bloke they recognize off the telly, Roland somebody, all poncey in a bright blue suit

it's the kid from their lecture last year, what's her name?

Morgan recognizes her from their first ever talk on being trans delivered at an International Women's Day event at a university in Norfolk last year

she'd been unmissable sitting in the front row of the lecture theatre with a crazy-ass afro and stunning face, clad in a tee-shirt with a blonde Barbie image on it, the words IRONY scrawled in black underneath

very witty, kid, Morgan thought, you're my kinda person

Morgan only agreed to do that first university talk because it supplemented their paltry salary serving in Drunken Nostalgia down the road from the cottage, the hangout for the local drop-outs who don't mind their glasses stained with lipstick, crockery chipped, tables left unwiped and toilets turning into rivers of urine through which they not so much walk as wade

Aaron, the owner, likes Morgan because they're a mardy cow and as a non-binary bald person with tattoos is cooler and edgier than most

all meant as a compliment, and taken as such

Aaron says he'll says lose his core clientele if his staff look normal and are nice to people, or if he smartens the place up, his happiest times were in the Student Union bar in Manchester just before closing time on a Saturday night

been trying to re-create the same vibe ever since

being trans is personal, Morgan began, trying to sound confident in the windowless lecture theatre, their first time actually inside a university let alone delivering a talk, and I interpret trans to include non-binaries like me, trans men, trans women and cross-dressers, others might interpret it differently

talk about scary, standing rooted in the spotlight, confronted by rows of unsmiling students, all of them more educated than the person they've come to hear

Yazz, *that's* her name, was different, grinning with pre-approval

it felt like the rest were staring down at a circus freak

as if *they* weren't alien youngsters from the world of normal by the look of what was obviously the fashion there for girlie dresses

although Morgan suspected a few might progress to khakis, combat boots and tattoos to rival theirs by the time they graduated

I can only represent myself, Morgan said, warming up by forewarning the audience against their doubtless assumptions that all trans people are the same, I'm not a spokesperson for everyone or the leader of a transgender movement, merely an explainer of my own unique journey into being non-binary, more specifically, I consider myself to be in the gender-free category

Morgan made eye contact with the fresh-faced youngsters who made them feel, at twenty-seven, incredibly worldly-wise

gender-free means I identify as neither male nor female, I also identify as pansexual, which means I'm attracted to individuals on the male-female-trans spectrum, although my long-term partner is a trans-female and I'm not trading her in any time soon, not that it's any of your business who I sleep with, if you really must know, I'm spoilt for choice, all bases are covered, yeh, I've got it made, peeps!

laughter erupted around the room, whew, ice broken, Morgan had managed to entertain a room full of people – a first

Sandy the lecturer, sitting in the front row, long hair dyed blue, wearing a medieval-style dress, who'd come across Morgan on

Twitter, beamed appreciatively that her untested guest speaker was delivering on the goods to her charges

Morgan talked for nearly an hour about their experiences of growing up

their rejection of feminine ideals (while simultaneously being ignorant about feminism), their nervous breakdown (the lost months at the Quayside), leaving home (for a hostel), finding a partner who was right for them, not mentioning Bibi by name (keep me out of it, love, I'm old-fashioned, I only want a private relationship with you, I don't want to be part of your public *brand*)

Morgan discovered it was actually enjoyable talking to the students, who were quickly and obviously rapt, especially when it came to their decision to get a pair of unwanted breasts surgically removed

Morgan hadn't planned this, it just seemed fair and honest to do so, knowing they'd be curious

they told them it was a relief to have their breasts departed forever, and as they'd been bound with a compression shirt for so long, nobody much noticed, their lover was fine with it, said they'd fallen in love with Morgan, not their body parts

Morgan said their body felt lighter after the soreness had subsided, the pleasure they get from being able to sleep comfortably face down

to never again see them bobbing up in the bath like two unsinkable buoys

they were going to get tropical bird tattoos inscribed on that part of their body in time, turn their chest into a spectacular work of art

when they'd finished, hands shot up for questions, Morgan was praised for being so brave, fascinating, educational, entertaining

Morgan felt that all the years of exploring gender in books and in discussion with Bibi had paid off, and has done a few more gigs since

so this Yazz came rushing up at the end of the class to exclaim that the lecture (lecture?) was mind-blowing, and she was thinking of becoming non-binary as well, how *woke* was that? she said excitedly, like she was going to embark on a trendy new haircut

Morgan let the kid down gently

she needed to know that being trans wasn't about playacting an identity on a whim, it's about becoming your true self in spite of society's pressures to be otherwise, most people on the trans spectrum felt different from childhood, they said, trying not to sound too harsh as the audience filed slowly out of the room, a few students hovered around to listen in, all friends of this Yazz it transpired, including a Somali-looking girl wearing a blinged-up hijab, a rosy-cheeked milkmaid who looked about twelve, and a Kardashian-Arab type with a designer handbag, cleavage, heels, and black hair so straight and glossy it looked like a wig made of plastic (weren't students supposed to be scruffy and smelly?)

it's something inside you, Morgan said to her, not a trend, although others might adopt a trans position as a political statement, which is okay when it comes from a place of integrity, of solidarity, when it's a genuine rejection of society's gender impositions

not because it's hip or woke

it's why women became political lesbians years ago, choosing to have sexual relationships with women because they'd had enough of sexist men

not because they no longer desired them

Morgan had come across this in the online archive of a long defunct, second-wave feminist magazine called *Spare Rib*

*

if they'd been too harsh on Yazz, it didn't show, she was nonplussed, insisted on dragging Morgan off to a campus café with her entourage

where they unashamedly pumped their visitor full of questions and cappuccinos and were so irreverent about transgender issues, Morgan loosened up

which didn't happen very often (according to Bibi)

Waris, who was Somali, joked it was easy in some Muslim societies for a man to pass as female because you just went out in purdah and nobody was any the wiser

Courtney, the milkmaid, said she'd like to transition to male because her father would have to leave the farm, if the bank didn't claim it, to her instead of her younger brother, it was the only reason she knew what the word primogeniture meant

Nenet, the Kardashian, said she couldn't become a man because she liked wearing high heels too much, barely finishing her sentence before the others pounced on her for getting it all wrong

as if *they* were suddenly the experts

and here was Yazz popping up again, at the National, rescuing Morgan from feeling isolated

it turned out that she was the daughter of Amma Bonsu, and like their first encounter Yazz was so excitable, it was infectious

fancy me bumping into *Mx* Morgan Malinga! how cool is that? all the way down from *oooop North, wey aye, man*, I bet you love being in London, are you going to move down? you so belong here, everyone will love you, wasn't the play great? have you met my mum? whadyamean you haven't met her? she's the Queen of the (*old*) Dykes, I'm well proud of her and relieved I won't have to stop her jumping off Hungerford Bridge tonight because the play's gone down like a lead balloon

I've been following you on Twitter, have you noticed? probably not with, like, a million followers, I retweet practically everything you post, no, not stalkin' just supportin'!

what do you mean you were just leaving, *no way*, come inside and say hi to Waris and Courtney who'll be mega-pleased to see you, and let's hope the prosecco hasn't run out because all the old pissheads are here and trust me

they don't know when to stop.

Hattie

I

Hattie
G G to her descendants
aged ninety-three and counting
sits at the head of the banqueting table in the Long Room of
Greenfields farmhouse built over two hundred years ago
her ever-growing gene pool crammed all the way down it
and their spouses

either side of her are her two children, both in their seventies
Ada Mae (named after Slim's mother) and Sonny (named after
Slim's brother what got lynched)
then there's the grandchildren in their forties and fifties
Julie   nurse
Sue   shop assistant
Paul   former body-builder turned gym manager

Marian	secretary
Jimmy	car mechanic
Matthew	plumber, self-employed
Alan	copper (who everyone gives a wide berth to)

a few of the great-grandchildren in their twenties and thirties are here too, God knows what most of them do

great-great-grandchildren are seated at a separate table, can't remember most of their names, a couple of adults are acting as minders to stop them using food as missiles instead of fodder for their mouths

then there's the newly-borns she's only just met – Riley, Zoe, Noah

she'll remember their names

for a few hours

everyone is digging into Christmas lunch, a giant turkey as centrepiece, selected for the honour for its inordinate size and robust demeanour

she overfed it all year, wrung its neck yesterday, plucked it, put it in the ice house and then into the stove first thing this morning

Morgan and Bibi helped with the rest: roast spuds (Hattie's Own from the potato pit), stuffing, Brussels sprouts, Yorkshire pudding and black pudding (both Hattie's Own), peas (Hattie's Frozen Own), gravy

Ma's mildewed tapestry of the house dominates one wall of the room

the blackened flagstone fireplace dominates the other, big enough for a person to stand inside

when it's not lit, which it is, flames hungrily attacking the air

*

there's a big Christmas tree which Young Billy (in his sixties now) from the village cuts down from what Slim used to call the Forest of Firs out back

Young Billy installs one every year: lights, fairies, tinsel, baubles, pine needles creating a mess, especially as she likes to walk barefoot inside the house, even in winter

it's one of the secrets of her long-lasting mobility, keeping her toes spread and feet grounded, same as all the other beasts of nature

hooves, that's what she's got

hooves

Polina soaks them once a week, gives her nails a scrape-out, file-down, pumice and moisturize – the latter against Hattie's better judgement, seeing as she stopped poisoning her body with chemicals after Slim went in 1988

Polina says your feet they will crack and the germs they will have the field day, Hattie

so she obliges, even though the body makes its own oil, if you allow the pores to breathe

although try telling that to the women in her family who slather themselves in unguents and other toxic substances in the name of beauty

then wonder why they get cancer

presents are piled underneath the tree, people giving each other things for the sake of it, nothing to do with religion, Christmas should be called Greedymas

a time when people over-eat and over-indulge in the name of Jesus Christ

she hasn't bothered with presents since Slim passed, has given up telling everyone not to bother with her they give her things she doesn't want like gloves, tissues, pill boxes, slippers, electric blankets and bottle grips, as if she can't still open lids with her strong hands

Young Billy takes it all to a charity shop for her

she's got what she needs, not the same as what she wants

Slim wrapped up in a parcel underneath the tree

waiting to jump up and surprise her

Hattie sits quietly at these Greedymas affairs

can't hear above the racket they're making anyway, hates putting in those wretched hearing aids that irritate her ears and distort sounds

they carry on without her, amusing themselves, happy to ignore her like she's of no consequence, most of them don't listen to what she says anyway

she sinks back, watches their performances, quite content to be left to her own devices, nodding off, until people prod her to see if she's all right, the equivalent of checking her pulse

she's sure they're disappointed when she wakes up and shouts, aye-what? aye-what?

Ada Mae and Sonny can't wait to get their hands on the inheritance they think is their right, except she's thwarted them – they're not getting their hands on Greenfields farm what's been in her family over two hundred years for them to sell off to foreigners like those Russians or Chinese to build a luxury hotel or turn it into a golf course

they keep pestering her to go into a home and sort out her 'power of attorney'

she knows full well it means giving them power over her life

*

far as she's concerned

if she falls down the stairs and nobody's there to call an ambulance, so be it, at her age death won't be prolonged anyway, one bad fall and she's a goner

if they try and force her to leave, she'll be meek and compliant, say, just a moment while I go to the loo for one last crap in my own house, if that's all right with you

once inside, she'll blow her brains out with the pistol Slim kept from the war

they'll find her brains splattered on the toilet walls

they won't forget that in a hurry

most of them don't deserve to inherit, anyhow, can't be bothered to visit from one Christmas to the next

even then the slackers try it on, complain they can't get up the hill from the village when it's snowing or icy

car won't make it up, GG, they say down the line of the crackling phone she's had since 1952

better than those mobile phones the young ones check hundreds of times a day which makes them go mental

she's read about it in the paper

besides, why replace her old phone when it's still in good working order, sits on the console by the front door, attached to a wire that's attached to a socket

telephone conversations should be kept short and had standing

far as she's concerned

she tells those lightweight relatives of hers to walk up the hill from the village instead, it's only a two-mile hike, a bit perpendicular, but none of them is suffering from vertigo, last she heard not that the village is a village any more, it's a ghost town, with one corner shop and a public house, even the Co-op (to think there were protests when it opened in the seventies) closed down a few years back

now it's an 'art gallery' that laughingly only opens for two weeks a year in summer, which she suspects is a tax dodge

let's not forget the post-box or rather the 'museum object from when people believed in writing letters by hand on paper and posting them'

oh and there's a farmers' market in the summer – as if there should be any other kind

the rest of the shops have been turned into holiday homes owned by rich southerners from York and Leeds, the lawyers, doctors and academical types who want to 'get away from it all'

for a few weeks every summer

who push house prices up that drive the youngsters out

that and the lack of farm jobs are the ruination of rural communities, as they say in *Farmers Weekly*

the rise of the combine harvester in the fifties started it

far as she's concerned

cheap foreign labour has continued it of late, good for farmers, not for locals who find themselves undercut by people who work twice as hard for half as much

as many a person has complained to her

she never resorted to bringing in foreign labour because she felt loyal to those self-same locals

who worked half as hard for twice as much

no wonder Greenfields went to pot, that and losing out to foreign produce coming into the country from the whole damned world

globalization? they can stick it up her arse

many farms around here had to rely on handouts, not her, she got nothing when she was struggling to run the farm alone, she applied to the EU and got knocked back after officials poked their nose around and couldn't hide their surprise at who they saw in charge

of course she voted to leave it, far as she's concerned, politics is personal, she voted Conservative when her father was alive because he expected it

she didn't want to let him down

she voted Labour when Slim was alive because he said he believed in 'the people', and she didn't want to let him down either

kept voting Labour out of loyalty to him

a few years back she made up her own mind for the first time and voted Green because she liked their environmental stance and hated the warmongering that was going on with Labour

she voted UKIP in the last election

Slim wouldn't have liked that

but he's not here

when her family do make it up the hill on two legs or four wheels, there's the brief honeymoon period before the drinking starts

they pile into the house in their party clothes: dresses showing off knees that should've gone undercover a long time ago, bellies spilling over belts, the younger ones wearing outfits so tight you can see their hearts beating

newborns in swaddling blankets are thrust into her arms for photographs, the parents looking anxiously as if she's going to drop down dead while holding the baby

it's starting to get lively further down the table

Jimmy, Sonny's son, her oldest grandson, turned up with a keg of beer and is proceeding to empty it, he might as well drink straight from the tap the way he goes on

others have brought multi-packs of wine and giant bottles of fizzy soft drinks for the children, to make them hyperactive and rot their teeth

there was an experiment on the telly where they put a tooth in a glass of fizzy drink

she's told them about it, do they listen?

that's modern-day parenting for you

Jimmy's on his feet now (been inside twice for GBH) and it's all about to kick off, he's usually the first, him and his two sons Ryan and Shawn are the worst hotheads

he's poking his finger at his younger brother Paul for a wrong he's done him, Paul won't take any lip from Jimmy so there might be a few cuts, bruises and cracked ribs

Hattie can't hear them properly and now Alan, the youngest brother, ever the copper, has stood up and is trying to calm things down in that bossy way he has, ready to prise his two older brothers apart

if he's not careful they'll set on him instead, it's happened before

no one likes Alan

not even his second wife, Cheryl

who left him last year

he joined the police when he left school, had been bullied by his brothers when he was growing up because he was a soft lad

that changed once he had the full force of the law behind him

he once asked her if she paid taxes on the farm's cash income

she wasn't sure whether it was a friendly enquiry or a threat

you don't know where you stand with Alan
not felt the same about him since

Jimmy, on the other hand, was born charming everyone who met him, he got his own way with Sonny who now despairs of him, who never listened to Slim telling him to discipline his boy before it was too late
when people said no to Jimmy he threw tantrums that turned into tempestuous rages as he got older, that involved getting into fights as a teenager, and it's been a rollercoaster ride of hooliganism ever since
it's why his first wife Karen left with the kids when they were little
he had to go to court to get supervised visits until they were adults
the number of broken marriages among her lot

Jimmy and Paul seem to have made up and are popping out to the yard to light up, Alan's eyes follow them as they leave, ever the outsider, aye, Alan?
she can see them through the window as they join the others freezing to death under the awning of the hay barn
so long as they're inhaling nicotine on a regular basis that'll eventually kill them, they'll consider these excursions worth it
she read in the paper that fewer people smoke these days
you wouldn't know it with her lot

her grandchildren all look more white than black because Sonny and Ada Mae married white people
none of them identifies as black and she suspects they pass as white, which would sadden Slim if he was still around

349

she doesn't mind, whatever works for them and if they can get away with it, good luck to them, why wear the burden of colour to hold you back?

the only thing she objects to is when they objected to Chimango when he arrived on the scene, a fellow nurse at the hospital where Julie worked, from Malawi

Hattie was sickened by their behaviour, they should've been more enlightened

but the family was becoming whiter with every generation

and they didn't want any backsliding

Chimango was a fine, hardworking man like Slim, he was patient, pleasant and he won them around in time

he didn't give up on them (he should have done)

she welcomed him on to the farm, apologized for the behaviour of her lot

it was Chimango who encouraged Julie to buy black picture books for his kids

Chimango said they had to see children who looked like them in books

when Julie told Hattie about this she felt terrible

had those books existed for her children in the nineteen-forties?

had she been a bad mother?

Morgan and Bibi, her *partner* (as they say these days), stay on until New Year, she likes their company best because they genuinely like her, help out, love being at Greenfields

she cherishes being on the farm – from when she was a wee, troubled bairn whose mother, Julie, didn't like her because she wasn't the Barbie doll she wanted her to be it wasn't surprising when Morgan became a sexual invert, not that it was a problem for Hattie

there used to be two women who ran the grocery store

Hermione (who was the wife, and dressed as such)

and Ruth (who was the husband, and dressed as such)

Ma said the village folk accepted them as a couple even though nobody mentioned it, and they, in turn, were the first to befriend her Ma, when she arrived as Joseph's wife

Ma said they'd call on her in the farm to see if you need any help, Grace

once Hattie was old enough, her and Ma were often invited to tea, would take down a basket of apples, pears and cherries from the farm

Ma said she'd once been told that Hermione came from an aristocratic family and Ruth had been the estate gardener's daughter, they'd eloped as soon as they were of age

they died within a year of each other shortly after the war

Hattie has put flowers on their graves ever since

so Hattie was never going to have a problem with Morgan being that way as well, but a while back Morgan took it to extremes when she declared, as they were taking their usual walk across the fields with Bibi, G G, I no longer identify as a male or a female

Morgan went into a big explanation of it, might as well have been talking Chinese

Hattie asked her outright if she'd been to see a doctor because you sound mental, dear?

Morgan didn't say another word, they walked back to the house in silence, her and Bibi left a day early

*

Hattie doesn't have a problem with Bibi who was born male, because she's never known her as anything other than female, which makes a kind of sense

to say you're neither is so far-fetched it's absolutely ludicrous

the next time Morgan showed up, two months rather than two weeks later (a big sulk, even for Morgan), Hattie sat her down and said, look, I was born in the nineteen-twenties, you're expecting too much of me to even begin to understand what you're going on about

just be who you want to be and let's agree not to talk about it

the funny thing is, nothing's changed about Morgan since she became a gender granary non-binding whatsit, other than changing her name from Megan to Morgan, which is fine, Hattie can live with that

at least she didn't name herself *Reginald* or *William*

Hattie absolutely won't pander to calling her *they* instead of *she*, as requested

Morgan looks the same (like a boy), acts the same (boyish) and to all intents and purposes is the same (Megan).

2

Hattie turns her attention to Ada Mae

sitting at the table all gnarled up from working in a factory as a clicker who cut out leather shoe shapes with a knife

what sort of job was that for forty years? the sort that gave her dowager's hump, rheumatism, that's what

she still straightens and dyes her hair, currently an unseemly grey at the roots, pulled back from a face that's gone slack except for a mouth that holds all her misery like a drawstring tightened around a pouch she's talking across the table to Sonny who's got emphysema, rattles as noisily as the washboard Slim used to play, worked down the mine at Bedlington until it closed, then as a barman, retired a few months before the smoking ban came in, too late, he'd inhaled more nicotine than oxygen

from lunchtime to closing time
for twenty-odd years
Hattie's as likely to outlast him
as him her

all of her family live in the diseased atmospheres that wash about the centrally-heated homes they insist on living in

greenhouses for bad bacteria

her usually windswept Long Room is too hot for her now, what with all body heat on top of the fire at full roar and cackle

the farmhouse has got so many cracks in the window frames it's usually warmer outside than in, keeps a person long-living and weather resistant, she tells the complainers, nothing wrong with being cold, she's been cold her whole life living in this remote part of the country near the Borders

number of times she's come downstairs to mounds of snow under the Long Room windows after a blizzard's blown in

shovels it out again, if it doesn't melt beforehand

(best not to have carpets)

she's not against a mild log fire, mind, heating the way God intended, the shirkers in the family complain when she gets them chopping up wood for a few hours in the woodshed

when they visit

*

when Hattie looks at her children these days she sees a pair of crippled wrecks who rejected life on the farm where they'd have stayed fit in body and mind

she's only ever wanted the best for them, but children don't listen to their parents, do they?

she admits it was tough for them growing up, she understands why they wanted to leave but once Ada Mae ended up working in a factory for so long and hating it, and Sonny went down a mine to work; they should have come back to live the outside life, to use their bodies as God intended, working on the land, and investing in an inheritance neither deserves

Ada Mae and Sonny got shoved down into mud once when they were young at the winter fair

one minute they were standing behind her, eagerly awaiting the candy floss she was buying, the next they were on the ground covered in mud and tears

the culprit had disappeared into the crowds

if it'd happened on the farm, she'd have gone after the bastard with an axe and beheaded him with the strength of a woman who's been chopping firewood since her father gave her an axe for her tenth birthday

she'd have thrown him in the trough for the hogs to demolish all traces, who'll go through bone like butter

she'd have thrown carrots and cabbage in while she was at it (meat and two veg)

any serial killer worth their salt knows you just feed your victims to starving sows

no need for the palaver of digging graves in the woods in the middle of the night, or dissolving bodies in metal drums full of acid, like

on those American crime documentaries that make her feel grateful
to be living so far away from such goings-on

Slim was less sympathetic when his children came home with their
'sob stories', as he put it, such as when a child pinched Ada Mae's arm
to see if she bruised, or scratched her with a compass to see if she
could bleed, and if so, what was the colour?

or the boys asked Sonny if his colour could be scrubbed off, held
him down, applied a scrubbing brush to see for themselves

rise above it, Slim said as they sat around the table at teatime to
have a glass of cold milk and jam sandwiches in the one hour of the
day they convened as a family before more farm work beckoned

cow-milking being first on the list

it's teasing, that's all, Slim told them, don't come crying to me
about it – if someone attacks you, attack them back and move on

y'all ain't living in the segregated society I come from where you
ain't got no rights

y'all ain't got a fifteen-year-old younger brother called Sonny who
was soaked in coal oil before he was strung up on a sugarberry tree
and set alight while still alive in front of thousands cheering

a boy called Sonny whose murder by mob was photographed and
sent across the country as a postcard because folks were so damned
proud of witnessing his lynching

y'all didn't discover that the woman who cried rape gave birth
nine months later to a child so white, even her daddy came round to
your daddy's house to apologize in person

y'all ain't been through that now, have ya?

so negroes, *please*, hold it down

Hattie asked *him* to tone it down with the stories, it was scaring
their children and would make them hate themselves, he said they

needed to toughen up and what did she know about it with her being high-yaller and living in the back of beyond?

you liked that I'm high-yaller, as you put it, so don't you go using it against me, Slim

he said the Negro had reason to be angry, having spent four hundred years in America enslaved, victimized and kept downtrodden

it was a powder keg waiting to explode

she replied they were a million miles from America and it's different here, Slim, not perfect but better

he said his little brother Sonny was the children's uncle and they needed to know what happened to him and about the history of a country that allowed him to be murdered, and it's your duty to face up to racial issues, Hattie, because our children are darker than you and aren't going to have it as easy

they had these conversations until she was able to see things from his point of view

they both followed the news about the civil rights protests, Slim said the Negro needed Malcolm X *and* Martin Luther King

when they were assassinated within three years of each other

he disappeared into the hills for a few days

Hattie saw that neither of her children liked being coloured and she didn't know what to do about it

Ada Mae painted herself as a white child in her drawings, and from the age of twelve Sonny never wanted to be seen with his father beyond the village, hated having to go to the cattle fairs with him as a teenager and he begged her not to bring his father to school events

she overheard Sonny telling a boy whose father dropped him

home one day that Slim, who was leading sheep out to pasture, was a hired labourer

Slim would have given his life for his children.

3

When Ada Mae and Sonny were sixteen and seventeen, they announced out of the blue one breakfast that they were leaving home

we're going today and you can't stop us, Sonny said, spreading his legs wide like he was a grown man, shoulders back, daring his parents to challenge him

we're not going to spend another day in the back of beyond baling hay, ploughing fields, milking cows and mucking out animal dung

for the rest of our lives

Hattie remembers it so clearly

Ada Mae wore her new orange mini-dress with a high neck she'd ordered though the Biba catalogue, white patent leather boots that rode up to her knees, hair sculpted into a beehive, false lashes, black pencil around her eyes making them appear huge

she was beautiful then, of course she didn't think so

it's only now, when they look at old family photos together that Ada Mae exclaims, with more than a touch of sadness, look at me, Ma, I was quite lovely, wasn't I?

Sonny was bone-thin in those days, in the way of teenage boys before they become men, his legs gangly and uncoordinated, he'd grown too quickly to the height of his father

357

he wore his purple velvet flare suit, his hair was trimmed almost to the bone back then, to hide its kinks, she suspected
with a side-parting that looked absurd
neither were dressed for the long ride to London

they left on Sonny's seventeenth birthday present – the Honda motorbike he'd begged them to buy him
said he needed it to come and go more freely
it cost them two bullhorns

Ada Mae sat pillion, Sonny revved the bike and the pair of them roared off out of the yard, down the hill, through the village and towards the glamorous streets that awaited them in London
Ada Mae was to become a secretary to a pop star, Sonny a rich businessman
they roared noisily out of their parents' lives leaving a plume of smoke and fumes
leaving her and Slim marooned on eight hundred acres of farmland

it took time to adjust to not hearing Ada Mae playing Dusty Springfield, Petula Clark and Cilla Black records on the record player in the Long Room, where she danced in the modern way
if one of them made the mistake of entering, she shouted at them to bloody well leave her alone for once
Sonny pretended to play the guitar in there, while listening to the Rolling Stones
they used to peep through the windows to amuse themselves

Hattie and Slim found it strange sitting down to meals for two instead of four, washing one set of sheets instead of three, to not taking the temperature of teenage moods when their kids were sloping about at home

they never stopped worrying about them being so far away in the capital city

where anything could happen to them

London didn't last, they didn't even make it to three whole months (lightweights!)

Sonny worked in a boutique in Carnaby Street that didn't pay enough to live on, Ada Mae washed dishes in the kitchen of the Regent Palace Hotel

it was impossible to get accommodation other than in a run-down house with coloured immigrants in a slum area called Notting Hill

the immigrants scornfully accused them of being like white people

Hattie wanted to say she thought they'd see that as a compliment and contemplated how her bairns had gone from the Scottish Borders to London, only to discover it was an alien country down there

she was happy when they settled in Newcastle, only seventy miles from the farm

instead of over three hundred

Ada Mae married Tommy, the first man who asked, grateful anyone would

she didn't exactly have suitors lining up in Newcastle wanting to proudly introduce their black girlfriend to their parents in the nineteen-sixties

Tommy was on the ugly side, a face like a garden gnome, her and Slim joked, none too bright, either

Hattie suspected the lad didn't have too many choices himself

a coalminer from young, he was apprenticed as a welder when the mines were shut down

he proved to be a good husband and really did love Ada Mae, in spite of her colour

as he told Hattie and Slim when he came to ask for her hand

lucky that Slim didn't lay him out

there and then

Sonny's experience was somewhat different, according to Ada Mae who reported back that women queued up round the block for him

they thought he was the next best thing to dating Johnny Mathis

he married Janet, a barmaid, whose parents objected

and told her to choose.

4

When she first saw him, Slim Jackson reminded Hattie of the Masai warriors she'd seen in the *National Geographic* magazine Pa had ordered monthly from America in her childhood

they'd pore over the photographs together on Sunday afternoons after church and explore the pictures and stories of places and people beyond the farm, village and surrounding towns

Pa had travelled across Europe in the army, he'd been to Egypt and Gallipoli, developed an appetite for things foreign

Hattie met Slim in 1945 at an afternoon dance in Newcastle for demobbed American Negro regiments who were due to be sent home it was her first dance in the big city, her parents sat outside in the farm truck, praying she'd meet someone

she'd had no luck so far

Hattie was astonished at the number of other coloured English-women there, who'd travelled from as far afield as Cardiff, Bristol, Glasgow, Liverpool, London

they were all kinds of mixtures, most with a white mother, which came out when they got chatting in the powder room

Hattie felt instantly comfortable among these girls, who all looked like versions of herself, she'd never felt so welcomed

they were surprised she worked on a farm, felt sorry for her as they re-applied lipstick and powdered their faces in the mirror, posing like they were all beauty queens whereas she looked plain, wore no make-up, which really won't do, one of the girls said, and set to brightening up features Hattie had thought of as plain

the women cooed over her and said now you look pretty, Hattie

when she looked at the red on her cheeks and her lips in the mirror, she agreed

the other girls wore glamorous taffeta dresses which showed off their waists, and long white gloves, and stilettos

Hattie felt embarrassed by the dowdy dress Ma had made her from *Woman's Weekly*

inside the hall the band played swing music, the dance floor was a swirl of girls in dresses as colourful as butterflies and smart green soldiers' uniforms, everyone pairing up, none of the girls were left as wallflowers, which had been Hattie's fate at local barn dances

only her father would take her for a spin

*

the girls agreed that most Englishmen wouldn't touch them with a bargepole, other than to expect easy sex, and African or West Indian men were few and far between

every one of them was a belle of the ball at this dance, as the soldiers made quite clear, in thrall to such high-class, light-skinned ladies

the women laughed at the compliments, were used to being treated as the lowest of the low

some said this was their last chance before the soldiers departed for the United States of America

some dreamed of being taken back there as wives

Hattie sat at a table with three Irish-Nigerian sisters, Annie, Bettina and Juliana, all training to be nurses, who were more full of life than anyone she'd ever met, she found herself giggling at their outrageous flirting with the soldiers

she invited them to visit her at the farm

they scoffed at the very idea, a farm? oh Hattie, how funny you are, we're going forwards not backwards, you're a pet

we're going to London once we're qualified, we'll write so you can visit us

to this day she wonders what happened to them

Slim approached her to do the foxtrot

she was flattered, shy at first, avoided his gaze, he openly admired her creamy complexion, girl, those blushing cheeks alone will give you high stock value back home in Georgia

he was long and thin, his skin shiny and silky

he was the first man to make her feel ladylike instead of like a workhorse who spent all day getting dirt underneath her fingernails

*

they married within the year, Ma and Pa approved, glad she'd found someone to look after her when they were gone

Slim liked her parents and they liked him for who he was

Pa said he was the son he never had, and once took Hattie aside, said he was relieved that Slim didn't try and boss her around

fat chance that, she replied

for his part, Slim didn't like the English weather, but he liked the people, said he felt more respected here, he hadn't been called boy once and when he rode his bicycle thereabouts, he wasn't worried folks were gonna don white hoods, burn crosses and lynch him

it's why I'm never going home, Hattie

Slim came from sharecropping stock, his people farmed land but never owned it

his father had to give half his sugar cane yield to the landowner, was in never-ending debt to the merchant who sold them seeds, clothes and tools, and ran the risk of eviction if the crop failed

Slim said many of his people left the land after slavery because it reminded them of it

the government had promised them all forty acres and a mule

it was the bitterest pill when it didn't deliver, folks had to stay wage slaves

now he was married to Hattie, the land he worked was one day going to be his

hers too, she reminded him

most people took favourably to Slim, he was confident and talkative, spoke to strangers, even hostile ones, diffusing their animosity, especially when they heard his accent, they praised his courteousness, his yes m'ams and no sirs, they liked the way he opened doors for women, tipped his hat at men, making them feel respected

especially when he sang in his stirring baritone in church, at harvest festivals, Christmas carols, birthday parties, barn dances, strumming a guitar or a washboard as accompaniment

she and him enjoyed their conjugals for the most part, once they discovered that him putting it in and taking it out wasn't enough for her

it only waned when his mental prowess did

they were together over forty years, she's not been touched in a sensual way in the thirty years since

she can still feel his manly farmer's hands holding her naked buttocks, complaining there wasn't enough meat on them

although he admired her physical strength

Slim boasted she could steer a plough as good as any man

hotdamn, Hattie, hotdamn!

5

Hattie started walking when Slim died

she bought walking boots as opposed to working boots, carved herself a walking stick with a Black Power fist on the knob – in homage to him

she wore thermals in winter, cotton shirts in summer, carried rainwear and a flask of the sweet tea Slim used to drink in her knapsack

as she trod her land and beyond

sometimes in high summer she'd go out to one of her fields at

364

night, lie on a blanket, watch the stars in the night sky, imagine Slim looking down at her

watching over her

waiting for her

she kept farm production going a long time, well into her eighties, at one point she had thirty farmhands on her payroll

it's only in the past ten years it's been reclaimed by nature, an aggressive beast consuming everything when you let it rampage unhindered

her land has become a jungle of rotten crops, grass, weeds, tangled bushes, foxes, roe deer and snakes

wild fields – where once grew wheat, barley, oats and winter linseed for market

wild fields – where once roamed Herefords, Ayrshires, the dray horses for the ploughs and carts, her Cheviot sheep, and her childhood Icelandic pony, Smokey

the two of them used to take off at a trot down the lane, around the lake, they'd canter through the woods and race at full gallop across the low-lying hills spread before them

if she fell off Smokey, she had to get herself back on again, she didn't wear a helmet or shoes

if she didn't come back, Pa would ride out with the dogs to find her

Hattie remembers she took her body for granted back then, when it automatically did what her mind instructed it to

she remembers when she could milk thirty cows every morning and every evening, slowly straining the warm milk into cans, then muck out the milking parlour, wash and sterilize the utensils and help the dairymen load the milk on to their horse-drawn wagons

without feeling tired

now her body fights her over the simplest things like putting on her overalls, getting out of chairs, and climbing stairs

Hattie remembers when her and Slim lived with Ma and Pa and Ada Mae and Sonny, when they were small children

it was an ideal set-up with two women and two men working together to raise the children and run the farm

her and Ma were more like friends than mother and daughter, from as young as she can remember they did everything together, Father said she could twist Ma around her little finger, he couldn't get a word in edgeways, which was true

Ma always said she missed her own mother, Daisy, who died young, and not a day went by that she didn't wish she'd known her own father, the Abyssinian

who was he, Hattie? who was he?

Ma fell ill when Sonny and Ada Mae hadn't yet started school

she was so unhappy that she'd miss them growing up, and that they'd be too young to remember her

Father struggled on, it wasn't the same after Ma passed, he said he wanted to join her

he went not long after, heart failure, she and Slim agreed it was broken

one of the last things he said to her was, you belong here, Harriet Jackson née Rydendale

you are my daughter and in your hands rests the future of this family this isn't just our *hyem*, Hattie, it's your forebears' who worked bloody hard to keep it going for us

so when the time comes, you must make sure you pass it on to Sonny, to do the same

that was about seventy years ago

she's lived in this place ninety-three years now, this farm isn't just her home, her *hyem*, it's her bones

and her soul

eight monarchs of the royal family have been on the throne since the first stone was laid by her ancestor Captain Linnaeus Rydendale in 1806

who'd made a large enough fortune to fulfil his life-long dream of landownership having started his life as a labourer's son in this district

having begun his career as a cabin boy on ships

Captain Linnaeus Rydendale

who returned to the district with a young wife, Eudoré, from Port Royal in Jamaica, the daughter of a merchant he'd done business with

according to family legend she was rumoured to be Spanish, and when Slim first saw her portrait in the library he said she's one of us, Hattie

she said he was imagining it, he insisted that he knew the full spectrum of how we people turn out and I'm telling you, Hattie, she's one of us

when Hattie looked at her through his eyes, a different Eudoré became apparent, something about her colouring, the shape of her face and features, the density of her hair

perhaps he was right

*

after Joseph died, Slim broke open an old library cabinet when he couldn't find the keys, said that as the man of the house he needed to know what was in it

he found old ledgers that recorded the captain's lucrative business as a slave runner, exchanging slaves from Africa for sugar in the West Indies

came charging like a lunatic into the kitchen where she was cooking and had a go at her for keeping such a wicked family secret from him

she didn't know, she told him, was as upset as he was, the cabinet had been locked her entire life, her father told her important documents were inside and never go near it

she calmed Slim down, they talked it through

it's not me or my Pa who's personally responsible, Slim, she said, trying to mollify her husband, now you co-own the spoils with me

she wrapped her long arms around his waist from behind

it's come full circle, hasn't it?

6

Hattie knows about secrets, never told anybody about the child she lost, the one she gave birth to when she was fourteen

her small bosom was growing larger and more tender, her stomach was swelling, she was sick in the mornings

Ma noticed, worked it out

Bobby was the father, the most popular boy in the village school, he was tall with a head of white hair, the butcher's son

boys paid Hattie no attention at all, so when this one did, there was no question she'd refuse his advances

the pair of them fooled about in between the church pews after
school
in those days churches were left open without fear of someone
walking off with the silver
she was the centre of his universe, for about thirty minutes
she can't remember it happening
it must have done

afterwards
he carried on ignoring her
as before

Father could barely speak to her he was that livid, she wouldn't tell
him the name of the boy who'd got her pregnant, which infuriated
him even more
Ma didn't seem to mind so much, after the initial shock, she seemed
pleased, they'd wanted another child, but it didn't work out for her and Pa
Hattie felt bewildered at what was happening to her body
and stupid for falling for Bobby
she didn't want to be pregnant, she wanted to be at school and to
go playing with her friends
Ma took charge, Hattie was to remain hidden from everyone,
they'd say she was sick
Hattie felt fine, wanted to walk around the house, at least, you're
not endangering this bairn, young lady, you'll do as you're told,
Ma said
the baby came quickly one Friday night, a girl, Ma delivered it
herself, she'd read a book about how to do it
she handed the baby over to Hattie, showed her how to
breastfeed

369

Hattie was fascinated, she'd made this child all by herself

Ma told her she must treat the child as the most precious thing in the world and not be clumsy with her

we have to make sure she survives, Hattie

because we love her very much

Hattie wasn't sure she loved the baby, she wasn't sure she knew what love was, it was a big word

she gave the baby a name, Barbara, which Ma accepted, it's yours to name and we're going to try and keep her

Ma spent all her time with her and the baby, she slept on the floor at night, was the first to wake up when the baby did, made sure Hattie didn't fall asleep while breastfeeding

she changed her nappies, bathed her in a tub in the room

Hattie heard her parents arguing downstairs, they never had before, not like this, it went on for hours, Pa shouting, Ma shouting back

Ma came in red-eyed, I'm not letting her go, I've told him

that day Pa came into the bedroom to see his grandchild for the first time since Barbara was born, Ma was getting herself washed in the bathroom

he said the baby had to go

Hattie said she wanted to keep her, just as he swiftly plucked her from her arms with his strong hands

before he left the room, he said, you don't speak a word about this, to anyone, ever, you must forget this ever happened, Hattie

your life will be forever ruined with a bastard child

men will have two reasons not to marry you

*

Hattie wasn't even thinking of marriage, she hated her father calling her baby a bad person, a bastard

she didn't really cotton on that she'd never see Barbara again

Hattie's still got the pink and blue blanket Barbara was wrapped up in, made from wool spun from their own sheep, dyed and knitted by Ma when they didn't know whether it was going to be a male or female baby

she's never washed it, keeps it in a shoe box

for a long time afterwards she could still smell Barbara on it, even when she knew it wasn't possible

she used to imagine Barbara had been taken in by aristocrats, become one of those debutantes, married a lord and lived in a castle

she kept her word to Pa and never told anyone

not Slim, not Ada Mae or Sonny – not anybody

*

Hattie wakes up, someone is prodding her arm, she opens the heavy lids of her eyes, she's back at Greedymas and her lot have got even drunker and louder

Ada Mae is peering intently at her, checking she's still alive

having spent her life unaware she had an older sister.

Grace

Grace
came into this world courtesy of a seaman from Abyssinia called
Wolde, a young fireman
   who stoked coal into the boilers in the holds of merchant ships
   the hardest, filthiest, sweatiest job on board
   Wolde
   who sailed into South Shields in 1895 and left a few days later leaving behind the beginnings of Grace hidden inside her Ma
   who'd just turned sixteen
   who didn't know she was with child until Grace was almost ready
to pop out, as Daisy told her little girl when she was old enough to
grasp how babies were made
   he was your Pa, Gracie, he was very tall, he walked like he wasn't
touching the ground, like he was floating on air, like he was from
another world

which he was

I thought he was very gentle, unlike the local lads who thought we girls were theirs for the taking

we used to flock down to the docks when the boats were off-loading

hoping we'd catch a seaman who'd take us far away to magical places with names like Zanzibar, Casablanca, Tanganyika, Ocho Rios and South Carolina

your father spoke the little English he'd picked up as a sailor, so we had half-conversations with each other, and full-on gesticulations

I come back for you, he promised, when I saw him off on the quay, walking backwards as I stood facing forwards

not wanting to see him leave

I come back for you

one day we'll take a boat to Abyssinia and find him, Gracie, I'll knock on the door of his hut, push you forward and say, hey mister, look what *you* left behind

Daisy

had given birth to Grace in the tenement block where she slept on sacks on the floor along with her brothers and sisters

her parents slept behind a curtain that divided the single room of their lodgings

a half-caste

Daisy's father said he'd never live the shame down at the pub

where he went directly after thirteen hours spent underground chipping away at rock to extract coal

before he staggered home to pick fights with Ma

give the bairn up to the church or you'll not stay, he told Daisy as if I could ever abandon you, Gracie, so innocent and pure and whole and one of God's blessed creations?

it was my job to protect and care for you, and I'd have murdered anyone who tried to prise us apart

Daisy

moved out, vowed never to talk to her Ma again, who was too weak to stand up to a father who cared more about what other people thought than helping his own child

she found a job making artificial flowers for a hat factory, shared lodgings with Ruby, another youngster who had a five-year-old son called Ernest for a sailor who'd come and gone

he came from somewhere called Aden next to the Red Sea

can you imagine, Gracie? a sea that's red?

Daisy

carried Grace everywhere in a sling because there was nobody to leave her with, nobody she trusted, enough

after her entire family had cut her off

certainly not Ruby, who didn't clean Ernest very often

I washed you every day, Gracie, in a bowl of water I collected from the standpipe and warmed in the hearth where the iron pot stewed vegetables

I washed you until you were squeaky clean and the lovely little curls on your head shone like dewdrops

poor Ernest's hair was matted into clumps and Ruby was often out late and I'd have to stop him wandering outside on to the muddy alley strewn with garbage and broken glass

I kept an eye on him but I couldn't take him on, Gracie, he wasn't mine

I don't know what happened to him because we moved into a room with Mary at the factory who was married, had three of her own, and needed the extra cash

Daisy
promised to take Grace to the countryside
what I'd give to see you run freely on the soft, springy grass with the sun shining on to your lovely caramel face, to hear you calling out, you can't catch me, Ma, you can't catch me
she promised Grace she'd find a husband who provided for them, a carpenter who'd build furniture for their cottage of three rooms plus a washroom, a proper inside toilet, real flowers on the kitchen table, bread baking in the oven, good-quality air and a clean river to bathe in every day
in summer

Daisy
who didn't reckon on starting up a wet, hacking cough when Grace was eight, made worse by the coal dust that swirled in the air
she couldn't afford to be ill, she told her daughter, I can't afford a doctor, and even so, if I take time off sick I'll not get paid and might not have a job to go back to
who will feed us, Gracie, who will feed us?
I'll feed you, Ma, I'll feed you

Daisy
was diagnosed with tuberculosis after the girls at work went in a group to complain to the manager that she was sick and was going to infect them
a doctor arrived to inspect her and she was taken to be quarantined in the sanatorium
with immediate effect

*

Mary took Grace under her wing until Daisy (hopefully, miraculously) recovered

only she drowned on the liquid and tissue
sloshing about in her lungs while they ate themselves
from the inside out

Mary, who'd been raised in the Northern Association's Home for Girls in the countryside

asked Mrs Langley who still ran the place, to take Grace in, it was perfect timing as one girl was going into employment

she delivered Grace to the front door that winter, gave her an affectionate squeeze

bye-bye, Gracie, they'll look after you here and teach you everything you need to know

Grace watched Mary walk away, black boots split at the sides, ripped dress trailing the mud of the path, brown shawl wrapped against her shoulders, hair like a bird's nest with a hat on it, an orange rose Grace had made specially for her stuck on its side

bye-bye, Gracie, she called out, her voice choked, not looking back, as she opened the gate and disappeared down the lane

the last person Grace saw who knew her Ma.

2

Grace wandered around the home as if in a daze at first, the girls crowded her, touching her hair, stroking her skin, couldn't stop staring at her, asked her why her skin was so brown

my Pa's from Abyssinia, she said proudly, pretending she'd known him don't you ever feel ashamed of where he's from, her Ma had told her, one day we're going to find him, if he's alive, that is, he didn't come back for me so perhaps he died

Grace told the girls Abyssinia was a magical faraway place where the people wore silken gowns and diamond crowns and lived in fairy-tale palaces and had feasts of roast meat and potatoes and cheese soufflé every day

the girls were impressed

but not when she woke up screaming, and matron rushed in to see what terrible thing was happening to her and when nothing was, told her off for making an exhibition of herself

the other girls told her to be quiet, you'll get used to it here, Gracie, we all did, it'll take a while, shut up now we want to sleep

Grace rolled herself up in her blanket, buried herself deep inside it so they couldn't hear how she felt when she thought of Ma

who'd wrapped her tightly in her arms when they slept

I'm never letting you go, Gracie, you're mine

yet one minute she'd been at her side at the factory working together, the next minute men with white coats and masks came to take her away

I'll come back for you, Gracie, I'll come back, she promised as they hauled her off kicking and struggling to free herself

whenever someone banged the shiny black lion's head on the front door, Grace hoped it might be Ma standing there, arms wide, smile wider, as if they'd been playing a game all along

hello Gracie, did you miss me? run and fetch your coat, love, we're going home

*

it took a long time for Grace to stop hoping her Ma might turn up
even longer before she stopped feeling her as a warmth spreading
in her stomach whenever she thought of her
longer still for her features to begin to fade

at night she began to dream of her Pa
who'd come back to rescue her
and take her to paradise

Grace was taught to clean herself and the house, she liked the former because Ma had said it was next to godliness, but not the latter
she was taught to sew her own dresses with buttons, ribbons and
pleats, to add lace to the collar of the white dress she made for church
she was taught to knit woollen stockings, a hat and a scarf to wear
in winter, to polish her black booties with buttons up the side until
they shone, which she wore with pride once she got used to them
because at first they gave her sores, never having worn shoes before
she was taught to cook meat, fish and poultry without poisoning
anyone, and vegetables from the garden, how to bake bread and
cake, under orders to never eat any of it while making it, or she'd get
her knuckles rapped
which happened
a *lot*

she was taught to wash the laundry in a wooden tub filled with
hot, soapy water, to stir the sheets with a big wooden spoon, to use a
washboard for clothes with ingrained stains, to make sure she hung
everything up to dry neatly with wooden pegs on the washing line,
not all higgledy-piggledy and half falling off

she loved going to bed when the sheets had just been changed and inhaling the outside wind and sun and rain on them

she liked drinking water from the taps that came from a well that didn't need to be heated up to be made safe

and the toilets were disinfected every single day

without fail

she was taught to tend the kitchen gardens, to grow cucumbers and lettuce, tomatoes, celery, carrots, parsnips and cabbage, to also not eat anything while doing it, which she disobeyed when no one was looking, especially when it came to the strawberry patches, blackberry brambles, plum trees

eating as much as she could then regretting it because purple lips and red stains down her smock also got her knuckles rapped

Grace was taught mental arithmetic, to read and write in the wooden classroom with the wooden benches and desks, to practise the beautiful patterns of letters that gave meaning to words

she was made to stay behind until she caught up with the others

she learnt to balance books on her head in deportment classes without any of them dropping, she was tall, imagined she was from Abyssinia and walking on air

you're possessed of a natural elegance, one of the teachers, Miss Delaunay, complimented her, then promptly told the other girls they walked like pregnant heifers

which made Grace feel very special

they went to church every Sunday unless the snow was too deep or the ice too dangerous or the rain too torrential they walked in a crocodile in their Sunday dresses, down the country lanes, holding hands, singing hymns

she collected flowers when they were allowed to play in the meadow, she pressed them in between the pages of her Bible and wrote poems about each one, 'Ode to a Rose', 'Ode to a Daffodil', 'Ode to a Hydrangea'

she took up embroidery as a hobby, and got quite good at it

the girls in the junior dorm became her friends, sometimes they stayed up talking past their bedtime, enjoying themselves too loudly, forgetting the rules of the home

Sally had the most musical voice, Bertha made up the scariest stories, Adaline was going to be an actress and liked to recite *The Rubaiyat of Omar Khayyám* which she'd found in the library and was memorizing

'Earth could not answer: nor the seas that mourn/In flowing purple, of their Lord forlorn; Nor rolling Heaven, with all his Signs reveal'd/And hidden by the sleeve of Night and Morn'

she'd orate dramatically for so long the others got bored and told her to shut up now, Adaline

Grace did the best impression of Mrs Langley, impersonating her stiff, hoity-toity posture, sticking her bottom out and going bandy-legged as she cavorted up and down the pathways between the bunk beds in her cream calico nightdress, adopting an exaggerated 'high-falutin' accent, delivering a silly speech made up of overly long, nonsensical words that nobody could understand, delighted at how popular she'd become, making the girls grip their aching stomachs in hysterics, begging her to stop it because they couldn't take it any more

at the very moment Mrs Langley flung open the door, shone her lamp in, caught Grace 'acting the clown as if in a harlequinade' it was lights-out ages ago, she scolded, accused Grace of corrupting the others, demanded to see her first thing in her office

you have too much personality, Mrs Langley said from behind the desk in her office, staring at Grace from behind halfpenny-round spectacles, hair pinned back, sat erect in mourning black for the husband everybody knew had died a long time ago at something called the Siege of Mafeking

too much personality is unseemly in a girl

Grace sat upright on the other side of the desk, legs dangling from it, hands placed correctly on her lap, feeling very scared, having felt safe in the home until now, she wasn't the only one being naughty, but she was the only one who was caught

everyone knew very naughty girls were sometimes 'let go'

well may you cry, Grace, and let this be a lesson to you, you are not like the other girls here, you have to be on your best behaviour at all times because life will be hard enough for you as it is, you will suffer much rejection by people less enlightened than we ladies who generously run this establishment

we believe in women's suffrage and want to give you disadvantaged girls the chance of at least an elementary education

I myself have never been one of those militant protesters, Mrs Langley continued, speaking as if to herself now, waving her hands dismissively in the air, because it only results in public opprobrium and governmental condemnation for the individuals concerned, and even imprisonment

I believe in achieving our goals for the vote through reasoned argument, do you understand?

Grace nodded, what was Mrs Langley talking about?

I am also a pragmatist, Grace, therefore please listen to me carefully, it is incumbent upon me to tell you, for your own good, that you must henceforth tone down your natural exuberance and desist from your larking-about laissez-faire attitude because it is unbecoming, we pride ourselves on maintaining decorum and emotional equilibrium in this establishment and expect our girls to carry themselves with poise and self-restraint, we do not tolerate the outlandish showing-off I witnessed first-hand last night

do you want me to send you packing on to the streets without protection? you'll likely end up in the disease-raddled environs of South Shields where girls such as yourself end up as 'ladies of the night' working for the Mohammedans, is that what you wish for yourself, Grace?

Grace decided that she was going to put a stop to her personality once and for all, she was going to have decorous emotions and be restrained

nor can we vouch for your domestic skills, modesty, diligence, trustworthiness and cleanliness in written references to future employers, and believe you me, Grace, without our endorsement you will never secure suitable employment

in respectable service

as a maid

at that, Grace tried hard to stop her tears turning into unladylike sobs

she'd wanted to be a shop assistant in Gillingham & Sons department store in Berwick-upon-Tweed where they were taken by Mrs Langley to see the Christmas decorations every year

the best girls from the home were employed there

she'd dreamed of wearing smart clothes, talking politely to customers as they made their purchases, people who'd leave the store complimenting the manager on what a charming girl Grace was, requesting to be served by her in future

it was not to be
at thirteen Mrs Langley found employment for Grace as a maid for the new Baron Hindmarsh, who'd returned to his ancestral castle a number of miles out of Berwick upon the demise of his father
after many years running the family's tea plantation in Upper Assam
returned with a retinue of Indian servants, including his Indian mistress and their two sons, who were housed in a cottage in the grounds
had no problem taking on a half-caste maid.

3

Grace
is shopping in Gillingham & Sons for material for a summer dress
it's the last shop on earth she wants to give any of her hard-earned money to, except it's the only one in town that's got what she wants
she'd written to the store manager a few years earlier requesting an interview for a position on the sales floor, determined to prove Mrs Langley wrong now that she was fully grown up and had several years' experience in service behind her

however, as soon as she presented herself to the manager, dressed in her smartest outfit, he said outright that she'd put his customers off
he didn't even give her a chance to open her flaming mouth
was quite sure she'd understand, he said
closing the door firmly behind her

for many weeks afterwards she dreamed of sneaking into the store one night and burning it to the ground

with the manager inside it, crying out for her to save him

Mabel and Beatrice from the home are working in Hosiery this Saturday, she's not seen them in ages, has a chat while their supervisor fawns over a very wealthy-looking customer, tells them she wishes she was working there

they tell Grace that standing all day without a break makes their legs and feet so swollen they can barely walk afterwards

that their room, clothes and food are all deducted from their wages leaving them with little money to spend and enjoy themselves

Grace doesn't buy it, she'd give anything to work in a swish department store where she can look sophisticated, meet interesting people, including future husbands (such as the ones they're courting), get to live in rooms at the top of the shop in the middle of town, enjoy the social activities on offer such as tea dances, and the playhouse, and the winter and summer funfair

you try working as a maid miles from anywhere, she says, giving it to them good and proper

you try getting up before the cock crows to shovel out the grates and having to be on call until they all turn in

in between it's non-stop scrubbing, scraping, shining, ironing, folding, fetching and carrying, because you're a nobody skivvy who has to wear a horrid uniform

even though I was as good as anyone in my last year at the home for reading, writing and arithmetic

Mabel and Beatrice really get on her nerves

she walks off, leaving them to it

*

at least she's found the right material for her dress – plum-coloured and soft in its brown paper package tied with string

it's so precious she holds it close to her chest in case it *dies* or something

she can't wait to get it home, will use the pattern all the maids are sharing for a dress that comes just below the knee rather than just above the ankle, considered very risqué, as she overheard Baron Hindmarsh's daughter Lady Esmée tell her weekend guests when she made her entrance at the top of the stairs for one of her parties

Grace peeped out from behind the secret door that connects the servants' passageway to the house proper as Lady Esmée made a show of herself to all her rich friends

the ladies in backless dresses that shimmied and sparkled, the gentlemen in elegant dinner jackets with satin collars, with their cigarillos in gold holders and mint julep cocktails

who watched admiringly as she walked slowly down the stairs showing off her slender legs and exquisite ankles

it's all the rage in London, my darlings, all the rage

Grace will never look like that; at least she'll soon have a new dress to wear when the occasion calls, not that it does very often

she's not allowed to get dolled up for church, but she is for the Hindmarshes' Christmas staff party

until she has to put her uniform back on along with the other maids to clear up the mess everybody's made

she's about to cross the road outside Gillingham & Sons when a swarm of men on bicycles swoop past so close they almost knock her over, workers cycling home from a factory for lunch, she suspects

next a packed omnibus lurches dangerously close just as she's about to step on to the road again

she's used to the busy town, still has to be careful every time she comes into it, seeing as the rest of her time is spent in the middle of the countryside away from busy roads with only the occasional car to be found on the country lanes, usually belonging to a Hindmarsh or guest

she finds she's not alone, a chap has sidled up to her

you must be the Lady of the Nile, aye, that's what you are, he says; she turns sharply, looking fierce, ready to tear down his impudence for calling her a lady of the night

reading her mind he says, Queen Cleopatra, you know, the Lady of the *Nile*

which is quite different altogether

Grace stops herself lashing him with her tongue or whacking him with her package

which she's done before now

he's got the brightest ginger hair which he's tried to comb flat, it's still sprung up all over the place; a ruddy, friendly face and honest blue eyes staring at her in admiration, he's not leering at her the way many men do on the streets

she looks at his tweed jacket, smart enough trousers, grubby boots, he's shorter than her, most men are

Joseph Rydendale, he says, and insists on helping her across the road, he's just had a profitable morning's business at the Friday cattle market and deposited a wad of crisp white notes in Barclays Bank

she suspects he's trying to impress her, which is working (when did a man ever try to actually *impress* her?)

he seems to be a man of substance, too, who'd normally not pay her any attention, as opposed to the scoundrels and wasters who do

Grace is right fed up of men who fancy their chances when she's alone with them, calling her a temptress, a tease, a seductress when she resolutely is not

it can happen anywhere, even at the castle, in the servants' back corridors or when she's working alone in empty rooms, one guest snuck into her bedroom one night, prompting her to get Ronnie the estate's blacksmith to put a bolt on her door the next day

she's managed to escape all advances without being ruined so far, despises those men who take ladies without their permission

those men who make children without marrying the mothers, and disappear to faraway fairytale places where they eat cheese soufflé every day

she's long ago resigned herself to eternal spinsterhood, to a future without the joys of marriage and motherhood

nobody wants a mongrel, which she's been called on the street before now, she lets the perpetrators have it back with, you're a mongrel yourself!

only she wasn't reckoning on meeting a Mr Joseph Rydendale, was she?

who, once they'd been chatting a while, asked her to walk out with him Sunday after next, and thereafter travelled to visit her every Sunday afternoon, then had to race home to milk his cows

can't milk themselves, Gracie, and I don't trust my farmhands

Joseph had returned from the Great War with his body and mind intact, unlike many of his comrades who'd survived but suffered amputations or still heard bombs exploding in their heads even though it was peacetime

comrades who slowly went mad with it

he'd returned to the family farm, Greenfields, to find both it and his father in decline, disease was decimating the emaciated livestock and crops, the equipment was rusty and broken down, farmhands were being paid every Friday evening and were nowhere to be found the rest of the time

his father, Joseph Senior, widowed many years earlier, had taken to wandering the upper fields at night in his long johns shouting for his wife to come and help with the lambing, Cathy, come and help with the lambing

Joseph put the farm to rights after years away, which took up all of his time and willpower, now he was ready for a wife for company and to carry on the family line

he'd fought in the Egyptian desert and in Gallipoli, had known Ottoman beauties of the Orient (she daren't ask him how)

when he came home from the war, none of the local girls appealed to him, until he saw her on the streets of Berwick

Grace could see that Joseph was a well-meaning fellow, she began to like him very much, spent the whole week looking forward to Sunday and the few hours they spent together, walking around the permitted areas of the estate in summer, sometimes wearing her best dress, just for him, lying in the grass in the sunshine, or sitting in the servants' kitchen in winter, where he joined everyone for Sunday lunch

Mrs Wycombe, the cook, allowed it, she'd taken to Grace as soon as she arrived and made sure she was treated well by the other staff

or you'll have me to answer to, she warned them

Grace couldn't believe her luck when Joseph asked for her hand in marriage, that he should behave as if she were a prize and not the booby prize they wed three respectful months after his father died

he brought her home to Greenfields for the first time

the old boy would never have approved, sane or insane, was stuck in the Victorian era and still listened to music hall songs on the phonograph

whereas I play jazz on a gramophone

when he brought her to the farm, he took her there via the only route through the bustling village in his horse and cart on a Saturday morning

past the shops lining the main street, past people out shopping who stopped and stared at this strange creature

most had never seen a Negro before, certainly not one capable of stealing one of the most eligible men in the district, as she was made to feel once she began taking the horse and cart into the village on her own

their Joseph Rydendale, the local farmer and honourable ex-soldier who most mothers of eligible daughters had hoped to have as their son-in-law

when they heard her speak, they were surprised she sounded just like them, a local-enough lass, and warmed to her

not the grocer, who threw her change on to the counter with such force it scattered and she had to crawl around on the ground to pick it up

next time she bought something from him, she threw the exact coins on the counter in the same way, and walked out with her Abyssinian nose in the air

her Ma would be proud.

Greenfields farmhouse was long, narrow, thatched and fusty

Grace was used to the Hindmarsh residence kept pristine by a legion of servants

she didn't like being inside the gloomy interior of her new home that smelled of old things that should have been thrown out a long time ago

surfaces felt sticky to the touch, the floor was covered in grit from the farm, nothing in the kitchen was clean enough to use

Joseph

had employed a very young girl as a maid, Agnes, ahead of her arrival, which amused Grace, seeing as she was one herself a few days previous

you don't need to work any more, Gracie, he told her, you're going to read books and do your embroidery, Agnes will take care of the house, me and the farmhands will sort out the rest

don't forget you're Queen Cleopatra, the Lady of the Nile

if you say so, she said, amused, saw no evidence of Agnes's house-work, and complained to Joseph who didn't seem to care, admitted he didn't notice dirt or messiness

I'd never have guessed, Grace replied, which he took literally, Joseph being a plain-speaking person without guile

she played at being the Lady of the Manor in the Long Room, started to embroider a tapestry of the exterior of the house as it was in 1806, newly built by Joseph's ancestor Linnaeus Rydendale

based on a painting of it in the hallway

it was going to be a gift for her *husband*

she tinkled the service bell whenever she wanted something from Agnes, a slothful child with no charm or wit, who slouched in, finger-nails dirty, pinafore un-ironed, hair unruly beneath her white cap, barely looking at her *mistress*

Grace reprimanded Agnes for her appearance, sent her back to the kitchen to scrub her nails and tidy her hair

ordered a pot of tea, make it strong and hot, but it turned up tepid and weak

Grace let her have it, I require you to perform your duties to the highest standards, she said imperiously, now bring me a pot of tea according to my precise specifications

Grace adopted the tone and vocabulary of any number of family members and guests at the Hindmarshes'

from the look the girl gave her when she picked up the teapot, Grace worried she might pour it over her new mistress

this was quite unlike her grovelling around Joseph

yes, Mr Rydendale, no, Mr Rydendale, let me lick your feet, Mr Rydendale, ridiculously curtsying when he came into the room

it became very clear to Grace that this slovenly scrap of a girl, of low intelligence, hygiene and ability, was never going to take orders from

a half-caste, a negress, Queen of the flaming Nile or not

Grace told Joseph to let Agnes go, she'd endured enough of her insolence and incompetence

she'd do the housework herself and might actually enjoy it as it was for herself, which she did, the pride she felt when she'd properly scraped all the blackened grease from the cooker the pride she felt when she'd been on her hands and knees and cleaned the flagstones on the ground floor until they shone like black ice, and polished the wooden floors upstairs so the daylight bounced off them

likewise with the numerous windows that were so filthy the yard and barns out front, and the fields sloping downwards out back, were invisible behind a slimy film of grime

she set to work with soap, water and vinegar, leaving the glass so clean it was invisible

she called Joseph in to look at the results of her endeavours and even he, who claimed not to be able to see dirt, praised her on how refreshed the house looked

not quite refreshed, Joseph, I suggest we refurbish the place in preparation for our children, most of the furniture will fall apart as soon as a child jumps on it, and a spot of paint won't go amiss, let's call in a handyman from the village to brighten the place up

when he started to protest, she said, you know an order when you hear it, Private Rydendale

Joseph loved it when she cheeked him

old was replaced with new, a china cabinet, oak dresser and chiffonier, art deco rugs, she went shopping in Berwick with him, smartened him up with new suits and shoes, bought yards of material for her own clothes, even popped into Gillingham & Sons to show him off to Mabel and Beatrice, boasted about the large farm of which she was now the mistress

they played Armstrong, Gershwin, Fats Waller and Jelly Roll Morton records on the new gramophone player and danced to them

on hot summer nights they opened the windows and took the party outside, watched only by the dogs, the village was two miles

down the hill, the pair of them moved their heads and legs and hands
to the energetic rhythms of the new American music

which she grew to love

or they'd sit reading and talking on the Davenport sofa, another
prized acquisition, log fire roaring, Grace's head resting on Joseph's
lap while he unpinned her hair so that its spiralled curls sprang out
from their containment

the curls he loved twirling around in his large farmer's hands

she couldn't believe how much he loved her thick, coarse hair

she'd been embarrassed by it

the most important purchase for Grace was a packed cotton mattress for the four-poster bed in the master bedroom, replacing the
decrepit, lumpy one steeped in all manner of excretions

it had been impossible to get a good night's sleep on it, especially
once he told her it was his parents' bed and their parents' before them

it had been hard for her to sleep on so much history

she wanted to clear out everything, including the old cupboard in
the library crammed with ancient ledgers; Joseph said no, they were
important deeds and records, he'd sort it out one day, and he put a
lock on it

he bought the roll-top desk and sat at it to do the accounts once a
week, pleased when in-goings topped out-goings, determined to keep
the farm in profit, with an eye on expanding into neighbouring fields

nights

they made love with the gas lamp dimmed

she was his expedition into Africa, he said, he was Dr Livingstone
sailing downriver in Africa to discover her at the source of the Nile

393

Abyssinia, she corrected him
whatever you say, Gracie

after he brought her to, she cried
from someplace inside herself she didn't understand
he wanted at least ten strong sons who'd work on the farm, the
eldest inheriting it
Grace would have settled for five, not sure she wanted to spend so
many years bloated by pregnancy
three boys for Joseph, two girls for her

the first two to announce themselves were washed out in clots of
blood
then there was a boy who started cooling down a few hours after
the midwife put him in her arms
until he slowly became marbled

unable to speak of it
a chasm grew in the marital bed
they slept back to back

Grace was unable to do little more than wash herself, to eat little
more than the bread and soup Joseph fed her as if she were a sickly
child
eat up, Gracie, eat up

then came Lily
who arrived perfectly healthy and was enchanting
she reached the age of one month, then two, then three
everyone said she was the bonniest of babies when Grace showed

her off in the bonnets, gowns, cardigans and knitted booties the ladies of the village made for her, who traipsed up the hill or rode up in carts to share her joy after the terrible bereavement

any lingering resentments or suspicions of the dark stranger had long ago dissolved

she was Grace now, their Grace, Joseph's wife

Lily was theirs too

four months, five months, six

Lily with the mysterious, bottomless eyes, what are you thinking, Lily? Grace wondered as they stared each other out, hypnotized

she's going to be a real Ethiopian beauty

Abyssinian, Joseph, Grace countered

they call it Ethiopia these days, Grace

seven months, eight months, nine months

her nourishing milk filled out her child, after feeding, Lily slept across her chest, light and warm, sometimes she whistled when she exhaled, face squashed to one side, lips tiny and puckered

Grace's own Ma came vividly back to her at this time, the remembered feeling of being deeply, utterly loved

of being the most important person in her mother's life

of being utterly safe

ten months, eleven, twelve months and one year

one year and two months and four days

Grace woke up early as usual, keen to begin another day with her daughter, delighted that

Lily had only needed feeding once in the night, they'd been told by the midwife this meant they could start to look forward to more uninterrupted sleeps

she got up and went to Lily's cot by the side of the bed

she reached out her arms to pick her little darling up, but Lily felt stiff, was cold, did not move, not when Grace stroked her cheek, or put her palm against her forehead

held her hands

cupped her toes

rocked her.

5

Joseph gave Grace no time, he wouldn't stop trying for another, there had to be an heir, he said, it was his duty to pass the farm on to the next generation

it had been in his family for nearly one hundred and twenty years at this point

it was only then that she realized how deeply he was attached to the property, perhaps even more than to her, he saw himself as the caretaker of it, his life would be a failure if he didn't have a child to hand it over to

he had to honour his ancestors

Joseph stormed around the house, knocked things over, bellowed at the dogs, swore at the farmhands, drank too much ale in the evenings

when they were in sexual communion, he entered her like a machine, not with the caresses of before

his only ambition was to ruthlessly pollinate her

396

she endured his merciless thrusting, looked up at the lampshade hanging from the ceiling, how thrilled they'd been when electricity was installed in the house

it was her duty to provide strong heirs for him, for the land, for his legacy, she understood that, and so far she'd failed

would he cast her out for dereliction of duty? to once more become a maid-of-all-work? replaced by another wife who could deliver on her obligations?

she endured him as the mattress bounced on the wooden frame of the bed that creaked on the wooden floor underneath the rug

they sat apart from each other in the Long Room in the evenings, the sound of the grandfather clock ticked

Joseph might read a farming journal or the *National Geographic* he ordered monthly

(how her husband loved an excuse to look at exposed native bosoms!)

she read *Woman's Weekly* or novels by Dickens, Austen, the Brontës, or any other she found in the study to preoccupy her

to take her away from this, from him, from herself

from a body that gave birth to death

when he went upstairs to bed, she lingered downstairs, as soon as she walked into the bedroom he'd wake up and it would start all over again

Grace gave birth to another one

Joseph named her Harriet when she refused to, after his grandmother, he said, who'd lived to a great age, never had a day's illness and died in her sleep

this one will survive, Gracie, I can feel it, she's a fighter, it doesn't matter that she's a girl she didn't care about the demon who'd almost killed her over three days of labour, who then angrily shouldered her way out of her battered body into the midwife's hands

who brandished her fists, screwed up her gummy face and bawled the house down with powerful lungs when she was slapped

Grace required morphine and stitching, too weak at first, and later, too unwilling to cradle the latest in a long line of doomed children

she refused to breastfeed it

Joseph refused to talk to her

Lily had been such a delicate, placid child, whereas Harriet's furious, taunting presence filled the house without respite

it was a demon screaming throughout the night, determined to wreck her mother's life from her cot in the room next to their bedroom where the wet nurse was camped

later, Flossie moved in, a nanny from Berwick

Grace spent months barely able to speak or haul herself out of bed, barely able to wash or brush her teeth, her hair tangled, skin paled without daylight upon it, she slopped about in nightwear, looked away when the demon was brought to her, felt physically sick whenever she thought of it

she dreamed of slicing her arteries to get rid of the pain, the same way she'd seen Joseph do to farm animals

she studied the kitchen knives to decide which one would do the job most effectively, quickly

she held each one up to the light in the middle of one night, was caught by Joseph who grabbed the knife

don't you dare, Grace Rydendale, don't you dare

*

she thought of walking out of the house, down the fields at the back and entering the lake until the water closed over her head

Joseph threatened her with the asylum, they'll chain you naked to a wall where you'll sit in your own toilet for the rest of your life

she didn't care, she was already in hell, she took to sleeping in another bedroom, that part of our lives is over, she told him

don't worry, he replied bitterly, I was only doing my duty, and you are now failing in yours

Grace remembered how he used to look at her with a love so powerful she could only return it, now he refused, just as she refused to touch the thing she'd given birth to

when Joseph thrust it under her nose, she pushed past him

don't you dare walk away from your daughter, you're a wicked woman, Grace Rydendale

the demon was sent to taunt her with the hope of motherhood, of fulfilling her role on this earth, to have something that was fully hers, only to take it away again

Grace remembered the suffering of when she was a little girl left alone in the world

she missed her ma who'd know what to do, who'd hold her and rock her and say, you can do this, Gracie, you can get through this, we'll get through this together

one year came and went	Harriet grew strong and sturdy
two years came and went	Harriet began to crawl/walk/ climb
thirty months came and went	Harriet was talking non-stop

*

Grace woke up one morning for the first time since the child was born and didn't feel full of dread, the clouds outside were a lovely light grey against a radiant blue sky

she'd not looked at sky for a very long time, or anything else, she'd only felt the heaviness inside her weighing her down

she hadn't seen Joseph either, not properly, the man who made her his Queen of the Nile, he'd be outside milking the cows

she arose and bathed, tried to comb out the tangles in her hair, had to unpick it with her fingers first

she dressed herself in proper clothes instead of keeping on her nightclothes

Grace walked into the kitchen

Harriet was sat there eating a boiled egg with bread soldiers for breakfast, prepared by Flossie who'd taken her to choose her own egg from the chickens earlier, their morning ritual

Grace usually waited until they'd left the room to have her own breakfast, spent the entire time avoiding the child, was expert at it, alert to wherever the child was in the house or outside it, and made sure their paths crossed as little as possible

ignored Flossie's disapproving glares when she did

Harriet and Flossie were silenced by her presence, Harriet looked up at her as if she was a new person

she imagined she was – with her hair combed and piled on top of her head instead of the wild tangled mess her daughter was used to, and she wore a white dress with yellow flowers on it instead of her washed-out dressing gown

Grace looked at Harriet as if for the first time, she was so plump and healthy with smooth glowing cheeks

her hair was in a single plait down her back, her eyes were almost golden, perhaps a little green, they were sparkling, curious, smiling at her

as if to say, hello my Ma, do you like me now?

Flossie, grey hair, rounded, stooped, wore a floor-length old-fashioned skirt from another century, she was a mother and grand-mother of many, made encouraging noises as she listened to Harriet's nonsensical chatter

which picked up again once the child became accustomed to Grace

she dipped the soldiers into the runny, yellow yolk and tried to eat without letting it spill down her chin

when she did, Flossie wiped it off with a cloth

they looked so comfortable together

so cosy, so close

too close

Grace

made herself a cup of tea, sat back down, this time closer to Harriet, carry on, she said when Harriet paused to stare at her again

I'd like to bake Harriet a birthday cake, Flossie, and you're to call her Hattie now, not Harriet, I've decided that Hattie suits her better

Flossie forced a nod, not quite hostile

Grace beckoned Hattie over, come and sit on your ma's lap, love, Hattie looked to Flossie for help, which hurt

go and sit with your mother, Flossie urged Hattie, mumbling, it's about time, loud enough for Grace to hear

Grace later took Hattie out to sit on the bench in the yard in the sunshine, she nestled her on her lap, read her stories from *The Fairy Tale Book* by the time she'd finished, Hattie was curled into her, asleep

Grace looked up and saw Flossie had fetched Joseph who was stood there across the yard by the gate that led to the front fields

sleeves rolled up, trousers tucked into mud-encrusted boots, leaning on a spade

watching

as if he was in the Egyptian desert again

looking at a mirage.

6

Everything changed, Ma, once me and my Hattie found each other, it was like I came out of the darkness and into the light and could love her as I should

I wish you'd seen me spoil her, Ma, let her get her own way with everything because I couldn't say no to anything she wanted, until Joseph stepped in and said I was ruining her

I wish you'd seen how Joseph and Hattie adored each other, how he made no concessions for her being a girl, how she followed him around copying everything he did

I wish you'd seen Hattie grow strong, tough and tall, Ma, seen her learn to plough, sow, thresh, drive bales of hay on the tractor from the fields to the barns

I wish you were around to be her grandma, to tell her what it was like for you growing up, and stories about me from when I was too young to remember

I wish you'd not died so young, Ma, seen how well I was looked after in the home, how I learned to walk in shoes, had clean water and fresh food and learned many things

I wish you'd seen me running in the meadows outside the home, Ma, just as you'd imagined, and pressing flowers in my flower book and writing little poems about them

I wish you'd learnt to read and write, Ma, gone to school as you really wanted to, you'd have liked reading books, Ma, especially all the famous novels by Mr Charles Dickens

I wish you'd seen how I learnt how to act with poise and ladylike decorum, Ma, I wasn't a pushover, just as you weren't, I could stand up for myself when I had to

I wish you saw how much I hated being a servant, Ma, how I resented every minute of it, until I had my own home and then thoroughly enjoyed keeping a clean and pleasant house

I wish you saw how much Joseph loved me again when I came round, how we decided together there'd be no more bairns and he used the withdrawal method instead

I wish you'd met Joseph, Ma, my man, who stood at my side for the rest of my life, he was my shelter and my companion and the best father of our little girl

I wish you'd seen how Hattie had no one ruining her personality, Ma, how she ordered the workers about, how me and Joseph laughed when she tried to boss us around

I wish you'd seen how I learnt to help out on the farm outside
    to fill the ice house with the ice we dug up from the frozen lake in winter
    to harvest fruit from the orchard, make preserves and jams
    to pick and pickle vegetables and store them in the ice house
    to feed the cows, goats, pigs, horses, chickens, turkeys, ducks, peacocks
    to put motherless lambs in boxes in front of the Long Room fire
    to muck out a whole winter's worth of dung from the horse shelter

to smoke meat and salt bacon with pork grease

to harvest fruit from the orchard, and make preserves and jams

to do the hedging, hurdle-making, basket-making, butter and cheese-making

weeding and weaning and beekeeping and brewing cider, beer and ginger ale

I wish you'd met Slim, Ma, the American man who married Hattie, how relieved we were she'd found someone we knew would look after her when we were gone

I wish you'd met Sonny and Ada Mae, Ma, your great-grandchildren, I only knew them for a little while

Joseph was so thankful that finally there was a boy who would one day carry on the family farm.

Chapter Five

The After-party

I

Roland
is the first to triple mwah Amma when she makes her *grande entreé* to the after-party of *The Last Amazon of Dahomey* in the lobby of the theatre
a crescendo of chattering voices and clinking prosecco glasses stilled
followed by rapturous applause
and
bravo! Amma, bravo!

she looks simply spectacular in a figure-hugging wraparound dress that shows off her toned arms, tiny waist and the mama-do hips that have emerged in the past few years
although she's gone and ruined the effect by wearing silver trainers
ever the rebellious teenager at heart – or rather *au coeur*

the play was simply wonderful, *wun-der-ful*, Roland effuses

which is all she ever wants to hear

which is all he ever wants to hear

which is all anyone ever wants to hear

a five-star review has already been uploaded online from one usually savage pit-bull of a critic who's been uncharacteristically gushing: astonishing, moving, controversial, original

rightly so, the production is indeed deserving of the highest praise and a far cry from the agit-prop rants of Amma's early theatre career

although the mother of his only child, writer and director, and dear, dear friend, could have made her name where it mattered a long time ago, if she'd taken his advice and directed a few multi-culti Shakespeares, Greek tragedies and other classics, instead of writing plays about black women which will never have popular appeal, simply because the majority of the majority sees the majority of *Les Négresses* as separate to themselves, an embodiment of Otherness

Roland decided long ago to align himself with *L'Établissement*, which is why he's a winner and a household name

among the educated classes

where it counts

Amma, on the other hand, has waited three decades before being allowed in through the front door

although she hasn't exactly been hammering on the castle walls for the duration

in truth, girlfriend spent much of her early career slinging rocks at it

he slides away, leaving Amma to the radico-lesbos who still follow her around like ageing fangirls, surging forwards to congratulate her

406

he *is* shocked to see one of them in a pair of denim dungarees

surely *La Dungaree* hasn't made a comeback?

just as he's cogitating on the relationship between sexuality and sartoriality, he's collared by 'Chairman Mao Sylvester', with whom he is cordial

at best

they've known each other since Amma introduced them at a party at her palatial King's Cross squat back in the day

when they were both young and beautiful and spent their weekends tripping on poppers and ecstasy and wearing nowt but leather hot pants and cowboy boots while dancing away under glitter balls to the pumping disco beats at Heaven before disappearing into the darker recesses of the Cellar Bar to satisfy their incorrigible cravings

even with each other

although once was enough because Sylvester shouting *Take that, Maggie T!* at the point of ejaculation was *quite* off-putting

Roland was one of the lucky hedonists to survive *El Diablo* which swooped in to kill so many of them

so many deaths ruined any sense of nostalgia, sadly, remembering the past also meant

remembering the

dead

grumpy old Sylvester is a survivor, too

resentfully admits that the play is Amma's best work yet, it's *such* a shame she's colluded with them, *them*, he points an enfuried finger at the Boring Suits, as he calls them, who line the party's perimeter, the representatives of the multinationals who beef up the theatre's finances with sponsorship, who stand apart, smiling awkwardly, desperate to be part of the luvvie fun

Sylvester says they sold their lefty student principles, if they ever had them, as soon as they left university and accepted an overpaid starter-salary in a morally objectionable corporate job offering lucrative career prospects and inflated annual bonuses which soon turned them into filthy-rich Tories with a hatred of the social welfare infrastructures they're actively *not* contributing to through tax avoidance *and* evasion while hypocritically scorning the underclasses as the scourge of society who sponge off the state when *they're* the ones who are the biggest scroungers on society with no sense of community responsibility other than a very self-aggrandizing, tax-deductible form of fashionable charity they like to call philanthropism!

Roland marvels that Sylvester has managed to make a prolonged stab at capitalistic corporate culture and the Tories within a minute of saying hello

it might just be a record

now it's his turn

The Last Amazon of Dahomey is a *tour de force*, he says, although I would never use such a cliché, you understand, when talking about it on Channel 4 News and the BBC's Front Row tomorrow, rubbing it in because Sylvester has never acknowledged the superb success Roland has made of his career

has probably never read a single one of his books and never told him he's seen him on the telly, when people often tell Roland they saw him on the box just the other day

it's wilful avoidance on Sylvester's part

and very undermining

*

the play is indeed ground-breaking, Roland continues, in spite of the fact that Sylvester appears to be more interested in grabbing the free prosecco in elegant flutes being passed around by waiters and knocking them back in one go before coming up for air

Amma, Roland says, could have paid homage to the original Amazons who were the archenemies of the ancient Greeks, according to mythology, and who the Benin, i.e. Dahomeyan Amazons, were compared to by adventurers of the West who travelled to Africa and wrote about their fearless ferocity over a period of one hundred and fifty years

perhaps the play could also have employed even more techno-dramatic devices in its production such as holograms of the original Amazons of Greek myth hovering as peripheralized spectres counterpointing the main drama thereby adding a more classical relevancy to its thesis? and while the myth that the real Amazons cut off their breasts to better fight the Greeks with ye olde bow and arrow cannot be proved, we do know that such women warriors existed in the region, courtesy of recent DNA testing and other forms of bio-archaeological analysis of the nomadic Scythian *kurgans* (burial mounds to the layman), which have revealed the historical presence of warrior horsewomen who lived in small tribes from the Black Sea all the way to Mongolia, although none had amputated breasts

furthermore, according to Herodotus, the Amazons of myth gathered herb intoxicants, threw them on to the camp fire, inhaled the smoke and got high as a kite, so do you see how Amma missed a trick here by not playing around with the source material? nevertheless, as for the wash of images projected on to the stage making it appear to be filled with thousands of dead Benin Amazons stampeding towards the audience brandishing weaponry and uttering war cries

it was terrifyingly realistic and without doubt a *coup de théâtre*

Roland pauses, he's done his research pre-performance so he can pontificate about it post-performance

before he can round off his disquisition, Sylvester lays a hand on his arm and says, I'm not one of your star-struck students, Roland, and stalks off, empty flute leading the way towards the waiters who, probably on instruction from the head waiter, have started to bypass their little spot

Roland is tempted to shout after Sylvester that he should be bloody grateful that he, Professor Roland Quartey, has even bothered to offer up his insights *free of charge* because guess what? who's the one being paid $10,000 to deliver an hour-long lecture in American universities, which is probably more than you earn in two years with your outdated 97% tin-pot theatre company that 1% of the general public has heard of

so you can keep your social conscience, *Comrade*, because he, Roland, has something far more powerful up his sleeve and it's called CULTURAL CAPITAL!!!!

Roland is, however, far too sophisticated to cause such a scene, he looks around, the volume and vivacity in the room is increasing as the prosecco loosens up everyone's inner theatricals

stage right from the kitchen, the canapés make their entrance, held aloft on gilded trays by tasty young men who enter like a buff chorus line

he spots Shirley across the room, still attired à la Women's Institute circa 1984 (dear heart)

Dominique is here too, he hasn't seen her in *ages*, still divinely sexy in a dykey-bikey way, even in her fifties, also being swamped by a group of drooling fangirls (*plus ça change*)

Kenny is prowling around the impossibly handsome and probably Nigerian beefsteak security man at the door who seems to be lapping up the attention

Roland prefers white flesh, Kenny likes black flesh, it's as simple as that

they're quite independent during the week, weekends they visit farmers' markets, catch up with friends, sometimes in the countryside

a few times a year they take long weekend breaks to their favourite cities: Barcelona, Paris, Rome, Amsterdam, Copenhagen, Oslo, Vilnius, Budapest, Ljubljana

summers are spent in the Gambia or Florida

'discretion not deception' is the motto of their twenty-four-year-old union, otherwise they're both free to do their own thing

which they both take advantage of when the urge moves them, so long as they don't bring anyone back to their sanctuary

home

Roland wanders out on to the promenade overlooking the Thames

the night sky is spangled with as many stars as pollution makes visible in this city

the river looks like a pulsating oil slick of viscosity at this late hour

the typical medley of buildings opposite are in silhouette

he simply adores London and for a long time now, in the increasingly rarefied circles of his existence, the city loves him back

as for the scorn currently poured on the so-called 'metropolitan elite', he's worked bloody hard to reach the pinnacle of his profession,

and it's infuriating that the term is now bandied around by a prolifer-
ation of politicians and right-wing demagogues as one of society's
evils, who ridiculously accuse 48% of British voters who voted to
stay in the EU of being just that

while the Brexiteers are preposterously described as ordinary and
hardworking, as if everybody else isn't

Roland was very willing to defend himself in an EU debate on the
BBC with a Brexit campaigner who accused him of being 'a metropolitan elite tosser'

to which Roland riposted that his family didn't last six months in
the great English countryside when they first arrived from the Gambia before they were hounded out of the village by the rabid racists of
the sixties

in other words, he said to his accuser, there's a reason why black
people (Roland usually avoids the descriptor 'black' in public as
much as possible – so crude) ended up in the metropoles, it's because
you didn't want us anywhere near your verdant fields and rosy-
cheeked damsels

nor is he ashamed to be elite, Roland added, why should he, Professor Roland Quartey, the state-educated son of African
working-class immigrants, be denied the right to rise up the ranks?

or are you saying that black people should only work on the assembly line, clean toilets or sweep up the streets?

the audience clapped and cheered

before his speechless interlocutor could think quickly enough to
counter-punch, the Chair called time on the debate

Roland had been given the last word, he should have felt
triumphant

except he was pissed off that he'd had to engage with *race* and was, in the aftermath of a debate that went viral (of course *that* one did), seen as a spokesman for cultural diversity

which he resolutely is *not*

an arm slides gently around his waist from the side, it's Yazz announcing herself in the nicest way possible, which is lovely, because he never knows whether she's going to hug him or berate him

Dad, she says, snuggling up, a bit tipsy, he suspects, in spite of her proclamations of being practically teetotal

hello darling, he replies, kissing her forehead

I was so worried the play was going to be awful and humiliating for Mum, you never know with her, we've been there before, right? she done good, didn't she, Dad?

she did, are we proud of her?

yeh, dead proud

did you tell her this, you know you have to

several times, while staring deep into her eyes so she knew I meant it, she's very needy deep down, although you and I know this success will go to her head and she'll become impossible to handle, Dad, *impossible*

he squeezes her ever closer to him

he loves it when she lets him hug her

feeling her warmth softening into him

Yazz is the reason he got his act together, his life is divided into the Before Yazz and After Yazz eras

before Yazz, he was an unexceptional university lecturer who'd gone to a rough Ipswich comprehensive, spent his teenage years working hard enough at school to escape his home town of Portsmouth and in his downtime drooled over his idols the dinky and adorable Marc Bolan, the surreally space age David Bowie, and the delectably pretty lead singer of Sweet, Brian Connolly

in that order of preference

when he made it to university in London he joined the Gay Society on the very first day and made up for lost time in gay clubs

still managing to graduate with a first class degree

he got his first lectureship after eighteen months' searching, and once there found he simply couldn't sacrifice his hard-won social life in order to devote the thousands of hours it took to sit down alone and write the damned books that would turn him from an anonymous academic into someone who was respected as a public figure

with Yazz en route he took stock, decided he needed to be a greater person for the child he'd consciously decided to bring into the world with his friend Amma, who was perfect for the job of mothering their child in that she was intelligent, creative and fun

he was deeply moved when she accepted him as her sperm donor

after his trip to Le Wank Bank, Amma quickly fell pregnant, by the time Yazz was born he'd begun writing his first book, intending it to be intellectual without being overly academic, popular without being populist, he wrote about what interested him – philosophy, architecture, music, sport, film, politics, the internet, the shaping of societies: past, present, futuristic

his first book made his reputation, by the third, it was sealed

however, unlike Amma, his career has never been predicated on his perceived identities, as expected of black intellectuals (even the term '*black* intellectual' gnaws)

he bemoans the fact that black people in Britain are still defined by their colour in the absence of other workable options

nor can he authentically call himself Gambian when he left when he was two

in any case, neither his blackness nor his gayness are the result of conscious political decisions, the former is genetically determined, the latter psychically and psychologically pre-disposed
  where they will remain, not as intellectual or activist preoccupations
  but rather as footnotes

  the university gig keeps him financially afloat in between book advances, he doesn't mind giving the odd lecture to mature students, won't teach classes any more, and as he's famous and on the telly, they can't make him
  so what if the students are disappointed, he didn't create the system (he just works it baby!), has a rule not to reply to emails unless they come directly from his bosses, whereupon he replies immediately and with great cordiality
  this works very well because everyone else in his department has given up asking him to do anything
  he knows he's loathed by his 'colleagues' who practically snarl at him when he walks down the Corridor of Long Knives
  what does he care?
  he's rarely there

  when Roland started writing the first of his three-part *magnum opus* he'd already decided he wasn't going to be accepted by *L'Établissement*, he was going to *become* it
  his bredren and sistren could damned well speak up for themselves
  why should he carry the burden of representation when it will only hold him back?
  white people are only required to represent themselves, not an entire race

*

Yazz stirs herself from their reassuring hug, he loves her more than anyone, even more than Kenny

the moment she was put into his arms after birth he was smitten, it's been the same ever since, he can't control his love for her, even though she can be such a handful at times, spiteful, when she feels like it

he worries about her going forth into a world that will punish her if she doesn't play the game to win by the rules

she needs to become proficient in the discourse of diplomacy, but she's so contrary

takes after her mother in that regard

this part of London is so special at night, isn't it, Dad? she says rather dreamily, isn't St Paul's so, like, majestic?

absolutely, it *is* majestic, darling, I think of it as the architectural heartbeat of the capital, dominating the skyline for hundreds of years until the city's skyscrapers challenged its powerful symbol of religious supremacy with economic prosperity

although, and this is a little-known fact, Le Skyscraper was actually indebted to various high-rise precedents such as the eleventh-century high-rises of Egypt, the Renaissance tower houses of Florence and Bologna, the five-hundred-year-old mud-brick constructions of Shibam in Yemen

you see, Yazz, the concept wasn't new at all, it was the ancient municipal solution applied to the mid-century population expansion that resulted in dense urbanization

before he's finished, Yazz is pulling away, just when they're getting into a great conversation

she's heading towards a tattooed man (or is it a woman?) standing alone, smoking, looking out at the river good to see you, Dad, she says distractedly over her shoulder, I've just seen someone I know

I'll be over to visit you and Kenny soon, promise

Yazz has no idea of the hollow he feels where she's been so lovingly nestled at his side, the way she did as a small girl who was devoted to him, never wanted to let go, even when she had to go to bed or go home, holding on to him, forcing him to prise her bony little arms off him

a small child who loved him just as he was

unconditionally

most people think he's remarkable so why doesn't she, his beloved only child?

all she has to say, and really, just *once* shouldn't be *too* difficult

you done good, Dad.

2

Carole stands quietly at the noisy after-party in a far corner of the room along with the other bankers and funders who, like her, look out of place in their smart business attire when the room is full of weirdly dressed arty types slobbering all over each other

this isn't her milieu at all so she declined Freddy's invitation to 'do the rounds and get to know the lesbian thespians'

he's working his way through the crowd, tie removed, shirt loosened, hair flopping about, charming everyone he meets from what she can tell, leaving them chuckling at his repartee

before he waltzes off to the next person who's going to be impressed with him

instead of upper-class reserve, Freddy exudes upper-class confidence, along with a bashful boyishness that endears him to people of all backgrounds

she wishes she had his effortless social skills

Carole had been intrigued by the play, set in Benin, although as she knew little about Nigeria, her parents' homeland, and had never been, she knew even less about its neighbour

it wasn't her fault, any close relatives were dead, according to her mother, having lost both her parents young, it made it difficult for her to return

her mother was never going to be one of those West African matrons one sees at airports who arrive with a trolley-full of excess baggage and get into arguments at check-in complaining the scales are wrong when clearly the scales are right

Carole is curious to visit Nigeria, hasn't been sent there for work yet, her desire to act on it isn't a priority at the moment, she'll take her mother back one day, maybe with Kofi for support, Freddy too

Carole loves Kofi, he's perfect for her mother

it was so odd seeing a stage full of black women tonight, all of them as dark or darker than her, a first, although rather than feel validated, she felt slightly embarrassed

if only the play was about the first black woman prime minister of Britain, or a Nobel prize-winner for science, or a self-made billionaire, someone who represented legitimate success at the highest levels, instead of lesbian warriors strutting around and falling for each other

during the interval at the bar she noticed a few members of the white audience looking at her differently from when they'd all arrived in the lobby earlier, much more friendly, as if she was somehow reflected in the play they were watching and because they approved of the play, they approved of her

there were also more black women in the audience than she'd seen at any other play at the National

at the interval she studied them with their extravagant head-ties, chunky earrings the size of African sculptures, voodoo-type necklaces of beads, bones, leather pouches containing spells (probably), metal bangles as thick as wrist weights, silver rings so large their wingspan spread over several fingers

she kept getting the black sisterhood nod, as if the play somehow connected them together

the thought crossed her mind it might be the black *lesbian* sisterhood nod, she scrutinized them more closely, guessed many of them *could* be lesbians, even the ones wearing head-ties were wearing very practical shoes

was this a predominantly gay gathering she found herself in?

she stopped making eye contact and grabbed hold of Freddy's arm

who took it a bit too far and nuzzled her neck

now, just as she's mentally preparing herself to dive in and drag Freddy away from the party, a woman walks towards her whom she hasn't seen in – how long?

oh crap!

oh double crap!

it's Mrs King

she hasn't seen her since she left school at eighteen

what on earth is *she* doing here?

*

meanwhile

Shirley is astounded to see her protégé on the other side of the room, barely recognizable, it's none other than Carole Williams

without thinking she gravitates towards her leaving Lennox and Lakshmi to continue enthusing about the jazz Lakshmi plays that Lennox likes enough to attend her concerts, which Shirley can't stand

as she makes her way through the crowd, she's astonished to see that Carole is no longer a grubby child but elegant, beautiful, refined, even from a distance

it must have worked out for her

then

Shirley feels a suppressed fury rise like bile up her windpipe

'keep in touch, Carole, I want to know how you get on, you can call on me at any time for support' – the ungrateful child had done nothing of the sort

Carole is wearing a peach-coloured skirt suit and tasteful pearls, both look expensively genuine, her hair is straightened into a ballerina bun, her make-up is perfectly understated, she's much slimmer than she'd been as a teenager and appears taller in high heels

Shirley feels frumpier than usual (which is saying something), even though she's wearing her new polka-dot dress from John Lewis, tied (*very*) loosely at the waist and done up with a nice bow at the neck

Mrs King, Carole exclaims, extending her hand rather regally

you must call me Shirley, Carole, it's Shirley

Carole's accent is barely recognizable, practically aristocratic, her perfume is fragrant, everything about her is

polished

*

it turns out she's a banker in the City, Shirley expects nothing less from this vision of success before her, she's here with her husband, Freddy, over there, his family are shareholders in a company that sponsors the theatre, although between you and me, this play isn't my sort of thing at all, Carole says

nor mine, Shirley replies, feeling she's betraying Amma by not raving about the play along with everyone else in the room

(unless they're all faking it, as luvvies are wont to do)

she herself would have loved to boast in the staff room about her friend's play at the National, but she can hardly do that when it's about lesbians

how are you keeping? Carole asks, you must be retired, I expect

not at all, I'm not *that* old, still teaching, for my sins, at the same insane asylum which has escaped compulsory closure many times, as you might have heard, yes, still there, still bringing on the next generation of prostitutes, drug dealers and crackheads

Shirley throws back her head in a guffaw expecting Carole to join in, who instead looks aghast, prompting Shirley to offer up a cheery, corrective smile to give the impression of *not* being embittered

I'm still mentoring the most able children, she says quickly, brightly, still rescuing those who have potential (and because she can't help herself), those who need my dedicated help over many years to set them on the road to success

there's an awkward pause during which Shirley feels a menopausal flush drown her face in sweat, dammit, not now, she should never have had a drink, a trigger, if she mops her face up with a tissue, she'll smear the make-up across it and look like a madwoman

what on earth must Carole think?

*

Carole tries to hide her discomfort at Mrs King's passive aggressiveness, she wishes Freddy would whisk her away, the woman's sweating like a pig, which is a bit odd, is she nervous?

Mrs King had exerted such power over Carole, it felt abusive

now here she is, a bit older, greyer, fatter, although it's hard to tell because from a child's perspective all adults are old and fat

therein follows a silence so long it becomes excruciatingly embarrassing, both women grimace at each other

Shirley breaks it, well, nice to see you after all this time, Carole

yes, nice to see you, too, Carole replies, and looks into Mrs King's eyes, expecting a devilish glint, instead they're watery, is she upset? she looks sad, hurt, does Mrs King actually have feelings?

it dawns on Carole that she's always thought of Mrs King through a haze of teenage rage, yet the woman was probably only trying her best, she just didn't go about it in the right way

Carole doesn't want to upset the woman, not now, yet she seems to have done just that, she needs to make amends

I know it's rather late in the day, Mrs King, I mean Shirley, I'm not sure I ever thanked you for your help when I was at school, well, better late than never, huh!

the huh wasn't intentional, Carole couldn't help herself

don't be silly, Shirley replies, you've absolutely nothing to thank me for, I did what I could to help you along, never in a million years did I expect or even want to be thanked, it was my pleasure, more than that, it was my duty as a conscientious teacher, I was just doing my job and it makes me happy that it worked out for you, that's thanks enough in my book

Carole sees that the watery eyes have become actual tears, it dawns on her that Mrs King really did help her when nobody else could or would, how could she have not realized this until now?

Mrs King takes a step backwards, embarrassed by her vulnerability, Carole suspects

I must fetch my husband or we'll miss the last train home, school tomorrow, Year 9, the worst, goodbye, Carole, it was lovely to bump into you.

3

Shirley walks back through the gathering lighter on her feet

she can't wait to tell Lennox about her encounter with Carole, even though he dismisses her long-held grievance as a negative waste of energy

life's so much simpler for men, simply because women are so much more complicated than them

Lennox never seems to get uptight about anything

she drags him away from Lakshmi to collect their coats and while the attendant fetches them, looks back at the party

large spaces packed with raised voices remind her of the cacophonous nightmare of hundreds of schoolchildren in the school canteen

the awful squeaking of voices and scraping of metal on crockery resounding and rebounding against the walls and ceiling

her idea of a good night out is still grooving to lovers' rock with Lennox in a corner of a party where everybody is like them and quietly smooching in the dark

rice, peas, curry goat simmering on the stove in the kitchen

she spies Roland walk in from the promenade, his carriage full of self-importance, although it entertains her more than annoys her these days

423

she only really got to know him a little when he fathered her god-daughter, Yazz, before then he, like many of Amma's friends, had no time for her

by the time Yazz started primary school he was becoming famous and she was, for a while, in awe of him, which was silly

she used to dread their encounters because he made her feel inferior as soon as he opened his mouth

this one time she was bundling little Yazz into the child seat of her car while Roland rabbited on about Piaget's stages of child development, about which he knew much less than her

she didn't feel confident enough to show off her knowledge, never did with him

then he got a call to say his mother, who'd returned to the Gambia years earlier, had died

one minute he was standing there pontificating, the next he'd collapsed on to the pavement

Shirley ushered Yazz and Roland back into the house and let him cry his heart out in her arms

thereafter she saw his intellectual showmanship as a performance, deep down he could be as vulnerable as anyone

these days they rub along quite pleasantly together, although not so much she's going to delay leaving the party to go over and say hello

next she spots Lakshmi wandering around anxiously, she must be looking for Carolyn, her latest twenty-something child bride, as Amma jokes

Shirley saw the child bride in a huddle with another much older woman a few moments ago, who seemed quite taken with her

Lakshmi had better watch out

*

424

just as she's thinking of finding Amma to say goodbye, she sees her heading towards the Ladies with Goddess Dominique, giggling conspiratorially

it reminds her of when they ran the theatre company together and they wanted to be with each other more than anyone else, even more than their lovers

until Nzinga came on the scene and whisked Dominique away to a glamorous life in America

although it wasn't that, from Amma's reports, apparently Nzinga took Dominique down a peg or two (that was overdue)

Amma insisted there never was an attraction between her and Dominique, yet Shirley never understood a friendship where you went to the toilet together in your twenties, as they did, let alone in their fifties

Shirley had tried to avoid Dominique tonight, who's far too edgy to be around a boring heterosexual suburban schoolteacher

unfortunately, they ended up standing beside each other at the bar during the interval and Shirley couldn't make a discreet escape

Dominique was the same as ever, still thin, tight white tee-shirt to show off her flat stomach (rubbing it in), biker jacket, knuckle-duster rings, earrings crawling up her ears like loops of silver stitches, black jeans, biker boots, boyish hairstyle, no grey

it would be age-inappropriate attire if Dom didn't look thirty-two

black women never look their age, except for Shirley

typical bad luck

they hadn't seen each other for many a year and true to expectation Dominique grinned mockingly at Shirley as if entertained by Shirley's pathetic little life

hey, how ya doin, Shirl? she asked in her almost-American accent true to form, Shirley had absolutely nothing exciting to tell her, and when she bounced the same question back at Dominique, it was, wow! where do I begin? just as Dominique's attention was diverted by the barman who chose to serve her first

of course he did

a wine glass in each hand, Dominique moved away, great to see ya, Shirl, she said, and disappeared

after serving Goddess Dominique the barman took an order from the person on the other side of Shirley who'd arrived later than her

Shirley said uncharacteristically loudly, *excuse* me, *I* was here first and the entire counter turned to stare at her

she hadn't resented Amma's friendship with Dominique when she came on the scene, because their paths had already forked dramatically

her friendship with Amma is based on historic loyalty and comfortable familiarity rather than shared interests and perspectives, they tend to see films together which Shirley believes should be thrilling entertainment (from what she can tell, billions of people in the world agree with her)

Amma likes *very slow* foreign films with *no* plot and lots of *atmosphere* because 'the best films are about expanding our understanding of what it means to be human, they're a journey into pushing the boundaries of form, an adventure beyond the clichés of commercial cinema, an expression of our deeper consciousness'

you can imagine what Shirley thinks of that

they compromise, Amma went to see *La La Land* with her, not admitting she enjoyed it (Shirley could tell she did), and Shirley sat (slept) through *Moonlight*, which Amma said was one of the best films she'd ever seen

*

426

she watches the two friends disappear into the Ladies – so confident, fun-loving, youthful and flamboyant

she wanted to say goodbye to Amma, they've hardly spoken all evening as she's been swamped by her admirers, Shirley isn't venturing into the toilet to intrude on her gossipy catch-up session with Dominique who'll give her a look that says, what is it now, boring Shirl?

Shirley's already had a quick chat with Yazz who seems to have caught the unseemly afro virus, her hair sticking up in a wiry frizz

back in the seventies people had tidy, symmetrical afros, it wasn't for Shirley even then, her mother put her under the hot iron comb at the age of twelve and she hasn't seen or felt her real hair since

Yazz didn't bother to introduce her godmother to the two friends with her, which was plain bad manners

they looked a bit attitude-y, and Shirley's used to teenagers cowering at the sight of her, not acting as if they're equals

one of them was wearing a very non-religious hijab with sequins on it, the other one was spilling out of a very low-cut top

Yazz is more like Roland than her mother in presenting an overly self-assured image, and it feels as if she only speaks to Shirley out of a sense of duty these days

you're my favourite godmother, Yazz used to tell her, perhaps she says that to all her godparents, all one million of them

she suspects Yazz doesn't find her very interesting

Lennox tells her to stop being silly

her and Lennox slip out of the lobby and on to the promenade where Yazz is leaning against the wall facing the river talking to someone, a man with vulgar tattoos up his arms, it could equally be a woman, hard to tell in this 'anything goes' environment

Shirley can't wait to get back home, to snuggle up on the sofa with Lennox with a cup of hot chocolate

and catch up on the *Bake Off* finale she missed tonight.

4

Amma

is crouched against the wall at the far end of the Ladies corridor at the National, toilet doors lining either side, keeping a lookout

while Dominique expertly cuts several lines of coke on her travel mirror

it feels like the old days when they'd sit and have a wazz in full view of each other while continuing whatever conversation they were stuck into

no matter how long since they've last seen each other, the distance of three thousand miles across America, plus another four thousand across an ocean, dissolves as if it was never a barrier in the first place

they pick up as comfortably as the time before, this is the real meaning of a friendship that lasts a lifetime

Dominique passes the mirror carefully over to Amma, here, ruin the lining of your nose with this

Amma snorts two lines up a nostril, as it hits the spot, she closes her eyes to savour the moment, feeling it infuse her bloodstream with heavenly sensations

remember this used to be the first night ritual for our plays? Dominique says, as she suctions up the rest of the powder

as the drug takes effect, she feels her own surge of euphoria as jet-lag is replaced with effervescent currents how could I forget? Amma replies, recollecting their shared past is often a rhetorical ritual, good of you to resurrect such a fine old theatrical tradition, Dominique, talking of which, you really did like the play and production? I mean you *really* liked it?

Dominique has already said she loved it multiple times, but not enough for Amma, who craves reassurance

it was sick, Amma, *sick*, you threw up all over the grand old knights of the theatre who'll be raging in their graves, my girl

you liked it then?

Dominique

showed up unannounced at the stage door to surprise her, whacked down to the bone, after ten sleepless hours from LA overnight, then an Uber from Heathrow to the National to take her seat just before the lights went down for an unmissable event in the herstory of our friendship

it's so good that you're here, Amma says, leaning back to enjoy the love the drug is giving her

it's good to be here although it's a whistle-stop visit as I'm crossing the ocean again tomorrow, twice in forty-eight hours, just for you, wouldn't do it for anyone else, Ams

it's been a long time since Dominique's been to any of her friend's first nights, the party outside is full of people she hasn't seen in ages, although for a very good reason

she had a brief catch-up with Roland during which he name-dropped recently having had lunch/dinner/drinks/whatever bollocks with two famous politicians, a rock star, and an artist whose work sold for millions

she said she'd never heard of him (she had)

Sylvester soared through the crowd like a homing pigeon when he saw her exit the auditorium at the end of the play, to tell her that he and she were among the few anti-establishment combatants of yesteryear who'd maintained their principles uncorrupted

it wasn't a coincidence that he waved his hand in Amma's direction

Dominique was about to mention her very capitalist festival when she was rescued by someone she'd worked with in the eighties, Linda, a stage manager who used to have urchin looks, and is now built like a Gulag prison guard

along with her entourage who stampeded in and elbowed Sylvester out of the way

Linda now ran her own film and telly props business, and her friends, who'd been diehard fans of Bush Women Theatre, were car mechanics, electricians, builders

she has a lot of time for these women who rejected femininity before it became fashionable

it was great to see them again

not so Shirley, Amma's oldest friend and the dreariest woman on the planet, who looked horrified when they ended up next to each other at the bar, and forced her lips into an alleged smile

she'd once caught Shirley watching Amma kiss a girlfriend at a party, the expression on Shirley's face when she thought she wasn't being observed

the woman is a closet homophobe, although Amma won't have it, says Shirley wouldn't be her friend if she was

Dominique greeted Shirley effusively, said goodbye effusively and said little in between, what she calls her 'hello-goodbye sandwich'

reserved for people she has to be nice to

*

430

Roland, Sylvester, Shirley

she'd once known them well, now when she sees them about once in a blue moon, sees that their worst traits have intensified

Roland is more intensely arrogant, Sylvester more intensely resentful, Shirley more intensely uptight

one of the exceptions is Lakshmi, still a great friend, who regularly pops into LA when she's touring to promote her latest album

the highlight was seeing Yazz who rushed up and proudly introduced her to two of her confident, articulate university friends, one of them wearing a hijab with sequins that screamed 'yeh, Muslim, funky and proud of it!'

the two friends gushed that they'd heard *all about her* from Yazz, *don't worry*, you can *rest easy*, it was all *good stuff*, nothing slanderous *much*

Yazz suggested Dominique pay for her to spend a month in LA next summer without *you know who*, as a way for them to bond because you *are* my Number One godmother who's been absent for most of my childhood, which was quite traumatic growing up with *you know who*

and the Professor of Fucking Everything

I could have done with a bit more support, Goddy Dom

don't worry, I'm not expecting first class tickets, economy will do and

a per diem

Yazz is downright feisty and Dominique loves her for it, of course she's going to pay for her to visit

she delves into her knapsack on the toilet floor, extracts a black and white photograph, passes it over to Amma

remember this? thought I'd bring it to show how far you've come

431

of course, Amma replied, how could I forget? just look at us, the
original riot *grrrrls* or is it *gurls* now? Yazz will know

they were standing on one of this very theatre's exterior balconies,
Dominique wearing a bashed-in trilby, old man's coat, ripped tee-
shirt, jeans, braces

Amma in a bomber jacket, ra-ra skirt, stripy tights, DMs

the pair of them scowling and sticking two fingers up at the theatre's thick black lettering high above them

look how young we were, Dom, it feels like so long ago

that's because it was, a bygone age, here pass the smelling salts, luv,
look at you now, Ams, at the *top* of your game, my girl, you're a power-
house, you're unstoppable, that's what you are, as for the closing
sequence of the play? afro-gynocentricism caused a femquake tonight

Amma feels herself melting against the wall as the flattery seeps
into her

this is just what she needs

everything is perfect

just

perfect.

5

The two women continue their conversation deep into the night
back at Amma's pad

Dominique is pleased that Amma's current squeezes haven't been
invited back, to their obvious chagrin when they had to say goodbye,
looking daggers at her for depriving them of their celebratory roll in
the hay

her friend is now into threesomes, as she admitted earlier
you're a filthy slapper, Ams
I hope so, I do try my best

Yazz and her 'squad', also staying over, have long gone to bed
what's the matter with the youth of today? Dominique called after
them when they left the room, yawning sleepily like five-year-olds
you're the ones who're supposed to be caning it, not us, come back
here you sensible little cows and get trashed
as they clod-hoppered up the wooden stairs, Yazz shouted down
over the banister that *some of us* have to be responsible adults when
there are naughty *children* in the house
not mentioning any names, *mind*

unlike the old days
she and Amma have only polished off two bottles of red and the rest of
the coke, which pleasantly counteracted the inebriating effect of the drink
best of both worlds, drink as much as you like and remain coherent
enough for a good chinwag
Amma is reclining somewhat grandiosely on a lumpy old sofa,
propped up by cushions
like a latter-day Sarah Bernhardt or Lillie Langtry
Dominique sits on the faded geometric shapes of the Habitat rug
on the floor
in lotus position

the house reminds Dominique of the lifestyle she's escaped, the
identical terraced cottages opposite are too close for comfort
the front garden is a three-foot-square yard taken up by black
dustbins and the back garden hardly bigger

the cottagey dimensions are claustrophobic, not helped by dark purple walls, painted against Dominique's explicit advice to Amma to paint them white to create the illusion of spaciousness

smoke-yellowed theatre posters are at least now preserved under glass

the mantelpiece displays a line-up of dusty African sculptures Amma has accumulated rather than inherited

the skirting is scuffed, the floorboards in need of a good varnish, the original hearth is home to a dusty altar candle grossly distorted by fossilized melted wax

Amma describes her house as shabby-chic, as if it's carefully designed to be so, but as one domestic slut trying to kid another, Dominique has suggested she drop the 'chic' bit

she herself has a maid who comes in twice a week to make up for her failings

she herself lives in an airy bungalow with walls of glass that extend the modest space outwards to include the pine trees on the hills below

thereafter the city lights in the distance

The Last Amazon of Dahomey is probably the pinnacle of my career, Dom, Amma says, no longer celebratory, as the night deepens she's going into the maudlin mode Dominique recognizes

I can't imagine it getting any better than this, maybe they'll invite me back to do another play if this one picks up a major award, or maybe not, I still have so much to give, I might still be scrabbling around trying to get jobs, and be in even more demand sitting on panels to discuss diversity in theatre

I've become the High Priestess of Career Longevity in the Chapel of Social Change preaching from the Pulpit of Political Invisibility to the Congregation of the Marginalized and Already Converted that's why it's my duty to help you escape, Amma, look at those black British actors who can't get work here, jump ship and end up Hollywood stars, and look at the life I lead? look at my Women's Arts' Festival? think of the size of the audiences over there, the support networks, the conversations, the high-powered black people operating at every level of society

America will make you expand into its expansiveness, Ams, you'll become louder, bolder, more intellectually and creatively stimulated, you'll reach new heights, for sure, I know it has more than its fair share of social and political ills, even so, compared to Britain, well, what can I say? I jumped ship a long time ago

I have to stay here for now until Yazz is ready to live independently

are we talking about the most cocksure young woman in the universe? Dominique replied, if anyone is capable of looking after herself, it's your daughter

not that I want her to, live independently, that is, not ever, really separation issues?

she's a monster but she's my little monster, and you know, I actually love it here, even if it frustrates the hell out of me, I'm not sure I want to become a foreigner anywhere else

so try it out like a new outfit that may or may not suit, life is about taking risks, not about burying your head in the sand

thanks

not a problem

you make me feel like a parochial Little Englander

that's because you don't know what's best for you, if I have to drag you kicking and screaming to the States, so be it

Amma gets up from the sofa, opens the window, lights up, blows the smoke out into the darkened, silent street

Dominique can never quite believe that her friend still smokes, that anyone over twenty does

I love Britain, too, Ams, although less so every time I return, it's become a living memory for me, Britain feels in the past, even when I'm in its present
    sounds like you've been talking to your therapist about this
    I pay her to sit and listen to me splurge without interruption for an hour every week, I've been seeing the same woman since I left Nzinga, it's wonderful, you should try it
    except unlike you I don't have any disturbing psychological problems, Dom
    that's because you haven't dug deep enough to find them
    right
    for me therapy is a form of consciousness-raising, Dom
    consciousness-raising is such a throwback term, Ams
    haven't you heard that throwback is making a comeback? it's really fashionable to be a feminist these days: blog, demos, crowd-funder campaign, I can't stand it

Amma closes the window, walks back, re-spreads herself languorously over the sofa, convince me why feminism getting a new lease of life *isn't* a good thing, Dominique? isn't it just what the doctor ordered?
    actually it's the commodification of it that bugs me, Amma, once upon a time feminists were so vilified by the media it turned generations of women away from their own liberation because nobody wanted to be denounced as one, now they're in a lovefest with it, have you seen all these glamorous photoshoots of stunning young feministas with their funky clothes and big attitude – until it's no longer on trend

436

feminism needs tectonic plates to shift, not a trendy make-over

Dominique wants her friend to agree with her, it's a no-brainer, but Amma, ever the contrarian, refuses to see the obvious, you're being way too cynical and doom-mongering, Dom

I'm being clairvoyant, any serious political movement that relies on beauty to sell it is doomed

oh come on, the media's obsession with beautiful women is nothing new, look at Gloria, Germaine and Angela in their youth, brilliant women but hardly ugly ducklings, if women are young, beautiful and fuckable, they get the coverage, whether they're musicians or paediatricians

paediatricians, Ams?

it rhymes, Dom, it rhymes

and another thing that bugs me are the trans troublemakers, you should have seen the stick I got when I announced my festival was for women-born-women as opposed to women-born-men, I was accused of being transphobic, which I'm not, I'm absolutely not, I have trans friends, but there is a difference, a man raised as a man might not feel like one but he's been treated as one by the world, so how can he be exactly the same as us?

they started a campaign against my festival which was taken up by someone with a million followers on Twitter called Morgan Malenga who kept up the attack for months, severely damaging my reputation until I backed down

Dom, you're so funny, er, troublemakers? protest? remind you of anyone? we'd have given people hell on Twitter if it was around when we were young, can you imagine? and the trans community is entitled to fight for their rights, you need to be more open-minded on that score or you'll risk becoming irrelevant, I've had to completely readjust my thinking having a 'woke' daughter who likes nothing

437

more than to educate me, in any case, I'm sure plenty of these young feministas *heroine* worship you over there, I bet you're a babe magnet

I'm not a babe to them, Ams, I'm an old-school has-been who's part of the problem, they don't respect me

then you need to talk to them, Dom, and we should celebrate that many more women are reconfiguring feminism and that grassroots activism is spreading like wildfire and millions of women are waking up to the possibility of taking ownership of our world as fully-entitled human beings

how can we argue with that?

Epilogue

Penelope

is hurtling towards her eightieth birthday in two days' time while hurtling north on an intercity train

she's trying to read the culture pages of the *Telegraph* and has come across a five-star review of a play about African Amazons at the National, her favourite London theatre

rave review or not, she'll be giving *that* one a miss

she's travelling first class, wants to enjoy her G&T and salted snacks in spite of her high blood pressure which is probably going through the roof right now with the rabble around her, the class of people who upgrade their tickets on the train for a few quid and then proceed to turn what's supposed to be a more comfortable and sedate environment for people who can afford it into a nightmare journey of howling brats, drunken beer revellers and the worst offenders, people having very public conversations about private matters on their mobile phones

she wants to tell them all to SHUT – THE – HELL – UP!!!

but even though she's an OAP, she wouldn't put it past a lout to attack her, the headlines in tomorrow's papers

Pensioner Hurled Off Moving Train By Drunken Thug

Penelope finds she has a little less tolerance for people these days except for Jeremy, her partner, who rescued her from the spinsterhood she'd endured for far too long

all those years being unhappily independent when all she ever wanted was to be co-dependent with a lovely man who loved her

just as she was

she met Jeremy at the Tai Chi classes she started in her late sixties which the lovely Dr Lavinia Shaw (sadly retired, a *Nigerian . . . man* replaced her) had recommended to improve her sense of balance because she kept falling over

the last time was in Waitrose when she hurt her shoulder so badly it took years to heal in spite of steroid injections

you shouldn't be falling over all the time, Dr Shaw warned her, you'll end up in a wheelchair, Penelope

point taken

Penelope first tried a local Camberwell Tai Chi class where she was surrounded by impossibly thin young women and beautiful young men with strange Samurai-style topknots – who were after the women

she found a much more suitable class in Dulwich proper (as opposed to East Dulwich) where there was an impressive supply of older gentlemen of a certain *ilk*

including the one she began to station herself beside, Jeremy, with silver hair and an aristocratic mountaineer face (*very* Ranulph Fiennes)

a few years older than her and divorced (quickly ascertained, best

440

to), she positioned herself next to him in class as the teacher instructed them to Part the Wild Horse's Mane, Grasp the Bird's Tail and Carry the Tiger over the Mountain

Penelope saw off all competitors, reviving the somewhat rusty skills she'd first employed as a teenager to ensnare Giles

she brought Jeremy pears from her garden, and cuttings for the horticultural gaps in his (also quickly ascertained) – hollyhocks, camellia, wisteria

he seemed to like her so she escalated her ambitions and brought him an extremely rare 78rpm recording of Maria Callas, whom he idolized

spent an age searching for it in West End record shops, and told him she'd come across it buried in her own (hastily assembled should he make it back to hers) classical music collection

she sat through numerous ghastly operas with him at the Royal Opera House, English National Opera, Glyndebourne, Aldeburgh, Garsington

as if quite enchanted by the caterwauling on stage

she joined him at Lords and Oval cricket matches and sat through innumerable and interminable said matches acting *very interested*, helped along by the regulatory Pimm's in an ice bucket

(it was her duty to uphold such traditions)

Penelope turned herself into a Fun Person, nothing was ever too much trouble where Jeremy was concerned, in truth most things had been too much trouble before she met him

with Jeremy, she became an attentive listener, offered soothing assurances, especially when he described his ex-marriage to Anne

who'd gone from a well-behaved mother and wife in the fifties and sixties to a manhating feminist in the eighties who picked fights with him and disappeared to Greenham Common with women who tried very hard not to look like they were

women she brought into their town house in Kennington as friends, until one day he caught her at it in their bedroom doing something only a man should do to a woman

he's had relationships since, will never marry again

well, feminism has a lot to answer for, Penelope said in commiseration, quite prepared to betray the cause if it meant finding personal happiness

Jeremy Sanders (MBE)

had enjoyed a distinguished career as a civil servant in the Palace of Westminster in charge of in-house publications, regardless of which political party was ruining, oops, *ruling* the country, as he often joked (GSOH, Jeremy!)

they were politically aligned (right of centre) and enjoyed debating the main issues of the day: law and order, the economy, the small state versus the nanny state, nationalism, immigration, discouraging social welfare, human rights, encouraging the growth of small businesses and tax breaks to big businesses and big earners, and the protection of personal wealth – her Camberwell villa, bought for a shining halfpenny in the sixties, was now worth seven figures

Penelope only allowed things to get intimate with Jeremy when they'd known each other eighteen months, she really wasn't going to jump into bed with him anyway, it had been a long time since she'd been seen in a state of undress by anyone other than the matronly bra-fitter at Marks & Spencer

her thighs, chunky and pock-marked, were no longer the streamlined contours of old, her breasts weren't the pumped-up balloons of her youth, and she'd spend sleepless nights wondering if she should dye her lady garden for him

when they did consummate their union, it happened quite unexpectedly when they ended up at it like teenagers on the sofa in the drawing room of his town house one night

after she'd endured three and a half hours of *La Traviata* at the Royal Opera House

and returned home to polish off a bottle of Vintage Bordeaux in order to recover from it

while he enjoyed a few shots of his favourite Metaxa cognac

one thing led to another and before she knew it, her cherry was popped by her seventy-something boyfriend

Penelope discovered then that Jeremy's feelings for her blinded him to her physical imperfections, he loved her just as she was, no complaints, he said, even when she allowed him to look at her buck naked on the bed one morning with the full force of sunlight streaming on to her through the windows

you're how I imagine Botticelli's Venus might look in middle age

middle age? she was seventy at that point

he was so *compassionate*

she certainly loved him as *he* was, neither a Michelin Man nor an ageing Adonis, his legs were his best physical asset, a walker all his life, she became one too which was nothing short of miraculous because until she met him she could barely manage five minutes without catching her breath

to and from her car and around the shops

she eventually worked up enough stamina to do a ten-mile round trip when they stayed at his cottage by the sea in Sussex, or hers in Provence

walking became one of life's pleasures

*

once all matters of compatibility had been determined, it made sense for her to move into his, which she decided to leave untouched, quietly disliking his grey and green colour palette, his fondness for original Edwardian furniture, wall-to-wall beige carpets and the preponderance of framed *Spectator* covers from the 1800s

in contrast with her own rather more eclectic sense of style that involved Balinese shadow puppets, glass sculptures, colourful Quaker quilts thrown over comfy white sofas, sheepskin rugs and light, sanded floorboards

they settled comfortably into life together, frequently dined out (neither cared to cook), regular visits to National Trust houses, theatre productions and West End musicals (for her) and, of course, the opera

they're both avid readers, her taste is in the realm of Joanna Trollope, Jilly Cooper, Anita Brookner and Jeffrey Archer, while he's a James Patterson, Sebastian Faulks, Ken Follett and Robert Harris kinda guy, as he puts it

Jeremy once said he'd never read a novel by a woman in his life because he'd never been able to get beyond the first chapter by one, he didn't understand why not, it must be biological, he said, looking crestfallen

she said nothing, doesn't nag him, that was her rule to herself, it's the secret of their harmonious relationship

they practise Tai Chi together every morning in his conservatory, in the garden in the summer, although he's less agile now he's deep into his eighties

she's survived a cancer scare that made her feel incredibly mortal (and grateful to avoid a mastectomy)

in contemplating her demise, however, she found herself

suffering restless nights about her birth parents, something she thought she'd laid to rest as a very young woman, once she'd overcome the shock of knowing that Edwin and Margaret weren't related to her by blood

who were the people who brought her into this world only to give her away?

Sarah was quite surprised to hear her talk about this during their weekly England–Australia Skype conversations

what's brought this on, Mum?

Sarah's middle-aged now, her visits to England infrequent, her children, Matty and Molly, are all grown up and *very* Australian

Adam has been living in Dallas so long, he's become shockingly Second Amendment, to the point she's rowed with him about the availability of guns for sale in his local Walmart, along with processed cheese and children's toys

Penelope thinks her children ran away from her, they'd never admit it, she wasn't a bad mother and she's saddened that she was never able to really bond with her grandchildren

she wanted to be a grandmother who babysat them every week

who is the second most important woman in their lives

she's still very close to Sarah who told her about the availability of Ancestry DNA testing, which is very popular in her part of the world, because so many people have roots in Britain and elsewhere, about which they know little or nothing

you must try it, seeing as it's on your mind, Mum, she said, I think it will at least tell you which parts of the UK your birth family came from

Penelope was keen on the idea, she'd been raised in York,

imagined her ancestors were from that region, going all the way back to the Stone Ages, probably

people didn't move around very much in the past except from the village to the town for work, and that only took off during the Industrial Revolution

up until then it was all very insular and cut off, especially in hilly territory so yes, her roots were likely to be in Yorkshire, Lancashire, Cheshire, Lincolnshire, possibly Durham, possibly with Viking ancestors, perhaps she's descended from a Viking warrior queen

that made sense

the kit arrived, Penelope deposited her saliva into the tube as per the instructions, sent it off in the post, and planned to surprise Jeremy with the results

except it didn't quite turn out as expected

now Penelope's suffering from post traumatic stress disorder because yesterday she went online to check her emails after her traditional Friday lunch of 'Penne & Pinot' with a gal pal divorcee, and there it was

Great news! Your Ancestry DNA results are in. The moment you've been waiting for is here . . .

in her case – all her life

Penelope clicked on the hyperlink without delay, relieved that Jeremy was out all day golfing in Surrey with Hugo, his brother

she found it hard to take it in at first, so many different nationalities

this was the science that was the deepest, most secret part of herself, and there was a collision between who she thought she might be and who she apparently was

Europe

Scandinavia	22%
Ireland	25%
Great Britain	17%
European Jewish	16%
Iberian Peninsula	3%
Finland/Northwest Russia	2%
Europe West	2%

Africa

Ethiopia	4%
South Sudan	1%
Kenya	1%
Eritrea	1%
Sudan	1%
Egypt	1%
Nigeria	1%
Ivory Coast/Ghana	1%
Cameroon/Congo	1%
Africa South Central Hunter Gatherer	1%

Penelope went straight to the drinks cabinet; a few hours later she made it to her bedroom to lie down

being Jewish is one thing but never in a million years did she expect to see Africa in her DNA, that was the biggest shock of all, the test didn't provide answers, it confronted her with questions

as she lay there, she imagined her ancestors attired in loincloths running around the African savannah spearing lions, at the same time wearing yarmulkes, eating open-topped rye sandwiches and paella, and refusing to hunt on the Sabbath

perhaps she should get a dreadlock wig in keeping with her new identity, become one of those Rastafarians and sell drugs

at least it explained one thing to her, why she tanned as soon as the sun hit her skin

only 17% of her was British which was a terrible disappointment, she was actually more Irish than British, which in all likelihood meant her ancestors were *potato farmers*

the Scandi element was all right so long as she was Viking, but how to tell? they too might have been potato farmers, Europe West must surely explain her great affinity with beautiful Provence

her African ancestors were probably nomads roaming over the continent killing each other before the British demarcated regions into proper countries and thereby imposed discipline and control

if she was 13% African did it mean one of her parents was 26% African? or was it divided between both of them?

as she didn't know who her birth parents were, she couldn't even begin to work out which strand belonged to which one

Penelope Skyped Sarah with the news, it was the early hours in Australia but this was an exceptional moment, Sarah got terribly excited

asked for the link to the site because you, Mum, aren't making a lot of sense, whether you have a thing for Scandi-Noirs has nothing to do with it

have you been drinking again?

(only a little)

*

448

within minutes Sarah was back on Skype saying not only did the website show her ethnic breakdown, it connected her with relatives who'd also done the test, how on earth did you miss this, Mum? okay, deep breath, are you ready for this? you have over a hundred genetic relatives listed on your page starting with fifth to eighth cousins, you've got no one under siblings or a grandparent, nor do you have a twin, but something else is showing, Mum, a parent — do you see what this means?

your birth mother or father must have had the test done and they've been biologically revealed to be your blood parent

they've got their name down as Anonymous25, last logged on two weeks ago in Yorkshire and, wait for it, there's an email link for you to get in touch with them directly to find out more

Mum, are you listening? you've gone really pale, oh God, I'm so sorry you're so upset, don't cry, Mummy, it's completely understandable, of course it is, I understand, I really do, I just wish I could hug you right now, look, I'll handle it, you go and sober up and we'll talk later

Sarah emailed someone called Morgan who replied almost immediately that he/she(?) was managing the DNA test for their great-grandmother, Hattie Jackson, in order to find out more about Hattie's own mother, Grace, who was half Ethiopian, they'd thought, only to discover her genes were spread wider in Africa, which was unexpected

the last thing Morgan was expecting was an email from someone who claimed to be Hattie's daughter because Hattie only had one daughter called Ada Mae, who lived in Newcastle

Morgan promised Sarah she'd call Hattie right away, and get back

after Hattie had recovered from the shock, she told Morgan she'd given birth to a girl she named Barbara when she was fourteen, who

449

was taken away from her by her father a few days after birth, she had no say in the matter and she never knew where the baby went, the only people who knew about her child were her parents and they'd died so long ago

Hattie had kept it secret all her life, thought of Barbara every day, and couldn't believe she was alive

Morgan emailed Penelope that her great-grandmother was in shock, she was very old, you must come soon

Penelope replied she was taking the train up the next day

Penelope takes a black cab from the station, she's usually a meter-watcher, this one can rack up a thousand pounds and it won't matter a bit

the taxi driver says the journey will take over two hours, he's African, which isn't quite what she expected to find so far north she's practically in Scotland

he makes her feel like she's back in south London, then she catches herself, it's not as cut and dried as it was before, he could be a relative, if there's one thing she's learned in the past forty-eight hours, anyone can be a relative

by rights, she should fall asleep, she woke up at four a.m. to get the seven from King's Cross, but she can't, her brain is completely wired

the car travels deep into the Northumbrian countryside

it's easy to forget that England is made up of many Englands

all these fields and forests, sheep, hills, comatose villages

she feels like she's going to the ends of the earth, while simultaneously returning to her beginnings

she's going back to where she began, inside her mother's womb

*

the taxi passes through another deserted village then the car climbs a hill so steep and long she's worried it won't make it up
at the top there's a sign above a high metal arch

Greenfields
founded
1806
by
Captain Linnaeus Rydendale
and his beloved wife
Eudoré

they pull into a yard so thick with mud the taxi has to slow down and trudge its way through, mud splattering on to the windows
it's like stepping back to pre-civilization
an ancient sagging farmhouse is to her right with a patchwork roof of mismatched tiles and mismatched bricks and vines creeping up it and out of it, looking as if with one hefty push it will all come tumbling down
the yard is otherwise surrounded by barns with doors flapping in the wind
a few chickens and hens are squawking around, a cow's head is sticking up out of a pen, a goat is tethered to a post, a plough is rusting at the far end with vines growing out of it
everything is falling apart and ruined and running riot

she disembarks from the taxi and pays the fellow the three hundred pounds on the meter, plus a tip, considering he's practically a sixth cousin or something the farmhouse door opens and someone steps out into the yard, her hair is a wiry grey and shooting up all over the place

she's wearing raggedy blue overalls with a cardigan over them, she's *barefoot*, in this place? in this mud? in this weather?

she walks towards her, she's old, bony, looks robust, is tall without being hunched, quite fierce, is this where Penelope gets it from? her imperiousness, as she's been accused of in the past?

the woman is unmistakably, ambiguously a light brown, the sort of colour that could place her in many countries

this metal-haired wild creature from the bush with the piercingly feral eyes

is her mother

this is she

this is her

who cares about her colour? why on earth did Penelope ever think it mattered?

in this moment she's feeling something so pure and primal it's overwhelming

they are mother and daughter and their whole sense of themselves is recalibrating

her mother is now close enough to touch

Penelope had worried she would feel nothing, or that her mother would show no love for her, no feelings, no affection

how wrong she was, both of them are welling up and it's like the years are swiftly regressing until the lifetimes between them no longer exist

this is not about feeling something or about speaking words

this is about being

together.

Acknowledgements

It's nearly twenty years since I first started working with Simon Prosser, publishing director of Hamish Hamilton, and I'd like to thank him for being such a great editor of the six books I've published with him since. I am so grateful and feel so blessed. I'd also like to thank the team at Penguin who work hard to get my books out into the world, including Hermione Thompson, Sapphire Rees, Hannah Chukwu, Annie Lee, Donna Poppy, Lesley Levene, Amelia Fairney, and all those people who make things happen behind the scenes. A special thanks is due to my agent Karolina Sutton at Curtis Brown. Big thanks also to my readers at various stages of the manuscript: Sharmilla Beezmohun, Claudia Cruttwell, Maggie Gee, Lyn Innes and Roger Robinson. And for checking my patois and pidgin, thanks to Chris Abani, Jackee Holder, Michael Irene and Kechi Nomu. I'd also like to thank Hedgebrook Retreat for Women Writers on Whidbey Island, USA, for my residency there in 2018.

Lastly but firstly, thanks to my husband David, who is always there to support me when I venture into creative waters unknown, and who is always a safe harbour when I come home.